PRAISE FOR THE ALASTAIR STONE

"The magic is believable, the characters c
and the twists, turns and mysteries to be solved glue your eyes to
the page. You will never forget these characters or their world."
—*Jacqueline Lichtenberg, Hugo-nominated author of the Sime~Gen
series and* Star Trek Lives!

"Alastair Stone is like Harry Potter meets Harry Dresden with a bit
of Indiana Jones!"
—*Randler, Amazon reviewer*

"Somewhat reminiscent of the Dresden Files but with its own
distinct style."
—*John W. Ranken, Amazon reviewer*

"I am reminded of Jim Butcher here...Darker than most Urban
Fantasy, not quite horror, but with a touch of Lovecraftian."
—*Wulfstan, Amazon Top 500 reviewer*

"An absolute delight for 'urban fantasy' fans! Smart, witty and
compelling!"
—*gbc, Bookbub reviewer*

"In Alastair Stone, author R.L. King has a major winner on her
hands."
—*Mark Earls, Amazon reviewer*

"Once you enter the world of Alastair Stone, you won't want to
leave."
—*Awesome Indies*

"You will fall in love with this series!"
—*Amazon reviewer*

"It's getting hard to come up with something better than great to describe how good this book was."
—*Ted Camer, Amazon reviewer*

"You cannot go wrong with this series!"
—*Jim, Amazon reviewer*

"Warning—don't start reading this book if you have other things to do."
—*ARobertson, Amazon reviewer*

"Once you start, you need to get comfortable because you will stop reading all of a sudden and discover many hours have gone by."
—*John Scott, Amazon reviewer*

"R. L. King has my purchasing dollars with fun-to-read, suspenseful, character-driven stories…Damn fun reads."
—*Amazon reviewer*

"I have been hooked on this series from the first book."
—*Jim P. Ziller, Amazon reviewer*

"Awesome and exciting. Love this series."
—*Cynthia Morrison, Amazon reviewer*

"Amazing series. The characters are deep and identifiable. The magic is only a small part of what makes these books great. I can't wait for the next one!!"
—*Amazon reviewer*

"Great series, awesome characters and can't wait to see where the story will go from here."
—*Amazon reviewer*

"I have read every book in this series and loved them all."
—*Soozers, Amazon reviewer*

"The writing is extremely good, and the plot and characters engaging. Closest author comparison probably Benedict Jacka and the Alex Verus series."
—*MB, Amazon reviewer*

"The Alastair Stone Chronicles is one of the best series I have read in years…"
—*Judith A. Slover, Amazon reviewer*

"A continued thrill to the urban fantasy reader…"
—*Dominic, Amazon reviewer*

"This a great series and one of the best ones I have had the pleasure to read in a long time."
—*Skywalker, Amazon reviewer*

ALSO BY R. L. KING

The Alastair Stone Chronicles

Stone and a Hard Place

The Forgotten

The Threshold

The Source

Core of Stone

Blood and Stone

Heart of Stone

Flesh and Stone

The Infernal Heart

The Other Side

Path of Stone

Necessary Sacrifices

Game of Stone

Steel and Stone

Stone and Claw

The Seventh Stone

Gathering Storm

House of Stone

Circle of Stone

The Madness Below

Boys' Night (Way) Out (novella)

An Unexpected Truth (novella)

Death's Door

Blood Brothers

Homecoming

Mortal Imperative

Balance of Power

Shadows and Stone (novella)

Turn to Stone (novella)

Devil's Bargain (standalone novel)

Stone for the Holidays (short stories)

Happenstance and Bron

The Soul Engine

Chariots of Wrath

By Demons Driven

Shadowrun (published by Catalyst Game Labs)

Shadowrun: Borrowed Time

Shadowrun: Wolf and Buffalo (novella)

Shadowrun: Big Dreams (novella)

Shadowrun: Veiled Extraction

BALANCE OF POWER

ALASTAIR STONE CHRONICLES: BOOK TWENTY-FIVE

R. L. KING

MAGESPACE
PRESS

Balance of Power: Alastair Stone Chronicles Book Twenty-Five
First Edition: March 2021
First Paperback Edition: April 2021
Magespace Press
Edited by John Helfers
Cover Art and Design by Gene Mollica Studio

ISBN: 978-1-953063-06-9

CHAPTER ONE

"**I** CAN'T SAY HOW GOOD IT IS to have you all here, together in one place."

Alastair Stone smiled. He couldn't remember seeing Aubrey this happy in a long time. He leaned back in his chair, letting his gaze travel over the massive bounty of food weighing down the dining-room table. "I see what you're up to, Aubrey: you're so pleased to have us here, you're planning to stuff us so full we won't ever be able to leave."

"Oh, dear, you've found me out, sir." The old caretaker's eyes glittered with merriment, his craggy, tanned face split into a wide smile. "But best get started, while everything's still hot. And you must blame Ms. Thayer, Ian, and Susan for some of the abundance. This was far more than I could have managed on my own."

"You heard the man," Stone said. "Let's get to it."

As the dishes were passed along and everyone loaded their plates with the components of a traditional British Christmas dinner, including turkey and stuffing, roast potatoes, pigs in blankets, Yorkshire pudding, cranberry sauce, and vegetables, Stone redirected his attention from the food to the company. He wondered how long it had been since this many people had sat at the long, antique dining table—quite possibly it had been during his father's lifetime, unless Aubrey had been hosting dinner parties while he was away.

The caretaker had insisted Stone sit at the head of the table as the house's master, but everyone else had sorted themselves out mostly randomly. Ian sat on Stone's right, with Verity to his left. Jason and Amber rounded out Verity's side, with Aubrey and his lady friend Susan Fletcher on Ian's. Selby had been invited too, of course, but had graciously declined since he had plans to visit family.

All day, the house had been full of warmth and delightful aromas. At first, Aubrey had protested Ian's and Verity's offer to help with the food preparation, insisting they should be enjoying themselves, but both had assured him they liked cooking and would be happy to assist. Stone, meanwhile, had made himself scarce (knowing Aubrey wouldn't want him anywhere near the kitchen) to meet Jason and Amber at A Passage to India so he could bring them through the portal to Surrey late that afternoon.

"You've done a beautiful job decorating the place, Aubrey," Stone said. "I'm not sure I want to ask how you got that tree in here." The Christmas tree in the main hall stood nearly fifteen feet high, and was decorated all the way to the top with tinsel, twinkling lights, and colorful ornaments.

"Don't worry, sir. I had a lot of help. I hired some lads from the village to bring it in, and Selby took care of any decorating that required a ladder."

"Good man." Over the last few months, Stone had gotten good at sneaking looks at Aubrey when the old man wasn't looking, and he had to admit he'd seen no increase—either physically or aurically—in any symptoms indicating his early-stage Parkinson's was getting any worse. Either he was diligently following his doctor's advice on his own, or Susan was encouraging him to do it.

Stone had kept his promise to himself, visiting Aubrey at least once a week since September. He'd sometimes felt guilty he didn't show up more often, but both he and Aubrey had quickly fallen into an equilibrium with visits frequent enough so they could catch up regularly, but not so frequent as to disturb both men's preference for solitude. That, and now that Aubrey and Susan seemed to have developed an enduring relationship, the caretaker was rarely lonely. The situation had worked out well for both him and Stone. Stone's only slight concern was to wonder what Susan might make of his frequent visits, since she knew he lived and worked in California, but she never inquired. Either she wasn't naturally nosy, or Aubrey had told her something to stave off suspicion.

"You guys outdid yourselves," Jason said after swallowing an oversized mouthful of turkey. He looked fondly at Amber. "I guess we're gonna have to start learning how to do stuff like this at some point. Once we have kids, we should have some kind of holiday tradition of our own."

Amber chuckled. "Don't worry, O Skeptical Hubby. Maybe I can't cook a turkey like this, but Jonah can. And my brothers' families put out a spread that, quantity-wise, makes this look like a light snack. You'd think they were part bulldozer, the way they plow through food."

Stone glanced at Susan, the only one at the table who had no idea about the supernatural nature of most of the evening's guests, but she merely laughed.

"Yes, young men are like that, aren't they?" she said. "My grandsons are the same way. Sometimes it's impossible to keep the refrigerator stocked when they and their friends are around."

Stone, Verity, Ian, Jason, and Amber all exchanged discreet glances, and kept the conversation fully mundane for the rest of the meal. They passed around anecdotes about Jason and Amber's home-renovation project, Verity's life in San Francisco, Ian's travels, and Stone's work at the University, and before long they'd worked their way through not only the main course, but the pies Aubrey had baked for dessert and a round of after-dinner drinks.

"Bloody hell," Stone said with a contented sigh, slumping back in his chair. "I didn't think I could eat that much. I'll have to run several laps around the village to work all that off."

"No kidding." Jason patted his trim belly. "I see some heavy gym time in my future."

"Can we help you with the dishes, Aubrey?" Amber asked. "Only fair, since you did the cooking."

"Oh, my, no." Aubrey waved her off. "You all go out in the main hall and enjoy the decorations. I'll just rinse everything off and pop it in the dishwasher."

"Are you sure?" Verity asked.

"Let him," Stone said. "He's looking for an excuse to run off and be alone with Susan for a while, so let's not bollix up his plans."

"Sir, of course I'm not—"

"Oh, you are." Stone rose from the table. "And I don't blame you one bit. This lot can be a bit much to take all at once. Come on, everyone—let's carry all this out to the kitchen and make ourselves scarce for a while, shall we?"

In less than five minutes, the group had cleared the table and moved all the dishes to the kitchen. After another assurance from Aubrey that he didn't need help—along with a sly look from Susan as she remained behind with him—the rest of the group adjourned to the main hall with their after-dinner drinks and took seats around the massive fireplace.

"Well," Stone said. "It has been an interesting year."

"You have a way with understatement," Verity said, grinning. Then she sobered. "Some good things—like Jason and Amber getting married. But some bad stuff, too."

"And some things that are sort of both," Jason said. "Like finding out V's got two other half-siblings. I'm still getting used to that."

"Have you met them yet?" Ian asked.

"Not yet. V's been down there a couple times, but..." He shrugged, looking uncomfortable. "I guess the time doesn't seem right yet. I'm sure it will, next year."

"Yeah," Verity said. "I guess there's no rush." She glanced at Stone. "You've had a pretty quiet quarter, haven't you? We've all been so busy with work and stuff, we've barely had a chance to see each other. How are you coping with all this calm?"

"Just fine, thank you." She was right: after the whole business with the dragons, followed by dealing with the ghouls and Richter and the shocking realization that James Brathwaite's echo was not only still alive, but had taken up residence in his female descendant and was continuing his necromantic activities, Stone had just about given up on the idea of any lulls in his breakneck life.

But to his surprise, the fall quarter had flown by without notable incident, at least in the supernatural sphere. He'd asked Kolinsky to keep an eye out for any signs of Brathwaite or Richter resurfacing, but neither had. The latter didn't seem odd, since he was fairly sure the failed ritual had killed Elias Richter, but Brathwaite was almost certainly still out there somewhere. Whether he'd taken over the Ordo Purpuratus was another question Stone had no current way to answer. He sometimes felt a bit guilty for not pursuing the issue with more effort, especially since the necromancer had a lot to answer for, but as long as Brathwaite stayed out of his way and didn't cause trouble, he'd decided a few months wouldn't make a big difference.

"How's Brandon Greene working out?" Verity lounged back in her chair, finished her drink, and used magic to levitate the glass onto the table.

"Oh, brilliantly. Couldn't be more pleased—and neither can Hubbard. He's already using his new free time to work on his latest book."

"Who's Brandon Greene?" Amber asked. She sat snuggled against Jason, her head on his shoulder.

"One of my most promising graduate students—not to mention my former cat-sitter. He finally completed his Master's last year, and he's taken on a position as an acting instructor in the Occult Studies department. It's only for a year, but he can handle a couple of the undergraduate courses and take some of the pressure off Hubbard and me."

"Hopefully they'll find somebody full-time by then," Verity said. "Are they stepping up the search?"

"They are. I've even agreed to do a bit of traveling to scout potential candidates and see if I can persuade someone to relocate." He shrugged. "I think Martinez has it in her head that I'm planning to retire."

"Any reason for that?" Jason slipped his arm around Amber and pulled her closer. "Are you?"

"Damned if I know. I love teaching, and if the quarters stay as calm as the last one I can certainly continue to fit it in. I'm only there two days a week now anyway. I'd feel guilty about leaving them up a tree if I left." He leaned back and put his feet on the table. "But I'd be lying if I said I haven't considered it."

"Not like you need the money," Verity said with a grin.

"I didn't need the money when I started. It's never been about the money."

"You just want more time to chase magical mysteries." Ian's grin was even bigger than Verity's. "You're jealous of all the time I spend traveling around the world, and now you want to do it too."

Stone shot him a mock glare. "You might be right about the mysteries. But as for gallivanting around the world living the playboy lifestyle…not really my thing."

"Yeah, that's true. I keep forgetting, you're just an old fuddy-duddy dad, lounging on the couch in Bermuda shorts and black socks with sandals, watching ESPN and drinking Budweiser."

Jason, Amber, and Verity all laughed.

"Oi," Stone said irritably, shaking his head. "If you're going to insult the host, you can all pop down to McDonald's or something."

Verity patted his arm. "Don't worry, Doc—if we ever see you in sandals, we'll stage an intervention."

"As well you should." Stone studied the Christmas tree, feeling content. "In any case, I'm glad we could all get together, and I genuinely hope the universe has decided to let up on the pedal for a while. I could get to like this peace and quiet."

"You're not fooling anybody, you know," Ian said.

CHAPTER TWO

THE NEW QUARTER STARTED a few days after the first of the year. Stone only had two courses and one graduate seminar, and he'd managed to schedule them all so he'd only have to work two days a week.

That didn't mean he didn't have to show up for meetings, though, including the one on the afternoon of the first day of the quarter. He didn't know what this one was about, only that Beatrice Martinez, the head of the Cultural Anthropology department, had put it on his calendar yesterday.

Brandon Greene was already at the conference room when he arrived. "Hey, Doc. Good holiday?"

"Very nice, yes." Stone looked him over. "Decided to skip the tie this quarter?" Ever since their first class together, Greene had always preferred a style that hovered somewhere between goth and skate-punk, preferring black, loose-fitting clothes and shoulder-length, perpetually messy hair. Last quarter—his first on the job—he'd gotten a haircut and worn a dress shirt, slacks, and a tie. This time, he'd swapped the more formal outfit for black jeans, a gray button-down shirt, and leather boots. Respectable, but not stuffy.

Greene shrugged. "Wanted to be comfortable, but not *too* comfortable." He grinned. "We can't all be rebel rock stars like you. Not yet, anyway. Working on it."

Stone chuckled. He wore his usual uniform of black pub T-shirt, jeans, and his long black overcoat. He'd wondered a few times in the past if Martinez ever wanted to say anything to him about it, but she never did. Even the late Edwina Mortenson, former head of their little Occult Studies department and well-known stickler for decorum, hadn't done anything more than shoot him disapproving glares when she thought he wasn't looking. He was damned good at his job, they all knew it, and he didn't mind taking advantage of a few harmless perks in return. Especially when it meant he didn't have to wear boring clothes to work.

"Any idea what this meeting's about?" He didn't take a seat at the table, but instead paced the room, looking out the window at the groups of students ambling by on the quad below.

"Nope. Maybe it's to congratulate me for doing such a good job. You know, with a cake, a full bar, and a twenty-one-gun salute."

Stone snorted. "You'll be lucky if you get a cup of lukewarm coffee and a personalized notepad."

"Hey, I've never had a personalized notepad before." Greene settled into one of the chairs.

Stone was spared answering by the arrival of Mackenzie Hubbard. The other Occult Studies professor sported his usual rumpled pants and a brown cardigan; he looked like he'd just rolled out of bed. He nodded to Stone and Greene, grunted a greeting, and dropped into a chair opposite Greene.

Martinez showed up a couple minutes later, cheerfully harried as usual. "Sorry I'm late," she said breathlessly, pulling a few folders from her briefcase and tossing them on the table. "I know this isn't our standard meeting time, so I hope I haven't pulled you from anything important."

"Other than making me drive over here, not really," Stone said. A couple of ley lines crossed the Stanford campus, and many times over the previous quarter he'd been tempted to skip driving and pop over the easy way, but decided he'd best not take chances. The last thing he needed was to get preoccupied, forget his invisibility spell, and have somebody spot him showing up out of nowhere in the middle of a vacant lot.

"Well, I'll keep it short. Just a few things, and then I have an announcement I think all of you might find interesting."

She got through the bits of administrivia quickly, to Stone's relief. He liked Martinez—she was a no-bullshit sort who didn't believe in dragging meetings out longer than they needed to go—but that didn't mean he enjoyed the meetings.

"Okay," he said when she'd finished and put her folders back in her briefcase. "So, what's this announcement? Did you finally find a full-time faculty member?"

She laughed. "You wish. *I* wish. No offense to Mr. Greene, who's doing a fine job—"

"Thank you, thank you," Greene murmured with a cheeky grin.

"—but that's been on my holiday wish list for the last several years."

"It's been on *all* our holiday wish lists for the last several years," Hubbard grumbled.

"*Any*way," Martinez put in, "I wanted to let you all know that we've acquired something you might want to check out."

Stone and Greene exchanged glances.

"A gentleman named Hiram Drummond passed away a few months ago. Mr. Drummond, as you probably don't know, was an alumnus of our fine university. He donated a lot of money to various departments over the years."

Stone didn't know, but then again, he didn't make a habit of memorizing the names of alums who'd been at the University before he was born. "I'm sorry to hear he's died. But what's it got to do with us?"

Martinez gave him an indulgent smile. "Patience, Alastair. Mr. Drummond was a historian. Obviously he wasn't part of the Occult Studies department, since it didn't exist when he was a student here. But he *was*, among other things, an aficionado of occult-related history and the objects related to it. He was also very wealthy and quite reclusive. He collected a large number of items, but never made them available to the public."

Stone sat up straighter. Even after Martinez's introduction, he still couldn't remember ever hearing about Hiram Drummond. That didn't mean he hadn't been a mage—some of them were serious hermits and didn't interact with the rest of magical society—but the possibility definitely existed. "Where did he live?"

"Near Boston. His only living family are a daughter and a niece. When he passed away, he left them his monetary and real-estate holdings, but neither of them wanted anything to do with what they called his 'creepy hoard.' Originally, they wanted to donate the collection to a museum, but they've had trouble finding the right fit for it—"

"—you mean, finding any museum willing to take it," Hubbard drawled.

"Well…yes. So far, they haven't found any interest, so they've decided to auction the collection instead. It will go up for sale in a few weeks in San Francisco. They've already taken pictures of the items and put out an online catalog. But because Mr. Drummond cared so much about our University, his heirs have suggested that our people might like a chance to look over the collection before it's auctioned off. I've arranged to have it brought here so you can examine it."

Stone raised an eyebrow. "They're just going to let us poke around to our heart's content?"

Mostly, yes. The daughter says she trusts us to show the objects the proper care. You'll have at least a couple of weeks to look through the items and see if you can find anything useful for your research, or perhaps to show your students." She fixed her gaze on Stone. "If you do find anything of particular interest, we can see if we can arrange with the daughter to remove those objects from the upcoming auction and set up an extended loan to us."

"Sounds brilliant," Stone said. "I'd definitely like to get a look at it. Where are they keeping it?"

"In one of the unused storerooms not too far from your office building." She gave them the details. "Some of the stuff is somewhat valuable, so the place is locked up tight and there'll be a security guard checking the area periodically, but you're all welcome to look around. Just sign the log outside the door." With a chuckle, she added, "You'll have your work cut out for you, though. The items have been tagged, but nothing's been arranged or organized. So it will basically be like hunting through the world's strangest storage locker. It's going to take them at least a week to get everything sorted out for the auction, hence the two-week window for us."

"Ah, a challenge," Greene said, grinning. "I want to get a look at that stuff too."

Hubbard grunted. "I suppose I'll stop by at some point, but I'd rather see it after it's been properly arranged. If I want to poke through a room full of dusty old crap, I'll go to my attic."

"Who knows?" Stone said. "Maybe you'll find something to inspire your next novel."

"Anyway," Martinez said, getting up. "I don't want to keep you any longer than necessary, so that's it for me. Let me know if you find anything interesting in the collection. I'd like to take a look, but I probably won't have time before it's sent on its way."

CHAPTER THREE

STONE, HUBBARD, AND GREENE left the building together, walking back toward the Occult Studies office building on the other side of campus.

"Don't tell me," Hubbard said. "You two are off to check the place out right away."

"Not me," Greene said. "Got a class in half an hour. Maybe later on, or tomorrow. We've got two weeks, and I don't think that stuff's going anywhere."

Hubbard snorted. "Never know. Martinez did say it was creepy. Maybe it'll get up and walk off on its own."

Stone was silent as he strode along next to them. He was itching to get a look at the collection, and grateful for both Hubbard's lack of curiosity and Greene's prior commitment. Both meant he'd be the first of the group to examine the items, which would give him a chance to check for anything that might be truly magical—or even potentially dangerous. It wasn't likely—most "occult collectors," even wealthy ones, didn't have an ounce of magical blood or talent, which meant their hoards usually consisted of equal parts overpriced tourist kitsch from "exotic" countries they didn't know any better about, and valuable but decidedly mundane artifacts.

Of course, there were always exceptions. He remembered the storage locker in San Francisco, where an old mage had unknowingly kept a set of ancient, deadly game pieces used by dragons hundreds of years ago, and the collection of tomes a dead mage's mundane family had donated to a used bookstore in Ojai. These things *did* happen. But not nearly as often as the movies wanted people to think they did.

The trio approached the building and separated, with Greene heading off to his class and Hubbard toward his office. Stone, at least ostensibly, turned in the direction of the parking lot.

"Heading home already?" Hubbard called. "Thought you wouldn't be able to wait to take a look."

"Eh, like Greene said, it's not going anywhere right away."

Stone continued down the path toward the parking lot long enough for Hubbard to disappear into the building, then turned around and hurried back. He felt a little guilty about deceiving his colleague, but the last thing he wanted was for the man to change his mind and decide he wanted to come along. Stone hadn't been kidding about Hubbard's novels: after the publication of his first one, he already had a second working its way through the publishing process, and his small-press publisher had bought a third. There were worse sources of inspiration for literary horror than an old cache of potentially supernatural objects.

The building was located in an even more obscure corner of campus than the Occult Studies offices, which was saying something. It was two stories, painted beige with the same sort of Spanish-tile roof that covered many of the other campus buildings. Stone had never visited it before, and judging by the lack of students milling around near it, it probably wasn't the site of any current classes. Probably overflow offices, or storage for hardcopy files and out-of-date lab equipment.

Stone stopped, switching to magical sight to give the place a quick scan. He didn't expect to see anything from out here, and wasn't surprised when he didn't.

Probably nothing inside, either. But still, it was hardly a waste of time. Even if he didn't find anything to pique his curiosity as a mage, there were almost certainly things he'd find interesting as an occult-studies professor. Mundane "arcane" artifacts could be fascinating in their own right.

The front doors weren't locked. He strode inside, noting the lights were kept low. That meant he was probably right about the place not being in regular use. Even wealthy universities like Stanford tried to save money when they could.

The room number Martinez had given them was on the first floor, down one of the side hallways branching off the main one. The door looked substantial, with a pushbutton lock. A clipboard hung on a hook next to it, holding a single sheet of paper with a sign-up table and a pen on a string. There was a name on the log, but Stone didn't recognize it. Probably whoever had checked the collection over when it arrived.

He paused a moment, trying to decide what to do. Martinez hadn't given them the code for the lock. She'd mentioned a guard, but he didn't see any sign of one.

He was debating whether to come back later or to use magic to open the lock when a voice called from down the hall. "Can I help you?"

He turned to face a middle-aged man in a guard's uniform. The man showed no suspicion; in fact, he looked pleased to have somebody show up to talk to. Given the building's deserted state, it was probably fairly boring here most of the time.

"Er—yes. I'm Alastair Stone." He pulled his faculty ID from his pocket and held it up. "I'm part of the Occult Studies department. Dr. Martinez said we could pop by to take a look at Mr. Drummond's collection. Is this a good time?"

The guard examined the ID, flicked his gaze up to Stone's face, and nodded. "Sure thing, Dr. Stone. Just sign the log there, and I'll open it up for you."

"Thank you." Stone stepped aside and scrawled his signature and the time on the sheet, then moved back, scanning the hall. He hadn't spotted them before, but the corridor included two security cameras—one near the entrance and one directly opposite this door.

Maybe this collection was more valuable than he'd thought.

The guard shielded the lock with his body, punched in the code, and swung open the door. It made a faint creak. "There you go. Take as long as you like. If I'm not here, you don't have to come lookin' for me. Just sign out and make sure the door's locked when you leave, okay? Just be careful not to move things around too much." He grinned. "And don't take nothin' with you. If you want to sign anything out to study, you'll have to clear it through Dr. Martinez."

"Of course. Thank you, Mr.—" He peered at the guard's name badge. "Kelso." Stone didn't show it, but he was relieved at Kelso's words. He'd half-expected the man to accompany him inside, and he didn't fancy spending the afternoon with a bored security guard dogging his every footstep and potentially asking annoying questions. "I don't know how long I'll be—it depends on how much there is to look at."

"Oh, there's a lot. Trust me. Freaky-lookin' stuff, too." He gave a little shudder. "Looks like a frickin' haunted museum blew up in there. I saw some of it when they were bringin' it in. You wouldn't get *me* in there by myself. No way." He grinned again. "Have fun. But if any mummies or ghosts or whatever come after you, don't call me." He patted his nightstick. "I only deal with *human* stuff."

"I promise, I'll handle the supernatural threats on my own."

Kelso reached through the opening and flipped on a light switch. "There you go."

"Thank you." Stone slipped inside, nodded to Kelso, and closed the door, then turned to face the room's contents.

"Bloody hell…" he murmured.

Martinez hadn't been exaggerating. Apparently, Hiram Drummond had been more of an avid collector than Stone had thought.

The storeroom was roughly fifteen by twenty feet, and every inch of it was stacked haphazardly with crates, boxes, bookshelves, and tables. Atop the tables were various statues, carvings, and figurines, and the bookshelves were stuffed with volumes, binders, and piles of loose papers. In the far corner stood an eight-foot-tall, closed sarcophagus that looked vaguely Egyptian, but not quite. A number of large, wooden boxes—obviously filled with things that hadn't been unpacked—were pushed back against the walls.

This was going to take longer than he thought.

Stone started by standing just inside the door, where he could get the best view of the room at large, and doing a mundane scan for any security cameras inside the room. He didn't see any, which didn't surprise him. If the only people with access to the area were professors from the University, he supposed nobody expected them to steal anything. Also, if anything turned up missing, they'd always have the footage from the outside cameras to show who'd been inside.

Next, he switched to magical sight, making a small bet with himself about what he'd see as he did it. Leading the odds was "nothing magically interesting." The fact that he'd never heard of Hiram Drummond didn't mean the man *hadn't* been a mage, but if a decent chunk of this stuff was the real deal, Stone was fairly sure he'd at least have heard of the man in passing.

It turned out he was mostly right.

If he'd gone with his next most likely bet—"Not much magically interesting"—he'd have won.

Starting on the left side of the room and directing his gaze in a slow pan across to the right, he spotted a grand total of three items that glowed with magical energy. One was a tome on one of the bookshelves, one a figurine at the far end of the leftmost table, and the last was a small assortment of what looked like quill pens in a wooden box on the middle table. Aside from those, the other objects in the room remained resolutely glow-free, including the sarcophagus. No marauding mummies here tonight. Even the things that *had* glowed didn't show the kind of blazing auras that would indicate powerful magic. The best of the lot was the tome.

Stone wasn't sure whether to be pleased or disappointed. On the one hand, he always hoped to find new magical artifacts to study, but on the other, he was glad nothing potentially malevolent had turned up. That way, he didn't have to figure out how to get it out of the storeroom without anyone catching on.

He crossed the room to the bookshelf, careful not to step on anything on the floor, and pulled the glowing tome free. It was bound in cracked brown leather with a strap holding it closed. Based on Stone's experience, he put it about two hundred years old, and probably European in origin from its design. There were no markings on the front, not even a title. As he held it in his hands, he didn't get any feeling of danger or unease.

"Probably some minor spellbook or reference volume," he murmured. Nothing to get worked up over, that was sure, but it still might have something useful from a mundane standpoint. He'd take a look at it, at least. Maybe Greene would want to give it a look.

As he passed the leftmost table on his way to the center of the room, he picked up the figurine that had also glowed. It looked mostly humanoid, possibly African in origin, with most of its features worn away. It had a small tag around its neck with a number printed on it, but no other identifying information. When Stone looked more closely at it, he got a sense of faint protective magic. It might have been powerful at one point, but like many magic items that didn't possess artifact-level power, most of its potency had long ago waned. He set it on the end of the right-side table and laid the book next to it.

Normally, when examining books this old and potentially fragile, he wore gloves and used a preservation spell to ensure the brittle pages remained supple while they were turned. He hadn't brought any gloves with him, though, and he hesitated to use any other magic on the tome until he'd determined more about its purpose. That was all right, though—it wasn't as if Hubbard or Greene would identify magic on the book, and he was certain there was nothing dangerous about it. If he put it back where he'd found it, he could return later with more appropriate gear and get a better look.

As a compromise, he pulled a clean handkerchief from his coat pocket and used it to undo the book's strap and carefully open the cover. It creaked a little, but didn't crack. Possibly someone had put a preserving spell on it before and it had mostly faded by now, but persisted enough to keep the book's spine from breaking.

When Stone got a look at the front page, though, he mostly lost interest. It had some text written in the quasi-Latin many old-time mages had used, and was surrounded by illustrations of twining leaves, berries, and vines. Stone knew the language but wasn't familiar enough with the precise terminology to do a proper translation, but it was obvious the book had something to do with magical herbs and plants. Perhaps he might sign it out and let Verity and Hezzie take a look at it for alchemy ideas, but it wasn't something that interested him personally. He pushed it aside next to a small group of odd-looking objects and used the handkerchief to pick up the figurine.

It wasn't any more interesting than the book, unfortunately. Its arcane glow was faint and flickering, and upon closer examination Stone verified his initial hypothesis that the thing had fulfilled some kind of protective role. Perhaps it had generated a ward to guard the home of a tribe's magical practitioner, or had been carried by a hunting party to keep them safe from predators. Fascinating stuff, true—even though African magical practices weren't one of Stone's areas of particular focus, researching its history might be interesting. *Might even justify a trip to Africa,* he thought. But Africa was a big place with many magical traditions, and first he'd have to figure out which specific area this figurine originated in. That would take a lot of research, and a lot of time.

Reluctantly, he pushed the figurine off to the side next to the book. So far, this trip was turning out to be a bit of a bust, at least magically speaking.

Last, he retrieved the box of quills, once again using the handkerchief to pull each from the box and spread them on the table. There were five in all, and once he had them separated he saw that only two glowed. The box itself was as mundane as most of the rest of the collection. Like the statuette, it had a tag with a number, this time inside the box.

He examined the two glowing quills, but once again quickly lost interest. They were another minor magical item used by mages long ago, enchanted to extend the usefulness of ink so the mage could write longer without having to re-dip the nib in the inkwell. A big deal in the olden days, but not much to speak of in modern times.

"Well, that's unfortunate," Stone murmured. He put the quills back in the box, this time shoving it to the left side of the desk. He supposed he should take a quick scan of the rest of the bookshelves before he left—even mundane books could contain information mages found useful—but aside from that, it appeared likely that Hiram Drummond hadn't been a mage. The three minor arcane objects among the collection could have been obtained accidentally, perhaps as part of smaller collections Drummond had bought from others. It happened all the time.

At least he knew now that he didn't need to spend a lot of time here this evening, making sure nothing in the room would enchant, eat, compel, or otherwise threaten his mundane colleagues. That was something, he supposed. But still, he couldn't help being disappointed.

He shifted back to magical sight, intending to give the room one last once-over before he left. This time he switched off the light, which sometimes made it easier to spot dim magical auras.

That's odd…

Instead of the three glows he'd expected to see, only one appeared, on the left side of the table where he'd put the box of quills.

He flicked the light back on, half-expecting the book and the figurine to be inexplicably gone, but no—there they were, right where he'd put them.

Frowning, he picked up the figurine and shifted back to magical sight.

It glowed as it always had.

Very strange…

Without dropping magical sight, he looked back at the book.

It too glowed, but only very faintly—far more faintly than it had before when he was examining it. So faintly, in fact, that he could easily have missed it before when he thought it was gone.

He wrapped the handkerchief around his hand and picked it up, pulling it to him.

The brighter glow instantly sprang into life.

"Bloody hell…" Stone murmured.

Perhaps something interesting was going on here after all.

Stone was a scientist at heart, so his first thought was to conduct experiments. The book and the figurine had glowed, and then they hadn't, and then they had again. The quills, on the other hand, had never lost their glows.

What had changed?

He'd shoved all three objects off to the sides of the table—but the quills had gone to the left side, while the book and figurine had gone to the right.

He shifted the book and the figurine to the left side of the table, then turned off the light again.

All three objects glowed as they had before.

"Hmm…" Stone murmured. This time, he didn't bother with the light switch, instead holding up his hand and summoning a glow around it. With his other hand, he moved the box containing the quills to the right side, leaving the book and figurine on the left.

The quills showed no sign of magic, while the other objects' auras remained, serene and untroubled.

"Okay…" Stone said under his breath, turning the light back on. He pulled a notebook and pen from his pocket and jotted down what he'd discovered so far.

This would bear more investigation.

There were several other objects on both sides of the table: more figurines, something that looked like an elaborate ashtray, a vase decorated with stylized images of animals, a brass amulet, and a six-inch-tall, chipped black pyramid with various glyphs and figures etched onto its visible surfaces. None of them glowed with magic, regardless of where Stone placed the original three objects. All of them either had tags tied around them or were sitting on a card with a similar tag attached to it.

Continuing to avoid using magic of his own in direct contact with the items in fear of contaminating his results, Stone moved the three magical objects to the next table over, then gathered all the other items to the right side of the leftmost table. Then, with the left side empty, he moved the book back there.

It continued to glow.

"Hmm…okay, so it's not the table itself. Could it be one of those other items that's interfering with magic?" Stone spoke barely above a whisper, his heart beating faster as it always did when he felt he was on the edge of a discovery.

One by one, he moved each of the non-magical objects into proximity with the book, starting with the figurines and the amulet. If one of the items *was* causing interference, he had a suspicion about which one it was—the pyramid with the etchings—so he saved that one for last.

None of the others had any effect on the book. It kept on glowing regardless of which of them was near it.

Finally, only the pyramid was left. Stone held his breath, picked the object up with his handkerchief-covered hand, and drew it closer to the book.

The closer it got, the more the tome's glow faded. By the time Stone put the two directly next to each other, the book might as well have been any other volume on the bookshelves.

"There we go…" he murmured. He was smiling, but also tense. If this thing truly *did* interfere with magic, that was a big deal. A bigger deal, in fact, than all the other magical items in the storeroom combined. Where had Hiram Drummond obtained it? *How* had he obtained it? Did he have any idea what he had, or, more likely, had he purchased it as part of an auction lot or from a fellow collector?

Stone looked around, checking again for cameras. His conscience twinged a bit about what he was about to do, but not much. This item definitely needed more study, and not here—and it definitely wasn't something he wanted to leave lying around protected only by mundane security. Even though the odds were extremely low that anybody would take an interest in it—it was nowhere near as impressive-looking as the amulet, the vase, or a couple of the statues—Stone wasn't willing to leave it to chance.

He switched off the light in case there *were* cameras hidden somewhere in the storeroom, then slipped the little pyramid and its tagged card into his coat pocket. It made a small bulge, but even if Kelso turned up unexpectedly he could always use an illusion to hide it.

Truly, pulling things over on uninitiated mundanes was almost embarrassingly easy.

He didn't have to worry, though—Kelso was nowhere in sight when he exited the room and carefully made sure the door was locked behind him. If all went well, he'd examine the pyramid at home, then have it back in the storeroom before anybody caught on that it was missing.

He was halfway home when his phone buzzed, showing Jason's number.

"Hello, Jason."

"Hey, Al. You haven't had dinner yet, have you?"

"Er…no." He glanced at the clock, surprised to see he'd spent nearly an hour and a half inside the storeroom. "Bit early, isn't it?"

"Yeah, but Amber's got a meeting tonight and I figured I'd see if you want to go have a beer or something before I head back over the hill. Maybe stop by and talk to Marta. It's been a while."

Stone patted the pyramid in his pocket. Truth be told, he was itching to get home and study it, but Jason was right—especially since he'd started traveling by ley line and no longer needed the portal, he hadn't seen Marta since well before the holidays. "Er…sure. Sounds brilliant. Let me just pop home and drop off a couple of things. Meet you in an hour?"

"Yeah, great. See you then."

It was tempting, when he got home, to take a few minutes to study the strange little pyramid, but he resisted. It wasn't going anywhere—especially when locked inside his safe, which had both a formidable mundane lock and a heavy-duty ward around it. He paused long enough to make sure the pyramid didn't interfere with the ward—it didn't, as far as he could tell—and then headed out. He'd have plenty of time to check it later tonight or tomorrow.

Dinner at A Passage to India was both delicious and pleasant, with a delighted Martha Bellwood taking some time off from her duties to join Stone and Jason at their table to catch up on their various activities. It turned out Marta *had* been considering the possibility of returning home to Leeds, but assured Stone that if she did it, she'd make doubly sure everything regarding the portal was taken care of before she did it.

"Don't you worry," she assured him. "I'd never leave you in the lurch. This is sort of a…long-term goal of mine, not something I'm going to do next week."

He and Jason had dawdled over dinner with her for a couple hours, then the two of them adjourned to a nearby bar for beers and more conversation. They didn't talk about anything momentous—mostly Jason and Amber's home renovation, which was proceeding apace, Stone's classes, and the latest cases at the agency. Stone didn't bring up Hiram Drummond's collection or the little pyramid, but it was on his mind for most of the evening. By the time the two of them said their good nights and Stone returned to Encantada, it was nearly midnight.

Sleep was the last thing on his mind, though. He didn't have any classes tomorrow, which meant he could stay up as late as he liked and sleep in a long as he wanted tomorrow. No reason not to get started examining the pyramid. He hurried upstairs to his attic workroom, pausing only to pat Raider on the head and make sure his food and water dishes were topped up. "See you in a bit," he told the cat on his way by. "Important things to do."

A small part of him had been concerned all night that somehow, someone had managed to break into his house and steal the pyramid. Even though that was absurd—nobody knew he had it, and even if they did, getting past his wards and other security wouldn't have been an easy feat—the thought had burrowed into his mind like a compulsion and refused to leave. When he opened the safe and discovered the pyramid exactly where he'd left it, he was almost surprised.

His studies didn't get him very far that night, however. He set the pyramid on his worktable and, wearing gloves this time, turned it in every direction. The three upright sides were all etched with the odd symbols and sigils. The bottom, while free of any writing, had two nearly identical round holes, one on each side. When Stone used a penlight to look inside them, he saw nothing of interest.

He didn't recognize the writing on the other surfaces. It looked remotely familiar, like he might have seen something similar to it at some point, but he couldn't remember where. That didn't surprise him: over his magical career, he'd seen plenty of odd languages and symbols, some of which he could read and some he couldn't. Whatever it was, it didn't look like any magical language he'd seen before. It also didn't look Egyptian, despite the object's shape.

He used his phone camera to snap close-up photos of all four of the thing's sides. After checking to make sure the photos came out properly, since sometimes magical objects resisted being photo-graphed, he pulled out a larger notebook and painstakingly sketched all of the sides, taking extra care to get all the symbols right.

Finally, he set the pyramid on the table and studied it. He'd saved his most potentially interesting experiment for last, on pur-pose. Back in the storeroom, the thing had seemed to interfere with magic, damping the arcane auras of the quills, the tome, and the statuette when he'd brought them near it. Obviously the power wasn't terribly strong, or it would have interfered with the wards around the safe he'd locked it into, but it existed nonetheless. He was sure of it.

With careful concentration, he reached out with a little magic and attempted to levitate the pyramid off his worktable. If it had been a normal mundane object, or even a normal magical one, he should find it an easy task. It didn't weigh much, and at Stone's power level, it should be no more difficult than picking up a mun-dane paperback book.

The little thing shuddered, trembling in place, but didn't lift.

Interesting indeed…

Stone added more power, gripping the pyramid and willing it to rise from the surface.

It shuddered again, but this time it rose, floating a few inches above the table.

It did it under protest, though, continuing to twitch and judder in the air as if resisting Stone's effort. Power-wise, instead of feeling like lifting a paperback book, keeping the pyramid aloft felt more like he was levitating a stack of heavy tomes.

So whatever else this thing was, it was both resistant to magic itself, and had an effect on other magic around it. Stone tested this hypothesis by bringing several more magic items of varying power levels in proximity to it one at a time.

Its response depended on the objects' magical potency. Powerful items seemed not to be affected by it at all, their auras shining strong and clear even when the two were touching. Mid-level objects reacted the same way those in the storeroom had: their auras dimmed relative to how close he placed them.

The most potentially interesting result came when he placed a weak object near the pyramid. He used a piece of paper he'd enchanted to display text only when examined with magical sight, and slowly moved the pyramid closer until he rested it on the sheet like a paperweight.

Its faint glow vanished, as Stone expected—but this time, when he removed the pyramid, the glow didn't return.

"Bloody hell…" he murmured, shoving the pyramid aside almost nervously. That thing had completely obliterated the paper's magical power. Not just interfered with it, but eliminated it. Sure, it had been a very weak object…

But still.

He would definitely need to do more study with this thing—but perhaps not under such informal conditions. Whatever this thing was, the mere *concept* of it was unsettling.

When he came up for air, he discovered two hours had passed and it was now after two a.m. That wasn't late for him, but his shoulders ached and a dull headache was blooming behind his eyes from focusing on the tiny symbols. He leaned back, stretching his arms above his head and reveling in the satisfying *pops* from his back, and decided perhaps this was enough study for the night. He didn't have anything on his schedule for tomorrow, so he could get started again as soon as he dragged himself out of bed. If he didn't get anywhere, he considered taking the pyramid to Eddie and Ward or Kolinsky—or perhaps all of them. He'd start with his friends in England, though. Any object that could interfere, even slightly, with magic was potentially an important discovery, and he wanted to know more about it before he revealed it to the dragons.

Hell, it was possible they already knew all about it. Stone wasn't sure whether that thought comforted him or made him nervous.

He locked it back in the safe along with his written notes, stretched again, and headed out. Raider, as was often the case, was waiting patiently outside the door. The cat fixed him with a calm, inquisitive stare, appeared satisfied, and padded along behind him as he descended the stairs toward his bedroom.

Stone's phone buzzed on his nightstand, rousing him from a sound sleep. He poked a hand from beneath the covers, startling Raider, and snatched it up.

The number was Beatrice Martinez's, and the time was barely after eight a.m.

What does she want this *early?*

As he fumbled with the phone, a sudden thought brought a surge of ice water along with it: *Does she know I took the pyramid?*

That was ridiculous, though. There was no way she could know. "Yes, hello, Dr. Martinez," he mumbled. "Bit early to be calling, isn't it?"

"I'm sorry to wake you." She sounded contrite, but her voice also held an odd, stressed edge. "I wouldn't do it if it wasn't important."

Stone was more awake now, sitting up against his pillows and glancing at Raider, who seemed as clueless as he was. "No, no, it's fine. What can I do for you?"

"Something's...happened, Dr. Stone."

Now he was fully awake, the last vestiges of his brain fuzz departing like fog in a stiff wind. "What is it?"

"There's been...an incident at the storeroom where Hiram Drummond's collection is stored."

Bloody hell, they do *know.* "What...kind of incident?"

"A break-in. And I'm sorry to report that Mr. Greene was injured."

CHAPTER FOUR

S TONE ARRIVED AT THE UNIVERSITY less than half an hour later, and the early-morning students must have thought it odd to see one of their professors dashing from the parking lot as though pursued by a pack of wolves. He ignored them, though, and didn't slow his pace until he skidded to a stop in front of the administration building where Martinez had her office. He managed to walk inside at a reasonable pace, but it wasn't easy.

"What's happened?" he demanded, after striding past Martinez's admin aide without acknowledging her presence and flinging open his boss's door.

Martinez didn't even look annoyed at his intrusion. Her pale face showed both worry and fear. "Thank you for coming so fast, Alastair."

"What's happened?" he repeated. "How's Greene? When did this happen?"

"Slow down." She held up a hand. "Please, have a seat. I've only got a few minutes—I need to meet with the police again."

Stone didn't sit. He couldn't. He stalked in front of her desk and forced himself to wait for her to speak.

She sighed. "We don't know much yet. Brandon will be all right. He's in the hospital for observation, and should be there for a couple days. Someone hit him pretty hard on the head, so they're watching for any complications, but they don't expect any. He's young and strong. And he was very lucky."

"Someone…hit him? Bloody hell. Do they know who?"

"No." She riffled through some papers on her desk, obviously as restless in her own way as Stone. "They…found him late last night, when the new security guard came on shift. He and the previous guard checked to see when Brandon would be done, but he didn't answer their knock. They went inside and found him unconscious on the floor."

Stone narrowed his eyes. "Wait. You're saying Kelso—the previous guard—was there, but he didn't see anyone come in? Didn't hear anyone break into the storeroom?"

"Apparently not." She looked grim. "Needless to say, both the police and campus security aren't very happy with him at the moment."

"They don't think he might have been involved, do they?"

"I don't know. But I do know he's been with the University for many years, and he's never had an incident before. His record's spotless. I've heard he feels terrible about what happened."

A cold knot was forming in the pit of Stone's stomach. "And Greene was still inside the storeroom?"

"Yes. The door was locked. When they got no answer to their knock, they figured he must have left when Kelso wasn't looking. The other guard insisted on checking inside. Thank God he did."

"Damn…" Stone slowed his pacing. "Do they know when this happened? Did anything show on the cameras?"

Martinez shot him a surprised look. "How did you know about the cameras?"

"I was there yesterday. I stopped by to look at the collection around four, just after our meeting. I have a friend who's a private investigator, so I've sort of got in the habit of looking for them."

She seemed to accept that without suspicion. "They don't know yet what time it happened. There was a log sheet outside the storeroom, but apparently whoever did this took it with them. Even if Brandon had signed in, we won't know when he was there until he wakes up. The only thing we know is it must have been before midnight, because that's when the new guard came on shift."

Stone gazed over Martinez's shoulder and out the window, which overlooked one of the campus's central quads. "Was anything missing? Do the police know why someone might break in? I didn't think it was common knowledge that the collection was even here."

"It wasn't. It certainly wasn't in the news or anything. In fact, we haven't told anyone other than a few faculty members who might be interested in viewing it before it's auctioned. So far, we don't know if anything is missing. It's going to be hard to tell, since the items weren't terribly organized in there to start with, and the thieves made even more of a mess." She sighed. "Perhaps you should come with me to the meeting with the police. If you were in the storeroom yesterday they'll probably find your fingerprints in there, so best if they talk to you so they can take you off the suspect list."

Yes, let's do that, even though I'm responsible for at least one theft. He let his breath out. "This is…horrible. I mean—we're not talking about King Tut's treasures here. As far as I could tell, some of the items in there were valuable, but not enough to nearly kill anyone over."

She nodded soberly. "I agree. I feel terrible for Brandon."

The knot in Stone's stomach twisted a little. "Yes, of course I'll come with you. I should go visit Greene at the hospital, too."

"I think he'll like that, but last I heard he was still unconscious. They're keeping him sedated to give him a chance to heal. He took a pretty good knock on the head." She rose from her desk, looking more sober than ever. "You're right, Alastair—this is horrible. I'd never have agreed to let them store the collection here if I'd thought something like this would happen."

"It's not your fault. Let's go see what we can find out, and go from there."

The police had cordoned off the area surrounding the storeroom's building. A crowd of curious students, reporters, and other onlookers had gathered, but so far everybody was behaving. As Stone walked through with Martinez, he was reminded of another, similar situation a few years back, when two men had been brutally mutilated inside a lecture hall by the demon he'd dubbed "Archie."

Martinez showed her identification and introduced Stone, and a uniformed cop let them through the cordon. "First room on the right is where they've set up," she told them. "Don't go past that."

The indicated room was another storeroom, empty this time except for a few metal shelves holding boxes of paper and other office supplies. The police had set up a table which was now covered with papers, and a few cops, both uniformed and dressed in the coveralls of crime-scene investigators, hurried in and out. Behind the table stood a purposeful-looking dark-haired woman in a business suit. She was talking to one of the uniforms, but looked up when Martinez and Stone entered. "You Dr. Martinez?"

"Yes. This is Dr. Alastair Stone, one of my colleagues. He's a professor in the Occult Studies department."

The woman's sharp gaze raked over Stone's black T-shirt, jeans, and long black coat. "You don't look like a college professor." She shrugged before either of them could answer. "Doesn't matter. Not important. I'm Detective Bertola, Palo Alto PD. We're working with the Stanford authorities."

Martinez shook Bertola's hand; Stone didn't.

"How can we help you, Detective?" Martinez asked. "Have you discovered anything else about what might have happened?"

"Still working the scene. It's going to take quite some time, I'm afraid. It's a mess in there."

"So you don't know what was stolen yet, if anything?"

Bertola snorted. "It'll probably be days before we figure that out, even with the list of stuff you sent us. Right now, we're more focused on the assault."

"Of course. I'm sorry—I didn't mean to imply otherwise."

"It's okay. This whole thing is unsettling, I know." She glanced at Stone. "I thought I was just meeting with you."

"I called Dr. Stone this morning—Brandon Greene is a friend and colleague, so I thought he'd want to know. He told me he was looking at the collection yesterday."

"Is that right?" Bertola's eyebrows rose. She pulled out a notebook, suddenly showing more interest in Stone. "What time, Dr. Stone?"

"Around three-thirty. I was inside for about an hour and a half."

"What were you doing in there that long? Just looking around?"

"As Dr. Martinez said, I'm a professor of occult studies. The entire collection was occult-related, so I'm sure you can see how I might find that fascinating. I sort of lost track of time, to be honest."

"Yeah, makes sense." She made another note. "So you arrived at three-thirty and left at five-ish. Did you see anything out of the ordinary when you were in the area?"

If you only knew, he thought, but didn't let any reaction reach his face. "Out of the ordinary?"

"Yeah—you know, anybody lurking around the building that you didn't recognize? Anything weird inside the room?"

"*Everything* inside that room would probably qualify as weird to most people. But as for anything else—no. The area was fairly deserted. A few students walking by, but nothing else."

"Did you see Mr. Greene or Mr. Kelso, the security guard?"

"I didn't see Mr. Greene after the meeting with Dr. Martinez. Mr. Kelso was on duty when I arrived. He's the one who let me into the storeroom."

She noted that down. "Did Mr. Greene say anything about wanting to visit the collection?"

"He did, yes. When we spoke yesterday after the meeting, he told me he couldn't go right away because he had a class, but mentioned he might pop in later yesterday or perhaps today. Nothing specific, though."

She looked him over again. "Okay. And you didn't see anything strange when you left?"

"Nothing. I didn't even see Mr. Kelso. He told me to make sure I locked up."

"And did you?"

"Absolutely. I double-checked the lock before leaving."

"Got it. One more question and then I'll let you go so I can get back to Dr. Martinez. You say you're an expert on this occult stuff."

"That's what it says on my business card."

She shot him a grumpy glare, but let it go. "In your…professional opinion…was there anything in that collection that might have been valuable enough for somebody want bad enough to kill for?"

Stone pondered, trying to think like a mundane. He closed his eyes for a moment, allowing his mind's eye to visualize the objects in the room. "I honestly don't think so. I don't recall seeing anything involving precious metals or stones, or anything like that. Most of the items I saw in that room were fascinating to people like me—perhaps to a few obscure collectors—but that's about it."

Her gaze sharpened. "Do you know any of these collectors, Dr. Stone? Anybody you can think of who might be a little… overzealous to pick up a few new acquisitions?"

He chuckled, once again wondering what she'd do if she knew the whole truth. "Honestly, Detective, most of the collectors I know are rather elderly, very strange, and wouldn't have the slightest clue how to pull off something like this—not to mention committing assault to do it."

"You'd be surprised what people can do when they want something bad enough." She flipped to a new page in her notebook. "Suppose you give me some names."

Stone paused as if thinking. "Let's see…well, there's Hubbard—the other Occult Studies professor here—but he wouldn't hurt a fly." *Too lazy to get out of his chair most of the time,* he thought but didn't say. "Plus, I doubt he'd be interested enough in the first place."

"Anybody else?"

He gave her a few more names, deliberately keeping to older mundane colleagues in both the United States and England whom he was certain would have ironclad alibis. While he thought it was possible this crime might be solved by mundane police work—he still wasn't certain the thief had been after anything but valuable items they could fence—his gut told him otherwise. Why would a mundane thief break into a building to steal bits of a collection nobody except a handful of people even knew was here in the first place, and why would they risk killing someone to get what they were looking for? Stranger things had happened, sure, but he didn't think they had this time.

Bertola dutifully wrote down all the names, then snapped her notebook shut. "Thank you, Dr. Stone. That's all for now. Will you be around if I have any other questions?"

"Of course." He took one of his business cards and a pen from his coat pocket and scrawled his cell number on the back. "I'm at your service, Detective."

She gave him another odd look, glanced at the card, and frowned, almost as if disappointed it didn't actually say *Expert on Occult Stuff.* Then she tucked it into her pocket and turned to Martinez. "Okay. Let's get started so I don't have to keep you too long."

"If you'll excuse me, then…" Stone nodded farewell and left the room, brushing past more uniformed cops and CSIs moving in and out of the room. He wished he could get another look inside the storeroom, but even with his best disregarding spell he didn't think that would be a good idea. Too many people around to spot him. Perhaps he could pop in later if he needed to.

Right now, he had other, more important, places to be.

CHAPTER FIVE

S TONE HAD FORGOTTEN to ask Martinez where they'd taken Greene, but since Stanford Medical Center was both close by and one of the best hospitals in northern California, he took a chance rather than interrupt her meeting with Detective Bertola.

He got lucky—stopping at the front desk and acting like he already knew Greene was there, he found out his friend's room number.

"Check in at the nurses' station up there to make sure he can have visitors," the receptionist told him.

He half-expected to see a police guard on the room's door, but didn't. The door was closed, though.

"Oh, yes," the on-duty nurse said, consulting her computer. "Mr. Greene is awake this morning and can have visitors. Are you a relative?"

"I'm a work colleague. I heard about what happened and came right over."

"Don't stay too long. He needs his rest."

"Of course. Thank you."

Stone knocked on the door, then pushed it partway open to reveal an empty bed on the near side and a privacy curtain drawn around another one near the window. "Greene? Are you decent?"

"No, I'm over here having a three-way with two hot nurses."

Stone smiled in relief. Greene sounded tired and a bit woozy, but he was still the same old Greene. "Well, then, suppose I join in? The more the merrier, they say."

"I'm not sure the bed can handle one more, but you're welcome to give it a shot."

"Let's find out." He pushed aside the curtain, and his smile died.

Greene lay in the bed, dressed in a hospital gown, a white bandage wrapped around his head. His normally-pale face was even paler than usual, except for the dark circles around them. An IV tube led to a bag of clear liquid suspended on his left side, and the usual assortment of beeping monitors stood mostly unobtrusively beneath it. He'd been looking at something on his phone, but put it aside.

"You'll do just about anything to get out of work, won't you?" Stone pulled up a chair and sat, keeping his voice light even though he felt anything but. He tried not to think about how easily Greene could have died.

"Yeah, you know me—finally got the job I've been working toward my whole college career, so I totally want to slack off and get fired." His smile faded. "I've been reading about what happened, since I don't really remember much. Nobody else got hurt, did they? The security guy?"

"No—he's fine. But as you can imagine, he's apparently not in anyone's good graces right now. Did you talk to him when you went in?"

"Yeah. He let me in and told me to find him before I left so he could make sure the place was locked up."

"How are you feeling now?" Stone wanted to get to the more pertinent questions fast before they made him leave, but he forced himself to slow down.

"Eh, my head hurts. They've got me on some good drugs, and they're pretty sure I've got a concussion. I'm pretty sure I've got one too. My brain feels scrambled, you know? But it sounds like I was really lucky."

"Yes, it seems so." He leaned forward. "Would you mind answering a few questions?"

Greene's eyes narrowed. "Questions? What are you, moonlighting as a detective when you're not teaching goth kids about the Mothman?"

"Just…curious, I suppose. I was in there yesterday a few hours before you were—it could easily have been me who got bonked on the head."

"Better you than me." Greene's tone made it obvious he didn't mean it. "But yeah, I guess I could answer a few questions. I doubt I'll be much help, though. I don't remember much about what happened."

"Let's give it a go, shall we?" Stone glanced toward the door to make sure the nurse wasn't coming in to kick him out already. "What time did you go to look at the collection?"

The younger man appeared to be having trouble organizing his thoughts. "Sorry…like I said, they've got me doped up and my brain's scrambled. Uh…I think I got there around nine. I had a late class, and stopped in to Coupa to grab a quick bite after that, then headed over there."

"Did you notice anything odd about the area? Anybody else lurking around? Anyone who seemed to be paying too much attention to the building?"

Greene snorted. "Are you kidding? That place is out in the middle of bumfuck Egypt, even worse than our building. There aren't any classes out that far, so nobody would be in the area that late. Unless they're curious idiots like me."

"Any particular reason you went tonight, instead of waiting until tomorrow?"

He shrugged. "I wanted to see it, I guess. And I'm glad I did. There were some seriously cool things in there. I was planning to talk to you and Dr. Martinez about maybe signing out a couple of them to show the Intro class."

"Okay." Once again, Stone checked the door. "Do you have any idea how long you were there before anything happened?"

"Not too long. Maybe a half-hour. I got a little distracted looking at the markings on one of the big statues, so I wasn't paying close attention to time."

"Did you hear anything? You know—the door opening, or Mr. Kelso talking to anyone outside?"

"That's the weird thing." Greene frowned, and although Stone couldn't see his brow furrowing beneath the wide bandage, he didn't have to. "I didn't hear a thing. You'd think I'd have at least heard the click of the lock or the door opening, but I didn't. Normally I wear my earbuds and listen to music when I'm studying, but it felt wrong to do it in there. It was really quiet. Kinda too eerie for me, if I'm gonna be honest. And you know me—I *love* eerie. It was quiet as a tomb. I would have heard a mouse fart."

"Are you sure you didn't get distracted? You know how we can be when we've got something interesting to examine."

"Yeah, no. I mean, I like this stuff—a lot. You know that. But I guess I wasn't born with the absent-minded professor gene. I pay attention to my surroundings, even when I'm studying. And I'm certain nobody came in through that door."

Stone wasn't so sure, but he let it go. "Go on."

Greene shrugged. "Not much else to tell. One minute I was looking at that statue, and the next my head felt like it was splitting and I was looking up at an EMT in the back of an ambulance."

"So you don't even remember being hit?" This wasn't what Stone was hoping to hear. If Greene couldn't tell him anything about the intruder, he didn't have too many other places to look. He doubted Detective Bertola would give him access to the recordings from the hallway cameras—if anything even showed up on them. If this thief was that good, chances were high they'd disabled the cameras before going in. There hadn't been any windows in the storeroom, so the door was the only way in. He didn't think it would have been all that difficult to evade Kelso long enough to pop the lock on the door and slip inside.

"Nope. I don't think so, at least." He rubbed his head. "I mean, like I said before, they told me I've likely got a pretty good concussion, and that can scramble short-term memory. I still feel like I'm looking at the world through a couple layers of cotton."

"I think that's normal. You're getting the best of care, so don't worry about that. Give yourself a few days to lounge about and watch rubbish television. We've survived this long without you before, so I'm sure we can manage long enough to make sure you're right as rain before you come back to work."

"Yeah, thanks."

"Has anyone else been in to talk to you today? Martinez? Anyone from the police department?"

"Dr. Martinez called. She sounded really worried, so let her know I'm doing okay, will you?"

"Absolutely. What about the police?"

"I don't think they really care how I'm doing."

Stone mock-glared at him. "Did you tell them anything?"

"Just what I told you. I wish I could remember more, but…"

He was starting to look even more pale and tired, so Stone stood. "That's fine. Don't worry about it. Your job is to rest and get better, so I don't have to deal with Hubbard grousing about taking time away from his writing. But take your time. We'll look after your classes for you."

"I will. Hey, thanks for stopping by."

"Take care. And if you remember anything else, give me a call or a text or something, will you?"

"Sure thing, Mr. Holmes."

Stone had reached the doorway when he remembered something else. "Oh, Greene?"

"Yeah?" Greene had already picked up his phone again, but turned from it to look up at Stone.

"You might not remember this, but it's worth a try. When you arrived—when Kelso let you in—you had to sign in on a log sheet, right?"

"Yeah. He said everybody had to sign in."

"Do you remember if there were any other names on it?"

Greene closed his eyes. Obviously, his concussion was making it hard to remember specifics. "Uh…yeah. There were three. One before yours, yours, and one other right before mine. I remember that because I noticed yours." He chuckled. "Not that anybody else would've been able to read it. You've got the most illegible signature I've ever seen."

Stone gripped the door frame, ignoring his last words. "One after mine?" So somebody else had stopped by the storeroom between five and nine p.m. "Do you remember who it was?"

"Sorry, I don't. Definitely not Hubbard or Martinez." His eyes were still closed, and now he clenched them tighter. "I think it might have been somebody from the Anthro department. Uh…oh!" He looked triumphant, like a little kid who'd managed the answer to a difficult math problem he hadn't expected to get. "Yeah. It was Dr. Inouye. Her signature is so neat, and she always makes that weird curlicue thing with her *I*."

"Brilliant. I'll get out of your way now. Feel better, mate."

"That's the plan."

Stone barely noticed his walk out of the hospital and to the parking garage where he'd left the BMW. He swirled Greene's words around in his mind, trying to make sense of the limited new information he had.

He was more convinced than ever that whoever had broken into the storeroom had magical capabilities, and probably strong ones. They could easily have clocked Kelso over the head too—maybe even killed him—but they hadn't, which suggested they were trying to be quiet about the whole thing. Maybe they hadn't even realized Greene was inside, since it was so late, and had panicked when they spotted him. Also, Stone remembered the faint creak when the door opened. If Greene had been right and the place was "quiet as a tomb," he definitely would have heard it.

The fact that he hadn't meant one of two things: either the thief had used magic to enter the room—probably a combination of invisibility and a sound-damping spell, both well within the capabilities of most trained mages—or else they'd already been inside the storeroom. Perhaps Greene's late arrival had interrupted their search, so they hid until they could get the jump on him. Either way, Stone didn't think he'd have much chance of convincing Bertola to let him have a look around the place, at least not while the police were actively investigating. In fact, it was likely Martinez might decide it was too dangerous to keep the collection on campus now, and insist Hiram Drummond's daughter have it moved somewhere else prior to the auction.

Come on—you're getting ahead of yourself. Stone got into his car and drove out of the parking garage. He had another class this afternoon; perhaps he could find time to talk to Martinez after that.

He wondered what the thief had been after, and if they'd found it. As he headed back for campus, he tried to come up with a plausible way to find out if the book, the quills, or the African statuette had been taken. Perhaps there had been more to one or more of those objects than Stone's initial scan had indicated, or perhaps one of the mundane objects had held magical significance. There had been a lot of books on the shelves, and not all books useful to mages were magical themselves.

He'd have to think about it later, though, after his class.

CHAPTER SIX

S TONE'S PHONE BUZZED as he left his class and headed back toward his office to call Martinez. He pulled it out and glanced at the text.

Hey, Doc. Call me if you have a minute.

He smiled. Verity. He supposed his questions for Martinez could wait a bit. He reached his office, closed the door, and tapped her number.

"Oh, good," she said without greeting. "I was hoping you were around."

"Something wrong?"

"That's what I was going to ask *you*. I saw on the news that they had a break-in at Stanford and somebody got hurt, but they're not saying much about it yet."

"So, of course you assumed it's got something to do with me," he said, amused in spite of the gravity of the situation.

"Well…yeah. Can you blame me? You *do* have a track record."

"I suppose you've got a point. And in this case, you're right."

There was a pause. "You're okay, right?"

"No, I was the victim. I died, and I'm speaking to you from the Great Beyond."

"Doc—"

He sighed. "Okay, sorry. You're right. I shouldn't joke about it. There's nothing funny about the situation. Remember Brandon Greene from the department?"

"Oh, God!" She gasped. She'd met Greene a few times in passing over the years. "Did he—"

"No, no, he's alive. He was the one injured in the break-in, though."

"What happened?"

He quickly gave her an overview of the events, telling her about the magic items he'd discovered in the collection but leaving out any mention of the strange pyramid. He planned to tell her about it at some point, but right now he had no idea whether the object had been the source of the thief's search. Without more information, the whole thing could have been nothing but an unfortunate coincidence. And even if the thief *had* been a mage, it made more sense that they were after one of the magical items.

"So…" she said slowly when he finished, "you were in there earlier? That could have been *you* who got hurt? Maybe even killed?"

"Unlikely. Even if the thief used magic, I doubt they'd have managed to get the drop on me. Plus, we've proven it would take more than a knock on the head to take me out these days."

"Yeah…you're probably right. But it's still kind of scary."

"It is, and I feel terrible about Greene. But it's probably just someone breaking in because they heard there were potentially valuable items being stored somewhat insecurely." He still didn't believe that, though, since there had been next to no publicity about the collection being held on campus prior to the auction.

"I guess so." She didn't sound convinced. "But be careful anyway. You know these things have a way of getting away from you."

"It *has* been a few months since anything's happened. I suppose I'm due."

"Now see, *that's* why you keep getting into the middle of these things." She sounded like herself again. "Hey, I'm coming down there to have dinner with Jason and Amber tonight. Want to come? That was the other reason I wanted to talk to you."

He considered turning down the invitation in favor of spending more time studying the pyramid, but once again reassured himself that unless the thief was considerably more powerful than he thought, they had no chance of getting anywhere near the inside of his home. To be doubly safe, he could pop it over to Caventhorne and store it in Desmond's heavily shielded secret vault before he headed to Santa Cruz. "Er—sure. That sounds brilliant."

"Jason said you don't need to bring any wine—they're busting out some of the stuff you gave them."

"Can't say no to an invitation like that, now can I?"

Stone thought about taking a bit of time to give the pyramid some further study before he left for Santa Cruz, but an accident on the road to Encantada slowed his trip home enough that he'd barely have time to take it to Caventhorne and put it in the vault before he had to leave.

It was too bad Jason and Amber's house was nowhere near a ley line, which would have made the whole thing more convenient. As it was, by the time he secured the pyramid, returned home, and drove across Highway 17, he was nearly late.

Verity was already there. All three of them were in the kitchen, chatting as they tended the pans and set the table. The small house didn't have a dining room and it was too cold to eat out on the deck, so they used the kitchen table.

"Hey, Al," Jason greeted, shucking off a pair of oven mitts after setting a serving dish in the middle. "Thanks for coming. Been a while since you've been down here."

"You *have* been busy." Stone looked around in amazement. He hadn't been to the house since mid-October, and in the meantime Jason and Amber had mostly finished remodeling the kitchen. It still wasn't fancy, but they'd replaced the cabinets, the floor, the sink, the light fixtures, and all the appliances, and now the small space looked neat and efficient while still being inviting and homelike.

"Yeah, it's taken some time because we had to work mostly nights and weekends, but we're pretty proud of it." He beamed at Amber. "Trust me, Al—when you get married, find yourself a woman who can do home repair. None of this shit about being threatened by it. She's better at it than I am, and I think it's amazing."

Amber grinned. "Now, there's a compliment I can work with."

"Indeed," Stone said, chuckling. "I'll put that at the top of my list of criteria. Especially given that I'm rubbish at it myself."

Verity laughed as she used magic to levitate another serving dish over. "Come on, Doc—you know as well as I do that you'd just pay somebody to do it for you."

"True enough. But I must say, I envy your skill. It's utterly beyond me how you could have managed going from…what it looked like before to this in such a short time."

Jason waved him toward a seat. "You don't have to be tactful—we know it was a dump. But that was fine—we saw *potential*."

"And now the rest of us see it too. Well done, both of you."

As they settled in and began eating, the conversation turned to more sober topics. "V was telling me about the break-in at the University," Jason said. "I saw it in the news, too. Have they got the people who did it yet?"

"No idea. They hadn't as of this morning."

"She also said there were magic items in the stuff."

"Yes. When I was in there, three of them were actively putting off magical energy. There was a book, a box of quills, and a statuette."

"Do you think one of those was what they were after?" Amber asked.

"No way to tell. I do think magic was involved with the break-in, so it's definitely possible. But I was only in there for an hour and a half, and I didn't move much around. There were a lot of things in that room, none of them very well organized and some still in boxes. It's possible the target was something I didn't even see." Stone debated whether to mention the pyramid. He didn't intend to keep it from his friends, but still wanted to learn more about it before he said anything.

"I wonder how they even knew the stuff was in there," Verity mused. "I mean, it kinda sounds like that situation a while back where those two salvage guys found the magical chess set—except they found it by accident. If somebody purposely broke in, they had to be looking for something, right?"

"That's my thought," Stone said. "Maybe tomorrow I'll give Leo Blum a call and see if he can manage to get a copy of the police report. If we can figure out what was taken, we'll be better off. But I think the detective was right: it's going to take quite some time to check the room's contents against the list of what's supposed to be in there. It—"

His phone buzzed.

He pulled it out, curious. Most of the people who would call him in the evening were sitting around the table with him.

He tensed when he saw the number: Brandon Greene.

Holding up a finger, he tapped the button to answer. "Aren't you supposed to be recuperating and watching mindless television?"

"Doing plenty of that." Greene sounded better now, less fuzzy than this morning. "My brain is sloshy enough without adding soap operas and old game shows. I think they're planning to let me out tomorrow, if nothing bad happens overnight."

"Brilliant. I'm glad you're feeling better. Is there something I can do for you? I'm not home at present, but if you need anything—"

"No, no, nothing like that. I just remembered something, and I thought you'd want to hear it."

"Oh?" Stone leaned forward, tightening his grip on the phone. "Did you see the thief?"

"I wish. All I know is that it was a man."

"How do you know that?"

"Because I heard him talking to himself, when I was drifting in and out. That's what I remembered."

At this point, Stone was barely aware his friends were in the room. "What did he say? Do you remember any of it?"

"Yeah. Stuff like 'Where is it?' and 'Why isn't it here?' It sounded like he was frustrated. Like he expected to find something in there, but he couldn't find it. He was throwing things around quite a bit. He even bent down and shook me, and I felt him poking around in my jacket pockets. I got scared and played possum. That's when I passed out again, so I don't know if he ever found what he was looking for. I know he didn't take my wallet, though, or my phone. Those were here in my stuff at the hospital."

Stone went cold. Could it be—?

"Right, then. Thanks for letting me know. Did you tell the police yet?"

"Not yet. Gonna call them tomorrow. But you said you wanted to know if I remembered anything, so there you go. I gotta go now—I hear the nurse. Maybe I'll get a sponge bath."

"Probably just a sleeping pill. Take care, Greene. Thanks."

Everybody was watching him expectantly as he put the phone back in his pocket. "That was Greene."

"We figured," Verity said dryly. "Any new developments? Sorry to be nosy, but you *were* sitting right here. Who heard something? Did he hear the guy talking?"

"Yes. Apparently, he was looking for something he couldn't find. Greene said the man even looked in his pockets."

"Huh." Jason rubbed his chin. "But he doesn't know what?"

"He says not. Says he passed out again, so he doesn't remember."

"So it had to be something small, if he thought Greene might have stuck it in his pocket."

A tingle traversed Stone's spine. "Yes…you may be right."

Verity was eyeing him suspiciously. "You know something about this," she said. It wasn't a question. "Something you're not telling."

He almost asked her how she knew that, but didn't. She was Verity, and she'd always been good at seeing through him when he tried to keep things from her. "You're right. I do."

Now they were all focusing on him, food forgotten. "What is it?" Jason asked. "You know what he was looking for?"

"I…believe I do."

"What is it?" Verity asked.

"A small, pyramid-shaped object with symbols etched into three of its sides, and a pair of holes on the bottom."

"That's…oddly specific," Amber said, frowning. "How do you know that?"

"Because I took it."

They all gaped at him.

"You…*took* it?" Verity demanded. "Why?"

"Because it was stranger and more interesting than anything else in that room, and I wanted to study it. Apparently I was right about it being interesting."

"Why is it interesting?" Amber finished the last of her chicken and washed it down with wine. "Before, you said there were only three magic things in there that you saw. Were you lying?"

Stone pondered his answer to that. "Yes…and no. It wasn't magic, *per se.*" He gave them a brief overview of the experiments he'd done so far, both inside the storeroom and at home.

Jason whistled. "So…you're saying it's *anti*-magic? It does something to interfere with magic?"

"Yes, but only in a minor way. I had to move the other items very close to it before it started affecting them, and it didn't interfere with the wards on the safe I locked it in."

Verity was frowning too. "But is that all that weird? Are you saying magical science hasn't figured out a way to block magic?"

"Not exactly. It's possible to *hide* magic, of course. Remember the tome Deirdre had? As powerful as it was, the reason nobody discovered it for all those years was because it was stored in a container that blocked its aura. Those are rare, but they exist. And..." he added more slowly, "...I know there are alchemical ways to temporarily block magic." He didn't want to go into what had happened with his grandmother in Windermere, since even Verity didn't know all the details, but he shivered a little at the memory.

"Okay," Jason said, "then how is this different?"

"Because it wasn't a container. It was an object that wasn't detectable as any kind of magic. If I hadn't accidentally brought those other items close enough for it to interfere with them, I'd never have noticed it."

"So, you're saying as long as it wasn't near any magic items, it just looked like any other mundane thing?" Amber asked.

"Yes, apparently. Not near any magic items and also not near anyone who could *detect* magic items. I want to do a bit more research into Mr. Hiram Drummond's history, but I'll bet my house he was nothing but a wealthy, eccentric mundane collector." He glanced at Jason, who was suddenly looking troubled. "Problem? You're not going to go all law-enforcement on me for nicking it, are you?"

"No." He appeared to be trying to get his mind around something. "But Al...doesn't it bother you that your colleague got hurt because that thing wasn't where it was supposed to be?"

"No, because I don't think it would have mattered. The thief didn't have any idea the item was missing when he struck Mr. Greene. I think the only thing that would have happened differently if I hadn't taken it was that he'd have made off with it successfully. If he knew what he was looking for, it was in plain view."

"I guess…" Jason didn't sound convinced, but he finally nodded. "Yeah. I see what you're saying, and you're probably right. So…now what? Are you going to tell the police you have the item?"

"Of course not. I told you—I need to do a lot more study, both of the thing itself and its history. It's quite obvious to me that it's not the only component of whatever this is."

"How do you know that?" Verity asked.

"Because of the two holes in the bottom. I suspect it's meant to join up with at least one other thing, though I haven't any idea what it might be." He pulled out his phone again and showed them the photos he'd snapped.

"Yeah, I see what you mean," Amber said. "It looks like it's supposed to fit onto something else. But you didn't see anything like that with the rest of the stuff?"

"No, but as I said, I didn't do a thorough search."

"Where's the pyramid now?" Verity finished her wine and poured another glass. "Is it at your house?"

"It's in Desmond's vault in Caventhorne. Easy enough to get to when I want to look at it, but I don't want to take chances on anyone trying to break in to the house here and steal it."

"They wouldn't have much success, would they?" Amber asked. "Isn't your house warded all to hell?"

"Well…yes."

"So isn't it kind of a pain to have to go down to Sunnyvale every time you want to look at it?"

Stone mentally kicked himself again. By this point, he'd fully acclimated to his ley-line travel method, but he had to keep reminding himself that he hadn't shared the knowledge with his friends. As far as they knew, he still needed to use the portal at A Passage to India when he wanted to return to England. "It is, but it's safer there than it would be here. Plus, nobody would suspect it's there."

"Nobody would suspect you have it, either, right?" Amber asked. "I mean, they found Greene inside the room, but that wouldn't necessarily lead them to you."

"Likely not." A slight chill rippled through Stone as he remembered another detail Detective Bertola had told him. "Unless…"

"Unless what?" Verity narrowed her eyes.

"There was a log sheet outside the storeroom. Kelso made me sign in before I entered. But when they found Greene injured, the log was missing."

"So the thief knows who else was in there," Amber said. "That's not good."

"Well…my signature isn't exactly legible, so they wouldn't know right away. They—oh, bloody hell."

"What?"

"Greene told me somebody else was in there between the time I left and he arrived. Dr. Inouye from the Anthropology department. And *her* signature *isn't* illegible."

Jason frowned. "You don't think the thief would think she took it, do you?"

"No idea. Obviously he didn't find it, because it wasn't there. The question is, does he attribute his failure to not looking hard enough, or does he think someone else took it?"

"Or maybe that it was never there in the first place," Amber said.

"Yeah," Verity agreed. "I guess it's possible he might suspect Mr. Drummond's relatives removed it before sending the rest of the stuff over."

"I'm wondering about something, though," Jason mused. His gaze was unfocused, fixed somewhere far away.

"What?" Stone asked.

"Well…how did the guy know about the thing in the first place?"

"What do you mean?"

"You said this Drummond guy was an old collector, right? So he probably had this stuff stored away for a long time?"

"Yes…I believe so."

Jason drummed his fingers thoughtfully on the table. "So why now? Why would somebody go after it now, instead of when Drummond still had it? You said you think he was a mundane, right?"

"I'm not certain, but I strongly suspect he was. Otherwise, I'd have likely at least heard of him in passing." Stone had no idea where his friend was going, but Jason had good instincts. "What are you getting at?"

"I think I see what you mean," Verity said eagerly. "You think if the guy was a mundane, and the thief easily broke into the locked and guarded storeroom without a trace, why didn't he just break into wherever Drummond was storing the stuff?"

"Yes," Amber added. "If you're right and the only reason Greene got hurt was because the guy was surprised he was in there at all, it sounded like he wanted to get in and out of the storeroom with this pyramid thing without anybody knowing. Right?"

"Yes…" Stone wasn't used to feeling like the slow end of the discussion, but he still wasn't following where they all seemed to be going.

"So he must have known—or strongly suspected—it was in there," Jason said. "How would that have been possible? You said hardly anybody knew about the collection being stored on campus, right, Al?"

"Yes. Dr. Martinez said that aside from a few of us from the department, nobody knew anything about it. Not because it was particularly valuable, but mostly because not many people would *care*."

"What about the people who delivered it?" Verity asked.

Stone shrugged. "Maybe—but I'm sure the collection was boxed up. Delivery people don't generally get detailed information about what's in the boxes they deliver. The manifest probably just said 'art objects' or something."

"Then how would the thief have…wait!" Jason flashed a sudden, triumphant grin. "You said they're auctioning the stuff in a couple weeks, right?"

"Up in San Francisco, yes."

"So somebody at the auction place had to have a list of the items, right? They must have catalogued them already. Did the stuff you saw have little numbered tags on them?"

His words energized Stone so much that he didn't even feel embarrassed it had taken him this long to catch on. "Yes, they did! That's got to be it! I saw the tags but didn't think anything of them at the time, but now I'm sure you're right. They'd have needed time to create the catalog and make it available to the people doing the bidding, which means the auction people must have gone through the collection before it was stored at the University."

"So you think somebody inside the auction organization might be in on this?" Verity asked.

"Possibly. Serious collectors—both mundane and magical— have been known to pay key people to slip them information about items coming up for sale. Antique dealers, auction personnel…it's not at all uncommon, and for the most part it's not even illegal. Why would anyone care about someone getting a heads-up about an object coming up for sale? In most cases, the collector simply shows up at the auction or sends an assistant, and they buy the thing legitimately."

"So why didn't they do that this time?" Idly, Verity began using magic to gather the empty plates into a stack in the middle of the table.

"Maybe they didn't want anybody to know they were interested in that specific item," Amber said. "My guess is if they pay these people to watch auctions, they're not looking for anything specific—just anything that might be interesting. The person they paid probably didn't even know what they were looking for, but just passed along the catalog for early peek."

"You could be right," Stone said. "If the item is particularly valuable or interesting to mages, the thief or whoever hired him wouldn't want to take the chance of any other mages finding out. Especially since a number of powerful mages are also quite wealthy, which could lead to a bidding war. They wouldn't want that—not only because they wouldn't want to have to pay extra, but because it's bound to raise attention in the wrong places."

"But wait a minute," Amber said, eyes narrowed as she rubbed her chin. "Now you're saying there might be *multiple* mages interested in this thing? That doesn't make sense. If it's been buried in some guy's collection for years, are you saying there's more than one mage actively keeping an eye out for it? And yet you've never even heard of it?"

"That's a good point." Some of Stone's ardor dimmed at her words. "And I *haven't* heard of it. There are a few lost magical items that every powerful mage knows about, and most of us are at least passingly keeping an eye out for them even though they probably don't exist anymore. But I've never heard even a whisper about this one. I'm planning to check with Eddie, to see if he remembers anything from the library, and Stefan and Madame Huan. But you're right. So why—" He stabbed a finger up as a snatch of conversation came back to him. "Hold on! Back when Martinez first told us about the collection and the auction, she mentioned they'd put out an online catalog!" Whirling on Jason, he said, "May I borrow your laptop?"

"Yeah, but I don't think that's the best idea."

"Why not?"

Jason shook his head. "Maybe it's just me being paranoid, but I've been learning a lot from Gina about the internet and how easy it is to trace stuff if you're not careful. If somebody *is* watching this pyramid thing—and especially now, since it's missing—it's possible they might have somebody keeping an eye on the traffic to the auction site. You know, checking to see who might be interested in it. Even the cops, possibly, if they figure out what's missing."

Stone frowned. "You're having me on. They can do that?"

"Sure they can," Amber said. "Don't know if they actually *are,* of course, but the authorities can definitely keep an eye on which IP addresses show up in searches for stuff they're interested in."

Stone felt like he knew now how his mundane friends must feel when he started tossing around specialized magical terms. "IP address?"

Jason chuckled. "Think of it as an identifier for something connected to the internet. If we do a search from here and somebody's watching, they'll know it was us. And since you and I are known to be associates, that could lead to some uncomfortable questions."

"Damn." Stone sighed. "So is there a way around it?"

"Sure. But you'll have to wait till tomorrow. I can ask Gina to look into it. She's got all kinds of ways to spoof that stuff. Come by the office and we'll do it then."

Stone didn't want to wait, but he also didn't want the mundane authorities deciding he was a person of interest in the theft—especially since they weren't even convinced yet that there'd *been* a theft.

"All right," he said reluctantly. "I don't have any classes tomorrow, so we can get started right away, if you're willing. In the meantime, I'll investigate some other angles. If you'll forgive me, I think I want to get started on this. Time may be of the essence. Thank you for a lovely dinner, all of you."

Verity grinned, making a shooing motion. "Go. We're used to you by now."

CHAPTER SEVEN

O<small>N HIS DRIVE HOME,</small> Stone made a mental list of his next steps. There were a lot of them. He wished Kolinsky could have taught him time travel in addition to ley-line travel, because it would make the whole thing easier if he could do them all at once.

Since he *couldn't* do them all at once, he'd need to prioritize each one based on three factors: how time-sensitive it was, how suspicious he'd look if he did it personally, and whether he could delegate it to someone else. By the time he reached Encantada, his mental list consisted of six items:

> *- Talk to Kelso*
> *- Talk to Eddie and Ward about the pyramid and any other items potentially connected to it*
> *- Talk to Kolinsky (and/or Madame Huan?) about same*
> *- Check the online auction catalog*
> *- Look into Hiram Drummond's history*
> *- Adjust the wards around the house in case the thief decides to break in*

He debated talking to Leo Blum, but put that aside for the moment. He didn't think Blum could get him anything he didn't already have, and didn't want to drag him into it unless it became necessary.

It was only ten p.m. and he wasn't tired in the slightest. He pat-ted Raider on the head as he breezed by, his mind far away, then paused in the living room to send a text to Eddie. He didn't expect an answer, and wasn't surprised when he didn't get one. The librar-ian was a night owl, but it was six a.m. in London and he'd no doubt be asleep by now.

Brimming with restless energy and nowhere to spend it, Stone decided to update the wards around the house now. His place had enough land around it, not to mention being surrounded by a wrought-iron fence, that it would be unlikely anybody would see him poking around the perimeter this late. He headed back outside, ignoring Raider's quizzical look.

Normally, Stone protected the house with relatively simple wards—far simpler than the potent ones surrounding his Surrey house, the Desmond house in London, and Caventhorne. He was proud of the design, though: they incorporated a version of the dis-regarding spell to make them unobtrusive, so even other mages would need to be looking for them specifically in order to notice them. He'd added a component to let him know if anyone passed any of the house's thresholds, but as yet hadn't supplemented it to take any action against potential housebreakers. That was his job, once informed of their presence. Besides, even if they got inside, they'd never get into his workroom or his library. Mundanes wouldn't even see them, let alone know they existed.

But if the mage who'd broken into the storeroom, and who had the log list, figured out he'd been in there before them, it was possi-ble they might think he'd taken it. If they knew who he was, they might not take the chance of trying to break in to his place, but not *everybody* in the magical world knew who he was.

After a few moments' thought and a bit more pacing, he finally decided on the simple approach. He hurried upstairs to his attic workroom to gather components, then spent the next couple hours adjusting the threshold wards to not only inform him if anyone broke in, but to implant a subtle mental compulsion to stay in the area. It probably wouldn't hold for too long, but it didn't need to. It only needed to hold long enough for Stone to return to the house and catch them. He could easily have made the ward more unforgiving—everything from rendering the thief unconscious to killing them—but he didn't want to go there. Yet, anyway. Whatever this pyramid thing was, he had no proof yet that it was anything worth hurting anyone else over.

Even after Calanar, wards still tired Stone. Creating and modifying them wasn't as much a question of raw power as mental horsepower, and his time on Calanar hadn't upgraded his brain. It was just as well, he supposed, since he couldn't do anything else tonight.

But still, when he crawled into bed with Raider, his spinning thoughts made it hard to fall asleep.

When his phone buzzed, it was still dark. He fumbled for it, yawning. Three a.m.

His mind cleared instantly when he saw the text's sender.

Sorry, slept in a bit. What's so important?

Eddie. Of course—it was eleven where he was. *Can I ring you?*

Figured you would.

Stone punched his number, sitting on the edge of the bed. Raider instantly curled up next to him as if to say *That's far enough, human.*

Eddie answered on the first ring. "Isn't it three in the mornin' there?"

"It is."

"Don't tell me—you've got yerself a new puzzle."

Stone chuckled. "Does it always have to be a puzzle?"

"With you? It's a damn good bet."

"Well, you'd win that bet. Do you have a few minutes? This one will take some time."

"Yeah, sure. Just potterin' around at the Library, gatherin' some information for a few folks from my backlog. Easy stuff. Can do it in my sleep."

Stone gave Eddie the whole story of the collection and the break-in. He wanted to get up and pace, but Raider had moved his head onto his leg and was purring contentedly. Cats made their own gravity, so he stayed put.

"Blimey," Eddie said with a soft whistle. "That's…quite a story. Is your friend gonna be all right?"

"He should be, yes. He took a nasty knock, but he's young and strong."

"That's good, at least. So what do you want from me?"

"A couple of things, if you wouldn't mind. First, do you re-member ever seeing anything about this object?"

Eddie was silent for several seconds. "Not off'and. You say it in-terferes with magic? That's bloody rare."

"Yes, and I know. It's fairly weak, but I have a feeling if it were connected to the other part, that might change."

"But you don't know what this other part is."

"No idea. I don't even know if there's only *one* other part. There might be more."

"And it's not in the collection?"

"Not that I saw—but remember, I wasn't looking for it."

"Are you plannin' to go back and take another look?"

"I'd very much like to, but I don't know if they'll let me near it again, since it's part of a police investigation. Dr. Martinez says she might arrange to have the stuff moved somewhere else prior to the auction."

"Hmm. And since you're connected with the University, you don't want to raise too many suspicions."

"Got it in one. So I'm hoping you and that incredible brain of yours can turn up some reference to this item and its history. And while you're at it, could you see if you can dig up any history on Hiram Drummond? I'm planning to see if I can talk to his daughter and niece, but I want to know if he might have been one of us." He chuckled. "You should know—you magical boffin types are great at staying under the radar. I'm still convinced there are a lot more mages out there than we know about, because they keep to themselves and don't make waves."

"Like you do." Eddie's tone was amused.

"Well—yes. I've been making too many waves lately, I know." Over the past three months, he'd been watching, along with Jason, to see if anything turned up in the news about the aftermath of the fight under the mall in Tennessee. Nothing had, which meant either the authorities were keeping it under wraps, or the Ordo people had managed to clean it up before anybody caught on.

"Okay. I'll look into it. I've got a few other little projects, but none of them are urgent. I'll give Ward a ring and see if he wants to 'elp."

"Of course he'll want to help. You two don't want to admit it, but you're both as curious as I am and you know it."

Eddie didn't even bother to deny it. "Speaking of that—you said you nicked the pyramid. Where is it now?"

Stone felt suddenly uneasy about admitting such a thing over the phone—too much time listen to Jason and his paranoid ideas, he supposed—but brushed it aside. *Nobody suspects you. They're not tapping your phone line.* "It's at Caventhorne. I have a few things I need to do today, but I can pop over later and we can all have a look at it if you like."

"Let's see." Eddie's voice dripped with good-natured sarcasm. "Do I want to 'ave a look at what might be an ancient bit of magical kit that could lead to knowledge that's been lost for 'undreds of years minimum? Nah, I think I'd rather go 'ome and watch something trashy on the telly."

Stone chuckled. "I'll talk to you later, Eddie. Thanks. Now let me try to get back to sleep, which I honestly doubt is going to happen at this point."

CHAPTER EIGHT

STONE HALF-EXPECTED TO GET A CALL from the University asking him to take over Greene's classes the next day. Apparently rank had its privileges, though, because by the time he left the house at close to ten a.m., nobody had contacted him.

When he arrived at Jason's agency and pushed open the door, Gina Rodriguez looked up from her computer. "Hey, Dr. Stone. Was expecting you."

"Oh?"

"Yeah. Jason said you wanted me to look into something, but he wouldn't tell me what it was until you got here."

Stone looked around. "Where is he?"

"Donut run. Should be back in a few—ah, there he is!"

The door opened again to reveal Jason bearing a box from Psycho Donuts. When he spotted Stone, he raised it in greeting. "Hey, Al. Didn't know when you'd get in. Want a donut?" He set the box on a nearby table and opened it, revealing a half-dozen large, elaborately-decorated confections that looked less like basic donuts and more like the baker had lived up to the place's name.

"Er…thanks, but I'll pass."

"Suit yourself, but you're missing out." Jason and Gina both grabbed one and began munching away. "Go ahead and give Gina the details about what we talked about last night."

Stone prowled the area around the assistant's desk as he told her about the break-in at the University. The only details he left out were anything about magic, obviously, and the fact that he not only knew what was missing, but had it in his possession. What she didn't know couldn't come back to bite her—or, more likely, him.

"Huh," she said, leaning back in her chair. She set the remaining half of her donut aside, wiped her hands on a napkin, and began tapping on her keyboard. "So, what is it exactly that you want me to do?"

Stone spoke carefully. "I assume, since the collection will be sold at auction in San Francisco in a couple of weeks, there's got to be some kind of online catalog showing the items available. I want to look at the catalog."

Her eyes narrowed. "Sure, we can do that, but why do you need me?" She grinned. "I know you're not exactly a computer whiz, Doc, but you're a college professor. Finding something like that on the net is easy-peasy."

"Not if he doesn't want anybody to know he's looking," Jason said.

"Ah." She nodded as light dawned. "I get it now."

"Yes. Well." Stone took a deep breath. "Given that I was one of the few people who was in that storeroom the day of the theft, it's in my best interests not to arouse anyone's suspicions by showing too much interest in its contents. I doubt the police suspect me of anything, but best if it stays that way."

"Got it. No problem. Give me a couple minutes, and I'll get you onto that site through a connection nobody can trace."

"Thank you, Gina."

Stone drifted to the front of the office, and Jason followed him. "Did you find out anything else last night?"

"Not too much. I'm going home to chat with Eddie and Ward when we're done here."

Jason lowered his voice, glancing over toward Gina, who was deep in concentration. "Are you gonna show it to them?"

"That's the plan. Maybe Eddie's heard about it, or seen something in one of the books in the Library."

"You're hoping he might find a reference to the other piece, right? The one it looks like it plugs into?"

"That would be more than I've got a right to ask for, but yes, that would help things along considerably."

"Got it!" Gina called.

They both hurried over to look over her shoulder. Her screen now showed the home page for a company called Pressman Auctions. The design suggested a staid, respectable operation.

"Brilliant," Stone said. "And they can't trace this?"

"Not unless they're a lot better than local police. I won't explain it in detail unless you want to get really bored, but trust me—unless they're watching the auction site for specific traffic, nobody will trace us. Especially since this is a public site, so they expect people to be checking it out. This would be harder if we were trying to break in somewhere we weren't supposed to be." She rose from her chair and picked up the remains of her donut. "Have at it."

Stone sat down and studied the page. It didn't take long to find the "Upcoming Auctions" link, and not much longer to find the Drummond Collection, slated for auction later in the month. The catalog was a PDF file, which he downloaded.

"Do you see it?" Jason asked, looking over his shoulder.

The catalog contained all sorts of interesting items, one or two per page. Each included a photo and a brief description, along with the auction tag number and any miscellaneous details. Stone quickly realized there were a lot more items in the catalog than he'd seen, probably because they'd either been in boxes or hidden behind other objects. "Going to have to give this a good going-over," he murmured.

"Yeah, but let's focus. Do you see what you're looking for?"

There was no table of contents, but the items were arranged sequentially according to their tag numbers. Stone pulled out his phone and checked the photo he'd taken, making sure to hide the screen from Gina. It wasn't that he didn't trust her, but the less she knew, the better. He flipped through the catalog until he reached the page.

"Huh," Jason said. "So that's it. Weird-looking thing."

"It is." Stone spoke distractedly, barely paying attention to his friend as he leaned in closer to get a better look.

The entry included several color photos of the pyramid, showing all three sides and the bottom with its two holes. The title was listed as *Carved Black Pyramid with Markings.*

"The purpose and origin of this object are unknown," Jason read aloud. "It is unclear whether the markings on three sides are an ancient, lost language or merely decorative. No documentation is available in Hiram Drummond's notes, except that it was originally purchased from the collection of Leander McGrath following his death in 1964." He looked up at Stone. "Ever heard of this McGrath guy?"

"No, but given he died over fifty years ago, that doesn't surprise me." Stone took out his notebook and jotted the man's name down. "I'll put that on my list of things to ask Eddie."

He flipped quickly through the rest of the catalog, which still took several minutes, looking for anything else with similar markings or prongs that might match the holes on the pyramid. He didn't find anything. "Gina," he called, "Can you send me a copy of this catalog?"

She came back over, wiping her fingers again. "Sure. Find what you were looking for?"

"Not sure yet. There's a lot of stuff here, so I want to look it over at home so I don't take over your desk for too long." He rose from the chair.

Gina plopped down, pulled up her email, and sent the catalog. "You want a copy too, Jason?"

"Sure, why not? I don't even know what I'm looking for, but maybe I'll take a glance through and see if anything pops up."

"Okay. Guess we're done, then? That was a lot easier and less exciting than I expected." She flashed Stone an amused smile.

"What can I say? It can't always be interesting."

As she returned to her work, Jason walked Stone to the door. "Let me know what you find out, okay? Keep us in the loop."

"I will. This still could turn out to be nothing, but I very much want to find out who was behind the theft. I'm convinced they—or the people who hired them—know more about this item than I do."

CHAPTER NINE

Eddie and Ward were waiting at the London library when Stone arrived.

"Find out anything else interesting?" Eddie asked.

"I was about to ask you the same question." Stone wasn't surprised at the eagerness on both his friends' faces. This was the kind of thing they lived for—an intriguing magical puzzle that required research into the past.

"Okay, fair enough. We'll go first." He waved Stone to a seat in the fussy, maiden-aunt sitting room that served as the library's receiving area. "Ward?"

Arthur Ward took a spot on the brocade sofa opposite Stone. "The first thing is, as far as either of us can determine, Hiram Drummond wasn't a mage."

Stone frowned. "That's a bit unexpected, but not entirely, I suppose."

"There are plenty of mundanes out there who collect odd stuff," Eddie pointed out. "Looks like in this case, Drummond was one of 'em."

"And I assume that means his daughter and his niece aren't mages either. They wouldn't be selling the collection if they were."

"No indication they are," Ward said. "Although I suppose it's possible, if they were, that they've held on to the magical pieces."

"Except I found three of them in the storeroom." Stone rose and wandered the room. "Four, if you count the pyramid. None of the other three were anything special, but they were definitely both old and magical."

"Speaking of the pyramid," Eddie said, "did you bring it?"

Stone chuckled. "You're not subtle at all, are you? I've seen starving dogs look less excited about a raw steak."

"What can I say?" He didn't look apologetic in the slightest, and neither did Ward. "That's the price for draggin' us into these things o' yours—we get to play with the fun stuff."

Stone had collected the pyramid from Desmond's vault before he arrived. He pulled it from his coat pocket and placed it on the coffee table.

Eddie and Ward leaned forward with identical expressions of interest. They both fuzzed out, clearly using magical sight.

"You won't get anything." Stone didn't bother to shift. "The thing looks as mundane as Jason's hat."

"It does…" Eddie murmured. "All right if I touch it?"

"Be my guest. I don't think there's anything dangerous about it."

He pulled a pair of gloves from his pocket, donned them, and lifted the pyramid. Ward moved closer, both of them examining it from all angles as Eddie turned it in his hands.

"You said it's 'ard to levitate, right?"

"Give it a go." Stone waved toward the table. "It took a lot more energy than normal for me to even move it—and still more to lift it."

Eddie placed the pyramid back on the table and concentrated on it.

Nothing happened.

His brow furrowed, his eyes squinting as he obviously poured more magical energy into the effort.

The pyramid jiggled slightly, but nothing else.

"Huh." Eddie didn't sound annoyed, merely interested. "You try it, Ward."

Ward, however, couldn't get it to move at all.

Eddie wrote something on a notepad. "Blimey. So it takes some significant power to even get the thing to wiggle. Stone, you said you were able to lift it?"

"Yes, a few inches off my worktable. But it felt like it weighed a lot more than it actually does. It was definitely resisting me."

"No surprise, is it? You're a bloody powerhouse compared to us magical weaklings." Once again, Eddie didn't sound like he resented the fact.

"You two are hardly weaklings." Stone resumed his seat across from them. "But you're right—that does tell me it takes a relatively large amount of magical power to overcome even this little thing's anti-magic properties."

Ward donned gloves—Stone found it amusing that the two of them always seemed to have at least one pair on them—and picked up the pyramid again, turning it over to examine the bottom. "It seems logical that the holes here are designed to line up with something else. But you don't know what that is, Stone?"

"No idea. I've got the auction catalog showing the rest of the collection, but a quick scan through didn't show anything else that looks like it might go with this."

"Can you send us a copy of that catalog?" Eddie asked.

"Of course." While his two friends continued studying the pyramid, Stone took out his phone, called up the email with the attachment from Gina, and forwarded it to both of them. "I'm planning to take a more in-depth look later, but I wanted to check in with you two first."

"Don't suppose you're willing to leave it with us for a bit, are you?"

"Probably best if I don't. One person was already almost killed over it. Even though I doubt anyone could track it here, I don't want to take the chance."

"I was afraid you'd say that. 'Ang on, then—let me snap a few photos of it. There's something about it that looks familiar, but I can't put my finger on it."

"I thought the same thing." Stone leaned in to look at it in Ward's hand. "But I thought you were the one with the photographic memory."

"I am, but it's not foolproof. Sometimes it takes a bit o' time for things to come back to me. In the meantime, anything else you want us to look into?"

"Yes. I found out from the auction catalog that Drummond bought this from the collection of a man named Leander McGrath, who died in the middle Sixties. Have you ever heard of him?"

Eddie and Ward exchanged glances.

"Not sure…" Eddie said. He jumped up from the sofa. "Sounds a bit familiar, though. Give me a few minutes—I want to check something in the library." Before either of the other two could reply, he dashed off.

Ward was still studying the pyramid. "What interests me about this thing," he said slowly, as if deep in thought, "is that you said it could literally destroy weak magical items?"

"Not destroy them. De-power them, is probably the better word. I wouldn't put it near any magical documents."

"Even so, that means it's got a lot of power all by itself. It makes me wonder if whatever the other object is—the one you think it might fit together with—would make it even more powerful."

"Interesting thought. You mean like some kind of amplifier?"

"Just a speculation." He put it back on the table.

"Do you have any idea *why* it has these properties?" Stone was tempted to pick it up again, but he didn't have gloves so he settled for staring at it. "Part of me wants to crack it open and see what's inside, but I'm not ready to do that yet."

"Could be something inside," Ward agreed, nodding. "It could also be something in the composition of the item itself, or the figures etched into the sides." He sighed. "It's really sort of a chicken-and-egg problem, isn't it? If it's magical, it should be detectable as such. And if it's *not* magical, it shouldn't be able to do what it's doing."

"That's why I brought it to you two. You're the best I know at twisting your brains around into all sorts of mad patterns."

"Thank you…I think."

Eddie bounded back into the room, now carrying a leather-covered book. "'Ere we go," he said triumphantly, slapping it down on the table. "I knew I'd 'eard that name before." He opened the book to a page he'd marked and turned it so Stone and Ward could read it.

The book didn't look like the typical magic tome, but rather a reference book. The page Eddie had opened it to showed a grainy, black-and-white photo of a white-bearded man standing in front of a bookshelf in a cramped-looking room. Below the photo were the words *LEANDER MCGRATH*. Several other photos showed the man in different poses—a couple obviously taken during his shows, a few in what looked like his home, and one next to a uniformed young man who was obviously his son.

Stone quickly scanned the text below them. "He was a magician?"

"Yup. Stage magician, sort of famous in the Midwestern part of the US during the early part of the last century. No 'Arry 'Oudini or anything, but 'e made a good living in the region. Retired after 'is only son was killed in World War I—'eart wasn't in it anymore, I guess. After that, 'e devoted 'is life and fortune, such as it was, to collectin' weird items."

"And when he died, it was sort of like Drummond," Stone said. "Nobody wanted his collection, so they auctioned it, and Drummond bought some of it."

"It's a surprisingly common occurrence," Ward said. "Even if someone isn't magically talented, they often pick up magical objects from unwitting heirs, auctions, or even junk shops, without ever knowing what they've got."

"We don't know if McGrath *was* actually a mage, though," Eddie pointed out. "It's possible 'e was. It's also not uncommon, especially in those days, for mages to hide in plain sight, posing as stage magicians. It was a decent livin', and there wasn't much chance of gettin' caught."

Stone shifted his gaze between the pyramid and the entry on McGrath. "I wonder…" he mused, stroking his chin. "Here's a challenge for you two: do you think you could find the auction catalog or the records for McGrath's auction? I know it's a long shot, but now I'm wondering if there might have been any other interesting things in his collection. If I'm right and there *was* another piece that goes with this pyramid, maybe it was there, and we can trace it."

"You're right," Ward said skeptically. "That is a long shot. Tracing a fifty-year-old auction…"

Eddie grinned. "But it's a challenge, too. And you know 'ow we love a challenge." He clapped Stone on the shoulder. "We're on it, mate. Leave that part to us. What are you plannin' in the meantime?"

"Not sure, honestly." Stone pondered. "I'd like to chat with the security guard to see if he noticed anything, though I doubt he did. And I'm still a bit nervous about the fact that the thief took the log sheet. That means he knows who else was in that storeroom."

"Do you think he might believe one of you took it?" Ward asked.

"One of 'em *did* take it," Eddie said. But then he sobered. "You're afraid they might try breakin' into these people's 'omes or offices, lookin' for it."

"The thought crossed my mind." Stone got up and began pacing again.

"Well, if they try breakin' into *your* place, they're gonna be in for a shock."

"True. I've already altered my wards so anyone who tries to enter the house without permission will alert me and end up wandering about in the yard until I get home."

"That's assumin' they'd even try. If the thief's a mage, especially if they're workin' for a stronger one, they're gonna know who you are. They'd be mad to try gettin' into your place."

"That's true, too. But that doesn't help Dr. Inouye, the other professor who was in there after I was. I'd hate to see her or any of her family get hurt over this. That thief has already proven he's willing to kill over this. Greene got luckier than he had a right to that he wasn't injured far worse."

"Can't exactly put wards around someone else's house, though, can you?" Ward asked, frowning. "For one thing, it would take too long to do. Someone would notice you."

"Unfortunately, yes. Even if I went over there in the middle of the night, my disregarding spell wouldn't conceal me well enough to be sure no one would notice me. Especially not for that long." He narrowed his eyes at Eddie, who suddenly appeared to be focused on something far away. "Eddie? Have you got something?"

"Maybe." He glanced at Ward. "Remember that little thing we were faffin' about with a couple months back?"

Ward looked confused for a moment, then smiled. "Ah. Yes."

"What are you on about?" Stone shifted his gaze back and forth between then.

Eddie shrugged. "It was just sort of a silly thing, to be honest. I read an article about some bloke who kept havin' 'is parcels nicked off 'is porch, so 'e rigged one with a camera and a glitter bomb. Thing went off on the thief when 'e tried to open it."

"Yes, and…? Not sure how that relates to the subject at hand."

"That's because you don't think like us anymore, mate." Eddie's grin widened. "You're over there doin' all that serious stuff—it's like you don't even remember the pranks we used to get up to during our University days."

"Eddie…"

"Okay. Okay. So I got to thinkin' about it, and wonderin' if there might not be a magical use for the same sort of idea."

Stone still didn't follow. Normally, he enjoyed listening to Eddie's farfetched thoughts, but right now he couldn't stop thinking about the pyramid and Greene in the hospital. "A magical glitter bomb?"

"Not exactly. Just 'ear me out." Eddie leaned forward, almost bouncing with eagerness on the old sofa. "You were just talkin' about alterin' your wards. What we were messin' about with was the idea of makin' a smaller ward that would go off when someone triggered it, coverin' them with somethin' that could be tracked. You know, magically."

"Magical glitter."

"Not glitter, precisely," Ward said. "It sounds fanciful, but it does have practical applications. Think of it as more like adding a dye pack to a briefcase full of cash."

Suddenly, Stone saw where they were going. Energized, he leaned forward. "You're saying this…magical dye pack could be traced using a tracking spell."

"Exactly!" Eddie looked pleased. "And the victim wouldn't 'ave any idea it even 'appened. It's not really a ward at all—more of a trap. And it's so small and well-concealed, even a mage would 'ave a 'ard time spottin' it unless they were specifically lookin' for it."

Stone looked at them in new light. "I'm impressed," he said, and meant it. "And here's me thinking you two are all about stuffy old research."

"Well…we 'aven't actually *built* any of these things," Eddie admitted. "But we've got the plans all worked out. Did it one night while we were at the Dragon. Shouldn't take long to put a few together, especially if you 'elp. We can pop up to Caventhorne—all the materials are there."

Stone wasn't sure he wanted to spend the time, but on the other hand, his friends' invention might solve a problem for him. "Let's do it. I can leave them at Dr. Inouye's house and near the store-room."

"Brilliant," Ward said. "And in the meantime, we can get started looking for any details about the McGrath auction."

"See?" Eddie asked with a cheeky grin. "We're good for more than research and gettin' potted with."

Stone mirrored the grin. "I never doubted you, Eddie."

CHAPTER TEN

THREE HOURS LATER Stone was back in California, where it was still mid-afternoon. He was grateful this was one of the times when the time-zone difference worked in his favor. He called Jason as soon as he popped back to his house.

"I need you to get me an address," he said without greeting. "You can do that, right?"

"Uh…sure. Not technically legal, but…"

"I promise I'm trying to help someone, not hurt them."

"Is anything wrong?"

"I don't think so, but I'm trying to make sure it stays that way."

"Okay, I guess. Who are you looking for?"

"Dr. Janice Inouye. She's a professor of anthropology at the University."

"Oh—right. The one whose signature was on the log sheet for the storeroom? Why do you need her address? And why can't you get it from the University?"

"The answer to your first question is that I want to put a bit of magical protection on her home. The second is because I don't want them to know I'm looking for her."

"You think the thief might think she took the thing?"

"Well…they didn't find it in the storeroom, so my guess is that they'll either go back there for another look, or else they'll check the sheet they took and assume one of us nicked it."

"What about your place?"

"Already protected. And if they're mages, they'd be fools to try breaking in there."

"Good point. Okay, give me a couple minutes and I'll look."

Stone paced his living room, followed closely by Raider, as he waited. The bag containing ten of the little devices he, Eddie, and Ward had built sat on his coffee table. It hadn't taken them long to put them together, since his friends had already worked out the details in their usual meticulous way.

"Don't look at these things as some sort of miracle device," Eddie had warned when they finish. "They've got a lot of limitations. They're bloody weak for one thing, which means any mage worth their salt will be able to neutralize 'em if they spot 'em. They *are* 'ard to spot and likely they won't be expectin' 'em, but keep it in mind. Also, once they trigger, the 'ink' won't last long—maybe a few hours at most—and it'll cut down your range considerably for trackin' 'em."

"So you're saying that if one of them triggers, I'll need to move fast."

"Yes," Ward said. "We could probably make something better, but it will take a lot more time. These are basically disposable."

"Better than nothing," Stone assured them.

"Al?"

He snapped back to the present at Jason's voice. "Yes? Have you got it?"

"Yeah. Wasn't that hard—not like she's tryin' to hide or anything." He read off an address in Mountain View. "You need anything else?"

Stone almost said no. "Er—yes, but only if you have time."

"It's a little slow today. What've you got?"

He told Jason about Leander McGrath. "I've already got Eddie and Ward researching him, but maybe Gina could turn up the auction catalog or records if they're online somewhere. Can't imagine why they *would* be, but it's worth looking."

"Got it. Don't hold your breath with something that old, but I'll call if we find anything."

Stone thought about waiting until after dark to go to Inouye's house, but decided against it for two reasons: first, if she and her husband were both at work, they couldn't catch him poking around outside their home. Second, he couldn't shake the growing sense of urgency that the longer he waited, the larger the chance that the thief would try something.

To his relief, Inouye's house was only a few blocks from a ley line, so he wouldn't have to drive and risk having his car picked up by some stray camera (*thanks, Jason, for making me bloody paranoid*). He used his disguise amulet to make him look like a boring, middle-aged man and walked the rest of the way to the address.

Another lucky break: the house was a small, single-story ranch. Mountain View was expensive, even by the standards of the University's generous salaries. The neighborhood was quiet this time of day, before most of the working people got home. There weren't even any children out playing in their yards. Still, he'd need to do this quickly, since it would require an invisibility spell and he'd never been any good at maintaining those for longer than two or three minutes.

With one final thought that he was being ridiculous and the thief wouldn't bother breaking into the house of an unassuming Anthro professor, Stone ducked behind a fence, pulled up his invisibility spell, and walked briskly toward the house.

The little trackers weren't hard to set. He, Eddie, and Ward had built in a component so they wouldn't trigger on a woman since they knew the thief was a man, but they'd still trigger on Inouye's husband when he entered the house so there was no point in putting one on the front door. Instead, he placed one on each window, starting in the backyard, and one on the glass door leading to the patio. It didn't look like the Inouyes used their backyard much, so he'd have to take a chance that nobody would exit through that door in the next few days.

By the time he finished, he was breathing hard with the effort of keeping the invisibility spell going. His Calanarian training had helped him a bit with it, but not much, and three minutes seemed like an eternity when it felt like you werc holding your breath the whole time. He ducked back behind the fence barely before the spell slipped, and let his breath out in a *whoosh* of relief.

Leaving the tracker on the door to the storeroom at the University was much easier. He didn't even need to disguise himself, since he had every right to be there.

When he arrived, he found a guard stationed at the door. Unlike Kelso, this one wasn't patrolling, but merely seated outside messing with his phone.

The guard looked up quickly as Stone approached. "Help you?"

"I was looking for Mr. Kelso."

"He's not here. Got taken off the post after last night."

"Ah. I'm sorry to hear that. I wanted to ask him something."

"Sorry, man."

Stone pulled out his university ID, noting that the log sheet hadn't been replaced, and showed the man. "I suppose they're not letting anyone in to examine the collection anymore, right?"

"Nope. They're moving it in couple days, after that guy nearly got killed in there."

"Bloody shame. He's a friend and colleague of mine. It's terrible what happened." He leaned against the wall near the door. "They haven't caught the thief yet, have they?"

"Not that I know of. They don't tell me much, you know?" He rose from his chair. "Hey, you probably shouldn't be here. Nothin' to see in this building."

"Yes, you're right. I'm sorry. I'll be on my way. Be careful."

"Yeah. They got new cameras set up, and anyway I doubt whoever broke in's gonna come back."

"Probably not. Have a good evening."

Mindful of the cameras, Stone kept the smile from his face until he was outside the building. His little trap wouldn't work if the guard had access to the storeroom, but he didn't think he did. But if anyone else tried to enter before the move, he might be in luck.

CHAPTER ELEVEN

NOTHING HAPPENED for most of the following day. Neither Jason nor Eddie got back to him regarding Leander McGrath, and his more in-depth perusal of the auction catalog didn't turn up any other objects that looked like they fit together with the pyramid. He spent the next early afternoon on campus, teaching one class of his own and taking over Greene's.

MacKenzie Hubbard caught up with him as he headed back to his office. "You talk to Greene at all?"

"Visited him at the hospital a couple days ago. He was very lucky."

"No shit. He could have been killed. Good thing I have no curiosity, I guess, or it could have been me in there." He shot a sideways glance at Stone. "Or you. You were in there before he was, weren't you?"

"Yes. And the thought had entered my mind."

"Yeah, I'm thinking I'll give this one a pass. Are you planning on checking out the auction? I know you collect crazy stuff like that."

Stone shrugged. "Haven't decided yet. There are some interesting pieces, without a doubt. I wish I could have had more time to examine them, but—"

He stopped as an odd buzzing sensation went through him. It felt like when he had his phone on vibrate, but in a whole-body way.

"Stone?"

"Er—sorry, Hubbard. I've got to take this." He yanked his phone from his pocket, carefully keeping it turned away from his colleague so he couldn't see it wasn't ringing. "Will you excuse me?"

"Sure, I've got a meeting coming up anyway. Talk to you later."

As soon as Hubbard had moved on, Stone put his phone back and hurried off the path. The buzzing was unfamiliar, but he knew what it was: Eddie and Ward had told him that would be the warning he'd receive when one of the trackers went off.

Since he was close to the storeroom, he checked that first. When he got inside, he found the same guard seated in the same chair, still scrolling on his phone, looking as bored as ever. The guard glanced up, nodded to Stone, then returned to whatever he'd been reading. It certainly didn't look like anyone had caused any recent trouble there.

That meant it had to be Inouye's house.

Don't get your hopes up, Stone told himself as he strode toward his car. It could merely be Inouye's husband deciding to exit the house through the glass door to do some late-afternoon gardening or something. But still, this was the first solid lead he had since this whole thing had started.

He was tempted to travel home using the ley line, but didn't. He'd need his car once he discovered the location, and he'd have to move fast. Even though Eddie and Ward had said he'd have at least a few hours, he didn't want to let any of that time get away from him. Still, he was almost running when he reached his car.

As soon as he arrived home, he swept upstairs, ignoring the indignant Raider, and began customizing the circle in his workroom. The little trackers worked the same way as a standard tracking spell: he had a bit of the same material used in the device, which would allow him to locate its counterpart out in the world. There was no way to tell *which* tracker had gone off, though.

It was already getting dark by the time he began the ritual, but the actual process didn't take long. The spell went off exactly as expected, sending its seeking tendril out in search of its mate. After only a handful of minutes, he had a location. "Got you!" he whispered, calling up the map on his phone to pinpoint it. Because it was so close—only a few miles away—and the tracker had been optimized for the purpose, he narrowed it down to a bar on Castro Street, a couple miles from Inouye's home.

At first he thought that was odd, but then he realized it might not be. Between the walk back to the car, the drive home, and the ritual preparation, it had been nearly an hour since the buzz had gone off. Certainly, the thief hadn't spent that much time inside—too much chance of someone coming home and catching him. If he had searched the house and found nothing, he might have gone off to have a drink afterward.

This might be a good chance to catch the guy off guard.

He threw on his coat, put out a hasty plate of food for the still-annoyed Raider, and hurried back to the car.

Castro Street in Mountain View was a bustling collection of bars, eateries, and shops. It was busy this time of day, as people got off work and headed there to have a few drinks or an early dinner with friends. As usual, the parking situation wasn't pretty, but Stone got lucky and managed to be in the right place when someone pulled out of a space in the lot behind the bar he was looking for.

He forced himself to walk normally, so he wouldn't catch anyone's attention. This was a bit of a long shot—even with the specially prepared tracker, he couldn't be certain he'd zeroed in on the correct location. He could only hope the guy would stay put long enough for him to look around. At least the arcane "glitter" would show up like a beacon to magical sight, so that might make things a little easier.

His phone buzzed as he stepped out of the walkway that led through to Castro Street from the parking lot. He considered letting it go, but he supposed it could be important. Impatiently, he pulled it out and glanced at it.

It was a text from Eddie. *Found something you might be very interested in. Ring me when convenient.*

Huh. It was two a.m. in England, so Eddie was either burning the midnight oil again or he'd had a sudden insight similar to the ones Stone got sometimes. Damn. He wanted to call his friend back now, but he couldn't risk letting the thief get away.

He dashed off a quick text: *Busy now, call soon,* and then shoved the phone back in his pocket. He melded into the crowd meandering along on Castro, and ducked into the bar.

He wasn't familiar with this one, but it was only a few doors down from one of the venues where The Cardinal Sin, the band he and three fellow professors played in, had performed a couple years ago. *The second time you should have died but didn't,* he thought idly, pushing open the door.

The place was more of a brewhouse/restaurant than a bar, with crowded tables and booths spread throughout a larger space than Stone had expected. The bar itself was along the right-side wall, its every stool occupied. Bouncy, jangly pop music played through hidden speakers, and several TVs showed mostly sports. A busy, cheerful place, and a perfect one to lose oneself after a spot of unsuccessful B and E.

"How many in your party, sir?"

The voice startled Stone from his thoughts. A woman stood in front of him, holding a tablet and eyeing him expectantly. "Oh. Er…no, I'm not looking for a table. I'm trying to find some friends. All right if I look around?"

"Sure, no problem."

Stone quickly headed further in as the woman moved to the next person who'd entered.

This wasn't going to be as easy as he'd hoped. The place included a lot of secluded booths and alcoves that would make it harder to spot even the telltale glow of magic. Also, the walkways were narrow and people were always pushing past. There was no way he could stand still long enough to do a full sweep. He'd have to settle for staying mobile and switching to magical sight every few seconds for quick scans. Even more problematically, the place had two levels, the second one accessible by a wooden staircase in the middle of the bar. A look up revealed more tables arranged around the railing overlooking the lower level.

So far, none of his scans revealed any hint of magic. It was hard to see through the overlapping auras anyway, which didn't help. Eddie had showed him what to look for—a silvery haze that hovered wherever the "glitter" had covered the target—but among the greens, reds, blues, yellows, and other colorful hues of happy auras, it was like trying to spot a single flashlight glow in the middle of a bunch of lighters at a concert.

Damn. What if I got it wrong? What if he's not even in *this bar?*

Mindful of the time ticking away before the tracker's glow faded entirely, he pushed further into the restaurant, risking leaving magical sight up longer as he pretended to be looking for his group of friends.

"Hey, Dr. Stone!"

Stone jerked his head up. *Oh, bugger. What now? Did he see me?*

But the voice hadn't come from the thief—not unless the thief was one of his intro Occult Studies students, seated at a booth with three other grinning young people directly in front of him. Their auras blazed with good cheer, blending with each other into a pleasant, brilliant haze. They were obviously having a good time.

He whipped his gaze desperately around, but he couldn't ignore his student without looking highly suspicious—not when the guy was three feet away. "Er—good evening."

"Didn't think I'd see you here." The young man's wide smile was more than a bit tipsy, the beer in front of him almost empty. "It's so weird, you know, seeing your professors out in public."

"Totally," said his female companion, whom Stone didn't recognize, and the other two laughed.

"Er. Yes. I suppose it is."

"Join us if you want," the young man said, waving him into the booth, apparently forgetting that it was full.

"Thank you, that's very kind." Stone spoke fast, once again mindful of the time slipping away. "Sorry, though—can't stay now. I'm trying to find some friends. I—"

He happened to glance up to the second level with magical sight still up.

There, amid the bouncing colors, was a small puff of glittery silver.

Bloody hell, he's up there.

"Excuse me," he said hastily. "Must go. Cheers."

He hurried toward the stairs before any of them could say anything else. He didn't think the man had seen him—and in any case, what difference would it make if he had? It wasn't as if he expected Stone to be following him. Still, he pulled a disregarding spell around him on his way up the stairs. Invisibility wouldn't be practical here with all these people, but this spell should be sufficient to keep him concealed long enough to get close.

When he reached the top of the stairs, he paused for another look. The silvery glow was still where he'd left it, at a table along the railing at the back of the restaurant. Stone couldn't tell for sure, but it looked like the man was alone. His aura, a vibrant orange, didn't appear agitated, but neither did it look as carefree and easygoing as most of the other customers. It was the aura of a man who was deep in thought about something.

Stone approached closer, careful not to draw attention to himself. If this man was the thief from the storeroom, he was almost certainly a mage. Stone didn't see any sign of illusion or other concealment around him, though. Probably because the man didn't expect anyone to be looking for him here.

He was about to move closer again when several thoughts occurred to him. The first was that perhaps he should call the police. This man *was* a thief, after all—and worse than that, an attempted murderer. Stone shuddered a little as he once again considered how easy it would have been for the outcome with Greene to turn out so much more tragically, if the thief had hit him a little harder or in a different spot.

But what could he do? What would he say? "Er…yes, I've cornered the man who tried to kill Brandon Greene. He's in a bar in downtown Mountain View. How do I know it's him? Er—yes. Well, he's got glitter you can't see all over him from a magical trap I illegally set at a fellow professor's house. You've just got to trust me."

Yes. *That* would go over well.

His second thought was to wonder how he even planned to apprehend the thief. He couldn't exactly walk up to his table and take him out with a spell. He was good with illusions, but not *that* good. He supposed he could wait until the man left, but he had no idea how long that would be. Was he expecting friends? Planning to sit here nursing his beer until the place closed? There were too many variables to make that a viable plan.

He wished now that he'd brought someone else with him— Jason, maybe, or Verity, or Amber, or ideally all three. They could stake out the exits, and even a mage would have trouble evading Amber's nose or Verity's magical tracking.

But he hadn't done that. It hadn't been practical even if he'd wanted to. So here he was on his own, and he'd better get on with doing something.

He moved a little closer, and as some of the other auras dropped away, it became obvious the man was talking to someone on his phone. He had the characteristic hunched posture of someone trying to hear in a loud environment, with his opposite-side finger stuck in his ear to block out the din.

That gave Stone an idea. Using an illusion to make it look like he'd pulled out a handkerchief to wipe his nose, he raised his own phone and snapped several photos of the man. They wouldn't be great in the dimness and at this distance, but they were better than nothing. Perhaps he could get better ones if he could get closer.

At that exact moment, the man looked up, almost like a deer at a watering hole who suddenly sensed a nearby predator hiding in the tall grass.

His gaze went unfocused, and then his eyes locked with Stone's.

He looked startled, then smiled—and disappeared.

Stone hesitated for a second, confused. The man couldn't have turned invisible—invisible people and objects, unless the mage was *very* good, still showed up to magical sight. But one second he was there, and the next he was gone.

Stone pushed past a group of laughing engineers on their way toward the stairs, picking up his pace and striding swiftly toward the table where the man had been.

He wasn't there anymore—just a faint hint of the magical glitter on the edge of the table where he'd pressed against it.

Damn.

Sharpening his sight, he looked swiftly around. There weren't that many places the guy could have gone. The stairs were the most obvious avenue of exit, but all he saw there were two groups of women, one going up and the other coming down.

Had he jumped over the railing? Levitated toward the door? That would have shown up too, though. He—

Elevator!

There had to be one here somewhere. Heart pounding, he hurried toward the restrooms and found it at the back of the hallway. The light next to the button was lit, indicating it was in use.

Stone growled in frustration. If the thief had taken the elevator and he waited for it now, the man would be long gone by the time he reached the ground floor. Forcing himself not to run and draw all sorts of unwelcome attention to himself, he jog-walked around the railing to the stairs and plunged down. Elevators in places like this tended to be slow—perhaps if he was lucky, he could make it downstairs before it opened.

"Hey! Watch where you're going, dude!"

Stone skidded to a stop, twisting his body to avoid running into a young man in a black vest, carrying a full tray of drinks. The tray teetered alarmingly, hovering between regaining its balance and crashing to the floor.

"Sorry!" Stone used a little nudge of magic to hold the tray steady until the waiter had regained control over it, then shoved past him and hurried on his way. Behind him, the young man muttered something that probably would lose him a tip if Stone had been his customer.

Stone reached the elevator as it opened. Shifting to magical sight, he stood in front of it, blocking the way so anyone coming out would have to pause before exiting. His heart pounded harder in anticipation.

The doors slid open, revealing an empty cubicle.

"What…?" Stone glared into the small space, confused. Where had the man gone?

Had he even been in here at all? Had he used the elevator as a diversion and ducked out another way?

He scanned harder, but spotted no sign of the glittery material inside. Either the thief hadn't been in here or the mix's potency was already fading. If the latter were true, Eddie had been off about how long he'd have, but he didn't blame his friend for that. It was what happened when you were testing new tech, magical or otherwise.

"Excuse me."

Stone spun to see two women, one of them with her lower leg in a walking cast, looking at him with veiled impatience. "Oh. Er…terribly sorry." He stepped aside with a sigh.

Damn!

He could look around, of course, but it was pointless. The guy had seen him, knew he was a mage—possibly even knew *who* he was—and had booked it out of there. If he'd been ready to do that, he obviously had an escape plan.

And now he knew somebody was after him.

Stone sighed. It was useless to return home and try another tracking ritual. The stuff was already losing its potency, and would probably fade completely before he could finish. Even if it didn't, the man had definitely realized something was up and would discover and neutralize the glitter.

Well. That was a bust.

He scanned the crowd with magical sight again as he left the bar, and did the same thing a few times on his way to the car, both to check for signs of the thief and to make sure nobody was waiting to ambush him. Neither happened, though. He made it back to his car without seeing anyone except a few couples and small groups heading toward Castro from the lot.

He slammed the car door closed in frustration and gripped the steering wheel hard. He wanted to pause here, to check out the photos he'd taken and get back to Eddie, but he allowed common sense to prevail. If the thief *did* know who he was, he might have accomplices. Better not to tempt them to try something they'd all regret.

CHAPTER TWELVE

T HE PHOTOS WEREN'T GREAT, but they were better than Stone had hoped. When he'd lost his phone the previous year, he'd replaced it with the most state-of-the-art one he could find, and that included an impressive camera. Even though he'd been standing at least twenty feet away in a dimly lit space, zooming in on a couple of the photos revealed a still-fuzzy but possibly identifiable face. The man looked to be in his thirties, with short, dark hair and an angular profile. Stone uploaded the photos to his laptop and examined them.

Then he called Jason.

"Are you home?" he asked when his friend answered. "Or still at work?"

"Home. Amber and I were about to settle down and watch some TV after dinner. Why?"

"Because I've got some photos of the thief who broke into the storeroom, and I'm not sure what to do with them."

"What the hell?" Jason sounded startled, and Stone heard a muffled sound as he readjusted the phone. "How did you get those? Hang on, mind if I put you on speaker so Amber can hear too?"

"No, that's fine."

More muffled sounds, then Amber's voice: "How did you get photos of the thief? And if you were close enough to take pictures, why didn't you catch him?"

"Long story, and I'm not very proud of it." He told them about Eddie and Ward's trackers, and how he'd traced the man to the Mountain View bar. "I tried to get close to him, but he noticed me and disappeared. Literally. He must have had some idea someone might be looking for him."

"That sucks," Jason said. "And now you're not sure what to do with the photos because you'd have to explain how you got them."

"Exactly. Do you think if I sent them to you, Gina could do whatever computer magic she does and figure out who he might be?"

"Not too likely, I'm afraid. That kind of facial-recognition stuff is harder. She'd probably have to look for help from other people, and I didn't think you wanted this getting out."

Stone sighed. "No, probably not. But I certainly don't recognize the man. I mean, the photos aren't perfect, but if I knew him, they're good enough I'd recognize him."

There was a pause, and then Amber spoke. "I have a suggestion, but you're not going to like it."

"At this point, I haven't got a lot of choices. Let's hear it."

"Call Leo Blum. Send them to him."

"Blum? This isn't anywhere near his jurisdiction."

"True, but if you tell him *why* you're sending them, maybe he can turn something up. You know, act like it's part of another case or something. It's either that or tell the cops in charge of the investigation down here, but I wouldn't advise that."

"No—I can picture trying to explain to Detective Bertola how I managed to work out who the thief was without being somehow involved in the whole mess."

He sighed again. He'd been sighing a lot lately. "Fine. I'll do that. I suppose it can't hurt."

"Oh—Al?" Jason again.

"Yes?"

"Before you do that, send me a copy of the photos. I'll have Gina scrub any of the identifying material off them."

"Identifying material? What are you talking about?"

Jason chuckled. "You know, I'm not gonna lie—I'm kinda loving that there's finally something I know about that seems like magic to you. But yeah, any time you take a pic with a phone or a digital camera or whatever, it gets tagged with all kinds of information you can't see unless you look for it. So if you send those photos to Blum without scrubbing it off, somebody could trace them back to you."

A little chill ran down Stone's back. "Bloody hell. You're right—this modern-technology stuff *does* seem like magic to me. You mundanes have made some fairly impressive strides."

"Hey, we gotta do something to keep up with you spell-slingers. Anyway, send 'em on and I'll have Gina fix 'em up for you and stick 'em out on an anonymous server. You can point Blum at that."

"Thank you, Jason. You might have saved me from a dangerous blunder."

"Not like you haven't saved *me* from a few of those. Talk you tomorrow, okay?"

"Yes. I'll call you. Oh—did Gina get anywhere with locating the catalog from McGrath's auction?"

"Not yet. Give her some time. If that even exists, it's gonna take serious digging. A lot of that stuff isn't even online."

"Fair enough. Sorry to be so impatient. You two go back to your…canoodling. I'm going to wake Eddie up and hope he doesn't get too cross with me."

Stone didn't call Eddie until he arrived at the London house. "Didn't wake you, did I?"

"No. I can sleep tomorrow. 'Bout time you got back to me."

"Sorry, but I have an excuse. The trackers worked, and I was following the thief."

"No kiddin'?" Eddie sounded impressed, and a little surprised. "Well, blimey, the things actually *worked*?"

"They did—though you were wrong about how long they'd be active. Either need to add more glitter or punch up the potency of the material you use. I wouldn't safely give it more than a couple hours as it stands."

"Good to know. I'll jot that down. Did you catch 'im, then? Who was 'e?"

"I…didn't catch him. He was at a bar, and he got away from me."

"Got away from *you*?"

"It happens. I couldn't exactly hit him with a concussion spell in the middle of a space full of mundanes, could I? I probably could have got closer, but I stopped to snap a couple of photos before I moved forward. He spotted me and took off."

"Well, damn. That's unfortunate, innit? Can I see the photos? Not much chance I'll be able to identify some random magical bloke from the States, but stranger things and all, y'know?"

"You're welcome to try. Is Ward around too?"

"Nah, the big baby went 'ome a bit ago. Said 'e was tired. No endurance, that bloke. Sad, really." Eddie's voice was laced with fond amusement. "Where are you now?"

"The London house. Want to come over, or should I come to the library?"

"Come over 'ere. I've got something to show you that you're gonna find *very* interestin'. I want you sittin' down in case you faint or summat."

"And of course you can't just tell me on the phone?"

There was a long, meaningful silence.

"Of course you can't. All right, I'll be right over."

Eddie opened the door at Stone's knock, his eyes wide. "Bloody 'ell, Stone."

"What?"

He looked at his watch. "I know it's three in the mornin', but how the *'ell* did you get here this fast?"

Damn. At this point, Stone couldn't even offer an excuse for getting so curious about Eddie's news that he once again used the ley line to travel between the London place and the library. As far as he knew, the library didn't have a portal—at least Eddie had never mentioned one—which meant he'd have needed to drive over or take a cab. The two locations weren't that far apart, but there was no way any mundane vehicle could have made the trip in such a short time.

He sighed. "Eddie…"

Eddie shook his head, and for the first time Stone had seen in many years, he actually looked angry. "Get in 'ere, mate. That's it. We're 'avin' a talk."

"Eddie, I can't—"

"You can and you will. Come on in and sit yer arse down. I'll get some tea."

Stone followed him in, mentally kicking himself. This wasn't the first time he'd forgotten about allowing sufficient time for normal travel methods. He wasn't sure why, exactly. Usually, his brain was a lot sharper than this, and he didn't make these kinds of careless mistakes. What was going on with him?

He took the seat on the brocade couch. Eddie returned with tea, poured two cups, and plopped into the chair across from him. His expression, serious and focused, was fixed on Stone. There was no sign of his usual cheeky good humor.

"Out wi' it," he said.

Stone looked at his hands in his lap and sighed. "I…can't."

"What do you mean, you can't? We're mates, aren't we? We've been through all sorts o' crazy stuff over the years. Are you 'oldin' out on me? 'Ow are you gettin' around so fast? You've been givin' Ward and me excuses about it for the past few months, but I'm not buyin' 'em. 'E's not either, but you know Ward—'e don't speak up like I do. Got better manners, maybe. But somethin's up, and I want to know what it is."

Stone ignored his tea. He got up and paced the room, gazing at the various bits of dusty décor without truly seeing them. "You're right," he said at last. "Something *did* happen. But I can't tell you much about it."

"Why not?" Eddie's tone was as resolute as ever.

"Because I'm not allowed to."

"What's that mean? Who's not allowin' you to?"

"I can't tell you that, either." He turned to face his friend. "I've made promises, Eddie. I can't break them." He waved around the space. "Any more than you can reveal to me who's got you searching for things in the Library, and what they're looking for. I wouldn't ask you to do that—and I'm begging you, as my old friend, to respect that I don't want you asking me too many questions about this."

Eddie's eyes narrowed. "Who else knows about this, whatever it is? Does Verity?"

"No."

"Ian?"

He almost said no again. But did he know for sure? "Not…that I'm aware of. If he does, it's not because I told him."

"'As it got anythin' to do with 'ow it seems like it's got 'ard to kill you lately?"

Stone thought about that. "I…can't say. Not because I've promised, but because I don't *know*. If I had to guess, I'd say no, they're not related." He was beginning to regret that he'd come here at all tonight. If he could have curbed his curiosity and waited until tomorrow, enough time would have passed so his friend wouldn't be suspicious.

"But you know 'ow it 'appened."

"Yes."

"And you know *when* it 'appened."

"Yes."

"So…when?"

Stone shook his head, suddenly annoyed. "Eddie, I feel like I'm under a bloody interrogation here. You want to tie me to a chair and shine a bright light in my face?"

Eddie looked away. "Fine, then. You don't want to tell me, don't tell me. I get it. Secrets are secrets, right?" Now, instead of resolve, his tone held disappointment and perhaps even a bit of hurt.

Something clenched inside Stone. Eddie was one of his oldest and most trusted friends. He would trust the man with his life—and had, on several occasions. "Look," he said. "I can't tell you everything. I'm sorry—if you're cross with me about it, you'll just have to be cross, because I can't. But…I can tell you *some* of it. If you give me your word you won't reveal anything about it to anyone else."

"Even Ward?"

Stone paused. Eddie and Ward were like brothers. Asking one of them to keep a secret from the other was cruel—and pointless, since Ward's discretion was every bit as impenetrable as Eddie's. "All right—no. You can tell Ward. But no one else. Give me your word, Eddie."

"You got it," he said immediately. "I'm surprised you even 'ad to ask. Come on, Stone—you know me."

And he did. He also knew it wasn't fair to dangle something like this in front of his insatiably curious friend and then snatch it away. It had, after all, been *his* carelessness that had let the cat—or the dragon—out of the bag.

"All right. But then you've got to tell me what you called me over here about in the first place."

"I'm dyin' to do that, mate. It's gonna seriously blow your mind, and I don't say that lightly."

"Okay." He ran both hands through his hair, considering his words carefully. "I've...learned a new travel technique."

"What?"

Under normal circumstances, Eddie's gape of astonishment would have been comical. As it was, Stone had an instant of regret at his decision. Would his friend be able to keep this to himself?

"What...kind o' travel technique?"

"I...can't tell you the details. But it's much more versatile than portal travel."

Eddie's eyes got even wider. When he spoke, his voice now held a kind of reverence—the sort of tone another man might use after a profound religious truth had been revealed to him. "You're sayin'...you don't need portals to travel?"

Stone inclined his head.

"So...you can go anywhere you want? Point A to Point B, bam like that?"

"Not...exactly. I can't go anywhere I like. Not by a long way. But I can go a lot more places than I could before."

"Just...like that?" He glanced around the room. "Like...you can pop from one side of this room to the other, or 'ome to the States, easy as that?"

"No. I could go home from here, yes. But some brief preparation is required. It's not instant."

Eddie sagged back in his seat. "Bloody....'ell," he breathed. His gaze came up. "And you can't tell me where you learned this?"

"No. That was part of the promises I made." Stone realized, even as he said the words, that they weren't correct. He hadn't ever promised Kolinsky he wouldn't reveal the existence of the dragons, or the ley-line travel method, or anything else they'd told him that night when he'd learned the truth.

But he might as well have.

"*When* did you learn it?"

"Last year."

Eddie was silent, staring into his lap.

"Eddie?"

"I'm thinkin'," he muttered.

"About what?"

"Tryin' to work out 'ow this might work." His gaze came up. "Stone, this is the 'oly grail of portal science. You know that, right?"

"Believe me, I'm aware."

"And…somebody's worked out 'ow to do it and just…kept it to themselves? Or mostly, anyway? No offense, mate, but what's so special about you that *you* get to learn this, but the rest of us poor sods 'ave to make due with reg'lar portals?"

"That's…part of the promise, too." Stone felt himself meta-phorically picking his way along the edge of a high precipice.

"*Is* there somethin' special about you? If it weren't for this promise, could you teach me 'ow to do it?"

"Eddie…"

"Could you?" Now, there was a strange kind of desperation in his friend's voice.

Stone understood it all too well. Eddie and Ward were two of the only people he knew whose scientific curiosity exceeded his own. If a wondrous secret like this was out there to know, they wouldn't rest until they'd figured it out. How could he tell them that, no matter how much effort and study they put in, no matter how brightly their intellects burned, they weren't going to get any-where with this one? It would be like a mundane genius trying to learn magic—they couldn't do it, because they didn't possess the necessary genetic prerequisite.

How could he tell them that, in order to learn this technique, they had to be directly descended from one or more dragons?

He couldn't, of course. And therein lay the problem.

"No," he said heavily. "I couldn't teach you. There *is* something about me, but I can't tell you what it is. That's part of the promise too."

Eddie studied him. "Somethin' special. And it's got nothin' to do with the 'ard-to-kill thing?"

"Not that I'm aware of."

"So you've got *two* special things now. Wow, Stone, you 'it the lottery, didn't you?"

Was that a hint of bitterness in Eddie's tone? "What are you talking about?"

Eddie shrugged. "Should be pretty obvious, shouldn't it? You're leavin' us behind, aren't you?"

"That's not fair. I didn't choose any of this."

As quickly as it had appeared, the bitterness dropped away. "Yeah, I know. Not your fault you got this 'ard-to-kill thing, and now you can apparently pop 'round the world whenever you fancy, and you're rich as Midas now't Desmond's dropped 'alf 'is fortune on top of the one you already 'ad." He gave a shaky grin as Stone drew breath to protest. "Nah, nah, seriously, mate. You're still the same ol' Stone. Got yer secrets, but don't we all? Right? And I can still drink you under the table, so there's always gonna be that."

Stone chuckled, some of his tension ebbing away. "Same old Eddie, too, thank the gods for small favors. So—are you satisfied?"

"No. Not even close. But at least I got somewhere to start."

"Start?"

"Well, sure. You don't expect me to just let you get away with knowin' summat like that without me and Ward tryin' to suss it out ourselves, do ya?"

Stone narrowed his eyes. "What do you mean?"

"Can't blame us for tryin' to work it out on our own, if you can't teach us, can you?" He raised his hands. "Don't worry—not gonna tell anybody else, or even bring anybody else into it. Just pokin' 'round the library, is all. 'Oo knows what kind o' info might be lurkin' in the deep stacks?"

"Be careful, Eddie. I'm telling you—I can't say there isn't a way for you to work it out, but I give you my word that my way won't work for you. Please take care. Don't try anything dangerous just to prove you can."

"Don't worry." Eddie shuddered. "I know portal stuff can be nasty. Don't want to end up like Daphne Weldon and 'er mates."

Now it was Stone's turn to shudder. He hadn't thought about his old girlfriend Daphne Weldon, the most brilliant portal scientist he'd ever known, and her three friends who had died years ago and unwittingly brought the extradimensional Evil into the world while trying to set up a temporary portal conduit. "Yes. That's the brightest thing I've heard you say all day. Now—can you please tell me what this is that you claim will 'blow my mind'?"

Eddie jerked his head up. "Oh. Right. Come on—let's go to the workroom."

Curious, Stone followed him through the fussy parlor and into the larger workroom area in the back. A series of books and papers were spread out across the long table, including blown-up versions of the photos of the four sides of the black pyramid-shaped object. A closed leather portfolio was at one end.

A little tingle ran up his back. "You've figured out something about the pyramid?"

Eddie grinned. "You know, if I were a right bastard, I'd make you wait for it. You know—maybe I should give Ward a ring and get 'im over here—the *normal* way, 'cause we normal blokes can't ride the ethereal currents or whatever to get where we're goin'— before I do the reveal. 'E'll want to see your face too, I'm sure."

"Eddie…"

"Yeah, yeah." Eddie waved him off. "But I'm *not* a right bastard. I'm just a lovable teddy bear, I am. And besides, this is too good to keep to meself. Sit."

Stone sat.

Eddie didn't. He struck a 'professor' pose, picking up a pointer from the table. "See, you said somethin' before you left, about me rackin' my photographic mem'ry for summat I might've seen that twigged an idea. Which is, of course, what I was plannin' to do. I figured there 'ad to be somethin' in the library somewhere, and all it would take was for me to remember where I'd seen somethin' like this before."

"And…did you?"

"You'd think so, wouldn't you?" He paced back and forth, clearly enjoying himself. "You've never been down in the stacks, Stone, but if you ever were, you'd probably wet yerself with joy. Thousands of volumes—magic stuff, mundane stuff, some stuff nobody's ever been able to figure out quite *what* it is. Obviously I 'aven't read it all—not even close—but it's all surprisingly well indexed, in both a magical and a mundane way. So I'm usually pretty good at puttin' my 'ands on what I need at any given time. In this case, though, that didn't 'appen."

"You didn't find anything in the library?"

"Not yet. Not sayin' it's not there, mind you—but you've only given me a day. I might be a miracle worker, but even the bloke up-stairs took seven days to make the Earth, right?"

"Er…"

"So. I got to thinkin', brainstormin' with Ward earlier tonight. I was certain I'd seen somethin' like those figures on that thing before. Not exactly like it, but close. But I couldn't put my finger on where. And then it came to me." He smacked himself gently on the forehead. "Boom, like a bolt from the blue, it 'it me. Where I'd seen 'em before."

"Where?" Stone leaned forward, his heart beating faster with anticipation. Like Kolinsky, Eddie didn't draw out reveals like this unless they were worth the effort.

In answer, Eddie used magic to pull the closed leather portfolio to him. He opened it with a flourish, took out a small stack of photos, and flung them across the table in an artful fan. "*Voilà*."

Stone recognized them in an instant, and went still.

"Bloody hell, Eddie," he whispered, astonished. "You're right. Why didn't I see that before?"

"Guess you're just not as bright as me, mate." Eddie grinned, obviously pleased. "Do try to cope. We can't all be mad geniuses, after all."

But Stone was no longer paying attention. He stared at the photos on the table, dread and anticipation competing with each other for his focus. "Bloody hell…" he said again. "This problem just got more interesting, didn't it?"

The photos were familiar, because he'd seen them before. They were copies of the same ones Jason had taken in the formerly sealed room they'd found in the catacombs beneath Stone's Surrey home.

The room that had held his dragon ancestor Aldwyn in stasis for nearly two hundred years.

CHAPTER THIRTEEN

S TONE WAS STILL IN A STATE of near-shock when he returned home an hour later. He had the leather portfolio full of photos with him, since Eddie had assured him he had copies, but didn't have any idea what he was going to do with them.

Eddie had been right: the symbols on the pyramid hadn't been identical to the ones in the sealed room. But they'd clearly been the same "language," and the two locations did share a few of them in common.

"I don't know what it means yet," Eddie had told him as they both studied the photos. "But it does seem a bit coincidental that your item and the room were both designed to nullify or block magical energy, dunnit?"

"Very much so…" Stone murmured, more focused on the symbols than on his friend's voice.

None of them had ever managed to work out what language the symbols in the sealed room had been written in. Eddie and Ward had searched the library for other examples, but found nothing. Eventually, his friends had moved the research to the back burner, trusting in Eddie's memory to resurface it if they ever encountered any new information. But what, if anything, did the two items have in common? Had there been more to the room than they'd thought? Perhaps another of these devices embedded in the walls or in a hidden alcove they'd missed?

That was all moot, though, since the whole catacomb complex had collapsed, burying any evidence.

Raider greeted him with a loud, insistent *meow* when he popped into the living room. Cats, apparently, didn't have a problem with their human servants appearing out of nowhere.

"Sorry, sorry," he murmured, bending to idly pet the cat. His heart was only half in it, though, his mind still firmly fixed on the odd characters and the odder correlation between them and the ones in the sealed room.

He got a Guinness and sat on his sofa, spreading the photos across his coffee table, where Raider promptly jumped up and sat on them. Eventually, after being gently nudged off several times, the cat settled next to him, his head resting on his leg, and fell asleep as Stone continued examining the photos.

Nothing came to him, though—at least nothing useful. The only potentially helpful thing he remembered was that the people behind the sealed room that had imprisoned Aldwyn had been led by his own ancestor and Aldwyn's son, Cyrus…and James Brathwaite, whom Cyrus's people had betrayed and murdered after refusing to go along with his suggestion that they use necromancy against Aldwyn.

And Brathwaite was quite probably still alive.

He sighed, running his hand through his hair in frustration, and tossed the photo he was holding down. What did it matter if Brathwaite *was* still alive? It wasn't as if he could find the man and compel him to talk. Brathwaite had disappeared ever since the battle at the mall in Tennessee, probably regrouping after the failure of the ritual and the loss of Richter. Maybe he was consolidating his power, trying to take over Richter's old job as head of the European branch of Ordo Purpuratus. Or perhaps he was on the run, hiding from the rest of the Ordo who were after him because his failed ritual had killed their leader. But either way, Stone had about as much chance of finding him and getting anything useful out of him as he had of figuring out the secrets of time travel.

But…

He sat up straighter as another thought struck him.

Yes, talking to Brathwaite was out of the question, even if he wanted to. But there *was* at least one other person involved in that incident.

One other person who was still alive after all this time.

He let his breath out. Last time they'd talked, Aldwyn had told him if he wanted to speak again, he had only to make it known he was interested. He had no idea how that worked, but he didn't doubt his dragon ancestor had ways of keeping tabs on him.

But did he want that? Was he ready to open *that* can of worms over this? Was a chance of discovering the pyramid's secret worth renewing a relationship with someone who had likely been responsible for murdering the forty-plus innocent people who'd been interred beneath the Surrey house?

Damn it, I don't know. He stroked Raider's head, and the cat stretched out along his leg and purred louder. "I don't know, Raider…" he murmured. "I'm tired. Suppose we head upstairs and try to get some sleep? Well…I suppose you're *already* getting some sleep. Nothing keeps you from your nap schedule, does it?" He rose heavily from the couch, picked Raider up, and settled him in the crook of his arm.

As interesting as this problem was, it could wait until morning.

He woke earlier than usual after an uneasy sleep marred by strange dreams of bizarre symbols, zombie dragons, and Raider perched on top of a giant version of the black pyramid.

When he checked his phone, he found a text from Jason: *Call me when you get up.*

He called on his way downstairs. "What's up?"

"Talked to Gina. She's fixed the photos and put them on an anonymous server for you. Got a pen? I could text you the address, but I don't want you to click on it."

"Er…hang on." He reached the kitchen and grabbed a pad. "Okay, go."

Jason carefully dictated a link, then made him repeat it to make sure he'd got it right. "Just give that to Blum when you talk to him."

"Thank you, Jason." Stone opened a can of food for Raider and put it on a plate. "I never asked you—what does Gina think of all this bizarre stuff we ask her to do? Does she ever get suspicious?"

"She's curious. What hacker isn't? But I think she enjoys the challenge. Beats the hell out of poking through a bunch of dusty old government and work records, looking for proof somebody's up to something."

"I suppose so. As long as you trust her…"

"I do. She's worked out better than I had a right to hope. She's a good kid."

"All right, then. Thank you for the information. I'll talk to Blum today."

"Keep me up to date with what's going on. Gina's still looking for that McGrath stuff. She has to fit it in around regular work, of course, but I'll text you if she gets anywhere with it."

He had another of Greene's classes later today, so he called Blum right away. "Detective. How have you been?"

"Hey, Stone. Long time. Crazy busy as usual. Don't tell me—you've got some weird magical problem you want to dump on me."

"Well…I wouldn't exactly put it that way. But there is something I thought you might be able to help me with."

"Wait. Hold on." He heard a door closing, and then: "Does this have anything to do with what happened at Stanford?"

Stone smiled. Good old Blum, always on top of things. "How did you guess?"

"Hmm. Let's think. Room full of oddball stuff gets broken into and a part-time Occult Studies professor gets whacked over the head. Can't imagine why I'd think you'd be involved. Only reason I haven't called you yet is because I've been up to my ass in the cases they actually pay me to work on."

"Yes. Well. As it happens, I am involved. The man who was injured is a friend of mine. He used to be my student."

"He doing okay?"

"He has a serious concussion, but I think he'll be all right."

"So…" Blum dropped his voice. "Is this one of *those* kinds of crimes?"

Stone hesitated, suddenly uncomfortable with revealing the details over the phone, and realizing he didn't have to. "Detective…could we meet somewhere? I'd rather do this in person."

Now it was Blum's turn to hesitate. "I'm pretty busy. Can you come up here? Only time I've got free today is in an hour. That's cutting it close."

"No, no, I can make it. Name the place and I'll be there."

"You sure?" He gave Stone an address. "I can't wait if you're late. I can only spare like twenty minutes."

"I'll be there, Detective. See you then. Cheers."

He hung up before Blum could ask any more questions.

The location the detective had chosen for the meet was a coffee shop a few blocks from the precinct. It was also, to Stone's relief, only two miles from a ley line. He took a cab to the shop and was waiting there when Blum arrived.

"Holy shit, that was fast." Blum dropped into the seat across from Stone in the back of the shop.

The place was packed. Stone normally didn't like crowds, but in this case the loud hubbub and clanking dishes covered their conversation. Even so, he quickly put up his "cone of silence" spell to make sure no one overheard them. "Good to see you, Detective," he said, ignoring the other man's statement. "Thank you for meeting with me."

"Well, like I said, you better make it quick." He glanced at his watch. "I gotta be in court in less than an hour, and unlike you, apparently, I can't fly across town on my broom or whatever you did to avoid traffic."

"That's fine. Let's get to it, then. In answer to your question on the phone, yes, I do believe the break-in at the University *was* magic-related. And I think I know what they were looking for."

"Oh, yeah?" Blum's interest perked up. "What's that?"

Stone took out his phone, cued up the best photo of the pyramid, and pushed it across the table. "That."

Blum looked at Stone, then at the photo, then back up at Stone again. His eyes narrowed in suspicion. "Why do you have a photo of it?"

"Because I've got it in my possession."

"What the fuck?" He glanced around to make sure nobody had noticed his outburst, then aimed a glare at Stone. "Are you sayin' what I think you're sayin'? That *you're* the one who took somethin' out of that room?"

"Yes. And before you're tempted to arrest me, hear me out." He quickly told Blum the rest of the story. The only part he left out was the exact nature of the pyramid, describing it only as a "powerful and potentially dangerous magical item, best not allowed to fall into the wrong hands."

Blum let his breath out in a loud, frustrated sigh. "You're a piece of work, Stone, you know that? So you took it away so you could study it, and later on somebody broke in looking for it, didn't find it, and bashed your friend over the head."

"Well, I suspect he probably hit Greene before he knew it wasn't there. I think Greene surprised him, and he panicked."

"Okay…" Their coffee arrived, and Blum paused to sip from his mug. "So what do you want me to do about it? You still have the thing, right?"

"For now, yes."

"What's that mean? You're expecting somebody to steal it from you?"

"No. I plan to study it, until I've figured out what it is and what its purpose is. I believe there might be at least one other related item, which probably isn't in the same collection. I've looked over the auction catalog, and didn't notice anything that looked suspicious."

"So you're gonna give it back?"

"We'll see. I'm still working that out. I honestly don't think it's inherently valuable to mundanes. It's old, yes, but it's not made of gold or precious stones or anything."

"You know that doesn't matter, right? Theft is theft, even if it's a piece of gum."

"True. But that isn't the point. That's not why I asked you here, and our time grows short."

"Okay, then why *did* you ask me here?"

"Because I found the thief last night."

Again, Blum looked at him sharply. "You did?"

"I did."

"Where is he? You…uh…haven't got him chained up in your basement or something, do you?"

"No. I tracked him to a bar in Mountain View, and unfortunately he got away from me. He's definitely magically talented."

"He got away from you? How'd that happen?"

"Crowded bar—and I think he spotted me. But…" He retrieved his phone, scrolled forward to the first of the photos he'd taken last night, and pushed it back. "I got some photos. I thought perhaps you might run them through whatever databases you police types use for that sort of thing, and figure out who he might be."

Blum gaped at him. "Stone…"

"Yes. I know." He tapped his watch. "Tick-tock, Detective. Can you do it?"

"Uh—yeah. I guess. I haven't got a fucking clue how I'm going to explain my interest, but I'll do it. Can you send me the pics?"

"No, but I'll give you this." He took out the slip of paper with the address Jason had given him.

"What's this?"

"Secure, anonymous server. You'll find copies of all the photos, with the…er… identifying information removed."

Blum grinned. "Jason's finally gettin' through to you, I see."

"I can neither confirm nor deny that."

The detective tucked the paper into his wallet. "Yeah. Okay. The pics aren't great, but we might be able to get something. What do you want me to do if I find him? This isn't exactly my jurisdiction."

"Honestly, my preference is for you to give me the information. I told you—this man is a mage, and he's obviously dangerous since he nearly killed Mr. Greene. I wouldn't want any of your colleagues' blood on my conscience."

"You make it really hard to do my job. You know that?"

"Hey, it's not my fault you decided to reveal to me that you're aware of the magical world. Find me someone else in law enforcement who is and who's willing to work with me, and I'll back off. But this is important, Detective."

"Yeah, yeah. I'll look into it, like I said. If I find anything, though, what I do with it depends on what it is."

"Fair enough."

Blum leaned in closer. "But I will tell you one thing, though, and you didn't hear this from me."

"What's that? And you needn't worry about anyone overhearing us."

He looked around like he expected to see a magical cloud swirling around them, but he resumed his former position. "Remember I told you I thought maybe you might be involved in this mess?"

"Yes…"

"Well, I've been watchin' it, just in case. Did you know another professor's place got broken into yesterday afternoon?"

"It doesn't surprise me."

"That right?" Blum looked disappointed. "I thought that'd be new information."

"I was actually expecting it. Janice Inouye, right? Anthropology department?"

"Yeah, that's the one. How'd you know?"

"Remember when I said I was tracking the thief? You didn't ask me how. You're slipping, Detective." Stone gave him an amused smile to take the edge off his words.

Blum waved him off. "I don't even wanna know how you people do what you do. But you were *tracking* him? You mean you *expected* him to break into somebody's house?"

"Either Inouye's or mine, yes. Possibly both, but any mage worth his salt wouldn't dare try breaking into my place."

"Why her?"

"She was the only other person who signed the log sheet outside the room after I did. The one, I might add, that the thief took with him after he left the storeroom."

"Shit." Blum stared into his coffee. "Nobody else on that sheet?"

"Just one, a couple days before me. Dr. Inouye was in after me, and Greene later that same evening. The thief broke into her place yesterday afternoon, according to my tracker. Probably trying to make sure nobody was home. I'm not sure whether that means he'd rather not cause any more injuries, or if it was simply more convenient not to have to deal with anyone." He looked up at Blum. "Did you see the police report? I hope he didn't cause any damage."

"No. Looks like a pro. Her husband got home and found the drawers tossed, that kind of thing, but no major damage. Likely the guy got in and out pretty fast."

"That tracks with what I know. My tracker went off when he entered the house, and it was only an hour or so later that I found him at that bar."

"Okay." Blum stood. "I'm not sure whether to thank you or not. This sure as hell sounds like another one of those cases the mundane cops aren't gonna have much chance at. Are you *sure* this doodad is dangerous? If it isn't and it's not valuable, maybe it would be better just to let them have the damn thing. Better that than risking anybody else gettin' hurt."

"That's the thing, though: I'm *not* sure whether it's dangerous. I doubt it would be dangerous to mundanes, but if I'm right and it's part of a larger artifact, *and* I'm right about what that artifact might be capable of, there are definitely people out there I don't want getting hold of it."

"So what do you suspect it's part of? What do you think it does?"

Stone paused, trying to decide if he wanted to give Blum that much information. He supposed it couldn't hurt. After all, the people who were looking for it almost certainly already knew or suspected what it was. That was *why* they were looking for it. "This is just speculation. But based on my and some friends' limited research, I suspect it might be an item that can nullify or attenuate magical energy."

Blum's eyes widened. "Holy shit. That's huge."

"Hence my concern, and my unwillingness to let this thing out of my hands until I've got more information."

"No, no, you're not gettin' it, Stone. That's not just huge for magical people. Depending on how it works, it might be huge for us mundanes too. Remember all that stuff Verity was going on about a while back, about doing something about magical criminals?"

Stone stared at him. He'd been so focused on the magical applications of the item, he hadn't even considered the broader ones. "You're right. If we manage to locate the components of this thing—assuming they still exist, of course—or work out how to build new ones, it could potentially lead to a way to incarcerate mages." Inwardly, he shivered a bit. The idea of being held in a cell at the mercy of mundane law enforcement didn't appeal to him in the slightest, but he couldn't deny the potential usefulness of such a capability.

"Yeah. If that kind of magical tech exists somewhere, maybe someday that might be a reality."

"Well. You might be right, but I wouldn't hold my breath about it. As I said, I'm not even one hundred percent certain I'm right about there being another component. If this little thing is all there is, the best we might hope for is using to wipe a few magically-written papers, or possibly conceal small, weak magic items. It's possible it's only useful for study purposes."

Blum looked dubious. "I dunno, Stone. People don't whack other people over the head and break into their houses for 'study purposes.'"

Stone chuckled. "Obviously you've never met some of my more zealous academic colleagues, Detective." He pulled on his coat. "Anyway, thanks for the chat. Let me know if you come up with anything, will you?"

"I will if you will."

"Did you hear Janice Inouye's house got broken into?"

Stone feigned surprise as he stood in Beatrice Martinez's doorway later that day. "Bloody hell, is that right? Is she all right?"

"She's fine. It happened sometime yesterday afternoon. She wasn't home at the time, and neither was her husband." Martinez sighed. She looked tired, with dark circles under her eyes and an uncharacteristic slump in her shoulders.

"Have they got any idea what they were looking for?"

Martinez waved him toward a chair. "She took a few days off, naturally—that's how I found out, when she called in this morning. She said they didn't find anything missing. The police have a suspicion, though."

"Oh?" Stone kept his expression carefully neutral.

"Yes." She glanced at him in concern. "And I'm afraid you might have cause for concern too, Alastair."

"Why is that?"

"They think it might have something to do with the break-in at the storeroom, where Brandon got hurt."

"Bloody hell. They still think the thief was looking for something specific?"

"That's their speculation—though they don't know what it is. Obviously if they're breaking in to Janice's place, they didn't find it in the storeroom."

"It was fairly jumbled in there, though. I don't think I saw half the items during the time I was inside."

"That's true—whatever it is, it might still be there, buried somewhere among the other items. But the police are speculating that, whatever it is, it's possible somebody who was in that room before the thief showed up might have taken it."

"Taken it? You mean stolen it?"

She shrugged. "I doubt it. I can't imagine anyone here would steal anything." Giving Stone a narrow-eyed glance, she added, "but

I wouldn't be quite as certain someone might not 'borrow' something for a little while if it struck them as interesting."

"I suppose it's possible."

"Janice claims she didn't, though. And I assume you didn't either?"

"Of course not." Stone was grateful once again that he was an excellent liar. It came with his extensive training in aura control from the time he was an apprentice. "Honestly, I didn't see much in there that struck me as particularly interesting. A few things I might like to show my students, but certainly nothing terribly valuable."

"Well, you might consider increasing the security around your house. The police might be able to provide a few drive-bys, but they're so busy I doubt you'll get much else from them."

"That's all right. The security around my house is fairly extensive. If they try anything, they might be in for a surprise."

Martinez shook her head, staring at her hands on her desk. "I don't know, Alastair. I'll be honest—I'm sorry I ever agreed to let them store the collection here. I thought it might be academically interesting to let some of the faculty examine the items before they move on, but look what that decision has caused. We have Brandon nearly killed, and Janice is understandably feeling violated...I'm glad the whole mess is leaving soon."

"Leaving?" Again, Stone feigned surprise.

"Yes. I've spoken with Hiram Drummond's heirs, and they've agreed to have the collection moved to San Francisco until the auction. It will have better security there, and we won't have to worry about anyone else getting hurt. They'll re-catalog everything when they get there, and hopefully determine if anything *is* actually missing. They're bringing in a truck the day after tomorrow to pack everything up and haul it off. Campus security will be sending some officers over to keep an eye on the process, and I think the

Palo Alto police department might even send over an officer or two to oversee things, just to be safe. I'll be glad when it's gone."

Again she looked up at Stone, almost as if coming out of a trance. "Anyway, what did you want? Sorry to drop all that on you, but you showed up and…" She gestured around.

"Of course. I'm happy to help, even if it's only to be a sounding board. I just came by to see if you've heard anything else about Greene. Is he out of the hospital yet?"

"Yes, I heard they let him go home today. His roommate is taking care of him. He's supposed to stay home and rest for the next few days." She drew a breath. "So…"

"So that means his classes will need looking after."

She gave him a faint smile. "Don't worry, Alastair—you and Mac are off the hook. I've arranged for a couple of TAs to take them over until he's back."

Stone didn't let his relief show. It wasn't that he minded taking the classes—he still enjoyed teaching, and was happy to help Greene—but he suspected he was going to be busy enough for the foreseeable future that it wouldn't be wise to add more commitments to his schedule.

He was already forming a new plan, and for that he'd need Eddie and Ward's help.

CHAPTER FOURTEEN

"I don't know, mate," Eddie said dubiously. "That seems like a bit of a dodgy idea—not to mention potentially dangerous."

Stone waved him off. "Dodgy, yes. Dangerous—I doubt it. If I can't fool a bunch of mundanes long enough to get this done, I should turn in my mage card. Can you do it?"

He exchanged glances with Ward. "Maybe, but not on such short notice. That's not exactly in our wheelhouse."

"But—"

"'Ang on," Eddie interrupted. "*We* can't do it—but I think I know somebody who can. Assumin' you're willin' to trust somebody else. And it'll cost dear."

"Cost isn't an issue. Trust—that's a bit more of a problem. If you trust this person that would normally be good enough for me, but we've already seen there are people out there willing to kill over this thing. I don't want to see anyone else get hurt over it. And I also don't want to let it out of my hands." Stone paced the sitting room, thinking. "It doesn't need to be exact—just good enough to fool the mundanes. Do you think your friend could work from photos and detailed notes?"

"Probably," Ward said. "The result wouldn't be as precise, though."

"Yes, well, I don't think it needs to be. Don't forget—nobody knows it's even missing, so it won't be subjected to close scrutiny.

Can you give him a call? I need it as soon as possible. By tomorrow if he can manage it."

"Yeah, yeah," Eddie said. "You don't want much, Stone, do you?"

"You love it and you know it. You both do."

"Well, I gotta say, life is certainly a lot more *interesting* wit' you around. I'm still workin' out whether that's a good thing."

With the day free of classes, Stone returned to California. Jason's agency wasn't anywhere near a ley line, so he drove down to San Jose.

"Hi Dr. Stone," Gina said as he entered. "Jason's not here. He's got a court appearance this morning and won't be back till lunchtime."

"That's fine. I was in the area, so I figured I'd check in to see if you've made any progress on locating Mr. McGrath's auction catalog."

She sighed. "Sorry, not yet. This isn't exactly the kind of hacking I'm familiar with. If you wanted me to break into a file system somewhere, that I could do easy-peasy. But do you realize how much of a needle in a haystack this thing is? Assuming it even exists?"

"I do. I know. Have you found *anything* yet?"

"A few things, yeah. You're lucky that this guy was semi-famous, even if it was only a hundred years ago in the Midwest. That will make it easier. But this involves a lot of looking through old newspapers and that kind of thing—a lot of which aren't even online. I'm hoping I can find out *where* the auction was held. At least that way if I can't find the catalog online, you might be able to go to wherever it is and search the library manually." She wrinkled her nose. "You know, work your way through boxes of dusty old microfiche records? Is this really worth it to you, Doc?"

"It could be, yes."

She leaned back in her chair and regarded him curiously. "You *do* know how hard it is for me to keep my mouth shut and not ask you about all this weird stuff, right? I mean, come on. Space aliens in Colorado, and now obscure auction catalogs from fifty years ago?"

"What can I say? I've got…eclectic interests."

"Eclectic interests would be crocheted toilet-paper cozies and NASCAR. This is just…weird. No offense," she added quickly, as if suddenly remembering he was a part-owner of the agency.

"None taken. Hell, if I got offended every time someone called me weird, I wouldn't have time to do anything else. All I can tell you is that it's got to do with the recent break-in up at the University. A good friend was injured, and I'm doing some investigation of my own."

She sighed. "Yeah. Okay. Like I said, I'm glad to help because I like tracking down stuff like this. But one of these days I hope you'll trust me enough to tell me the rest of the story."

Eddie didn't get back to Stone until late the following day.

Stone called him instantly after the text arrived. "I was starting to worry you wouldn't be able to do it."

"You'll worry when you 'ear 'ow much it's gonna cost you. I 'ope you were serious about money not bein' an issue."

"It's fine. Can I come and pick it up now?"

"Oh, sure. It's only three in the mornin'. Early yet. Especially with your new flittin'-around-the-world thing."

This time, Stone didn't bother trying to hide anything. He re-appeared outside the library less than five minutes later and knocked on the door.

Eddie stared at him. "Okay, that's bloody incredible. The other times I could almost rationalize that you were 'avin' me on. You weren't over 'ere already, were you?"

"No, I was in my study in California with Raider. Come on," he urged, hurrying inside. "Let's see it."

It was on the table in the sitting room, atop a stack of random papers. Stone hurried over to it and used levitation to bring it up where he could study it. He whistled softly. "Impressive, Eddie. Very impressive."

"Told you 'e was good." Eddie looked pleased. "I think 'e did a bang-up job matching it from nothin' but photos and notes."

Stone didn't answer, too busy examining the replica of the black pyramid from every angle. It wasn't perfect—he was familiar enough with the real thing that even without having it handy to compare, he could see small differences in some of the symbols on the sides. But Eddie's craftsman had managed even to duplicate the signs of the pyramid's advanced age—the rough edges, the chip out of the top, and the slightly asymmetrical sizes of the two holes in the bottom. Obviously, he hadn't duplicated the thing's magic-damping properties—Stone had no trouble levitating it and manip-ulating it with magic—but that hadn't been a requirement. The mundanes who'd be cataloguing it wouldn't know about the magic anyway. He had, however, somehow imbued the pyramid with a faint aura of magic. "It's brilliant," he said at last. "Thank you."

"Thank Mr. Khouri. He's a master craftsman, and the best mag-ical artificer I know. I'm honestly surprised I managed to convince him to work on this. He's usually scheduled for months in advance." He handed over a piece of paper. "There's what you owe, and the bank account number to send it to. 'E says 'e trusts you if I do, but don't wait too long."

Stone glanced at it. "You weren't kidding. Worth every penny, though." He pulled a cloth from his pocket, used it to pluck the floating pyramid from the air, and put it in his pocket. "Thanks again. No time to spare, either. They're going to be loading up the collection starting tomorrow morning."

"You sure you want to do this? If they catch you—"

"They aren't going to catch me. I've got all sorts of tricks up my sleeve. I'd best get going, though. Lots to do, preparations to make."

Eddie tilted his head. "Can I watch?"

"What?"

"You know. Can I watch you leave?"

Stone chuckled. "You want to try working out what I'm doing."

"Do you blame me?"

"Sure, why not? Give me a moment, though. It does take a bit of preparation."

Eddie watched him closely, obviously using magical sight while he visualized the pattern in his mind. He nodded, offered a cheery wave, and disappeared.

The last thing he saw before he was gone was the look of wide-eyed amazement on his friend's face, but he couldn't pause to let it amuse him. He hadn't lied to Eddie—he had a lot of things to do before the morning.

CHAPTER FIFTEEN

THE NEXT DAY dawned bright and chilly.

Stone crouched on the roof of the building across the way from the one containing the storeroom. He'd been there for half an hour already, watching the activity milling around the large truck parked at the back of the opposite building. They had the double doors propped open; a pair of campus security officers stationed on either side watched as coverall-clad workmen wheeled crates outside and into the truck. Two other security guards patrolled the area around the truck's rear, and Stone had already determined two more were watching the storeroom door. If any of the workmen had plans to steal anything, they'd have no chance to do it between the storeroom and the truck. Even if the campus security guards didn't deter them, the uniformed Palo Alto PD cop hanging out near the truck's ramp would probably do the job.

They weren't taking any chances. Stone supposed it made sense, since they probably still had no idea how the original thief had managed to enter the room without a trace and someone *had* been nearly killed during the commission of the crime. But as far as they knew, this was nothing more than a collection of dusty old artifacts that probably weren't worth that much to anybody but a collector. Stone wondered if this was Martinez's doing, beefing up the security to help her deal with her guilt over what had happened to Greene.

It was a Saturday morning, so far fewer students drifted by this obscure corner of the University's grounds than usual. Even so, a small group of them had congregated near the truck, watching with curiosity from behind a makeshift barrier. One was taking photos with an actual camera—perhaps someone from the *Daily* staff looking for human-interest stories.

Stone checked his coat pocket, rubbing the fake pyramid with a gloved hand. He still wasn't entirely sure how he was going to accomplish his mission. So far, everything that had come out of the storeroom had been boxed up in large wooden crates, some of which hadn't even been opened before being initially stored. With all the activity going on inside the storeroom, Stone doubted even his magic could guarantee no one would notice him if he tried slipping the pyramid inside one of the boxes before it was sealed.

He'd already discarded the idea of trying to sneak into the storeroom before the truck arrived. He probably could have done it, but he had no idea how many other security measures they'd put into place in the wake of the break-in and attack. The last thing he needed was to be caught on some hidden camera. This pyramid was intriguing and he wanted to know who'd attempted to steal it, but not so much he was willing to put his position at the University at risk.

Not yet, anyway.

The workmen continued steadily loading crates into the truck and hurrying back with their empty carts to collect more. Based on Stone's knowledge of the storeroom's dimensions and the size of the collection, he estimated they'd probably be at it for another thirty to forty-five minutes, minimum.

He considered waiting until they were finished, then using invisibility to enter the truck. Once the workmen closed the doors, he'd have until they reached San Francisco to pry one of the crates open and slip the pyramid inside. It was definitely an option, but he didn't want to remain here on top of this building for that long.

The odds were almost nonexistent that anyone would see him, but he didn't want to take chances. Better to get this over sooner rather than later.

He scanned the group again, including the spectators and the immediate surroundings, looking for any sign of magic. If he was hiding, it made sense someone else might be as well. But he saw nothing—no magical energy hovering around anyone, no illusions, no invisible presences lurking behind trees. If the thieves were planning anything, this apparently wasn't when they were going to do it.

And even better, if nobody around here was magically active, their chances of spotting anything he tried were low. He'd have to devote some extra energy to avoiding the cameras, but that was fine. Energy, he had.

Another pair of workmen came out, wheeling two more large, wooden boxes. So far, all those that had come out had been wooden, which meant they were probably the ones that hadn't been opened since they arrived at the University. Stone had spotted them when he was inside the storeroom, pushed back against the wall.

Would the workmen crate up the rest of the collection in more wooden boxes? That seemed a bit old-fashioned. Did people even *use* wooden boxes for shipping anymore?

Stone sighed. This was getting him nowhere. Even with his magic, trying to open one of those sealed crates and slip something into it would be risky, as would trying to stow away in the truck. He didn't like it, but he was rapidly reaching the conclusion that his only viable option was to get into the storeroom and put the pyramid inside one of the crates before it was sealed.

That was assuming, of course, that all them weren't *already* sealed. They could have already finished the packing inside before he got here.

He pulled out a small pair of binoculars and observed the workmen for a while. They moved at a steady pace, shuttling boxes to the truck and up the ramp on moving dollies. They were taking obvious care with what they were doing, leading Stone to believe these weren't your typical house movers. Knowing Martinez, she'd probably hired a specialized crew. More guilt, no doubt.

He wished Jason and Amber were here. His friends were a lot better than he was at this sneaking-around thing. Perhaps he should give them a call. If they could—

Hello. What's this?

A pair of workmen finished unloading their boxes into the truck, but instead of going back inside, they milled around in the courtyard outside the building. After a moment, four other workmen emerged. One lit a cigarette, and a few others drifted over to a table where a blue plastic coffee jug and a series of cups had been set out.

They're on a break!

Stone smiled. Well. Perhaps the Universe was offering him an opportunity after all. Best not to squander it.

Two campus security guards were stationed on either side of the storeroom door. They frowned as the coverall-clad workman walked past them into the room.

"Aren't you guys on break?" one asked.

"Yeah. Forgot my phone in there. Be right out."

"Hurry up," said the other. "I gotta take a leak and I don't want anybody in there while we're not both here."

"No problem."

Stone didn't smile again until he was past them and inside the storeroom. Of all his magical toys, his disguise amulets were the most useful for things like this. He'd even gotten to try out his new American accent—a deeper one he'd been practicing with Jason's help. Combined with a disregarding spell, it should make him both unobtrusive and uninteresting long enough to do what he needed to do.

But he'd still need to hurry.

There were a lot fewer boxes in here now. The tables where the loose items had been laid out were gone, and several more boxes stood lined up near the door, waiting their turn to be loaded.

Stone ducked behind one of the larger ones and looked around. Surely there had to be at least one that hadn't been sealed yet. He didn't think his disregarding spell would hide the sound of a crate being pried open. His heart beat faster—he didn't know how long the workers' break was, but he doubted it would be more than five or ten minutes. He could hear the two guards out front, talking to each other about last night's Warriors game.

His gaze fell on a box on the other side of the room. It was still open, its lid balanced askew on top to reveal a few tufts of packing straw poking out.

There we go…

With a glance toward the door to make sure the guards weren't coming in to check on him, he hurried across the room. To be doubly safe, he cast an invisibility spell over himself as he reached the crate. Now the clock was ticking.

He pulled the pyramid from his pocket and examined the crate's interior. Several other items, all carefully wrapped, were nestled in the straw, double-cushioned against any bumps or mis-haps. Sticking the pyramid in there "naked" might look suspicious, but there was no helping it. He definitely didn't have time to wrap it. He took another look at the door, then jammed the fake pyramid down as far as he could, making sure it was fully covered not only by the straw, but by another item.

There. It was done. Now all he'd have to do was get out of here and away, and he'd be home free.

Sudden voices startled him. He jerked his head up in time to see two more workmen enter the room, pushing carts.

Oh, bloody hell.

One of them was the same guy whose face Stone had "borrowed" with his disguise amulet.

"Hey," one of the guards called. "How'd you get out here?"

"Huh?" Both workers turned back.

The guard appeared in the doorway and pointed. "You just came in. Lookin' for your phone."

Stone crouched behind the box, struggling to keep his breathing quiet. Already, the invisibility spell was starting to wear on him, and the guard was blocking his only exit.

"What are you talkin' about, man? I was outside havin' a smoke."

"What the hell? You were *in* here. Just now." The guard waved his counterpart toward the door. "Watch the door," he ordered, then entered the room and stalked over to the stack of boxes Stone had been hiding behind.

"You okay, man?" the worker asked. "Maybe *you* need to go have a smoke?"

"You were *here,*" the guard insisted. His head swiveled as he tried to look everywhere at once. "You just came in here. Said you had to find your phone."

"He wasn't in here," the worker's partner said. "He was out with me. We were talkin' about some stupid thing his kid did last night."

"Well, *somebody* was in here." He raised his voice. "Right, Chuck? Somebody came in?"

"Yeah," Chuck called back. "Went right in. Like five minutes ago."

"Well, he ain't here now."

"Listen," the second worker said. "You didn't hear it from me, but I heard this crap in here is haunted. I'm serious. Lotta old weird shit from some crazy collector. The spook department was all over it. One of 'em even got clocked over the head during the break-in. I just wanna get it all loaded up and get the fuck outta here, okay?"

He stalked over, snatched up the cover for the crate Stone was hiding behind, and began nailing it into place. "Can we do that?"

The security guard looked like he didn't know what to do with himself. Obviously nobody was in the room, but Stone could see from his expression that he was still certain someone *had* been. "Yeah, whatever," he finally said wearily. "Get movin'. I want to get home too. Told the wife and kids I'd take 'em to the mall this afternoon."

The workman was less than two feet away from Stone. He could smell the man's combination of sweat, cigarette smoke, and after-shave, and hear the huff of his breathing.

He hoped the man couldn't hear *him*. His heart raced and droplets formed on his forehead. If it hadn't been three minutes yet, it was damned close. He'd have to do something now—the alternative was appearing out of thin air in front of at least three witnesses.

As his desperation grew, an idea occurred to him. This would take some effort and carried a risk, but he was out of options. He fixed his focus on the other side of the room, where someone had left a hammer on top of a sealed crate. A quick nudge of magical energy sent it scooting off the side, where it crashed to the floor with a loud *thud*.

The effect on the two workers and the guard was instantaneous. They all whirled toward the sound.

"What was *that*?" the guard demanded, his voice a bit high and shrieky.

"I *told* you this shit is fuckin' haunted!" the second workman yelled. "Didn't I tell you?"

"What's going on in here?" The second guard appeared in the doorway as Stone ducked out from behind the box and headed toward him. "What was that sound?"

Waiting for the guard to move into the room and clear the doorway seemed to take about an hour and a half. Stone was sure someone would hear his desperate panting as he struggled to keep the invisibility spell up. Sweat ran down his back now, and he feared his heart would burst free of his chest.

If the man didn't move soon…

The guard strode inside. "Did you guys drop something?"

"Wasn't us," the first worker said in a shaky voice, pointing. "That hammer just—"

Stone didn't wait to hear the rest of the sentence. He ducked out the door and took off at a run down the opposite hallway toward an empty classroom. A quick flick of magic opened the lock and then he was inside, bent over with his hands on his knees, panting like he'd just gone a few rounds in the boxing ring.

Bloody hell, that was close.

But close was fine. He'd done it. The fake pyramid was now safe inside a sealed box, ready to be moved to San Francisco. If the thief tried again, he'd be in for a surprise. And if he didn't…

Well, there was nothing at all suspicious about a prominent and wealthy Occult Studies expert turning up at an auction full of fascinating occult-related objects, was there?

With any luck, he wouldn't be the only one.

CHAPTER SIXTEEN

A FEW DAYS PASSED with no further updates about the collection. Martinez told Stone on Monday that the collection had reached San Francisco without incident and been stored in a more secure location.

"There was only one weird glitch," she told him. "One of the guards said he let one of the workers into the room during their break to get his phone, but then he says the guy strolled in with his buddy a couple minutes later."

"That's...odd," Stone said noncommittally.

"Isn't it? They're saying the collection is haunted." She shook her head, amused. "I'm not surprised, given what it is. But everything made it where it was going just fine, so I'm not going to worry about it anymore. As one of my students said recently, 'Not my circus, not my monkeys.'"

"Indeed. Probably for the best, though I would have liked more time to examine some of the artifacts. The bits I saw were fascinating."

She smiled. "Why am I not surprised? Are you planning to attend the auction?"

"Who knows? I might. I'll see if I can fit it into my schedule."

He'd also called Leo Blum, asking him to keep an eye on any reports related to the collection. Now that it was physically in San Francisco, the detective had a better excuse for checking up on it.

"You expectin' somebody else to try breakin' in?"

"I don't know what to expect. They might have given up, or believe whatever they were looking for wasn't actually there at all. Or they might be waiting for the auction. If they can't steal whatever it is, maybe they can buy it. I've got no idea. I'd just like to know if anybody else breaks in, assuming anyone even finds out. If they're mages, they can probably get in and out without being seen."

"I'll check every morning. Hopefully they shot their wad and that'll be it."

Stone didn't think that was true, but he shared Blum's hope that it was.

On the Tuesday morning following the collection's movement, Stone got a text from Jason. *Hey, I think Gina's got something for you. Can you come down?*

When he arrived at the agency, Gina was at her desk, leaning back in her chair and regarding him with a smug expression. Jason came out of his office and joined her.

"So, what did you find?" Stone fought to keep the eagerness out of his voice, but wasn't very successful.

"I told you I could do it. Well, I *think* I did it."

"What are you talking about? Did you find something online?" It was more than he could dare to hope that she'd managed to find a digital copy of the McGrath auction catalog.

"Yes and no. Have a seat and I'll show you."

Stone didn't sit, but instead hovered over Gina's shoulder. "Yes and no?"

"Well, I found some references to something. But it's not online." She tapped a few keys and called up an image.

It was a blurry photo of a newspaper article, and seemed to be referring to a museum in a town called Tilley, Nebraska.

Stone leaned in closer. "What's this?"

"This is the town where Leander McGrath was living when he died. As you already know, most of his valuable stuff was sold at auction. But he also had a lot of less valuable stuff from his career as a traveling magician. Posters, props, scrapbooks, that kind of thing."

"Yes, and—?" Stone glanced at Jason, who shrugged.

"Sorry, man. She didn't tell me anything yet either."

Gina tapped the screen again. "Apparently Mr. McGrath was kind of a local celebrity. He *did* have pretty good success as a magician in the early part of last century, and his home town thought he was interesting enough to create a permanent exhibit in their museum about him after he died." She clicked her mouse and the blurry photo disappeared, replaced by a modern website for the museum. "The exhibit is still there. It doesn't look like too many other interesting things happened around Tilley, Nebraska, so it's a minor draw for tourists and school kids doing reports."

"I still don't see—"

She clicked again, pulling up a page with a few photos showing parts of the exhibit. In one, a series of lurid but faded posters hung on the wall behind a covered table featuring an old top hat, a magic wand, a faded bouquet of fake flowers, and a layout of old-fashioned playing cards. In another, a glass case covered what looked like a collection of programs from McGrath's shows.

Stone was about to ask his question again, more impatiently, when something caught his eye. "Wait a minute," he murmured, leaning in closer. He pointed at one of the documents in the case. "That doesn't look like a program."

"It's not," Gina said triumphantly. "Look at the caption."

He had to lean in uncomfortably close to read the tiny print. "*A number of programs from McGrath the Magnificent's shows are on display in our exhibit, as well as newspaper clippings and reviews, photographs of notable celebrity guests, and an actual copy of the catalog from the auction of many of his valuable items. Several photos from its pages show some of the fascinating artifacts and apparatus from the collection."*

Stone grinned. "Gina, you're a genius!"

She returned the grin. "Ah, shucks, man. T'warn't nothin'." Then she sobered. "But what good is it going to do you? They didn't digitize it. I couldn't find any references to any online copies. That's probably the last one in existence."

"Yes, I suppose you're right." He exchanged a significant glance with Jason. "Not as if it's worth taking a trip to Nebraska for a closer look."

"I doubt it would matter," Gina said. "I mean, you could look at the photos, I guess. But that catalog looks pretty thick, and even if you *did* go there I doubt they're gonna take it out of the case so you can look through it."

"Good point." He straightened and pulled back. "Please send me the information about the museum, and copies of the photos showing the pages. Perhaps we'll get lucky and find something interesting in one of them."

"Yeah, good luck. I'll try to blow them up as much as I can, but it won't be great. You won't be able to read them or anything. Wish I could have got you more."

"No, no, it's fine. I owe you one."

"Okay," Jason said. "Great work, Gina, but can you get back to the stuff on the Kaufman case now? I need it by the end of today."

"Yes, *sahib.*"

Stone followed Jason into his tiny, cluttered office. He closed the door behind him.

"So," Jason said, gathering papers into a stack. "Don't tell me—you're going to Nebraska."

"I am, yes."

"You honestly think you'll find something in that catalog that goes with the pyramid?"

"I think it might be our only chance, if McGrath had the other piece."

"Or pieces," Jason pointed out. "You don't know it's only one. It could be a whole bunch of them."

"I hope not. Finding *one* other is probably going to be hard enough."

"But how are you gonna get it?" He dropped his voice. "You're not gonna steal it, are you?"

"Borrow. Not steal."

"Al—" Jason glared at him, taking on a warning tone.

"Yes, yes, I know. It's unethical. But I didn't tell you what I found out from Eddie."

"What?"

Stone paused to cast the "cone of silence" spell before speaking further, just in case Gina decided to get nosy. "I thought some of the markings on that pyramid looked sort of familiar, but I couldn't put my finger on where I'd seen them. Eddie, of course, came through. Remember the sealed room in the catacombs under the Surrey house?"

Jason's eyes widened. "Holy shit. You think they're related to *those*?"

"I think they might be, yes. And if they are, that makes this little thing dangerous. Especially now that at least one other person seems to be aware of its existence." He leaned in closer and told Jason about what he'd done Saturday morning at the University.

"Wait. You…made a *fake* pyramid?"

"Had it made, yes."

"And put it *back* with the other stuff?"

"Yes."

"Why?"

"Well, my hope is that if nobody tries stealing it again, perhaps someone will show up at the auction trying to buy it."

"And you're gonna be there to catch them."

"To identify them, at any rate."

Jason considered. "Not a half-bad idea. Want me and Amber to come along? Maybe V, too, if she wants? We could help keep an eye out if anything goes down."

"I think that's a brilliant idea. Having more eyes on the area will reduce the chance of anyone getting away. Thank you, Jason. I'll ask Verity, too, and we can discuss our plans when it gets closer."

"And in the meantime, you're going to Nebraska to steal an auction catalog from some podunk museum."

"Borrow."

"Steal."

Stone sighed, shaking his head. "I don't—"

His phone buzzed with an incoming text. Idly, he pulled it out and scanned it. "Bloody hell."

"What is it?"

He held up the phone. "Blum. Apparently they've found the thief who broke into the storeroom."

"Hey, that's great. Maybe you can find out why he did it. Where are they holding him?"

"At the morgue. He was hit by a truck last night."

CHAPTER SEVENTEEN

S TONE WAITED until he got back to his car to call Blum.

"What's going on?" he demanded without greeting. "You found the thief, and he's dead?"

"Yeah." Blum sounded tired, like he'd been up all night. "Thought you'd want to know."

"Of course I want to know. But how do you know he's the thief? Those photos I gave you aren't good enough for a definitive identification, are they? You don't want me to come up there and try to identify him, do you?"

"I don't think you need to. When they found him, he had one of the items from the collection in his backpack."

Stone froze. Was it possible the guy had managed to get back inside the storeroom, or sneak into the truck when it was en route to San Francisco? "What item?"

"Hang on, I'll send you a photo."

His phone pinged, and a thumbnail photo popped up. He clicked it, expanding it to display a familiar form.

He let his breath out. "That's…odd."

"Why? That *is* something from the collection, right?"

"Yes. But…"

"But what?"

Stone examined the photo again. It showed the African statuette he'd seen the night he was inside the storeroom—one of the three items he'd identified as having magic. It had a ruler next to it and a tag with an evidence number. "Well…it's not what I'd have expected him to have in his possession."

"You mean because it's not that pyramid thing you showed me the photo of."

"Exactly."

The line crackled. "Maybe he stole more than one thing. Either to cover up what he was really lookin' for, or because he thought it might be valuable. Was that thing magical too?"

"To a minor extent, yes. They didn't find anything else in his backpack? A book, perhaps, or a box of quills?"

"Nope, not according to this. Just that figurine. It was wrapped up all nice and safe in a cloth."

Stone pondered. "And you said he got hit by a truck? Where?"

"In Pacifica."

"Any witnesses?"

"Nope. Another driver spotted him lying in the road. The investigators figure it was a truck because of how high the bumper was, and the damage to the body. It's not pretty."

"Damn."

"Yeah. You know…are you *certain* the guy was looking for that pyramid thing? You don't have anything other than your own speculation to make you think so, right?"

"I suppose I don't." Stone spoke reluctantly. Listening to Blum's matter-of-fact words, it occurred to him the man was right: he *didn't* have anything else. Discovering the pyramid and its strange properties had led him on a convoluted flight of fancy that might not have been anything but his own mind forming patterns where none existed.

Except…

"Wait!" he said. "Hang on. That's not possible. I mean, it *is* possible he wasn't looking for the pyramid, but something's dodgy."

"What?"

"You said this figurine was found in his backpack."

"Yeah…"

"But when I talked to Greene—that's my colleague who got hit over the head—he says he remembers waking up a bit and hearing the thief muttering something like 'where is it?' and 'it's got to be here.'"

"Yeah, and—?"

Stone gripped the steering wheel tighter. "When I was inside that storeroom, before the thief and Greene were in there, I saw that figurine. It was sitting on a table in the middle of the room. That's where it was when I left."

"I don't—Oh. Wait. Yeah, I do. You're sayin' that if the thief was lookin' for that figurine and it was right there in plain sight, how could he not see it when he was in there."

"Exactly." Stone's heart rate increased. Something was going on here. "Greene is young, and this is his first job at the University. He wouldn't dare move anything around, and he certainly wouldn't have taken it. I doubt Dr. Inouye would have either. So if it wasn't there when the thief arrived…"

"Then somebody else took it?"

"Yes, or someone planted it on our thief."

"Wait—you're sayin' you think the thief was *murdered*?"

"Who knows, Detective? That's for you lot to work out. I assume there'll be an autopsy?"

"Already done, and preliminary results in. Injuries were consistent with getting hit by a truck." Keys clicked. "I'm lookin' at the report now. Assuming nothing wonky comes back from the tox screens, massive blunt-force trauma is probably our COD. Initial investigation says they didn't find any skid marks in front of the body, which means whoever hit him didn't brake."

"That sounds like murder to me."

"Maybe. But remember, it was dark, and the guy was wearing dark clothes. It could be hit and run, which is bad enough—the driver hit him, got spooked, and took off. That's still bad, but it's not the same thing as deliberately murdering him."

"True. I suppose this could be a coincidence. Though I do wonder why the thief was carrying the figurine around several days after the theft, if that's all it is."

"Maybe he was planning to fence it somewhere. That happens too."

"In Pacifica?"

"Okay, fair enough. Not exactly your hotbed of criminal activity. But one thing you learn in my line of work, Stone—you can't expect things to make sense all the time. People are funny like that."

"I won't argue with that. Did the victim have any identification on him?"

"Nope. No wallet, nothing else in his pockets or the backpack."

"Don't you think that seems odd?"

"Yeah, I do. But then again, if he *was* tryin' to fence that thing, maybe he didn't want anybody to know who he is if he got caught."

"I suppose…"

Blum sighed. "If you're right about the guy lookin' for that pyramid, though, this might be a problem."

"Why is that?"

"I submitted those photos you took of the guy at the bar—said they came from one of my anonymous sources. They're part of the case now. And from what I've seen of the autopsy photos, it's pretty obvious it's the same guy. Obviously they're not gonna just believe one anonymous tipster, but I suspect this'll take the heat off that case. As far as they're concerned, they've found the guy who broke in, and they found what he took."

"Bloody hell. So they'll stop looking?"

"Probably they won't stop, but trust me—I know Palo Alto doesn't have the caseload we've got up here, but they still won't prioritize a case that looks like it's mostly solved. Unless they find anything else missing when they unpack that stuff in SF—" Blum paused. "But wait. They *are* gonna find something else missing, aren't they?"

"Actually, no."

"No?" He lowered his voice. "You put it *back?* Is that safe?"

"I put back…a reasonable facsimile. Nobody mundane will be able to tell the difference without a closer examination than I think they're likely to do."

Blum sighed loudly. "Stone, I don't know what the hell to do with you. You're gonna get my ass fired one of these days."

"I'll do my best to prevent that." Stone started the car. "Thank you, Detective. You've given me a lot to think about."

"No problem. I guess it does mean one good thing for you, doesn't it?"

"What's that?"

"If the police back off on investigating the case, it'll be easier for you to do your magic thing."

"If there's anything else that needs to be done. You could be right: I could have assumed the thief was after the pyramid when he wasn't."

"Here's hoping. I gotta go, Stone. Talk to you later, okay?"

"Yes. I—oh, Blum?"

"Yeah?" He sounded distracted now, as if he'd already mentally moved on to the next item on his to-do list.

"Can you send me a copy of the autopsy report, and the photos, if possible?"

"Why?"

"No particular reason, except I still think something dodgy might be going on here and I want to see if anything pops out at me."

Blum hesitated. "I feel like I'm goin' down a real slippery slope here, you know."

"I know, and I do appreciate your help. I can make it worth your while, if it will help you feel a bit more comfortable with it."

"Offerin' me bribes now?"

"Of course not. Call it a…gift in recognition of our productive professional relationship."

"Yeah. A bribe. And no, I don't need one. I suppose the report'll be public record in a few weeks anyway, so this is just jumpin' the gun a bit. It won't be complete yet, but most of the good stuff should be there." He sighed again, loudly. "Listen to me twistin' my brain into all kinds of knots to justify this."

"Thank you again, Detective. This may end up being nothing. I hope it is."

"But it won't be. Because nothing you've got your fingers in *ever* ends up being nothing."

By the time Stone arrived at the Encantada house, Blum had already emailed him the files he'd requested. He headed to his study accompanied by Raider and pulled up the email, which he noticed was sent from an anonymous throwaway account. The title was *stuff*.

It included two zipped files: one was screen shots of the two sides of the autopsy report, and the other was a series of photos. He glanced over the report itself first. It included what Blum had said it would: an initial cause of death of extensive blunt-force trauma to the chest and abdomen. There was also a post-mortem head injury. The medical examiner stated that the injuries were consistent with being hit by a vehicle with a high bumper and tossed away by the impact. Several parts of the report included only *Pending* or *TBD*, including the results of the toxicology report.

Stone was about to put the report aside when one of the fields caught his eye. Under *Marks and Wounds,* below the descriptions of the various wounds found on the body, the examiner had written:

> *Tattoos: Wolf's head on left thigh. Small cross with letters M N P V on left chest.*

That's odd. Stone wasn't exactly a religious scholar, but he didn't recall ever seeing those letters in conjunction with a cross. He was about to call up a browser and search for them when the answer locked in.

A tiny chill ran up his spine and settled at the back of his neck.

It couldn't be.

He was seeing things where they didn't exist again.

With a shaking hand, pulled up and unzipped the photos, paging through each in turn. Blum was right, they weren't pretty. The truck had done significant damage to the man's body. Stone barely noticed, though, nor did he pay much attention to the thief's face. Instead, he located the clearest shot of his chest and examined the tattoo there.

It was small—perhaps an inch and a half high on the cross's long axis. The cross itself wasn't elaborate, but merely the simple sort of thing any devout Christian might sport. It also didn't have the crude appearance of a homemade or prison tattoo. This one had been done lovingly, by a professional.

What chilled Stone even further, though, were the letters. They were arranged with one at each of the corners where the cross's two bars intersected. Each one was a capital: *M*, *N*, *P*, and *V* arranged in a square around the crossed beams.

He leaned back in his chair with a loud exhalation. "Bloody hell…that is *not* what I expected."

MNPV.

Maleficos non patieris vivere.

Thou shalt not suffer a witch to live.

CHAPTER EIGHTEEN

IT TOOK A BIT OF EFFORT to arrange a meeting between Jason, Amber, Verity, Eddie, and Ward, but all of them put aside their plans when he told them how important it was.

"What's this about?" Verity asked. "Can't you tell us now?"

"Better to get everyone together," he told her. "That way I don't have to tell the story multiple times."

They met at the London house early that evening, and gathered around the big table in the dining room. "Okay," Eddie said. "We're all 'ere. What's this bug you got in your knickers now, Stone?"

"Is Ian coming?" Verity asked. "Did you tell him?"

"No point in getting him involved in this," Stone said. "He's off in South America somewhere with Gabriel, and this doesn't really concern him enough to pull him away from that."

"So, what's up?" Jason asked. "This have something to do with that guy Blum told you about? The one who got hit by a truck?"

"What's this, now?" Eddie leaned in, his curiosity obviously piqued. "Who got 'it by a truck?"

Pacing around the table, Stone filled them all in on the latest information Blum had given him, stopping before he got to the part about the thief's tattoo.

"So…somebody *murdered* him?" Verity asked. "And they found something from the collection in his backpack, but *not* the pyramid?"

"That's weird," Jason said. "Especially since you said the statuette was still there when you left."

"Any chance the other two could have taken it?" Ward asked. "Your colleagues?"

"I can ask them if it comes to that, but I'd put a lot of money on no." Stone paused his pacing and gripped the back of his chair. "They're scholars. Curious, sure, but theoretically they'd have had all the time in the world to study anything that caught their interest. The heirs were willing to remove things from the auction if any of us decided we wanted a more in-depth look. So why risk their careers on getting caught nicking something?"

"Like you did," Verity said.

"Yeah, well, ol' Stone's a special case," Eddie said. "You lot should all know that by now."

"Anyway," Stone continued, "that's our first question: who killed this man? We still don't know his name, by the way. They didn't find any identification on him."

"That implies there's a second question," Ward said.

"Yes, and a much more interesting one. Blum sent me the preliminary autopsy report. I didn't notice anything out of the ordinary until I got to the bit about marks and wounds." He'd snapped a close-up photo of the thief's chest tattoo on his phone, which he pulled up now. He slid it across to the center of the table. "Take a look at that."

All of them stood and leaned in for a better look. "It's a cross," Jason said. That's not all that odd, is it? Maybe he's religious."

But Eddie and Ward had both tensed.

"You see it, don't you?" Stone asked.

Eddie nodded wordlessly.

"What is it?" Amber asked. "What do those letters mean?"

"They're almost certainly an abbreviation," Ward said. "For a Latin phrase: *Maleficos non patieris vivere.*"

"Sorry…I'm a West Coast kid. I took Spanish in high school. What's that mean?"

"It's from the Bible," Eddie said. "Thou shalt not suffer a witch to live."

Jason and Verity exchanged horrified glances.

"Holy shit," Verity said, turning back to Stone. "Are you saying—"

"I'm saying I think our thief might have been a member of Portas Justitiae."

"Portas what, now?" Amber was the only one at the table who still appeared confused.

"Portas Justitiae," Stone said. "It means 'Gates of Justice' or 'Gates of Righteousness.' They're an organization dedicated to wiping mages off the Earth."

She looked around at the others. "That sounds pretty bad. Why hasn't anybody mentioned them before?"

"We've got no idea how big they are." Stone resumed his pacing. "We dealt with them once a while back, before you and Jason were together, but haven't heard anything from them since. I thought they were likely some sort of small lunatic-fringe outfit. They might still be."

"But you said the guy was a mage. Why would a mage be in an organization like that?"

"That's what we thought initially, too," Stone said. "But last time we dealt with them, they had another mage working for them. They seem to attract quislings—mages who, for whatever reason, want to betray their brethren. Or who don't want to be associated with them."

"Why would they want to do that?"

"Who knows? In the last case, the woman chose to toss her lot in with Portas because she felt ashamed of her magical abilities."

"They likely look for mages raised in strict religious environments," Ward said. "The sort of people who've been indoctrinated since childhood to believe magic is evil or of the Devil."

"Exactly," Stone said. "Some of those types are masters at rationalizing ideas and practices that further their ends, even though they ostensibly go against their core beliefs."

"The enemy of my enemy is my friend." Amber nodded. "Okay, so why is this guy breaking into a collection of occult artifacts?"

"Easy," Eddie said. "They're anti-magic. They want nothin' more than to see every mage on the planet—including their own, eventually—destroyed. Or neutralized," he added meaningfully, with a significant look at Stone.

"Oh, bloody hell, yes." Stone stopped again. "I saw the first part, but the second makes even more sense."

"Huh?" Jason frowned. "I don't get it."

Stone spread his arms. "Portas Justitiae is a religious organization. We've seen before that they go to great lengths to avoid killing mundanes. Remember when they cornered you at that construction site and beat the stuffing out of you?"

"Shit…yeah. They easily could have killed me, but they didn't. They even *said* they didn't want to, when they were talkin' to each other."

"Spot on. They don't want to kill mundanes. I'll wager they'd prefer not to kill *anyone,* if they can help it. The only reason they kill mages is because they consider them both evil and irredeemable, as long as they possess the power they consider Satanic."

"Wait, I get it now," Verity spoke up excitedly. "So, you're saying if this thing you're looking for really *can* neutralize magic once the pieces are put back together, they might think they can use it to…I don't know…de-magic mages and make them redeemable again?"

"It makes sense, doesn't it?" Eddie asked. "They probably figure they'd be doin' us a favor by turfin' the Devil out o' us."

"Or at least doing the world a favor by keeping us safely imprisoned," Stone said. "I strongly doubt this thing could literally remove a mage's powers." He thought of Aldwyn when he said this, although his ancestor might be a special case because he was a dragon. "But I wouldn't be surprised if, properly deployed, it could create a prison that most, if not all, mages couldn't breach."

"So how did they find out about the pyramid?" Jason asked. "How did they know it was there in the first place?"

"Probably the way we were speculating about before," Stone said. "If the organization is older and more far-reaching than we thought they were, it's possible they do have long-standing arrangements with people to watch upcoming auction lots and keep their eyes out for any other odd items resurfacing. It's also possible they've found other things in the past, but we didn't know about it so it never rose high enough to attract any mages' attention."

All of them sat silently, mulling over what they'd just heard. Finally, Amber spoke up. "But there's still part of this that doesn't make sense to me, though. Sorry if I'm being dense, but this isn't exactly the kind of thing I normally deal with. All this twisted intrigue isn't exactly what we bears excel at."

"Quite all right," Stone said. "What doesn't make sense?"

"Well...assume you're right and this thief *was* a member of this organization. You're right, that part does make sense, especially with the tattoo, though he might just be a guy who was working on his own who just happens to be religious."

"It's possible."

"But anyway, if it *is* true...who killed him?"

The others looked at each other.

"Maybe some other Portas member did," Jason suggested. "He *was* a mage, after all, and if they did send him after the pyramid, he didn't succeed in his mission. Maybe they killed him to get the cops off their tail. You know, made him a scapegoat. If the cops think they have the guy who committed the theft, they'll stop looking, right?"

"Not sure," Stone said. "Blum said they'll probably put the case on the back burner, but there are still too many questions for them to stop completely."

"Better than nothing," Verity said. "But what about Brandon Greene? You said the guy almost killed him, and Greene's a mundane. If the thief is part of Portas, would he have done that?"

"Good question." Stone pulled out his chair and sat, though he wondered how long he could remain still. "The working theory is that the thief was already inside the storeroom when Greene arrived and surprised him. Maybe he panicked. Even if our thief was some high-powered practitioner, people *do* panic—even mages."

"Maybe that's why they killed him," Jason said. "*Because* he almost murdered Greene. Sort of a kill two birds with one stone thing—they get the cops off their back, *and* they take out a potentially dangerous mage who might get spooked and off somebody else."

"If that's the case," Stone said, "they must have at least one other mage working with them."

"Why do you say that?" Verity asked. "It doesn't take a mage to run somebody down with a truck."

"No, but it might take one to get back inside that storeroom and nick the African statuette. Remember, at that point the room was under much heavier guard. If someone got in there and took something later on, they were either a mage or connected with the security company. And nobody's reporting any camera glitches or anything, which leads me to believe it's got to be a mage."

He glanced at Ward, who was suddenly looking pensive. "Something on your mind, Ward? You don't agree?"

"I'm…not certain. It's possible you're right—but it's also possible something else is going on here."

"What's that?" Jason asked.

"It could be that Portas aren't the only people looking for the pyramid."

"That's a good point," Stone admitted. "Any number of people or groups could be looking for it. Though I think it might be stretching credibility a bit to think a relatively obscure and low-value auction would draw multiple players out of the woodwork."

"Dangerous to assume it didn't, though," Eddie said.

"True enough. But since we've got no idea who might be involved, our best course of action is probably to continue looking for the other component or components. Even if anyone suspects I've got the pyramid, there's no way they'll find it in Desmond's vault. So that should give us some time."

"What about the Ordo?" Verity asked. "This seems like it would be exactly the kind of thing they'd want—even if it's just to keep it under wraps so nobody uses it against them."

Stone nodded. "I thought about them, and you could be right. But after the whole business with Richter and Brathwaite, I think they might have more pressing matters on their plates." He spread his hands. "There could be any number of organizations looking for this thing. I think we might be spinning our wheels trying to work out which of them are, so until we have more information, we'll go forward with what we have for the time being. Oh—and Eddie: speaking of, you can stop hunting for McGrath's catalog. Jason's computer whiz located it."

Eddie and Ward both perked up. "That right? Can we see it? Did you bring it with you?"

"Well…I don't actually have it yet. It's on display in some little nothing town in Nebraska. I was planning to pay them a visit, but this information from Blum sidetracked me a bit."

"You're gonna break in there and nick it?" Eddie asked. The thought didn't seem to bother him.

"Borrow it. I don't need the actual catalog—just photos of any relevant pages."

"Can I come along?" Verity asked.

He almost said yes, because having some magical backup couldn't hurt. But then he remembered why it wouldn't be a good idea. If his sense of middle-American geography was accurate, the closest public portal to Nebraska was either Chicago, Santa Fe, or Dallas—none of which were terribly close. He was certain there were ley lines that would get him closer, but to use that method he couldn't bring anyone else along. "Er...not this time, I'm afraid."

"Why not?" Her eyes narrowed, and she looked at him suspiciously. "You're not being protective, are you?"

"Of course not. You trained me away from doing that ages ago."

"Well, why, then? It makes sense not to go alone. What if Portas or one of these other groups have figured out the same thing you did? It would be better to have some backup."

Jason and Amber were shooting him odd looks now, too.

"I can handle Portas. But first of all, I doubt anyone else has got this far yet. And second, the odds they'd show up at exactly the same time I do are fairly low. That's why I've got to move fast. I was thinking of going as soon as we're done here. Verity, you'll need to take Jason and Amber back through the portal."

He didn't meet her gaze, but he did catch the significant glances Eddie and Ward shot him. They got it, which apparently meant Eddie had shared Stone's secret with his colleague.

Verity glared at him, but then sighed. "Okay, fine. I can't go tonight anyway—got a job with Scuro. But I still think you should wait for me."

"I can't." He added an apologetic note to his tone. "I'll be fine, Verity, but we can't wait on this. If Gina found the link to the catalog, one of these other groups might have as well." *And I can get there a lot faster than they can,* he thought but didn't say.

"Right, then," Eddie said briskly, obviously trying to move the conversation along. "Is that it, Stone, or 'ave you got more bombshells to drop on us?"

"I think those are enough to be getting on with for now."

"So, what do you want us to do in the meantime?" Jason rose from his chair. "Not much we *can* do, is there? We're kinda back at square one on who else is after the thing."

"If anyone else is at all." Stone stood too. "I'll keep in touch with Blum in case they figure out our thief's identity. Jason, you stay up to date with your law enforcement contacts. I don't know if anyone will try breaking in to wherever they're storing the collection in San Francisco, but if they do I want to know about it."

"What about us?" Eddie asked. "Not much else for us to do until you've got more information."

"Keep checking the library, I guess—and the reference material at Caventhorne. See if you can find any references to magic-damping devices."

"Are you going to do any checking about your ancestor and that sealed room?" Verity asked. Jason had already filled her and Amber in on the latest news. "If they're related to this thing, maybe there's a connection."

Stone shivered a little at that. Checking into Aldwyn's history was one thing—but none of his friends knew the real deal was still alive. Would his ancestor be willing to talk to him about it? Would Stone even *want* to talk to him? The last thing he wanted was to incur any sort of perceived debt to his murderous forefather. "I'll see what I can find," was all he said. "There might be something in my library at the Surrey house."

"It's too bad we can't get down there to that chamber," Jason mused. "If the place hadn't all collapsed, maybe you could look around magically and see if there was...I dunno...a hidden alcove or something with another one of those pyramid things in it.

Maybe even the whole gizmo, if you think it has more than one part."

"Yes, well, that's a bit out of the question, I'm afraid. Someone's bound to get suspicious if I start bringing in heavy machinery to dig up the property." Stone pushed his chair in. "Anyway, thank you all for coming. Part of me is afraid the whole thing might turn out to be nothing but a wild-goose chase, but part of me hopes it *is*. I can't say I'm comfortable with the idea of something like that being out in the world—and even *less* comfortable with it falling into Portas Justitiae's hands."

CHAPTER NINETEEN

TIME ZONES WORKED in Stone's favor again. It had been early evening when he and the others had met in England, but only early afternoon when he returned to Encantada. After gathering a bit of gear including his disguise amulet, he consulted an online map and one of his ley-line atlases. Tilley, Nebraska, it turned out, was in the north-central part of the state. The nearest ley line that passed through a reasonably-sized town was ninety miles to the south.

That meant he'd need to rent a car, or take a cab. He thought again of what Jason and Amber had told him about concealing his identity. It was even more important now that he could travel to many more locations more quickly, but so far he hadn't done anything else about it except pick up a small collection of burner phones. He'd still need to figure out how to set up a fake identity, complete with things like driver's license and credit card, but there was no time to do that now. He'd have to take a chance that nobody looked too closely at his activities.

Sometimes he wished Jason had never brought up all these problematic considerations. He'd been popping around through the portals for years, and nobody had gotten too suspicious about it. But now that he'd been made aware of all the ways it could come back and bite him, he couldn't continue on in blissful ignorance.

The trip was as quick and easy as always. Since he didn't know where he'd be reappearing, he used an invisibility spell to conceal himself.

It was a good thing he had. He reappeared in the middle of a street, and barely had time to gather his wits and levitate himself before a pickup truck ran him over. Puffing, he spared only a moment to contemplate the irony of being run down by the same kind of vehicle that had taken out the thief back in California, then floated back down to the street and hurried into an alley where he could hide behind a dumpster before his spell fizzled. He leaned against the wall, panting, and looked around for anyone else.

One thing seemed to be going his way, though—he was alone. He let his breath out, forcing himself to relax. Now that he was here, nobody was going to be suspicious. Both his disguise amulet and his disregarding spell were working fine, making him look like a boring young man in a down jacket, jeans, and Chuck Taylors. He'd picked the right outfit, because it was *cold* here. It wasn't snowing, but it looked like it might start any minute. His black wool overcoat was barely sufficient to keep him from shivering. He needed to find a ride to Tilley.

At least it appeared he was in the business district, which would make things easier. He'd decided to take a cab instead of trying to rent a car or take a rideshare, because cabs took cash. He had a stack of it in his pocket. He spotted a bright-green one and waved it down.

"Can you take me to Tilley?" he asked the driver, an older man in a Cornhuskers sweatshirt. He used his American accent.

"Tilley?" The man's eyes narrowed. "That's like a hundred miles away."

"Ninety-four, actually. Yes. Can you take me?"

The driver looked him up and down. "That's gonna cost around two hundred and fifty bucks, and take an hour and a half."

"I know. I can pay."

"You're gonna have to prove it."

Stone pulled cash from his pocket. "Listen—I need to get there fast. I can't wait for the bus. Too slow. I'll tip you well, I promise."

"Well…" The man didn't look convinced, but finally sighed. "Okay. Hop in."

By the time they made it to Tilley, Stone had firmed his resolve to talk to someone—either Jason or possibly Kolinsky—about doing something to improve his fake identity.

The cabbie had been right—the drive took an hour and a half, and throughout the entire trip the man had alternated between playing bad country music and sports reports on the radio, and trying to engage Stone in conversation about his two favorite topics: Cornhuskers football and how he was convinced space-alien lizard people had taken over the top positions in world government. Stone didn't even have a magazine to read, and since his real phone was shut off to prevent it from pinging his location, he couldn't even use that to entertain himself. He had just about lost the last of his resolve not to tell the cabbie to shut up and drive when they reached their destination.

"Here we are. Tilley. You got an address?"

"No, this is fine. Thank you." *Let me out of this damned car before I go mad.* They were driving through what looked like the town's small downtown area, which should be as good a place as any to stop.

"That'll be…two hundred and forty fifty-three."

Bloody hell, it's a good thing I'm rich. Stone peeled off four hundreds from his stash and handed them over. "Keep the change."

"Hey, thanks, friend. You're all right. You ever in Kearney and need another ride, give me a call."

Not much chance of that.

He watched the cab trundle off and considered his next options. It was even colder here than it had been in Kearney, with a light dusting of snow beginning to fall. It was also only a few minutes after two p.m., which meant it would be a while before he could safely break in to the museum. He supposed it couldn't hurt to do a little recon in the meantime.

After ducking into a nearby coffee shop for a hot cup, he took another cab to the museum's address.

"This is it?" he asked dubiously. The place looked less like a museum and more like someone's two-story home.

"That's it." The driver pointed at a small sign out front, barely legible from the cab. It read *Tilley Museum and Historical Society.*

Well. This could make things easier, or more difficult. He wasn't sure which yet.

The bored-looking old woman at the table inside the door perked up as he arrived and put down her magazine. "Oh, hello, dear. Welcome to the Tilley Museum." She studied him. "I don't think I recognize you. Are you new in town? We don't get many tourists up this way."

"I'm—just passing through. Killing some time. Someone told me about the place."

She looked pleased. "Oh, that's nice. The donation's five dollars, and you can stay as long as you like. We have some lovely things here."

Stone paid her and she handed him a folded paper. "There's your map and a list of our exhibits. If you need anything, let me know. We've got a troop of Girl Scouts going through some-where—I think they're upstairs. Other than that, it's just you."

"Thank you."

Stone almost felt guilty about what he was planning to do—almost like breaking in to the place would be an affront against this very nice old woman. "Ah—what time do you close?"

"At five. That should give you plenty of time to see everything, don't you worry." She giggled. "I'm proud of our little museum here, but we're hardly the Louvre or anything."

He drifted off, deliberately taking his time feigning interest in every display. The place looked like it *had* been someone's home at some point. The displays—everything from a detailed history of the area's farming, crops, and agricultural implements to several well-researched presentations on prominent local dignitaries—were arranged in the individual rooms. Stone had to allow that whoever had put this place together had obviously done it with love: they'd even taken the care to arrange the exhibits in a logical manner, with the agricultural and food-related displays in the kitchen and dining room, the dignitaries each in their own bedrooms, and the general history of the town in the large sitting room facing the street.

He passed the Girl Scouts, a small gaggle of five chattering nine-year-olds and their chaperone—coming out of one of the bedrooms. They all waved cheerful greetings and thundered past on their way upstairs.

The McGrath exhibit, the highlight of the collection, was displayed in a large, finished attic. Stone noted, as reached the stairs to it, that someone had painted "mystical" symbols, rabbits in hats, stars, and similar artwork on the walls leading up. *THIS WAY TO MCGRATH THE MAGNIFICENT* was painted in old-fashioned script, with a fancy arrow pointing up. *BE AMAZED BY TILLEY'S MOST FAMOUS CITIZEN.*

"You're gonna like that one, Mister," said a piping voice from behind him.

He turned to see one of the Girl Scouts who'd dropped back a little from the rest of her group. "Is that right?"

"Oh, yeah." Her eyes shone. "I wish I coulda seen him do magic. I love magic."

Stone smiled at her. "I love magic too."

"Do you know any?"

"I do."

"Oh, wow. Will you show me a trick?"

"*Rachel!* Come along!"

The Scouts' chaperone had looked back and spotted them. She shot Stone a suspicious glare.

"But he was gonna show me some magic!" Rachel protested.

Her glare intensified, taking on a protective "*I'll just* bet *he was*" aspect. "*Now, Rachel.*" She caught the little girl by the shoulders and chivvied her back to the group, and they all hurried off. Rachel, looking disappointed, glanced back over her shoulder at Stone before they disappeared down the hall toward one of the bedrooms.

Stone continued up to the McGrath exhibit.

This was more like it.

The attic encompassed the entire top floor of the house, and every inch of it was taken up with various displays behind velvet ropes, arranged to take the visitor in a circular path around them all. A flat-screen television displayed a grainy, black-and-white recording of one of McGrath the Magnificent's performances, obviously in a large hall in front of a sizable audience. There was no sound, but it was easy to follow what he was doing. He was clearly a talented magician, and even more clearly—if you knew what to look for—he'd been "enhancing" his performance with some of the real thing. Stone stood there for several minutes watching, until the recording looped and started at the beginning. Then he moved on.

He didn't have to feign interest in these exhibits. He'd always enjoyed both stage magic and its history, so he paused to read each of the placards in front of the different sections. The displays started with Leander McGrath's early days in Tilley, then progressed through his magical career as he moved from small local shows to traveling all over the Midwest. He'd even performed for the state governor at one point. The displays included framed, black-and-white photos, various bits of gear from some of his magic shows, costumes he and his wife (who was also his assistant) had worn, and ephemera like programs and clippings of reviews from area newspapers. Each section was separated from the others by jewel-hued drapes decorated with golden stars and moons.

By the time Stone reached the end of the circular path, he had a much better idea of what Leander McGrath must have been like: a born showman who delighted in entertaining crowds, and a devoted family man who loved his wife and son. The second-to-last display included clippings describing how, despondent at the death of his beloved son in World War I in 1918, he'd lost all his motivation to perform and retired. He'd been only thirty-eight years old at the time. After that, he'd dropped out of public life for many years, traveling all over the world with his wife to collect magic- and occult-related items. He eventually returned to Tilley in 1955 to live out the rest of his days following her death. He himself had died in 1964 at the age of eighty-five.

Stone moved to the final display, which included a few photos of the white-haired, bearded McGrath in his later years, several obituaries from different regional papers, and a report describing how, after his death, it had been discovered that he maintained a storage facility where most of his odd collection had been archived. Since he had no heirs, the bulk of the items had been sold at auction with the proceeds used for various local and veterans' charities as his will stipulated. The remainder had been donated to the museum, where they'd been on perpetual display since.

It didn't take long to find what Stone was looking for: the catalog from the 1964 auction. It was in a glass case along with several black-and-white photos from the collection. The cover had a photo of an elaborately-decorated magician's disappearing cabinet, flanked by a collection of what looked like African and Egyptian artifacts. The images were blurry and faded and the text hard to read, which wasn't surprising given the catalog's age and the state of printing techniques at the time. It had never been meant to be retained, like a book.

But there it was. So close.

Stone resisted the temptation to use magic to pop the flimsy lock holding the case closed and simply take the catalog right now. Two things stopped him: first, the room was so cluttered he couldn't tell for sure there weren't cameras trained on the area, and second, he had no way to ensure nobody else would come up and catch him in the act. If Rachel or one of the other Girl Scouts decided to ditch their troop for another look at McGrath's finery, he'd be in trouble. He could use illusion or invisibility to make things easier, but it would be safer all around to simply come back later when everyone else was gone. It was four p.m. now—the place would close in an hour. He could grab an early dinner and a drink, wait for it to get dark, and come back then.

On a whim, because he had time to kill, he returned to the beginning of the McGrath exhibit and switched on magical sight. There wasn't much chance of anything magical here, but it was never wise to take that for granted. He walked slowly forward, scanning the items in each of the displays, looking for any faint sign of arcane energy.

He found none, as expected. All the photos, posters, and stage-magic paraphernalia were every bit as mundane as he'd expected them to be. If McGrath had truly been a mage and owned anything with power, he'd either gotten rid of it before or it had been sold as part of the auction.

Stone was about to switch off the sight and head out when a faint glow caught his eye. He turned, surprised to see it was coming from the last display—the one with the catalog. That was odd, since that part of the exhibit had been nothing but posters, news clippings, and the catalog itself. What could be magical over there?

He hurried back, but before he even reached the display, he knew what it was.

The catalog was glowing with a hint of magical energy.

"What's going on with you…?" he muttered, leaning in for a closer look, sharpening his sight.

When he realized what he was looking at, he nearly slammed his fist down on the top of the display case. "Bugger!"

"Are you okay, mister?"

He whirled to find two of the Girl Scouts staring at him, wide-eyed, from the other end of the display.

"Oh. Uh…yes. I'm fine. Sorry." His heart was beating fast, his nerves jangling, but he forced himself to release his balled fists and unclench his jaw. "Didn't mean to scare you."

"Are you upset about something?" They didn't look scared, but they didn't come any closer, either.

"Er…yes, that's it. I just got a…er…mean text from someone."

"Melissa! Hannah! We're leaving!" came a voice from below. "Hurry up!"

"Oh! Sorry, mister, we gotta go. You sure you're okay?"

No. I am most certainly not *sure I'm okay,* Stone thought. But he plastered a smile on his face and nodded. "I'm fine. You'd better go, though—don't want to be late."

They exchanged glances. "Yeah. Bye!" And then they were gone, dashing back down the stairs.

Leaving Stone to glare impotently at the glass case, which contained a credible illusion of the auction catalog.

Someone had beaten him to it.

CHAPTER TWENTY

S TONE STORMED DOWN THE STAIRS, still fuming. He wasn't sure whether he was angrier at himself for waiting too long and missing his opportunity, or the unknown thief who'd reached the same conclusion he had, only faster.

Whoever this person was, they were no minor-league mage. That had been some fancy illusion work, and most people, even other mages, wouldn't have spotted it. It would likely fade away over the next week or so since there was no ley line to sustain it, but by then the thief would be long gone.

It was four-forty. The museum closed in twenty minutes. The Girl Scouts were already leaving, laughing and shoving each other as their leader nudged them out the door.

Think, he told himself angrily. But no matter how hard he tried to come up with a way around this, nothing was presenting itself. He had no idea who might have stolen the catalog. He paused at the foot of the stairs and stared into nothingness.

"Did you enjoy the museum, dear?"

He jerked his head up. The old woman behind the table was watching him curiously, so he did his best to pull himself together and look cheerful. "Oh. Yes, it was very interesting. Especially the McGrath exhibit."

She smiled. "Oh, yes, that's the one everyone loves." With a giggle, she added, "I know people don't come here to look at a bunch of stuffy old politicians and dusty photos of cornfields. McGrath the Magnificent was quite a character."

He looked at her in a new light. She appeared to be in her late sixties to early seventies—probably a retiree doing volunteer work to keep her spry and get her out of the house. "You…didn't know him, did you?"

"Leander McGrath? I did, actually."

"Is that right?" He didn't have to fake the interest in his tone.

"Oh, yes. It was a long time ago, of course—he died more than fifty years ago. But he used to come into the little market I worked at when I was just out of high school, before I got married. We'd chat sometimes, when it was slow. He'd tell me stories about his time doing the traveling shows. He was a sweet, kind man, but I don't think he ever got over losing his boy in the War. Not even after all those years."

"That's fascinating. I do a little stage magic myself, which is why I'm interested in him. I'm doing a paper on him for one of my college classes." Grateful he'd chosen a young man as his illusionary disguise, Stone spun out the lie with ease, turning on the charm. It was harder when he was using a fake American accent, but he seemed to be getting through to her.

"Oh, I wish you'd mentioned that before! I could have taken you through the exhibit and given you some more of the history. Perhaps you could come back again?" She looked at her watch. "We're closing soon, but I'd be happy to do it some other day."

"Thank you. I wish I'd said something too, but I'm just passing through." Another ruse popped into his head and he went with it. "Could you answer a question for me, though?"

"Of course, dear."

"I've got a friend—they're interested in magic too. They said they might stop by here, but we didn't connect. You mentioned that you recognize almost everybody who comes through."

"I do. I've lived in Tilley all my life, and it's not exactly a big town. I know pretty much everybody, and we're not really a tourist attraction, so I notice new folks."

"That's good. So…did anyone new come in here in the last few days?"

"Hmm. Let me think." Her gaze went fuzzy for a moment, and then she gave a brisk nod. "Oh! Yes. Just this morning, in fact. A man came in shortly after we opened. He was very pleasant. Kind of distant, though." She frowned, her brow furrowing. "I…think he might have been the only one. It's been really quiet this week except for the kids' tours. You know—school groups, Scouts, a few kids doing reports on local history. That's the bulk of our visitors, honestly."

"What did he look like?"

"Hmm. Older than you—maybe middle thirties. Definitely too old to be a college student. Clean-cut fellow, dark hair, thin, wearing a sweater and nice slacks."

The description wasn't enough to give Stone any ideas, but he played along. "That sounds like him. Did he stay a while?"

"Not too long. He went straight upstairs—that makes sense now, since he was probably interested in the McGrath exhibit too."

"He didn't happen to say where he was going after he left, did he?"

"No. As I said, he didn't really have much to say to me. Pleasant but standoffish. I'm sorry, dear. Perhaps you should give him a call."

"I'll do that. Thank you."

"I'm sorry I couldn't be of more help. But I was serious—if you're ever in town again, come back and I'll give you a real tour. I can tell you lots of stories about Leander McGrath."

"Thank you, I'd like that. Have a good evening."

Stone headed outside, his thoughts still spinning in frustration. That had to have been the man who'd stolen the catalog. But if he was here this morning, several hours had already passed. Stone was certain he wasn't in the area any longer. He wondered if the man had come alone, or if he'd had one or more accomplices.

It didn't matter, though. He was gone, and Stone was out of luck. Damn it, he'd been *so close.* There he'd been, looking through the cluttered room packed full of McGrath's old junk, and all that time, the thief had been—

Stone stopped.

Cluttered room packed with junk.

Could it be possible?

He reversed direction and hurried back inside. "Excuse me…"

The woman had put aside her magazine and was counting the small amount of money in the cashbox, probably preparing to close the place. "Yes? Did you forget something, dear?"

"No, but I just had a thought. Something I wanted to ask you."

"Of course. I hope you don't mind if I keep doing this. I know it's not much money, but I feel better when it's safely put away."

"That's fine. The McGrath exhibit—it looked fairly crowded up there. Lots of things packed into the space."

She beamed. "That's right. I helped set it up. It's not easy arranging everything in a pleasing manner that still makes sense."

"You did a beautiful job. But what I was wondering was—do you rotate the collection periodically? I read somewhere that it's been here since shortly after Mr. McGrath died. I'd imagine the local people might get tired of looking at the same things."

"Oh! You're a smart young man. Yes, of course we rotate it. Usually around once a year. We've got enough items to do around three complete exhibits. Mr. McGrath had a lot of stuff in his house and storeroom, and quite a lot of it wasn't suitable for auctioning."

"Where is it kept? The items that are currently out of rotation, I mean."

She pointed down. "In the basement. Everything's all boxed up and carefully arranged on shelves down there. Why?"

Stone swallowed, hardly daring to believe he might get lucky this time. "Well…I know this is asking a lot, but one of things I was really interested in for my paper was the items related to his magic show—the ones that got auctioned."

"Oh, but they aren't down there, dear. They've been gone for fifty years." She tilted her head, confused. "I already told you—"

"Yes. I know the actual items aren't here. But I noticed a catalog in the display upstairs, from the auction. I'm guessing it listed all the items that were sold?"

"Well, of course it did."

"I would love to get a look at that catalog. I'm sure there are a lot of things in there that could make my paper really amazing."

She frowned. "That would be nice, wouldn't it? But I'm afraid I can't open the display case. That catalog is like an old magazine—it's brittle and requires special handling."

"I wouldn't ask you do to that. I understand. But I thought maybe there might have been another one in the collection, stored away in a box somewhere?"

"Hmm." She pondered. "It's possible, of course. Now that you mention it, I think I might remember seeing another copy in one of the boxes. We rotated the collection only last month, so I was down there with Candice, sorting through things."

Here goes… "Ms…"

"Mrs., it is. Mrs. Hodges."

"Mrs. Hodges…" he said carefully, "would it be possible for me to take a look at that catalog, if it's down there? I know it's late, but it would mean so much to me."

Her frown deepened. "You mean now? Oh, no. I'm sorry, but that wouldn't be possible. We're closing in a few minutes, and I've got to—"

Stone held up a hand. "The thing is, Mrs. Hodges, I need to get a good grade on this paper, and I think this will do it. What if

I…made a generous donation to the museum fund? Would that convince you?"

He could almost see the wheels turning in Mrs. Hodges's head. On the one hand, she was seventy-year-old woman and he was proposing a trip down to the basement with a young man she didn't know. On the other, she'd clearly seen a kindred spirit in him, someone who shared her interest in Leander McGrath. "Well…what sort of donation did you have in mind? I won't lie— we can always use money. But you're a college boy."

Stone smiled. "I'm a college boy, yes. But my family's got money." He pulled two hundred dollars from his pocket and offered it to her. "Suppose I give you that for a half-hour of your time. If you're worried about being down there alone with me—"

"Oh, no. Nothing like that," she assured him. "I've got two boys of my own, and I can tell a bad one when I see one. But…" She still looked hesitant, then brightened as she reached a decision. "Oh, why not? I haven't got anything else to do tonight except go home, feed my cats, and watch TV. I suppose Muffin and Blueberry can wait an extra half-hour. They'll hardly starve." She stood. "Thank you very much for your kind donation, Mr.—"

"Michael Townes. You can call me Mike." Stone struggled to keep his voice calm as his insides thrummed with anticipation. He wouldn't let himself get excited yet, but if he could get hold of the catalog without having to steal it, the thief might have done him a favor.

Except, of course, that the thief already *had* it, which meant he was hours ahead on finding anything useful in it.

First things first, though. He gave her the money, and she tucked it away in her box and locked it, then locked that in another cabinet.

"All right, Mike. Let's go. I'm afraid I can't give you much more than half an hour, though. My cats get cranky if I don't feed them on time."

"I understand. I have a cat back home, too." He followed her through the kitchen to an unmarked door, which she opened with a key from her pocket.

"I warn you, it's a little dusty down there, and there are probably spiders."

"Not a problem. I'm very brave when it comes to spiders."

She laughed as she descended the stairs. "You know, I like you, Mike. You remind me of my oldest boy, Fred, when he was your age." She flipped a switch at the bottom of the stairs and two hanging bulbs flickered to life, illuminating a space half the size of the attic.

The place was actually a lot neater and better organized than Mrs. Hodges had implied. A series of metal shelves lined the walls, each one stacked with rows of bankers' boxes and lidded plastic tubs. A closed armoire stood on the far side next to a few larger boxes that wouldn't fit on the shelves, and a big, empty table took up the middle part of the room.

"Okay," she said, bustling around. "Let's see, let's see…we've got everything sorted by stages in Mr. McGrath's life, so if we had another catalog, it would be…here." She hurried over and pulled a box from a top shelf near the door. "Let's start with this one."

Stone stood back and watched as she carefully unloaded the box onto the large table, spreading the items out. There were more laminated clippings, copies of regional magazines, loose photographs, folded posters, and scrapbooks. "Anything I can do to help?"

"No, no, it's fine. I need to be careful so I don't tear anything. It should be…aha! I was right. Here it is!" In triumph, she pulled out what looked like another magazine and held it up.

It was identical to the one in the case, except more ragged-looking. It had a large coffee stain on the cover, as if some long-dead person had used it as a coaster. "That's it. I'm impressed, Mrs. Hodges. First box!"

She preened. "Oh, now, it's nothing. I'm *supposed* to know where things are." She studied the catalog. "I can certainly see why we never used this in an exhibit. Look at it. It's a mess, especially with that big, ugly stain on the front."

An idea seized Stone, and he went with it before he lost his nerve. His heart thumped hard—this would be a lot easier with his normal appearance and accent, but there was no helping it now. "Mrs. Hodges…are you serious about that? This isn't one of the items you rotate in and out of the displayed exhibit?"

"No, of course not. There's no point. We've already got the other one, so why would we substitute this ratty one for the nicer one that's already upstairs?"

"Is it complete? No pages torn out?"

She riffled through it. "Nope, looks like everything's here. Just a little raggedy and yellow around the edges. Kind of like me," she added, chuckling.

He smiled. "I was hoping you'd say that. Not the raggedy part. The part about the catalog."

Her gaze came up, and her brow furrowed. "Why is that?"

He took a deep breath and plunged forward. "Mrs. Hodges…is there any chance I could buy that catalog?"

"Buy it?" She frowned at him. "Why?"

"Well…it would be a very nice addition to my paper. And it's fairly thick, so it would be easier to look through it later at my leisure than to waste your time doing it now, wouldn't you say?" He smiled. "I wouldn't think of keeping Muffin and Blueberry waiting too long for their dinner."

She wavered. "But—I don't know, Mike. It's not really my decision to make. I just volunteer here, you understand."

"But you said yourself that the catalog is too damaged to put on display."

"Yes…but…"

"Listen, Mrs. Hodges. I know this is going to sound very odd, that I'd be so interested. But if I could copy some of those pages and put them in my paper, I think my professor would really be impressed." He reached in his pocket again. "I was serious about my family having money. What about a five-hundred-dollar donation to the museum? Certainly this old thing isn't worth even close to that."

Her eyes widened. "Five hundred…dollars? For an old catalog?"

"What do you say? If anyone asks, you could just tell them that someone was impressed with what you're doing here and wanted to help." He glanced at the box. "Would anyone even know it was gone? Would they care, even if you told them?"

"I…" She swallowed, still unsure. "I suppose they wouldn't. And five hundred dollars—seven, with what you gave me before— *would* help us make some improvements around here. We had a pipe burst last month in one of the bathrooms that took quite a chunk out of our funds…"

"It's up to you, Mrs. Hodges. But it would really help me out, and it sounds like it would help you out too." Stone put the money on the table and backed up, giving her space.

She slowly began packing the other items back into the box, leaving the catalog lying on the table. When Stone shifted to magical sight, he saw her clear, blue aura roiling with indecision.

Finally, she put the lid back on the box. "All right," she said decisively. "You're right—that money *would* help us, and that catalog is basically worthless. You take it, Mike. I think old Candice—she's in charge of the museum's operation—will be so happy to see the donation, she won't ask too many questions."

"Thank you. You're helping me more than you know." He pushed the cash toward her and picked up the catalog. "I'll get out of here now, so you can go home. Tell Muffin and Blueberry I said hello."

"Oh, I will. They're going to hear all about it."

Stone was tempted to try finding someplace where he could hole up and look through the catalog before heading back, but it was already getting dark. Even if he caught a cab instantly and convinced the driver to take him back to the ley line, it would still be close to two hours before he could return to Encantada. He slipped it into the interior pocket of his coat and called the number on the side of the local cab he'd taken, which he'd memorized.

While he waited for it to arrive, he altered his illusionary appearance again and called Jason on his burner phone. "Greetings from Armpit, Nebraska."

"Hey, Al. They don't really have a town called Armpit, do they?"

"Might as well. Though the lady looking after the museum was quite nice."

"So…did you find it?"

"I did. Not quite the way I'd originally intended."

"Have you got it? Did you have to break in?"

"Yes, and no. Unfortunately, somebody *else* has got it too." Watching the road for the cab, he quickly told Jason about the day.

"Holy shit, so somebody else is already as far along on this as you are? And you have no idea who? Do you think they're with Portas?"

"No good idea. But I've got another copy of the catalog that they had in storage, which I got for a handsome donation to the Armpit Museum and Historical Society."

"Damn, Al. It's a good thing you're loaded. It's a lot easier to do things when you can just pay your way through."

"Beats breaking in. Anyway, must go. Just wanted to update you on the latest."

"I'll tell V and Amber. Take care, Al. That guy's still out there somewhere."

"I suspect he's long gone by now, which means we need to get moving. My cab's here. Talk to you soon."

It took a bit more persuasion to convince the driver to take him back to Kearney, and he ended up being very glad he'd brought along as much cash as he had. This was getting inconvenient. He added speaking to Kolinsky to his mental to-do list. He'd been intending to do it about the pyramid anyway, since the alternative would be tracking down Aldwyn.

It was fully dark now. Once again, he was tempted to pull out the catalog and give it an initial once-over, but the light back here was bad. It could wait until he got back home. He leaned against the seat, which thankfully didn't smell like anything unpleasant, and tried to pass the time with some meditation techniques. The cabbie's aura, bright green and steady, showed no signs of subterfuge or potential threat.

There wasn't much traffic out here. The scenery, such as it was, consisted of mile after mile of flat, rolling farmland dusted with snow. A light snowfall swirled in the air. Stone wondered how anyone could live out here and not go mad from boredom, but he supposed it had to be different for the people who'd grown up here. Aside from a car or a speeding semi passing them every few minutes, it was quiet and dark out here. Peaceful. Stone wished he could let himself fall asleep, but he could never do that unless someone he trusted was driving.

"What are you doing way out here?" The cabbie, a clean-cut young man not much older than Stone's illusionary disguise, glanced over his shoulder. "I don't get too many fares to drive this far. Cheaper to rent a car, isn't it?"

"It's…a long story. And there weren't any rental cars in Tilley."

The driver laughed. "Not much of anything in Tilley."

Not much of anything in this whole sodding state, Stone thought but didn't say.

"You want some music or something?"

"No...thanks. I'm fine."

"Suit yourself."

They kept driving into the night. Stone spotted a few bright spots off the highway—probably tiny towns like Tilley—but aside from that it was more endless farmland on both sides of the road. He considered calling Jason or Verity again just to have something to do, but decided against it. All he'd have to do was be patient for another hour, then he could return home and get started working on the catalog. It felt late out here under the oppressive darkness, but it was only six p.m. It would only be five when he got home. Plenty of time.

Headlights appeared behind them, reflected in the rearview mirror. Stone glanced at them, then lost interest. He focused on his meditation, trying to calm his temptation to start paging through the catalog in the dimness. *Patience.*

The lights behind them drew closer, moving over to the right lane to pass. It wasn't a semi, or even a truck, but merely a boring, dark-colored sedan with two occupants. It was catching up with them, but not quickly.

Why isn't it passing us—?

"Holy *fuck!*" The driver's shriek of terror came at the same time as the car suddenly wrenched sideways with a wild screech of brakes.

Stone snapped his head up, and got an instant's impression of a human figure standing in the middle of the road directly in front of the cab before it slewed to the side. The left-side wheels dropped over the edge of a ditch running along the roadside. The world tilted crazily end-over end as the car rolled over once, twice, then came to rest on its roof.

CHAPTER TWENTY-ONE

S TONE WAS UPSIDE-DOWN, and for a moment he couldn't figure out why.

It was dark, the air full of the acrid odors of scorched rubber, gasoline, and dirty water.

Thoughts flooded his mind, making his head throb.

Bloody hell, we crashed.

There was something in the road.

No—someone in the road!

What was a person doing standing in the middle of the road in the middle of the great bugger-all, Nebraska?

He was hanging from his seatbelt, which had held him in place during the rollover, but his body still felt like it had done several rotations inside a cement mixer.

The driver!

Stone blinked a few times, focusing on the seat in front of him. The driver's seatbelt had also held him, but he hadn't been as lucky as Stone. His airbag had deployed, and he now hung limply against its deflated remains, unconscious. In front of him, the windshield was a mass of spidery cracks. The headlights were out.

A glance at his watch told Stone he'd only blacked out for less than a minute. He didn't think anything was broken or he was bleeding anywhere, but it was hard to tell for sure in the darkness. He switched to magical sight, ignoring the stabbing pain in his head when he did it. He had to see what was going on.

The driver, thank the gods, was still alive. His aura fluttered, weak but steady, with angry red flares around his shoulder and the back of his neck. Stone couldn't see the rest of him from where he was.

He himself had fared better. His purple, gold, and silver aura shone bright, with only a few red patches indicating mild injury. Apparently he'd been knocked around, but suffered no life-threatening trauma.

Tell that to all my muscles that won't shut up.

He'd have to get himself out of here. He had no idea if anyone was coming to help them, or if anyone would even spot them here in the dark at the bottom of this ditch.

There was another car behind us. They must have seen what happened. Maybe they stopped and called for help.

Fighting pain and the cotton in his head, Stone struggled with the seatbelt. Even though it hurt to use magic and he was afraid of passing out again, he risked using a small levitation spell to ensure he didn't fall on his head when he popped the belt free. Instead, he landed in an awkward, sideways position against the car's roof.

"Are you awake?" he called to the driver in a weak, croaky voice. His disguise amulet was still active, but he'd forgotten about his American accent.

The cabbie groaned, but didn't stir. His radio crackled, emitting pops and static but no intelligible voices.

Cabs have GPS, right? His dispatcher must be tracking him. Someone will see we're not moving.

But he couldn't be sure of that. The rollover might have damaged the GPS. The cab company would probably investigate eventually, but that could take a long time.

Both rear doors were stuck shut. He couldn't push either of them open from his awkward position, even when he pulled his legs back and slammed his feet against them, shooting more waves of pain up through his torso.

Rear window, then.

The rear window was shattered into the same spidery patterns as the windshield. Stone tried to push it out, but his shaking arms didn't have the strength to do it. Reluctantly, he summoned more magic and sent it tumbling away, then slumped for a moment as his whole body throbbed anew.

He couldn't let himself rest for long, though. He had to assume nobody was coming for them right away, and the driver needed help. He scrambled through the rear window, feeling uncomfortably like some large, ungainly beast being born—a feeling reinforced when he slid off the back deck and landed with an awkward splash in a few inches of dirty water crusted with ice.

"Oh, *bugger!*" Now ice-cold water was seeping through the back of his coat.

The catalog!

Ignoring the pain, he scrambled up before the water could soak through to his front and reach the catalog in his pocket. Suddenly, irrationally convinced it wasn't there anymore, he patted his coat, then let his breath out in a rush of relief when he felt it there, safe and still dry.

Shivering, leaning against the cab for balance, he first scanned the area for any other vehicles. He saw nothing. No lights as far as he could see from either side.

Even more concerning, there was likewise no sign of the car behind them, nor the person who'd been standing in the road and caused the cabdriver to swerve to avoid him.

Where had they gone?

He couldn't think about that now, though. The cabbie needed help. Stone didn't think the man would die, but he wasn't a doctor. It was cold out here, and shock could do unpredictable things to human bodies.

Including mine.

But he was still running on adrenaline, so he could worry about that later. He scrambled to the driver's side of the car and tried to wrench the door open.

It, too, was stuck, and this time the angle at which the car had come to rest meant the bottom part—the part closest to the roof—was deeply dug into the trench, enough that Stone couldn't get it open even with magic. Not now, anyway. It was one of the small negative side effects of Calanarian magic: his body had to be in good shape to get the best effect from it, and moving earth had always been difficult for him even at his strongest.

"Okay…next plan." His voice came out as a weak, ragged mutter.

Carefully, to make sure he didn't get any glass fragments on the injured man, he focused his magic and popped out the driver's-side window. While he waited for the next wave of pain and lightheadedness to pass, he examined the cabbie.

This was going to be tricky. He realized he had no idea what to do. He didn't have Verity's healing gift. Sure, he could do a bit of healing, but the man had a neck injury. Should he even try pulling him out of the car?

His gaze fell on the driver's phone, lying on the headliner near his head where it had no doubt fallen from his pocket or the dashboard in the crash. He snatched it up, used the man's finger to unlock it, and tapped 911.

"Nine-one-one, what's your emergency?" a brisk female voice answered immediately.

"Er—yes." This time, Stone remembered to use the American accent. "We were in a cab, and there's been an accident. A rollover. I think the driver's hurt badly. He's still stuck inside the car, and I think his neck might be injured."

"Are you all right, sir?"

"I'm…mostly fine, yes. I was his passenger. But the car's upside-down in a ditch, and he's hanging from his seatbelt and his face is bleeding. Should I try to get him out?"

"Is the bleeding severe?"

"Doesn't appear to be, no."

"Is he breathing?"

"Yes."

"Is the car in danger of catching fire or being struck by other vehicles?"

"There *aren't* any other vehicles." Stone looked the cab over. He could still smell gasoline fumes, but didn't see signs of imminent fire. "Doesn't look like there's a fire risk."

"All right, then. Don't try to move him—if he has a neck injury it's safer to leave him where he is. We've got your location. It will take around fifteen minutes to get to you. Stay calm, sir. Do you want me to stay on the line with you?"

"No. Just—get here as soon as you can. Thank you." He disconnected, wiped the phone free of his fingerprints, and tossed it back into the car.

He couldn't be here when the EMTs arrived. His disguise was good, but it wouldn't hold up to too much scrutiny, especially since he had no ID on him and wasn't thinking as clearly as usual. But he couldn't leave without at least trying to help the cabdriver. After all, it was his fault the man was out here in the first place.

He crouched next to the window, using a light spell to examine the driver more closely. He was still unconscious, his skin pale and blotchy, his breath slow and labored. This couldn't be a good position to be in for too long, with all the blood rushing to his head.

Stone drew a few deep breaths, focused his mind to ignore his own whole-body pain, and then reached out with his power. He tried to remember what Verity had taught him about effective healing, going back to the time when he'd done his best to make the dying Edwina Mortenson comfortable after the cave-in at Brunderville.

Hard to believe that's already been three years ago…

Focus, damn you!

There were two skills a mage had to master to be a good healer: the ability to view the body both as a system and as a series of sub-systems, and the empathy to reach out to another person and channel the desire to heal into the energy to get it done. The first one, Stone could manage easily. His extensive magical training made him adept at thinking in systems, at multi-tasking his thoughts to maintain more than one pattern at the same time. The second, though, he'd never been good at. Verity joked sometimes that it was because he was, at his core, a self-centered person. She was probably right. But whatever the reason, he'd never got the knack.

Fortunately for him, the cabdriver wasn't gravely hurt. He concentrated on the neck injury first. The process of magical healing involved taking something that was out of balance and returning it to the state where it was meant to be, and this particular system was definitely out of balance. Stone couldn't tell for sure, but although he didn't think anything was broken, the man's neck muscles had been cruelly wrenched in the crash. A bad case of whiplash, maybe.

He tightened his focus to a pinpoint, blocking out everything else around him until the only thing that existed was the angry red aura hovering around the driver's neck. Then he slowly, carefully directed his magical energy to nudge the system back into its proper pathways.

The fuzzy, lightheaded feeling rose again, and his head began to throb worse than ever. He recognized the feeling: it wasn't an injury *per se*, but rather his body's response to trying to channel arcane energy in unfamiliar ways when he was nowhere near at top form. He pushed past it, pouring the power in until at last the red, roiling miasma around the driver's aura began to recede. The man moaned softly, but didn't wake.

Stone let his breath out and settled back in his crouch, swiping a hand across his forehead. He'd rest for a few moments, then tackle another injury. That was probably all he'd have time—or energy—for before more qualified help arrived.

Behind him, the snow crunched.

He whirled, losing his balance and falling sideways—which probably saved his life.

A loud *crack* split the silence. A bullet flew through the space where Stone had just been and *spanged* off the side of the cab.

Stone scrambled for a look, pulling a magical shield around himself despite the pain.

A car was parked just off the side of the road, its headlights off. A shadowy figure stood near the open passenger door, pointing a handgun toward Stone. He fired again, but this time the bullet hit the shield and ricocheted away.

"Oi!" Stone yelled, trying to get to his feet before the figure fired again. He struggled to gather power for an answering shot, but his response came too slowly. The figure dived into the car, slammed the door shut, and the car took off, throwing a plume of dirty snow behind it.

What is going on? He must have been concentrating so hard on the healing spell that he hadn't noticed the car approaching. But why would someone want to kill him out here in the middle of Nebraska? Nobody except his friends even knew he was here.

When the possible answer struck him, he shook his head.

That was ludicrous.

A man appearing in the middle of the road, directly in front of their cab.

A car following closely but not passing.

Stone let his breath out in a cloud of billowing steam.

Could it be?

Had the figure in the road been an illusion, designed to make the cabdriver do exactly what he'd done: swerve in panic and veer off the road?

If it *had* been an illusion, had someone known he, Stone, was in the car? He couldn't imagine why anyone would use magic to kill a nobody cabdriver.

Could this have something to do with the man who'd stolen the catalog?

Perhaps he'd been keeping a watch on the museum to see if anyone else showed interest. Even if he didn't know Stone had managed to obtain a copy of his own, he still might see value in eliminating any competition looking for the pyramid's companion.

"Bloody hell…" he murmured.

In the distance, red flashing lights appeared, accompanied by the faint yowl of a far-off siren.

Damn.

He looked at the cabdriver again. The man's breathing was stronger and more steady even now, and his aura, while not clear, looked better. He'd be all right—or at least he was unlikely to die before the ambulance arrived.

Stone pulled his coat closed and stumbled to his feet, risking a bit more magic to alter his amulet's illusionary disguise. Now, he looked like a young, Latino drifter with an Army jacket, scraggly beard, knit cap, and backpack slung over his shoulder. He used a disregarding spell to conceal him further, not wanting to risk invisibility, and hurried away as fast as he could manage. By the time the ambulance and its accompanying fire rig and police car reached the cab, he'd already made it a half-mile from the scene. He kept low, walking off the road and keeping an eye out for the gunman's car up ahead, until he was far enough away that he could only faintly see the lights behind him.

When he couldn't walk any further without a rest, he stopped and turned back again. The lights weren't visible anymore. Stone didn't think the EMTs had extricated the cabdriver already, so he must have made it farther than he'd initially thought. *Score one for motivation, I suppose.* He wondered what the authorities would think when they found the bullet hole in the side of the car. The cabbie wouldn't remember the shooting or the man from the other car, but he might remember the figure in the road who'd caused him to swerve.

And what about his passenger, the man who'd called for help? Would they look for him, thinking he'd wandered off in disorientation?

Stone didn't have time to worry about that now, though, aside from being grateful he'd had the presence of mind to change his appearance before calling the cab so the cops didn't make a connection between the young man at the museum and the one in the cab. His body was already aching, and it was getting worse the more he walked. He wasn't going to make it much farther on foot. But he didn't think curling up in a snowy cornfield was a great idea, especially since he was still shivering from the water seeping through the back of his coat.

You don't make anything easy, do you?

The thought reminded him of Jason, which reminded him he still had his burner phone in his pocket. If the water hadn't got to it, he could call somebody. He wasn't sure exactly what good that would do, but the thought comforted him nonetheless.

One thing was going his way, at least: the phone was dry, and when he flipped it open, its tiny, primitive screen lit up with a satisfying glow. He wished he could sit, but the wet, snow-covered ground didn't lend itself to that. Shivering, he tapped Verity's number and plodded forward.

He feared she wouldn't answer. The burner's number would come up as blocked on her phone, so she might let it go to voicemail. *Please, Verity, pick up...*

"Hi, it's Verity. Leave a message and I'll get back to you..."

Damn.

He looked at the phone. He'd chosen a bare-bones, no-frills option on purpose, but that meant its texting capabilities were limited to the old-fashioned, phone-style keypad. His hands shaking from the cold and from shock, he carefully tapped out a quick message:

V pls pick up. Nd hlp. AS

He sent the text, waited a few moments for her to receive it, then called again.

This time, she answered instantly, breathlessly. "Doc? Is that you?"

Relief flooded him. "Gods, Verity, it's good to hear your voice. Thank you for answering." His weak voice shook as much as his hands had.

"Are you all right? You sound terrible. Where are you?"

He forced himself to keep walking, though he wasn't sure how much longer he could keep it up. His limbs felt like painful blocks of ice. "Nebraska. There's…been an accident."

"Accident? Oh, God! What happened? Are you all right?"

"I…will be, I suppose. I'm feeling ghastly right now, but nothing life-threatening."

"What town are you in?"

"I'm not. I'm walking along the road out in the middle of nowhere right now. It's bloody freezing, and every part of my body hurts."

"*What?*"

"Listen…" He swallowed hard, trying to put some strength in his tone so he didn't worry her. "I can't talk long. Need your help."

"Anything. What do you need?"

"Go…to my house. You still have a key, right?"

"Yeah, of course."

"Go there…and wait. I'll be along as soon as I can. I need healing, Verity. Will you help me?"

"Of course I will. I'll leave now. But...you're in Nebraska. You're nowhere near a portal, are you?"

"Please. Just...do it. Wait for me." He was slowing down. The idea of curling up in the snowy field was starting to look more appealing. He glanced back over his shoulder, afraid he'd see the approaching red lights of the police or the ambulance. Instead, he saw a set of normal headlights off in the distance.

Did he dare try to flag the vehicle down? It could be the gunman from the car again, tracking him. But it was a long way to the next town, and he knew there was no way he'd make it if he had to walk the whole way. "Verity—listen. I've got to go now. I'll see you soon. Thank you."

He flipped the phone shut before she could reply. She couldn't call him back because his number was blocked. He hated doing that to her—she'd probably give him an earful about it when he got back—but there was no helping it.

The lights were getting closer now. Shivering, he staggered to the road's edge and adjusted his disguise amulet again, this time making himself look like a stocky, dark-haired farmer type in jeans, plaid flannel shirt, heavy jacket, and work boots. If this vehicle didn't stop for him, he had no idea how much longer it would be before another one came by.

Gathering all his remaining willpower, stepped into the road and stuck his thumb out. It had been years since he'd hitchhiked anywhere—he had fond memories of doing it around the UK and Europe with friends during his summers at University—but he'd never been this desperate before. He concentrated on looking more like a man down on his luck and less like a serial killer and waited, heart pounding with anticipation.

The headlights drew nearer, and now Stone could see the outline of the vehicle more clearly. It wasn't a sedan, but a mid-sized box truck. Bigger than a pickup, smaller than a semi. For an agonizing second, he didn't think it was going to stop, but then it slowed and carefully rolled off to the shoulder, its bright lights dazzling his eyes.

He hurried over as fast as he could and opened the door. "Thank you. Thank you for stopping." He remembered to use his American accent—the deeper one this time.

The driver, a gruff-looking fiftyish man in a denim jacket, looked him over and waved him inside. "You're a mess, son. You okay?"

Stone's every muscle protested as he climbed up and settled into the seat. "Car broke down. Been walking for a while."

"That ain't too smart. Shoulda stayed with it, called the cops or Triple A or somethin'. Too cold to be walkin' out here in this, 'specially at night." He eased the truck back onto the road and stepped on the gas, then cranked the heater. "Just sit back and warm up. Where you headed?"

"Kearney."

"You're in luck. That's where I'm goin'. There's coffee in the thermos there on the console, and a blanket on the floor if you don't mind dog hair."

"Thanks." Stone tried to keep the shiver out of his voice, but couldn't do it.

The trucker snorted. "I ain't gonna leave a fella out here in the middle of God's armpit in cold like this. My wife'd have my hide. You ain't a murderer, are ya?"

"No." Stone shook his head. "Too cold to murder anybody." He hadn't taken the guy up on the blanket, but he did pour a cup of coffee into the big thermos's lid. It wasn't hot, but it was warm and right now it tasted better than anything he ever ordered from one of the upscale shops he frequented in Palo Alto.

"Well, that's good t'hear. Just sit back, warm yerself up, and we'll be in Kearney before ya know it."

Stone settled back, letting the heater warm his outside while the coffee warmed his insides. The cab smelled like coffee, sweat, fast-food burgers, and a hint of wet dog, and the radio played some political talk show at barely audible volume. Despite the throbbing in his head, he risked a quick look at the driver with magical sight, and was relieved to see a clear, medium-yellow aura with only the few minor darker spots he'd expect to see in somebody that age.

He tried to stay awake. Between his all-over body aches, the shock from the accident, and his fear that the man from the car would somehow find him and take another shot at him while he wasn't prepared, he didn't think it would be possible for him to sleep.

Maybe he'd just rest his eyes for a few minutes…

Somebody was shaking him. "Hey, son?"

"Uh?" He jerked awake, sending another bolt of pain through his head. "What?"

"We're here. Kearney." The guy chuckled. "You slept like a baby the whole way in, but this is the end of the line, I'm afraid. I gotta head home."

"Oh. Er—" He looked around. The truck was idling in a gas-station parking lot. With a sigh of relief, he opened the door. "Thank you. You're a lifesaver."

"Told ya—the wife would kill me if I passed somebody by out there. You take care, son. Good luck with your car."

"Thanks." He fumbled in the pocket of his coat, pausing to verify that the catalog was still there, and pulled out one of his last hundreds. "Here. Take this. It's the least I can do."

The man's eyes widened. "Oh, no, I couldn't do that. I'm happy to help."

Stone smiled and dropped it on the console next to the thermos. "Buy something nice for your wife, then. I might owe my life to her."

From there, it was easy to catch a cab to the ley line. Fortunately, ley-line travel wasn't any more tiring than walking through the Overworld portals. Stone spent a few more moments gathering his energy and visualizing the pattern to make sure he didn't pop out at the wrong location (at least Kolinsky had assured him there was no chance of appearing in the middle of a solid object—if he tried that, the spell simply wouldn't work). The ride in the truck and the sleep had helped, but not much. He wasn't cold anymore, but the shock and pain were catching up to him.

Never gladder to leave a place than now, he released the energy. An instant later, he was standing in his upstairs study.

"Bloody hell..." he murmured, slumping against the desk. Raider, who'd been curled up on his leather sofa, raised his head and opened one drowsy eye, then went back to sleep.

"Yes...nothing to see here..." Stone pushed off the desk. He couldn't afford to stay here, as appealing as the sofa looked. Verity was probably waiting for him downstairs. He quickly stashed the catalog in a locking desk drawer, then left the room.

Somehow, he managed to make it down without tripping and going arse-over-teakettle to the ground floor. He threw off his coat, dropped it in a heap on the floor, then slumped onto the living-room sofa before he noticed Verity wasn't there yet.

The key turned in the front-door lock, and a moment later, she strode into the living room, looking worried. She didn't call for him, though, and her eyes widened in shock when she spotted him on the sofa.

"Doc?"

Oh, no...

CHAPTER TWENTY-TWO

S TONE SUPPOSED this time he had a valid excuse for not, as his students were fond of saying, "braining" properly tonight. When he'd talked to Verity, he'd expected to have to walk for a lot longer before someone turned up willing to give him a ride. The trip back to Kearney had taken just shy of forty-five minutes—in other words, barely enough time for him to have made it home if he'd stepped into a portal immediately after he talked to her.

And he couldn't have done that, of course, because the nearest portal in any direction was hundreds of miles away from Nebraska.

He decided his best course of action was to pretend he hadn't noticed. "Hello, Verity." This time, he did nothing to hide the pained shake in his voice. "Thank you for coming."

As he hoped, her concern for him overshadowed her suspicion—for now, at least. "What *happened* to you?"

"Rollover accident in a taxi. I guess I'm the new poster child for wearing seat belts."

"Oh, God. How bad are you hurt?"

"Don't know." He let his head drop back to the sofa pillow. "Didn't really have time to do a thorough check. I don't think anything's broken, though."

"Come on—let's have a look."

He felt only a hint of regret when she began removing his clothes. Her touch now was concerned, almost but not quite clinical. Not the touch of a nurse, but not of a lover, either.

The touch of a friend, which was exactly what he needed right now.

She got him down to his shorts and looked him over with a healer's eye, then shifted to magical sight and scanned him. "Looks like you might be in mild shock. But I don't see any signs of anything too bad—no internal injuries, and you're right, nothing broken. Just bruised and banged up quite a bit. You didn't hit your head, did you?"

"No. I was hanging upside-down from the seat belt when we landed."

"Okay. Let me see what I can do for you. Hang on and be quiet so I can concentrate."

He was happy to obey. It felt good to be back in his own home, safe behind his wards with the prize he'd gone out to secure. He could finally let himself relax.

"Doc?"

He blinked as she gently shook his shoulder. "Did I fall asleep?"

She smiled faintly. "Yeah. Not surprised. It took me a while to fix you up, but you should be feeling better now. I think you did some of the work, though—whatever that weird new thing you've got now is, I mean."

She'd covered him with a light blanket, and Raider was now curled on his chest. He *did* feel better, too—the lightheadedness was gone, and so was most of the pain. He sat up experimentally. According to the mantel clock, he'd been asleep for twenty minutes. "You are good, Verity. You've even improved, I think."

"Maybe. Haven't had that much chance to practice lately. Most of my *other* friends don't make a habit of getting put through manglers as often as you do."

"Well…I'm glad to be of assistance as your training dummy, then." He sat up the rest of the way, gently tipping Raider off, and pulled on his jeans and shirt.

"Don't move around too much yet. You're still not a hundred percent. You should get some sleep."

"Yes, I suppose I should." Was he going to be that lucky? Had she been so focused on his injuries that she'd forgotten about the rest?

"But first we need to talk." She rose from the sofa edge and dropped into a chair directly across from him. Her expression was sober.

"Talk?"

"Yeah."

"About what?" *That's it—play dumb. Because that's always worked* so *well before…*

"About you. And how you got home this fast."

Damn. He sighed.

"And please, Doc, don't insult me by pretending you don't know what I'm talking about. Unless you were lying to me, you called me from Nebraska. The closest portal to there is in Chicago. And there's no way I know that you could have gotten from Nebraska to Chicago in forty-five minutes. Especially not in the shape you were in."

"Verity—"

"Not to mention it would have taken you at least half an hour to get home from A Passage to India. But yet you managed to get here before I did."

He stroked Raider in his lap and didn't answer.

Her eyes narrowed. "So…*were* you really in Nebraska when you called me?"

"Yes." He didn't look at her.

"I want to know about what happened. Did you get what you were looking for? How did you get into an accident? But even more than that, I'd like to know the answer to this question."

Again, he said nothing.

"Is this something else you can't tell me? Like why you can't close the rifts? Is this *related* to the rifts?"

"No. It's got nothing to do with…that." Even now, Kolinsky's oath wouldn't let him say the words.

"So, you're not…I don't know…finding more of them and somehow using them to travel between?"

He glanced up. "That's a brilliant thought, actually. But…no."

"So, you're saying that as far as you know, this whole business with the thing from the collection and Mr. McGrath and all this isn't related to the rifts at all?"

"Yes. No. It's not related at all."

She let her breath out. "This isn't the first time you've done something like this. I've been suspicious for a while that something new is up with you. Can you tell me *anything?* I know—you don't have to. I don't have any right to ask, except I'm still your apprentice, even if it's not official anymore, and I thought we trusted each other. I hope you'll tell me *something.*"

He thought about Eddie. He'd told *him*—and by extension, Ward—part of his secret. And Verity was every bit as good and loyal a friend as they were. He sighed. He wished he could tell his friends everything. He was tired of keeping secrets from them. But that wasn't possible. Not yet, anyway.

"All right. Honestly, this is my fault. I haven't been as careful as I should have been, and my friends are all too bloody bright for their own good."

She chuckled. "Hey, you *did* pick us."

"Yes, that's my fault too." He looked her over fondly, still stroking Raider, who was now purring. "The truth is, I've got a new magical travel method. It lets me move around more easily than before."

"What do you mean, more easily?" She leaned forward, looking every bit as interested as Eddie had been.

"I can't tell you everything. But I can go places without a portal now. Some places. Not everywhere."

She gasped, her eyes widening. "You're *kidding*."

"I'm not."

"How did you learn to do that? Who taught you?" She sharpened her gaze. "Wait. Don't tell me, let me guess. It was Harrison, wasn't it?"

Stone didn't smile, but he wanted to. "I…can't say."

She snorted. "I should have known. This is some extradimensional thing, isn't it? It's related to wherever that other place is that you went for your training?"

He looked back down at Raider. Sometimes the best way to avoid having to lie to friends is to let them think they'd figured out the answer on their own.

"That's…amazing." She paused, and when she spoke again, her tone was tentative. "Do you…think you could teach me?"

"I don't think so," he said gently. "There's…more to it than you know. Things I can't tell you."

"I was afraid of that." She sounded resigned. Then she looked up again. "You said you can go *some* places. And one of those is *Nebraska?*"

He shrugged. "I can't exactly choose the places."

"I guess not—because I can't imagine you'd choose that one." She got up and paced. "Doc, I have to tell you, it's hard being your friend sometimes. You know I'm always gonna love you, but…it just seems like you're keeping so much from me—from all of us— lately. That's hard to deal with, sometimes."

"I know it is." He stood too, and pulled her into a hug. "I know it is. I hope you'll forgive me for being such a prat."

She returned the hug, squeezing hard, then backed off. "You know I do. Even with all the secrets, you're still more interesting than pretty much anybody else I know. But just try to remember it's tough for us, okay? And maddening. And frustrating."

"I will."

She jammed her hands into her pockets. "I should go—I still have that thing with Scuro tonight. I told him I might have to skip it because I didn't know what you'd need, but if you're doing okay now I shouldn't bail on it. The client's coming all the way from Zimbabwe for her tattoo, and I'm sure she'd prefer it to be as pain-free as possible."

"Yes, of course you should go. I'll be fine. Just going to get some sleep, I think."

"You do that. I healed you, but your body still needs rest."

"I promise, Doctor."

"Good."

"And thank you again for your ministrations. I'm very lucky you're as good as you are."

She turned away, then back. "Oh—a couple more quick things you didn't tell me, before I go."

He tensed. "What?"

"Did you get what you were looking for? The auction catalog?"

"Yes."

"That's good, at least. And how did you get into a rollover accident in a cab?"

Stone thought about the illusionary figure in the road and the gunman from the car. "It's certainly looking like more people are interested in our little puzzle than I'd originally thought. And at least some of them are willing to kill to get what they want."

CHAPTER TWENTY-THREE

STONE TRIED TO SLEEP, and actually managed to do it for almost three hours before the lure of the catalog, combined with a lingering fear that somebody would figure out a way to get past his wards and steal it, dragged him from his bed.

It wasn't even late. His sense of time had been thoroughly messed up by everything that had happened over the last few hours, but in California it was only nine-thirty. He padded downstairs for a cup of coffee, then shoved the rest of the papers and his laptop from the middle of his desk and unlocked the drawer.

With everything that had occurred, he still half-expected the catalog not to be there. But there it was, right where he'd put it, coffee stain, ragged pages and all. He spread it out, gave Raider a gentle magical nudge to keep him away from it, and began paging through.

To his disappointment, it wasn't as helpful as he'd hoped. He'd been picturing something similar to the one for the Drummond auction, with photos (albeit grainy, faded black-and-white ones) and detailed descriptions for each item. Some of those did exist—a quick flip-through revealed perhaps a third of the pieces had photos and write-ups—but the other two-thirds had to make do with a heading and a small paragraph of text. There had been a lot of items in the auction.

He wished Jason, Verity, and Amber were here, or Eddie and Ward. Dividing the catalog, with everyone taking a subset of the entries, would make things go faster. Did whoever had stolen the other copy have people to help him? If he was part of Portas Justitiae, odds were good he did, not to mention that he'd had several hours' head start.

Quit whinging and get on with it, he told himself angrily. If he didn't get through it all tonight, he could enlist his friends tomorrow.

He didn't allow himself to think about what might happen if, after all the trouble he'd gone through to get it, he *didn't* find what he was looking for in the catalog.

He'd made it a few more pages in, squinting at the tiny, blurred print until his headache threatened to return, when his phone rang.

He picked it up, certain it had to either be Verity or, if she'd told them about this evening, Jason and Amber.

The number showed up as blocked. Neither of them, then.

"Yes, hello?"

"Stone?"

He recognized Leo Blum's voice—but he sounded odd. "Hello, Blum. Is something wrong?"

"Uh...not sure. I need to talk to you."

Stone frowned. "Well, here I am. What's going on?"

"In person."

Uh oh. "Tonight? I'm sort of in the middle of—"

"Doesn't have to be tonight if you don't want. But it should probably be soon."

This wasn't looking good. "What's this about? Can you tell me anything?"

Blum hesitated. "I'd rather not. I don't think anybody can trace this call, but I don't want to take a chance."

Stone looked at the catalog and sighed. He'd waited this long—he could wait until tomorrow. "All right. Tell me where to meet you and give me an hour."

"There's a little coffee shop called The Mean Bean on Hyde. I'll be in the back. Thanks, Stone. Oh—and if you've got a way to disguise yourself, might want to use it."

The line went dead.

"Well…" Stone murmured to Raider. "Life is nothing if not interesting, is it?"

Blum was already at the shop when Stone arrived, disguise amulet once again active, after moving the catalog to Desmond's vault along with the pyramid.

The detective was sipping a cup of coffee and doing a good job of not looking nervous—at least until Stone got a look at his aura. The place was fairly busy at ten-thirty, mostly full of college students and groups of twentysomethings.

Stone got his own cup and took the seat across from him. "All right—what's going on?" He used his normal voice so Blum would know it was him.

Blum's shoulders slumped in relief. "Nice disguise. Wish I could do that—it would help out a lot in my job. Anyway, thanks for coming, and sorry to drag you out so late. I guess this could have waited, but…"

"I'm here now, so tell me what's on your mind."

The detective cocked his head. "You sound a little off, but I can't put my finger on why."

"Long night."

"Yeah, okay. None of my business. That's fine." He sipped his coffee, leaned back, and met Stone's gaze. "I got a visit tonight."

"A visit? From whom?"

"That's just it. I don't know exactly. They didn't introduce themselves." He leaned closer. "And I gotta tell you before we go on—they told me not to tell you we talked."

Stone tensed. "Is that right?" He shifted to magical sight and glanced around the room, pausing at each of the groups. Nobody's aura looked agitated, and no one appeared to be paying any attention to them. Almost without thinking, he cast the "cone of silence" spell around their table.

"Yeah. They were waitin' for me when I got back to my place. Wanted to go for a drive."

"And you let that happen?"

Blum let out a slow breath. "I'm pretty sure they were some kind of law enforcement. They didn't give me names, but I know the type."

"So you went with them."

"Yeah. Didn't have a lot of choice." He looked up. "They asked me about you."

"About me?" This wasn't good. Stone thought back to Glenn Turman, who'd come to his house, and Matthew Fischer, who'd wanted to know what he was up to regarding the "space alien" he and Harrison had busted out of the government facility. Were they connected to these people tonight? "What did they want to know?"

"I'm not sure how they figured it out, but they knew you were interested in the stuff from Hiram Drummond's collection."

"It wasn't exactly a secret. It would be odd if I *weren't* interested in it, given my line of work."

"Yeah, but I got the impression they were aware you were more interested than you should be."

"I...see." Stone sipped his coffee and tried to think. "What did you tell them?"

"I said I didn't know anything about that. Not my jurisdiction."

"Did they believe you?"

"I don't think so, but they didn't push it."

"What did they look like?"

Blum shrugged. "Pretty generic. A guy and a woman, both in their thirties, clean-cut, nicely dressed. If I had to guess, I'd say they might be feds."

This was getting better and better. Stone had managed to fly under law enforcement's radar for years—why all of a sudden did everybody seem to be interested in him? "Did they say anything else? Did you get any impression that they thought the collection—or I—had any connection to the magical world?"

"You know..." Blum sipped again, obviously choosing his words carefully. "They didn't, *per se*. But I've been a detective for a long time, and you learn to pick stuff up. I honestly can't imagine they *don't* know something. Why else would they be taking this kind of interest in some mostly worthless auction of a bunch of old spooky junk?"

"And in *my* interest in it..." Stone mused. Sometimes he wished he'd remained in "hobbit mode," focusing on teaching, magical studies, and keeping his head down. Eddie and Ward didn't have to deal with this kind of nonsense. But that particular cat had not only emerged from the bag, but fathered a few generations of kittens by now.

"All right," he said. "Thank you for letting me know. I appreciate it, even though they asked you not to."

"Yeah, I figured I owed you that, at least. You getting anywhere with your problem?"

"I hope so. I've got a new lead I was in the process of investigating when you called, which I hope will point me to the other piece that goes with the pyramid. The only problem is, someone else has the same lead, so now it's a race. Possibly a three-way race now, or even four-way, with these people you spoke with. Did you hear anything else about the dead thief?"

"Nope. He's still a John Doe, and nobody's turned up to claim his body. They were hoping that weird tattoo might give them a lead, but no luck so far."

Stone considered whether to tell him, and decided it was only fair. "They probably won't. It's the symbol of an organization called Portas Justitiae. I don't know how big they are or how long they've been around, but they hate mages. The letters around the cross are an abbreviation for the Latin words *maleficos non patieris vivere,* which means 'Thou shalt not suffer a witch to live.'"

Blum whistled. "Shit."

"Don't tell anyone you got that from me, though."

"So they…what…kill mages?"

"Yes. They're very religious, but they don't consider killing mages to be murder."

"But wait—wasn't this guy who died a mage? The thief?"

"He was."

"So they have mages in an organization that hates mages?"

"Apparently, those who hate their own magic. They rationalize it by making themselves believe they're using their evil gifts to help the cause of righteousness." Stone shrugged. "I don't know—the whole thing doesn't make a bloody bit of sense to me. Anyway, I doubt anyone *will* claim him. He's served his purpose, so Portas will have washed their hands of him."

Blum finished his coffee and slapped the cup down. "You think these Portas guys are after the whosit? The one you have?"

"Without a doubt. And it's possible they're not the only ones. That's why it's so important I find out if there truly *is* another piece to this thing. As you might guess, having possession of an item that can block or negate magic is a bit of a big deal—especially for an organization that wants to eradicate mages."

"No shit."

"Anyway, thank you for letting me know about your little visit. Not that I can likely do anything about it, except be more vigilant than I already am, I suppose. This new lead I've got might get me somewhere, but I've got to get back to it. Is there anything else you wanted to talk about?"

"Isn't that enough?"

"*Touché.*" Stone slid out of the booth. "I'd best head home, then. Still got a lot to do tonight."

Blum tilted his head. "You sure you're okay? Like I said, something looks off with you."

"I suppose having someone try to kill you can do that."

"You're kidding."

"I wish I were. Good night, Detective. Let me know if your little friends contact you again."

Stone had a hard time concentrating when he returned home and went back to examining the catalog. He paged through it, focusing most of his attention on the pages with photos, but part of his mind wandered far away.

Who were these people who'd talked to Blum? How much did they know? Was there some government agency out there, tasked with keeping tabs on mages or magical artifacts? If so, why had he only learned about them recently? Were they watching *him* specifically now?

Damn it, he didn't have *time* for this. The last thing he wanted was for a bunch of nosey mundanes to be interfering with his affairs. Hell, he was trying to *help* them. The least they could do was leave him alone.

But he supposed, if they'd somehow managed to find out about an artifact that would interfere with magic, they'd be every bit as interested in it as Portas was. Mundanes were terrified of mages, and with good reason—most of them had little defense available if the mages decided to target them. Having something like this on their side could be a game-changer, and it would be hard to resist trying to find it.

"Bugger them," he muttered, as Raider leaped onto his desk and settled into a loaf on the corner. If they wanted to play these kinds of games with him, he could play too. If they wanted something from him, they could bloody well reveal themselves and their purpose to him. Until then, they weren't his current problem.

He continued paging through the catalog, pausing now and then to examine some interesting item. Leander McGrath's collection had been both larger and more varied than Hiram Drummond's, consisting of equal parts stage-magic paraphernalia and exotic, occult-related items he'd obtained during his travels following his retirement. Every now and then, Stone's heartbeat would quicken as he spotted some item he'd like to get his hands on—only to remind himself that this auction had taken place over fifty years ago, and most of the collection was probably scattered beyond recovery. Even if he found what he was looking for—assuming it was here at all—tracking that single item after all this time would likely be a nearly-impossible task. Trying to find *more* of them was out of the question, at least until this problem was solved.

He fell into a rhythm: flip a page, scan it, pause a few seconds longer if it contained a photo, then flip to the next one. The catalog had almost two hundred pages, and by the time he was three-quarters of the way through, his eyelids were drooping. Verity had been right: she might have healed most of his physical damage from the accident, but the body still held on to shock. He needed to get some sleep.

Just a few more pages.

Flip.

Scan.

Flip.

Scan.

Flip—

Wait!

Stone went stiff, pausing in mid-flip.

Something had caught his eye on the previous page, but his brain had been on autopilot and he'd nearly missed it. He flipped back. The page didn't have any photos, but some bit of text must have flashed past. He scanned the page more slowly, looking for anything related to the item.

Beveled black sculpture with unknown markings, a heading halfway down read.

Stone spun in his chair, summoning a magnifying glass from a nearby shelf with barely a thought. He pulled the desk lamp closer and bent over the page.

The text was sparse, since whoever had written it clearly had no idea what the thing's purpose was. It listed the item's dimensions, and made a cursory attempt at describing the symbols on all four sides. *Speculation is that the object was used as a platform or base on which to display some other item*, it continued, *but its actual purpose is unknown*.

His gaze fell on another small block of text at the end. *Two small protuberances, ½" in height, extend from the top surface of the sculpture, 3" apart*.

Yes!

Stone almost pumped his fist. This had to be it! Unless anything else turned up later in the catalog, this had to be what he was looking for.

The only problem now was finding it before Portas or someone else did. He—

His head snapped up. Raider was looking at him with wide-eyed curiosity, and he realized he must have nodded off for a few seconds. If he could do that in spite of his excitement about his find, that had to mean he needed sleep now. He'd get nowhere with this if he wasn't at his sharpest.

If he put it aside now, he'd have just enough energy left to pop to Caventhorne and store the catalog in Desmond's vault.

Tomorrow, he had two stops to make.

CHAPTER TWENTY-FOUR

HE WOKE LATER THAN HE EXPECTED, but by the time he got out of the shower, he felt mostly back to himself. He reached his first stop at eleven-thirty.

Gina looked up from her desk. "Hi, Dr. Stone. What's up? I think Jason's on a call right now if you want to wait for him."

"Good morning, Gina. That's fine, but I'm actually here to see you."

She grinned. "You come to see me more often than Jason anymore. People will think we're in love."

"Don't tell Jason—he'll be terribly jealous." He pulled out the catalog. "Listen—I need you to do something for me. This isn't related to your work, so I'll pay you extra for it. I suspect it's going to take a fair bit of your free time."

"I'm intrigued already." She nodded at it. "What's that? Looks like an old magazine." Then her eyes got big. "Holy shit, is that what I think it is? The catalog from the McGrath auction?"

"The very one."

"How…did you get it? You didn't steal it, did you?"

"No. I bought it. It wasn't the one from the photo you found. They had another one in storage." He held it up so she could see the coffee stain on the cover. "It was damaged, so they don't put it on display. I made a…generous donation to the museum fund."

She laughed. "Must be nice to be able to solve all your problems by throwing money at them. Anyway, what do you want me to do?"

At this point, Jason came out of his office. "Oh, hey, Al. What's up?"

"I'm in the process of hiring your assistant away from you for a side project."

He shrugged. "That's nothing new. As long as she keeps up with her real job, it's fine with me. What kind of side project?"

Stone glanced at him, looking for any sign Verity had told him about last night, but saw none. Maybe she hadn't had time to call him yet. He opened the catalog to the page he'd marked and dropped it on Gina's desk, pointing at the entry for the item. "I need to find out where this ended up."

She looked at it and frowned. "What *is* that thing?"

"Something I need to find, and quickly. If I leave the catalog with you, do you think you've got any chance of tracing it?"

Gina was studying the page. She flipped back to the front. "You don't want much, do you? This is fifty years old."

"If it was easy, anybody could do it. And I promise, I'll make it worth your while if you can manage it."

Jason picked up the catalog. "I think your only hope is if the auction company still exists. Maybe they've kept hardcopy records, but that's a long shot."

"It's the best we've got," Stone said. "Do your best, Gina—but keep this under your hat. I don't want it getting out that I'm look-ing for it, so don't spread it around with your…hacker collective, or whatever you call it."

She laughed. "Old people are so cute."

"Oi. I'm the old person who's planning to give you a nice bit of cash if you get me what I want, so show some respect."

"You're right. Those are the best kind. Sorry. Leave it with me and I'll do what I can. If it's out there, I'll find it."

Stone had already looked through the rest of the catalog this morning and determined there weren't any other items of interest. He'd also used his phone to snap photos of the cover, the information about the auction company, and the page with the sculpture's entry. "Be careful with this thing. When you're not looking at it, keep it hidden and locked up."

"You think somebody's going to come in here and try to steal it?" She frowned, tilting her head. "Doc, are you some kind of international spy or something? Don't take this wrong, but you're way more interesting than a college professor should be."

"We all have our secrets. Thanks for your help."

He nodded farewell to her, then followed Jason into his office and closed the door.

Jason settled behind his desk. "I can't believe you found that thing. I'm kind of impressed."

"Well, don't be too impressed. It was a lot less fun than I'd hoped." With the "cone of silence" spell active so Gina couldn't overhear, Stone told him about last night's adventures, and his meeting with Blum.

Jason stared. "Shit. So somebody else really *is* on the trail of this thing. You aren't just being paranoid."

"On the trail of this thing, yes—but also, apparently, on *my* trail more than I'm comfortable with. It's beginning to feel like I don't have much time to solve this little problem. If Portas or the Men in Black or whoever else is looking for this thing manages to get to it before I do…"

"Yeah, but it might not help them, right?"

"What do you mean?"

"Well…you've still got the other piece. You swapped a fake one into the collection that's going to auction, so even if they get their hands on that, it won't help if they need to put the two pieces together to make it work. You said there's no way for them to get to the real one, right?"

"Correct. I'd pit Desmond's vault against any mage I've ever met—up to and including Kolinsky. But if they get hold of the fake and realize it *is* a fake, that will lead anyone with half a brain back to me, won't it? And depending on how desperate they are, that could put others in danger."

"Don't worry about that now. Let's focus on finding it before they do. Gina's good, but do you have any other leads you can pursue?"

"I'm about to go pursue one, actually. Someone I've preferred to keep out of this, but I'm realizing it might not be possible anymore."

CHAPTER TWENTY-FIVE

S TONE HADN'T VISITED Stefan Kolinsky's shop in more than three months. Partly it was because nothing much magically interesting had been going on and Kolinsky wasn't the kind of guy one dropped in on for social visits, and partly because he didn't have anything he needed the dragon's help with. Kolinsky had, likewise, not contacted him recently.

When he reached the East Palo Alto shop, he found it closed and locked, but there was no sign on the door behind the wards indicating how long Kolinsky would be away. Since this wasn't an emergency, he decided not to enter the shop and call; instead, he took out his notebook, scribbled *I need to talk to you about something. Dinner tonight? AS,* along with today's date. Then he left for campus, where he had one class to teach that afternoon. There wasn't much else he could do in the meantime, since Gina had a better chance of tracking the location of the new artifact than he did.

He stopped by his office after class. Laura, the department's admin aide, looked up from her computer. "Oh, Dr. Stone?"

"Yes?"

"Your…strange friend dropped off an envelope for you. The one who sends messengers in funeral-director suits." She took it from her drawer and offered it to him. The face was blank, but she'd put a sticky note on it that said "Dr. Stone."

Good old Stefan. Stone wasn't sure how he knew to send his reply to the University instead of his home, but he'd given up wondering how Kolinsky knew things. "Thank you. I was hoping he might."

He was about to turn away when she spoke again, her voice full of worry. "That's a terrible thing, what happened to Brandon, isn't it?"

Stone paused. He liked Laura, but she was the chatty type who loved to gossip and he didn't have time for a lengthy discussion. "Yes. Yes, it is."

"He won't be back till next week. He's home now, but he's supposed to take it easy for a few days. I hope he's got someone to look after him."

"I'm sure he's fine. I'll give him a call. Must go, Laura, sorry. Thanks for the message."

He got out of there before she could say anything else, and opened the envelope as soon as he got out the door. The card was blank too, as usual, but magical sight revealed a concise message: *I will join you for dinner tonight. I suggest La Maison Noire in Los Altos. Eight p.m.*

Stone smiled. Good old Stefan, indeed. Still picking the most expensive restaurant around. He couldn't blame the dragon, though—he hadn't suggested a place himself, after all.

He was surprised to find himself looking forward to seeing Kolinsky. Despite his misgivings about involving the dragon in this situation, perhaps his old friend could shed some light he couldn't find anywhere else.

And again, it was better than talking to Aldwyn.

La Maison Noire was a far fancier restaurant than Stone tended to frequent. Tucked away at the end of a tiny side street, it had a small, dirt parking lot full of high-end cars. He was glad he'd chosen to wear one of his best custom-tailored suits.

Kolinsky was waiting at the bar, sipping a glass of wine. He stood when Stone entered, before even seeming to notice him.

"Hello, Stefan. Your lavish taste in restaurants hasn't changed, I see."

"Life is too short to indulge in low-quality cuisine." Kolinsky was dressed, as usual, in one of his familiar old-fashioned black suits. Stone occasionally wondered, now that he knew more about what his friend really was, if the suits were the product of a draconic illusion generator, and Kolinsky was really wearing sweatpants and an old T-shirt.

"Especially when I'm paying for the good stuff." *And especially when you're functionally immortal.* He smiled, taking the edge off the words. It was their old game, and as always, he didn't mind plying the dragon with fancy meals and wine if it meant he got the answers he sought.

A slim waiter in black took them to their table and gave them leather-bound menus. Stone ordered a glass of wine of his own as he perused his. "How have you been? It's been a while. Have you missed me?"

"I have not."

"You know, from anybody else I'd take that as an insult."

"You may take it as you will."

They placed their orders and sipped their wine. Kolinsky regarded Stone over the top of his glass. "How may I be of assistance?"

"Well…that's an interesting question." Stone had been turning the situation over in his mind ever since receiving the card today, trying to figure out how he was going to describe the situation to the dragon—and how much he wanted to reveal. He'd also remembered he had another topic he wanted to discuss with Kolinsky, so perhaps it was best to lead with that. He might even combine the two to work things out to his advantage, if he was careful.

He leaned forward. "I actually have two things I want to discuss. They're not related, but I know how much you enjoy your *quid pro quo.*"

Kolinsky said nothing, but merely watched him expectantly as he swirled his wineglass.

Stone didn't bother with the "cone of silence" spell for this conversation, since he was certain his friend had better concealment magic active than he could manage on his best day. "So…first of all, I've been finding the new travel method very useful."

"I am not surprised."

"But…" He paused, choosing his words carefully. "It's brought up certain…difficulties for me."

"Difficulties?"

"They aren't unique to traveling by ley line—I've experienced some of them while using normal portal travel. But the speed and versatility of the new way has made them more…obvious."

Kolinsky remained silent, his face still and calm.

Stone let his breath out. Might as well just put it all out there. "I'm getting noticed. Naturally, I've been traveling more now that it's easier, and even before this, my friends have been concerned about things like my cell phone popping up in places it shouldn't be, my IDs and credit cards being used thousands of miles from where I'm supposed to be, that sort of thing. I've taken to using disposable phones and doing as many transactions as I can with cash, but that can be inconvenient too. Some places don't even take cash, and some still require valid identification."

"Ah. I see." Kolinsky didn't look surprised. "And why are you bringing this problem to me?"

"Well…I don't imagine you lot have to deal with the issue, but it would make my life a lot more convenient if I didn't either. So, I suppose I'm going back to our original arrangements, before I found out—" He spread his hands, encompassing the table. "—everything."

"Indeed. And which 'original' arrangement are you referring to?"

"I thought you might be able to point me toward someone who's an expert at setting up false identities. I need everything: identification, credit cards—probably multiples of each—I don't know. This isn't exactly my area. Basically, I need someone who it *is* their area to set this up for me. Of course, I can pay them handsomely."

"No doubt you can." Kolinsky steepled his fingers and shot Stone a significant glance.

And there it was. Stone gave a sly smile. "Don't worry. I can pay *you* handsomely, too. And not in money. I know you don't give a damn about that. Or, more precisely, you have more of it than you could ever spend in *your* lifetime." He buttered a piece of warm bread and took a sample bite. "So…is that something you can do?"

"Of course."

"Brilliant."

Kolinsky continued to watch him.

"All right, then—let's discuss the details later. And for your payment, I think I've got some information you're going to find highly interesting."

"I hope so, for your sake. What you ask will not be a simple or inexpensive undertaking."

"As I said, don't worry. I think you'll like this." He leaned in. "Stefan…have you ever heard of a magical device that…negates magic?"

Kolinsky's expression stilled. "Negates?"

"Yes. Blocks it. Interferes with it."

"I…have heard stories of such artifacts, yes. Why do you ask?"

"Because I think I've found one. Or part of one."

Kolinsky's face didn't change, but it didn't have to. Stone knew him well enough to know interest when he saw it. "I see. Is this perhaps related to the recent theft at the University?"

Stone chuckled. "So you *have* been paying attention."

"I pay attention to everything around me. I take it by your response that it is related?"

"Yes." He felt a sudden relief that he was finally addressing someone he could speak freely with. "Sit back and get comfortable, Stefan. This is going to be a long story."

Their meals had arrived by the time he finished telling Kolinsky about the break-in, the pyramid, the auction catalogs, a little about Portas Justitiae, and his attempted murder in Nebraska. For now, he left out only Eddie's revelation regarding the pyramid's markings and the chamber buried beneath the Surrey house.

The dragon listened silently while picking his slow and deliberate way through his coq au vin. When Stone finished, he didn't reply.

"So…" Stone prompted. "What do you think? Does it sound like something you might have encountered in your travels?"

"As I said, I have heard of such devices. Not recently, though. I believed that, like necromancy, the expertise for designing and building them had been lost long ago."

"Yes, well, we all know how well that worked with necromancy, don't we?" When Kolinsky still didn't reply, he said, "So…you don't have one of these things in your possession?"

"I wonder why you would expect me to tell you if I did. But no, I do not."

"I want to show you a couple of things. Can you make sure no one else might get a stray look?"

"Of course. You need not concern yourself with that. You may safely assume all aspects of our conversation are fully private."

"That's…comforting." Stone pulled out his phone and cued up the best photo of the pyramid. "Here's part of it. It was included in the collection on loan to the University. When I saw what it was, I 'borrowed' it for further study, and later replaced it with a fake version."

Kolinsky took the phone and studied the photo, but didn't attempt to swipe forward to view more. Stone wondered if he even knew how a mobile phone worked.

"What do you think?"

The dragon didn't reply, but merely leaned in closer, trying to get a better look. "This image is far too small to reveal any significant detail."

Stone grinned. "You're such a Luddite, Stefan. Seriously—you do need to get with the twenty-first century one of these days." He took the phone back, set it on the table facing Kolinsky, and used two fingers to zoom in.

The dragon's eyebrow rose. He picked up the phone and tried the same thing, nodding once. "Fascinating."

"Want one? I can recommend a few places where you can get a good one."

"No. Thank you." He focused in on the photo, turning the phone in several directions. "Are there more of these images?"

"Yes." He showed Kolinsky how to swipe forward. "A few more of the pyramid from various angles, and some I took of McGrath's auction catalog."

As the dragon slowly swiped through the rest of the photos, Stone said, "I've been discussing this with a couple of colleagues back in England. They think the second device—the larger base— might serve as a sort of amplifier for the top part. What do you think?"

Kolinsky gave him back the phone. "They are almost certainly correct. The devices were, as you might guess, highly forbidden. By dividing them into parts, they could be more easily hidden and transported."

"Forbidden by whom? Other mages? You lot?"

"In the past, there was a great deal more rivalry between various wealthy and powerful mages. Even though their aims often coincided, leading to dangerous alliances—"

"—like Ordo Purpuratus."

"Just so. But even with these alliances in place, the various practitioners continued to work in secret, individually and in small groups, trying to gain power and advantage over the others."

"As humans are prone to do—and not just mages."

"Yes. These devices were rare, even in those days. Possession of one could most certainly give one faction an advantage over others."

"You mean, by grabbing an enemy and…what…imprisoning him with it?"

"It was done, yes."

"Hmm. Interesting." He finished his wine, then refilled both his and Kolinsky's glasses. "So, how do they work? My colleagues and I were speculating about that too. How can an item that interferes with magic not show up *as* magic?"

For a long time, Kolinsky didn't reply. He swirled the wine in his glass, appearing to consider his words carefully. "It is not magic…not precisely. There is another component involved."

"Another component? What do you mean?"

"A substance."

"What kind of substance?"

"An exceedingly rare one. One that does not originate on this dimension."

Stone stared at him. "Bloody hell, Stefan."

Kolinsky inclined his head. "This is why I feel secure in sharing this information with you. If any of this substance remains— perhaps beyond this item you seek—it is highly unlikely you could find it."

Stone pondered his words. This was huge. So, his original hypothesis about the pyramid—that it had something inside it that made it tick—might be closer to the truth than he'd suspected. He narrowed his eyes, thinking. "What about you lot? How do you feel about these things? Do they *work* on you?"

Kolinsky gave him a look. "Again, I wonder why you would presume to think I would tell you if it were so."

"Because you're as curious as I am—and because you know I've got more to tell you. And because you trust me."

He considered, then nodded toward the phone on the table. "That one likely would not. It would take a much larger and more powerful version to hope to imprison us."

"But it *would* it work? Some version of it?" Stone heartbeat quickened as he pictured the room under the Surrey house.

"Potentially, yes."

"But it wouldn't…destroy a dragon's magic, right? Only interfere with it as long as one was in its proximity? What about a human mage? When I put the pyramid near a weak item, it de-powered it completely, but it only affected stronger items until I moved them farther away. Does it work that way for mages, too, if the item were combined and the amplification ability activated?"

"I do not know. I doubt even a potent one could do more than inconvenience a dragon as long as they remained in proximity to it. As for human mages…I do not have enough information to give you a definitive answer."

Stone nodded.

"You have something on your mind." Kolinsky's gaze sharpened, boring into his eyes, and once again Stone wondered if dragons could read thoughts.

"I…do. I think what I've already told you has been enough to convince you to help me with my identification problem. But if it isn't, this will be."

The dragon leaned back in his chair, steepling his fingers, and waited.

"I know what happened to Aldwyn now."

Both Kolinsky's eyebrows rose, and once again he went as still as a statue.

"You get it, don't you?"

"You…believe he was imprisoned by one of these devices."

"Not *by* one. *Inside* one. A much larger one."

Stone cued up more photos, this time of the room beneath the Surrey house, and pushed the phone back across the table. "The symbols look similar, don't they?"

Kolinsky looked at the first photo for a full minute before he spoke. "They do. Where was this taken?"

"Before I tell you that—can you read the symbols?"

"Yes."

"What do they say? Why are they different, if it's the same sort of device?"

Once more, Kolinsky hesitated as if trying to decide whether to answer. Finally, he set his wineglass back on the table. "They are different because their purposes are different. The smaller device is more…generic. It was designed to function in a broad range of situations."

"And the other one?"

"Purpose-built, for a highly specialized application."

"Imprisoning a dragon."

Kolinsky inclined his head, and his gaze sharpened. "Where was this taken, and when?"

"A year and a half ago. At my home in Surrey."

The dragon's hand was resting on the table. Now it tightened, clenching into a fist. "This chamber…is in your home."

"Under it, yes. And yes, apparently Aldwyn was imprisoned under there for almost two hundred years before something happened to break the seal and let him escape."

"You knew this and did not tell me?" There was something dangerous in his eyes now.

Stone glared at him. "Why would I? I don't tell you everything going on in my life any more than you tell me. Until I saw you two acting like a pair of spitting cats at the Caventhorne opening, I didn't even know you knew each other. I certainly didn't know you were a couple of dragons who couldn't stand each other. And when you revealed the truth to me last year, I had…more pressing things on my mind at the time."

Kolinsky subsided, and his fist relaxed. "True. Forgive me. But…this chamber exists at your home?"

"Not anymore. That whole situation was a big mess. James Brathwaite was also interred under my house, in a different area. Really dead that time, though—except his echo somehow managed to hang about. He and Aldwyn's son Cyrus were the ones who betrayed Aldwyn and locked him up in that chamber. But the whole thing's collapsed now. There was a network of catacombs under there, and it all came down around our ears. We barely survived it. Sorry to disappoint you."

Kolinsky nodded. "It is probably for the best. For such a thing to exist in the modern age could lead to…complications."

"You mean if a chamber existed that can bugger up a dragon's power."

"Yes."

Stone sighed. "Okay. Well, I suppose I'm glad it's gone, then. But that still leaves the smaller one, and at least two groups I know of looking for it, aside from me. So, what I want to know is: will you help me find the other piece?"

But this time, Kolinsky's answer came immediately. "No. I will not."

"No?" Stone blinked in surprise. "Why not? I thought you'd find it intriguing. And honestly, I'd rather have it in my hands—or yours—than a bunch of religious nutters or some shadowy government organization."

"On that, we agree. But nonetheless, it is not something with which I can assist you."

"But why?" Stone leaned forward, gripping the edge of the table. "Wait. I think I get it. It's because of the other dragons, isn't it?"

"It is."

"Because of the little dance—the agreements—you've all made among yourselves to keep anyone from getting too far out of hand."

"Yes. If it were to become known that I provided any material aid to you in locating this device, the consequences could be…unpleasant."

Stone considered his words. "Okay. I get it, I suppose. But you don't want these other groups getting their hands on it either, do you? I've got no idea how strong Portas is, or how many of them there are. Do you?"

"I was not aware of their existence in the modern world. Like the Ordo, they appeared to die out many years ago."

"But, like the Ordo, it's possible they just went under-ground…scaled back their activities. Right?"

"It is possible. They had significant backing in the past."

"How significant?"

Kolinsky shrugged one shoulder. "There were rumors of the Vatican being involved."

"Bloody hell."

"I do not know if it was true—or if it was, if it is any longer."

"But if you had to take a guess?"

"I do not 'guess.'" He looked mildly put out, as if even speaking the word was offensive to him.

"Okay, if you had to *speculate*."

Again, he shrugged. "Almost certainly not the mainstream Church. But even in the modern age, shadowy sub-groups with specific agendas remain."

Stone nodded slowly. "So they're possibly more dangerous than a few random nutters. What about the other group—the one I suspect is connected with the mundane government?"

"That, I do not know. I have not heard of them. I rarely involve myself in the affairs of mundane humans."

That was unfortunate, but Stone knew it was true. Kolinsky had never been actively hostile to mundanes as many of the Ordo were, but he tended to treat them as nonentities, unworthy of his attention. "Probably because they haven't got a chance in hell of touching you or any of the other dragons. Right?"

"Yes."

He sighed. "But they've got a chance of touching *me*. Which brings us neatly back to my original request. Was what I've told you sufficiently interesting for you to put the wheels in motion to find me some help in that regard?"

"Yes. I will look into the situation. I have a few contacts who might prove useful. I will put one of them in touch with you soon."

Stone tossed his napkin on his plate. "Thank you, Stefan. I appreciate it. And if there's *anything* you can do to help me find the other half of that device—even indirectly—I'd appreciate it even more. I wonder if there *are* only two halves, actually. I've got no way to know that."

Once again, Kolinsky appeared to be considering something with care. When he spoke again, he didn't look at Stone. "From the appearance of the design, I believe there to be only two parts to the device itself. Although it is possible there is a third, of a different nature."

Stone snapped his gaze up. "Oh?"

The waiter came by, and Kolinsky ordered a glass of the finest cognac on the menu.

"Thank you, sir. And you?"

"Might as well," Stone said. When the waiter left, he shook his head, amused. "Getting your money's worth, I see. What did you mean about a third part?"

"I do not know if this is true. It is, as you say, pure speculation. But some of these devices were rumored to include what the mundanes would call an…operations manual."

Stone frowned. "You're having me on. A magical artifact with an owner's manual?"

"The concept does not map precisely. The devices' creators did not wish them to fall into their enemies' hands, so they sometimes enchanted them in such a way that they would not function without a specific ritual. These rituals were documented in volumes kept separate from the device itself."

Their cognacs arrived, and the dragon paused to swirl the amber liquid in his glass. He sniffed appreciatively, then sipped. "Ah, this is exquisite. Spirits are one area where mundanes do excel."

Stone didn't bother asking any other questions. He knew from past experience that Kolinsky was done talking about anything beyond his opinion of the food, the liquor, and the restaurant's ambiance.

As the two of them exited the restaurant after he'd paid the hefty check, his mind was already spinning. If Kolinsky was correct—and when was he ever *not* correct?—he might have not only one, but two mysterious components to find. Even if Gina and her computer wizardry could locate the first, how was he going to track down one book that might have been lost for centuries, or might have been destroyed long before he was born?

If it was easy, anybody could do it, he'd said before. That was proving to be even truer than he'd suspected.

CHAPTER TWENTY-SIX

S TONE'S IMPATIENCE GREW as more days passed and the date of the auction approached.

Despite his and his friends' best efforts, no new or helpful information had turned up. Gina had located the auction company, only to find out they had been bought sometime in the Nineties by a larger company. When she reached that company, they told her the records did still exist, but any files that old would be stored in hardcopy form in one of three warehouses. Even when she took the liberty of promising a hefty finder's fee if they could locate the record, they told her they would try but couldn't promise anything.

Stone had told Eddie and Ward about the possibility there might be a book or other document containing the ritual needed to activate the device, which had sent Eddie off into the Library stacks in the faint hope it might have found its way there.

"That's a tough one," he said ruefully. "First, we don't even know if it existed in the first place. If it did, we don't know if McGrath 'ad it—obviously he didn't 'ave the pyramid, so 'e wasn't collectin' the set. And if it's not in the Library—which I don't think it is, honestly—we've got no bloody idea where it might be. You know I like a challenge, Stone, but I think maybe I might've finally found my match."

"But you'll keep looking, right?"

Eddie grinned. "Try to stop me, mate."

Leo Blum hadn't gotten back to him, which was probably a good thing. It meant as far as the detective knew, nobody had tried to break in to the secure facility in San Francisco where the Drummond collection was being stored. Stone didn't even know where it was, and hadn't asked. Perhaps whoever was interested in it had decided to lie low and try buying it legitimately. Stone doubted it would be as easy as sitting back at the auction and waiting for the trap to spring, but he could always hope.

With everything going on, he'd almost forgotten about another item he had on his calendar. When it popped up on the Friday morning a few days prior to the auction, he'd briefly considered begging off, but the impulse didn't last long. The Cardinal Sin had been booked for a couple of months to play at a bar in downtown Palo Alto, and they couldn't very well go on without their lead guitarist. Despite his preoccupation with more important matters, he couldn't let them down.

To his disappointment, neither Verity nor Jason and Amber could attend the show.

"Sorry, Doc," Verity told him when he texted. "You know I really hate missing your shows, but I already made plans with the Harpies. I could bail, but—"

"No, don't do that. You have fun. Next time, maybe."

"For sure," she promised.

He didn't bother contacting Jason and Amber, because he knew they were planning to head to Lake Tahoe for the weekend to visit Amber's brothers. Jason had made him promise to get in touch if anything came up with the Drummond situation, but that wasn't the same thing as missing a concert.

He was on his own tonight, but that was fine. It might even be good to get his mind off things for a while. Sometimes his brain worked best when it was otherwise occupied.

"Looking a little glum tonight, Stone," Gerry Hook called. "You okay?"

The rest of the group was already there, setting up on the small stage. Stone leaped up and unlatched his guitar case. "No, no, I'm fine—just have some things on my mind."

"We need to get you loosened up." Radha Unger, the lead singer, grinned at him. "Go get yourself a beer."

"I'll get one during the break." He plugged thc cable into his red-and-black Strat, scanning the crowd as he fondly remembered when Jason and Verity had "given" it to him for his fortieth birthday. It hadn't exactly been a gift since he already owned it, but they and Aubrey had braved the Surrey house's dusty attic to locate it and then had it restored to its former glory. The faded sticker on the back said *Fever Dream,* the name of the previous band he'd been in during his university days. Things had been so carefree back then, full of studies and magic and drinking too much and hanging out with Eddie and Ward and Imogen…

At least until his father had been killed, and everything had changed.

"Hey."

He glanced up to see Gerry Hook giving him a sideways look. "Oh—sorry. Woolgathering a bit, I guess."

"You sure you're okay? I forgot there was that business with your friend getting hurt recently—"

"I'm fine, Gerry. Really." He pulled up his best imitation of a cheery grin. "Ready to rock."

Hook shook his head, amused. "We have *got* to get you laid, Stone."

That stung a little. He hadn't been with anyone since he and Verity had broken up, mostly because every time he thought about going out to a club, his motivation had deserted him. Still, he kept his tone light now. "Yes, well—that's not something I need your help with, thanks."

Hook snorted. "Yeah, not that I *could* be any help. Been out of the game for years." He clapped Stone's shoulder. "Come on—let's make some music."

As always, most of Stone's stress and unease melted away as soon as he hit the first riffs of "Highway to Hell," their opener. He forgot about the pyramid and Brandon Greene and Leander McGrath, and even Portas Justitiae, in favor of letting the pounding beat of the music resonate through his body. How had he ever even considered skipping the gig? Music didn't give him the same high as magic, but it wasn't as far off as he remembered—and it was a hell of a lot less complicated.

None of the Sin's songs, mostly covers with a couple originals written by Radha and bass player Jake Cohen, were musically rigorous. The band was about having fun, playing hard-rock favorites and getting the fans moving. Stone's fingers flew over the Strat's strings without his conscious thought, leaving him free to continue scanning the crowd. He shifted to magical sight, reveling in the brilliant, mingled auras of happy people. Some were dancing in the cleared-out space in the middle, some tapping their feet or bobbing their heads at the tables or the bar, a few focused more on their companions than the music but still looking unworried and relaxed. It was a good show, and just what he'd needed.

When it was over, including an encore following the crowd's enthusiastic applause, he helped the others take down the gear and then headed to the bar for another Guinness. Some of the crowd were already drifting out now that the show was over, but most had remained. A couple even came over to congratulate him and his bandmates for a great show.

As was usually the case, the other three left before he did, citing family obligations the following day. "Next one's in a month," Hook reminded him as he prepared to take his drums out to his van through the back exit. "And don't forget the pub next week."

"I wouldn't think of it." During the previous, uneventful quarter, Stone had gotten back into the habit of attending the Friday-night pub-crawling group with several fellow professors, and realized how much he'd missed it. "Good night, Gerry."

He sat at the bar and finished his Guinness, enjoying the relaxed feeling of coming down off the show's energy. Now that he was no longer performing, some of his more immediate thoughts began trickling back in again, but he refused to focus on them. For tonight, he could put them aside and pretend he was a normal, mundane man out for a pleasant evening.

Even so, he decided against another beer. He wasn't even close to tipsy enough to worry about driving home yet, but as he looked around and saw no one else he knew, he decided it might be best to go home rather than hanging about here like a lost dog. Perhaps he could pop over to England to pick up the pyramid and spend some time studying it. Ever since Kolinsky had told him of the extradimensional substance, he'd been meaning to take a closer look.

He left his empty glass on the bar, slipped off the stool, and bent to retrieve his guitar case.

Something careened into him, nearly knocking him off his feet.

"Oh, I'm so sorry!"

Stone took a staggering step back as a slim arm shot out to grab his in an attempt to steady him. He jerked his gaze up to find himself facing a dark-haired woman in her middle thirties. She was staring at him with wide-eyed, flustered concern.

"I am *so* sorry," she spluttered again. "I wasn't looking where I was going, and—"

"Oh, sure, I get it," a drawling male voice spoke from behind her. "I see how it is. You'll fall all over the guy in the band, but you won't let *me* buy you a drink."

Stone regained his balance and scanned the man and the woman. She was still looking concerned, shooting glances back and forth between him and the other guy. She wore a fashionable blouse, designer jeans, and a loose-fitting, flattering blue jacket, her shoulder-length hair pulled back from an attractive, intelligent face. A pendant with a large blue stone and a silver setting hung around her neck.

"Er—quite all right. No harm done."

From behind her, the guy grabbed her upper arm. "C'mon back to the table, honey. Let's have that drink." He glared at Stone. "And *you* mind your own business, okay?"

Stone shifted his gaze to him. He was in his late twenties, clad in typical club-bro gear: jeans, black polo shirt, leather jacket. He had short-cut hair, a goatee, and heavy brows which were currently beetling over angry eyes. Even from where he was standing, Stone could tell he'd had too much to drink.

"I think you should do as the lady asks and let her go. Suppose you sit down and have another drink? I'm buying. How would that be?"

"Suppose you fuck off, asshole." The man glared hard at him, but didn't let go of the woman's arm. "This isn't your concern."

"It's okay." The woman wrenched free of the man's grip, but otherwise ignored him and focused on Stone. "I was just headed to the ladies' room anyway. Really sorry I ran into you. I didn't hurt you, did I?"

"No, of course not. Honestly, it's fine."

"Great show tonight, by the way." She flashed him a smile. "Your band had the place rocking."

"Thank you, that's very kind. I—"

"I *said* to mind your own business, fuckwit," the bro said. "The lady's with me."

"Where did you get that idea?" She glared back at him. "Get away from me. You're drunk, and I don't even know you."

"Stuck-up bitch." He lashed out snake-quick, pressing his flat palm into Stone's chest and shoving hard.

This time, Stone held his ground. "Best if you don't do that again."

"Oh, yeah? And what are you gonna do about it if I do?"

At this point, the guy was getting loud. Stone wondered if he'd need to use a bit of subtle magic to discourage the guy, but to his relief their altercation had attracted the attention of the bar's bouncer, who slipped up behind him with far more grace than a man his size should have been able to manage.

Stone nodded past the bro toward the bouncer. "Me? I probably won't do much. But *he* might."

"Hey, buddy." The bouncer's large hand closed around the bro's shoulder. "I think you've had a little too much tonight. Come on, time to go. I'll call you a ride."

To nobody's surprise, the guy sputtered a token protest but deflated when confronted by somebody who could obviously take him apart without breaking a sweat. "Yeah, fine, whatever. Get your hand off me. I'm goin'. Ugly bitch isn't worth my time anyway," he muttered. He was still muttering as the bouncer escorted him out through the front door.

The woman watched them go, then turned back to Stone and rolled her eyes. "Well, *that* was awkward. Sorry you had to see it."

"Glad I was here to be of at least some help."

She shook her head. "He's an asshole. He bought me a drink without asking if I wanted one, then got pissed when I told him to get lost. It sucks that a girl can't sit at a table by herself and have a beer without that type sniffing around and refusing to take no for an answer."

"I'm sorry. I hope the rest of your evening is more pleasant."

He expected her to thank him and continue on toward the restrooms, but instead she gave him a sideways glance. "You know, that really *was* a good show. Bar bands can be hit or miss, but you guys were great."

"Thank you. We have a good time, but we've got no illusions of greatness. Just four university professors making a bit of music in our spare time."

"University professor? Really?" She looked him up and down. "I never would have guessed. You don't look like a professor. But I suppose you get that a lot."

There was no mistaking it now, even without a glance at her aura: her interest wasn't feigned, and neither was the way she was looking at him. He took a chance. "I'm Alastair Stone. At the risk of sounding like our obnoxious friend, may I buy you a drink? I promise if you'd rather not, I will absolutely take no for an answer."

She considered, then flashed an easy grin. "Eleanor Newman. And sure, why not? It'll give me a good story to tell at work, anyway. Not often a rock star buys you a drink."

He laughed. "Not on my best day, I'm afraid. The 'rock star' bit, I mean. But I suppose you can stretch the truth…to make a better story."

They got beers—he ordered another Guinness, and she got a local microbrew—and he nodded toward the other side of the room. Most of the band's crowd had thinned by now, leaving a few open tables. "Shall we sit over there instead of at the bar? Bit quieter."

"Sure. And you can tell me all about how a college professor ended up playing bar gigs."

He watched her as she sat across from him, shifting briefly to magical sight. Her aura was golden yellow, touched with a few red patches that clearly indicated she found him at least somewhat interesting. "Not much to tell, really. I go out pub-crawling periodically with some fellow professors. Gerry, our drummer, was already in the band, and their lead guitarist left when his wife fell pregnant. Gerry knew I played, so he asked me. And the rest is history. Of a sort, anyway. The sort no one cares about except us and a few of our students."

Her grin was infectious. "And me, apparently."

"Well, I wouldn't presume to think so, but I certainly won't object. And what about you, Eleanor Newman? What do you do with yourself?"

"Nothing nearly as exciting. I'm a marketing manager at a tech startup in Sunnyvale."

"Sounds fascinating."

"No, it really doesn't. But it pays the bills, and it's easier on the feet than waiting tables."

He watched her as she talked. She had a trim, athletic figure and sparkling honey-brown eyes. "What brings you out here? I can't imagine you came all the way from Sunnyvale to see a bar band you've never heard of."

"Came with a friend, actually, but she had sitter issues and had to leave early. By then, I was enjoying the music so I figured I'd stay for the rest of the show." She glanced around, taking in the old movie posters decorating the walls. "Do you live around here?"

"Not too far. Little town called Encantada, a few miles from the University."

"Wow. I'm impressed. That's a nice area."

"It's quiet, which I like." He sipped his Guinness and watched her as she was looking around. He hadn't gotten out of the habit of scanning the women he found attractive with magical sight, even after Deirdre had been so long ago. Her aura remained unchanged, except possibly the red patches might have grown a bit larger.

"My place is quiet, too—a little too quiet, actually. I used to work at another startup in the City. They offered me more money to come down here, but Sunnyvale is basically a bedroom community. Not much going on. I'll probably move back up again if I can find a better offer." She grinned. "You know us startup people: always job-hopping."

Stone didn't know, actually—despite the area being taken over by the technology industry, he'd never spent much time learning about it. "I suppose that could be exciting."

"But not for you." She gave him a knowing, sidelong glance. "How long have you been at the University?"

"About ten years now."

Her eyebrows rose. "Really? You don't look old enough to have been a professor that long."

He shrugged and smiled. "What can I say? Good genes, I suppose."

The returned the smile and fixed him with an amused, slightly predatory gaze. "You know, I was just thinking something."

"And what's that?"

"Well…I was thinking we could sit here and keep making small talk over a couple of beers, or we could…continue our discussion somewhere a little more private."

Stone risked another quick look with magical sight. He wasn't misreading her signals. "What did you have in mind?" he murmured.

"You *did* say your place wasn't far from here…I'd love to see it."

"And I'd love to show it to you."

"Sounds like we're both on the same page, then."

"Indeed we are. Shall we?" He set his glass back on the table, rose, and picked up his guitar case. "Do you have a car here?"

"No, I came with my friend. Was going to get a rideshare home."

"Brilliant. Makes things easier, doesn't it?" Part of Stone was wondering if this was a good idea, preoccupied as he was with other things. But he *did* think better when his mind was relaxed, and what Eleanor was clearly proposing was definitely relaxing.

"Wow." Eleanor looked up as Stone tapped the button to swing open the wrought-iron gates to his house. "I've heard Encantada is nice, but I wasn't expecting something *this* impressive." She chuckled. "I know it's none of my business, but they must be paying professors a lot better than I thought."

"They're not. It's…a bit of a long story."

"Oh, that's all right. It's none of my business, and it doesn't matter. As long as you're not a Mafia don or something."

"I promise, I'm not. Or any other sort of criminal mastermind. As dons go, I'm closer to Oxford than Mafia." He pulled the car through the gates and parked it in front of the garage.

"Aww." She sounded mock-disappointed as she got out. "That's too bad. A criminal mastermind could be intriguing. Certainly a lot more exciting than the usual engineers and marketing guys I date."

"Don't say that yet. I'm really a bit of a homebody most of the time. And you haven't met my cat."

She laughed. "You're serious."

"Oh, quite. I warn you, you'll have to meet with his approval. But that's not hard to do. Offer him a bit of tuna and he's all yours."

She eyed him appraisingly when they reached the front door. "And what about you? What can I offer you?"

"Well…I don't care for tuna, but I'm sure we can find something."

Raider was nowhere to be found when he pushed the door open and waved her inside. "Sorry—he's a bit skittish around new people."

"That's all right." Her voice had a new huskiness. "I'm sure I'll see him."

"Probably. Shall I get us some wine?"

"Yes, but let's not drink it now. Let's save it for…later."

"I like the way you think. Give me just a moment."

Heart thumping in anticipation, he hurried to the dining room to retrieve one of the bottles he kept in a small rack on the sideboard, a corkscrew, and a pair of glasses. He thought about Gerry Hook's comment from earlier that evening, and wondered briefly if it might be possible his friend had set him up. But Hook had already left, and Stone knew if he *had* tried, he'd have remained behind to watch from afar to see if he'd succeeded.

No, sometimes these things just happened when you least expected them. He'd brought home women he'd met at clubs before—just not since Verity. *I'm out of practice.*

Best way to get back in *practice, though.*

He was about to call to her from the doorway, but then he stopped in mid-breath.

She was in the living room where he'd left her, but instead of sitting on the sofa or looking out the window, she was standing in front of one of his bookshelves, examining the collection of objects he had on a shelf. As he watched in silence, she quickly moved to the next one and appeared to be giving it a quick scan.

Tensing, he shifted to magical sight. The red patches still flickered at the edge of her golden-yellow aura, but they were smaller now, overshadowed by a clear sense of purpose or focus.

Hmm. Interesting indeed…

"Here we are," he called cheerfully, striding in.

She didn't look startled, but turned and smiled back at him. "I was just looking at your shelves. You have some interesting books. Are they related to whatever you teach?"

"They are. Anthropology." It was the usual thing he told women when he first met them, so he didn't scare them off with Occult Studies. It wasn't even a lie: his department was under the same umbrella—just perhaps a bit farther out near the edges than the others.

"That's really fascinating." She drifted over toward him, and the red flashes were back as she drew closer. "Maybe you could tell me all about it…later."

"Later," he agreed. But this time, the husky murmur in his tone didn't come as easily.

They'd barely reached the bedroom when she pulled him close, pulling his head down into an insistent kiss. "Mmm…" she whispered. "I didn't run into you on purpose tonight, of course. But as soon as I saw you, I was hoping you'd feel the same way I was. I don't mind admitting I was checking you out while you were…performing."

He let her shove his coat from his shoulders as he slipped off her jacket and dropped it on the floor. His heart was still pounding, but now it wasn't sexual anticipation—not completely, anyway. He didn't know what to make of her aura: the interest was definitely there and he didn't think she was feigning it, but there was more he couldn't read. Always, in every relationship he'd ever had, his aura-reading skill had guaranteed he'd never misread a woman's signals, or press things farther if she showed any hint of reluctance or misgivings. It was the reason why he had the somewhat contradictory reputations of being both a sexual tomcat and a perfect gentleman. But with Eleanor, he couldn't tell *what* she wanted. Her aura was all over the map.

And why *had* she been examining his bookshelves so closely—and so furtively?

For that matter, why had she been so insistent to come back to his home when they'd barely had a chance to get through the initial, flirting pleasantries?

It had happened before, of course. Stone had no illusions about some women being as eager to move to the next level quickly as he was.

But why tonight? And why after she had (conveniently?) run headlong into him at the bar?

He was very much afraid he knew.

He couldn't help feeling disappointed—but if he handled this just right, he might learn something.

She was pulling his T-shirt up. She deftly slid it over his head and started on his belt, her hands moving with expert insistence. Despite his uncertainty about her motivations, he was still human, male, and straight—and she was still very attractive. As she unbuckled his belt and tugged his jeans down, his heartbeat increased further and his body responded to her touch. She didn't resist when he reciprocated.

Before they removed the last bits of each other's clothing, though, he pulled her into a kiss, rolling her over onto the bed. Her arms snaked around him, pulling him on top of her. Her lips, soft and willing under his, still tasted faintly of her microbrew from the bar.

How far would she let this go? Had he been wrong? *Had* she merely been examining his bookshelves because she was interested in discovering bits of his life? Was he seeing problems where none existed?

"Wait…" she murmured, turning her head just a little to break the kiss but still continuing to stroke his back.

"What?" He couldn't entirely keep the roughness from his voice, but he forced himself to tilt his head back. "What's wrong?"

"I…I'm sorry. I want this, but…I think we're moving a little too fast."

With reluctant effort, he pushed himself up on his arms, looking down at her. His breath came in short, sharp puffs. "Of course. I'm sorry—"

She traced her finger over his chest. "No, no, it's not your fault. I *do* want to."

"It's all right. If you don't, I mean."

"I do," she insisted. "I'm glad to hear you say that. It makes me feel safer. But I do." She glanced at the wine bottle he'd left on top of the dresser. "Tell you what—why don't we have that glass of wine and talk for a little longer? I promise, I'm not leading you on."

"It doesn't matter if you are. If you've changed your mind—"

She lifted herself from the pillows and pulled him into a passionate kiss. "I haven't. But you're sweet to be so understanding." Tapping the tip of his nose playfully, she said, "You stay here. Doing a show like that must be tiring. I'll pour the wine."

"Sounds brilliant." He rolled over, releasing her, and made a show of languidly stretching, but something in the pit of his stomach tensed at her words.

Before, he thought he might have been wrong.

Now, he was sure he hadn't been.

The thought disappointed him more than he'd expected.

She swung her legs around and stood, walking unselfconsciously to the dresser in her black silk wisps of bra and panties. Stone watched her, not surprised when she turned away from him, blocking the scene with her body as she picked up the bottle and the corkscrew. A moment later, a faint *pop* sounded in the dim silence. "There we go…" she murmured. "Won't be long now…."

"I can't wait." He kept his voice husky, but he'd already switched to magical sight. As he expected, the red flashes melted away again as she poured. He didn't miss the way she reached up toward her neck, then poured two glasses of wine and brought them back to the bed.

She carefully crawled back in, sitting with her legs tucked under her, and offered him one. "I wonder where your cat is. You'd think he might be jealous. Unless you bring a lot of strange women home…" She sipped her wine, extending her other hand to trace his chest with a long-nailed finger.

Stone sat up, pressing his back against the pillows and taking a sip of his own. "Would you believe me if I told you I hadn't had a date in months?"

"No. I can't imagine that."

"It's true."

She tilted her head. "You just don't want to scare me away. But why would it? You're an attractive man, Alastair, and I don't think you're married…are you?"

"No. Never married, actually." He took another, larger sip and swirled his glass contemplatively.

"Waiting for the right woman to come along?"

"Something like that, I suppose."

She held up her wineglass. "This is excellent, by the way. You have good taste in wine."

"Thank you." He held his expression to neutral interest, but didn't miss that her gaze never left his face.

She was waiting for something.

All right—let's give it to her, then.

He stretched again and drained the glass. "I think I might have another, actually. Would you like one?"

"No, thank you. Not yet. I think I'll make this one last for a little while."

She was still watching him as he stood. She didn't seem at all surprised when he stumbled, nor did she cry out or jump up in alarm when he staggered forward, caught himself briefly on the edge of the dresser, and then slumped awkwardly to the floor. His empty glass rolled beneath the bed.

CHAPTER TWENTY-SEVEN

STONE GAVE HER TEN MINUTES after she gathered her clothes and left the room. He remained where he lay sprawled on the floor, then rose and quickly pulled on his jeans.

The room was empty as he'd expected, but the wards hadn't buzzed to indicate she'd left the house.

He glanced at the bed. He'd need to clean up the puddle of wine from the glass underneath, but that was a small price to pay. Apparently, his illusion had fooled her.

Good.

He wondered if she'd only been trying to knock him out, or if she'd intended to kill him.

Using a levitation spell to avoid any creaking floorboards, he floated to the doorway and paused to listen. For a moment there was nothing, but then he heard a soft *thump* coming from his study down the hall. The door, which he always left closed to keep Raider out when he was away, was open.

He added an invisibility spell to the levitation and floated the rest of the way down the hall until he hovered in the doorway.

She was there, dressed now, crouched on the floor where she'd just pulled a whole row of books off the lower shelf and now seemed to be hunting for any hidden catches. Raider sat on the corner of the desk, watching her as if this were the most normal thing he'd seen all evening.

Stone's anger rose . Even now, he'd hoped he'd been wrong—that somehow he'd completely misread her cues, that perhaps she'd gone off to call an ambulance and was downstairs waiting for it. But no, here she was going through his things—and he knew exactly what she was looking for.

He shimmered back to visibility, still hovering two inches off the ground. "Raider seems to like you, though I can't imagine why," he said in a calm, conversational tone. "If you've done anything to hurt him, I'll kill you. And no one will ever find the body."

She moved fast, without even wasting the motion to turn toward him, leaping toward the closed window. She'd made it half-way across the room before he plucked her in mid-jump and held her suspended in midair, her arms locked at her sides.

She glared at him. "You caught on, didn't you?"

"It wasn't difficult. Your aura gave you away. Either you're rubbish at controlling it, or you're mundane. I've got no idea why they'd send a mundane against me." He shook his head. "Foolish."

Her glare didn't soften. "So, what are you going to do with me now? I didn't touch your cat. *Are* you going to kill me? I'm expected, you know. People know I'm here."

"I'm not sure I believe you. But let's assume for the moment that you're telling the truth." Stone entered the room, descending until his bare feet touched the floor. "What should I do with you? I've got a lot of options." He began pacing back and forth in front of her, holding her immobile with next to no effort. "I *could* kill you. I don't know if you know how easy it would be—and I wasn't having you on about no one finding the body."

He glanced at her aura again, and was pleased to see it flaring fear, even though she wasn't showing it in her expression or her body language. She was good, without a doubt. He kept pacing, thinking back to the encounter at the bar. "Don't tell me—you were in league with the obnoxious gentleman who was bothering you. That whole thing was staged for my benefit, wasn't it?"

She didn't reply, but she didn't have to. It was obvious. Her eyes flashed.

Raider licked his paw and looked back and forth between them.

"Anyway," he continued, "that's one thing I could do with you. Possibly the easiest. I could also pop you somewhere remote, where if you *were* found, it wouldn't be any time soon. That would get you out of my way long enough to make you irrelevant. Or I could turn you over to the police. I'm willing to bet if I let them test the wine you gave me, they'll find—what? Poison? Knockout drops of some kind?" He stopped in front of her, a few inches away. "Were you trying to kill me, Ms. Newman—or whatever your real name is?"

"No." She snapped it out quickly. "Just knock you out fast. That's the truth."

Stone thought it probably was. Her aura didn't flare when she said it, anyway. "I see. You just wanted to put me out of commission for a time, while you looked for…what?"

"I won't tell you."

He resumed pacing. Back and forth. Back and forth. "That's all right. You don't have to tell me. I already know. And you wouldn't have found it, because it isn't here. I haven't got it."

"You're lying."

"Am I? You've got no way to tell, but I promise you—it's not here, so all this cluttering-up you've been doing in my house is all pointless. And annoying."

She still seemed mostly unaffected by his words, her eyes flashing defiance. "So what *are* you going to do with me? You can't hold me up here all night."

"Oh, you know that, do you? So you know something about magic. But you're mundane, so if I *did* plan to hold you, a simple length of rope or a couple of heavy zip ties would do the job nicely. No need for magic. Who do you work for?"

She snorted. "You can't believe I'd tell you that."

"I do, actually." Once again he stopped in front of her. "I could make you tell me."

"No, you can't."

"Is that right? As I said, I'm not sure that's true—I've got some fairly persuasive methods. Hmm—let's have a better look at your aura, shall we?"

He moved closer, taking care to hold both her arms and her legs immobile so she couldn't take a shot at him, and shifted to magical sight.

"What are you looking for?"

"Just be quiet a moment."

What he was seeking was hard to spot, but he was getting better at it after a few sessions with Verity, and this time he knew what he was looking for. "Aha. There we go…" He shifted back and flashed her a triumphant grin.

"What?"

He walked behind her and dropped into his desk chair, turning her slowly so she continued to face him. "Whoever sent you is good, I'll give them that. But I'm better."

"What are you talking about?" she snapped.

"A magical oath. They've put one on you, so perhaps you're right—you *can't* tell me who you work for. But no matter. There are ways around that."

Her aura flared fear again, but her face remained calmly annoyed. "You're bluffing. Nobody made me take any oaths."

"I'm not, actually. I can tell you're lying. I can see it in your aura." He tilted his head at her. "But you see—here's the thing. I *can* break magical oaths. You should be angry at the people who sent you after me, especially if you're a mundane."

"Why is that?"

"Because I'm almost certainly a better mage than any of them are—especially if you work for who I think you do. They should know that, if they've got half a brain, so perhaps they simply don't care what happens to you if you get caught." He got up again, making a show of turning her so she kept facing him as he paced the room. "But in any case, while I can break even strong magical oaths given enough time…I'm not that good at it."

He stopped in front of her again. "Let me give you an image, Ms. Newman. Picture a safe. A heavy safe with a good, strong lock on it. And it's got something inside that I very much want. Now, if I had the expertise, I could crack that safe—work out the combination, open it up, and get what I'm after without any harm to the safe itself. Or, if I *didn't* have that expertise, I could use explosives. I'd still get the same result, but I wouldn't count on anyone using that safe again afterward. Do you see where I'm going with this?" He continued speaking in a pleasant, conversational tone, as if he were lecturing to a hall full of students.

This time, he was pleased to spot a hint of the fear reaching her eyes. "Look," she said. "I don't know what group you think I'm with, but I'm not. I'm a freelancer. People hire me to do things. I do the job, get paid, and that's the end of it."

"Is that so?" Stone had been watching her as she said it, and was surprised to see no hint of deception. Either she was better at controlling her aura than he'd thought, or she was telling the truth. "If it *is* so, then it's in your best interest to save yourself. Because I don't take kindly to anyone coming into my house to steal from me—and that's not even discussing whatever you put in my wine." He leaned in. "So tell me, Ms. Newman—who sent you after me, and what did they want you to do?"

She shook her head. "I can't."

"Why not? Because they'll kill you if you tell? But they're not here, and I am."

"You won't kill me." She sounded certain, but again her aura betrayed her.

"Can you be so sure? How much did they tell you about me? I'd be insulted, if I were you, to find out they sent you in here like a defenseless kitten, with nothing but a knockout potion to protect you." He snorted. "Ms. Newman, you're lucky I caught you before you got very far. If you're looking for what I think you are, it's not here—but a lot of very nasty things are."

"Look," she said, glaring. "You're not going to kill me. If you were, you'd have already done it. I've seen plenty of cold-blooded killers before, and you're not one of them."

"That's true," he admitted. "I won't kill you. But I *will* find out what I want to know. And I'm not having you on about being rubbish at finesse when it comes to mind-work. I can't promise you won't end up sitting in a corner counting your toes and drinking juice through a straw instead of wasting a glass of exquisite wine. So what's it going to be, Ms. Newman?"

She said nothing. But her aura was roiling, more red than yellow now.

"All right, then. Suit yourself. Don't say I didn't warn you." He approached her, one hand reaching for her forehead.

She *was* good, he had to give her that. She lasted until his fingers were only an inch away. "Wait!" she snapped. "Stop."

He paused, but didn't pull back.

"I'll tell you. What I know, anyway. Which isn't much, and that's the truth."

"All right, then. Start talking."

"You're right—they *will* kill me if they find out."

"Let's worry about that later, shall we? We'll start with what you were hired to do."

She wrenched against his telekinetic hold. "You could let me loose, you know."

"I could—but I won't. Not yet. Answer the question."

Her eyes flashed again. "It should be obvious. I was supposed to seduce you and convince you to take me back to your place. Which wasn't hard, by the way."

Stone shrugged unapologetically. "You're attractive, intelligent, we seemed to hit it off—not that surprising, is it?"

"Men are so easy to manipulate," she said with a smirk. Her gaze traveled from his eyes downward, then back up again. "*So* easy."

"Keep going."

"Once I was inside and past your wards, I was supposed to seduce you, drug you, and search the house while you were out."

"Ah, so you know about wards, then."

"Yes. Not much, though."

"You're a mundane. From a magical family?"

"Yes, I'm a mundane. No family, though. Learned about it years ago from a fellow…freelancer."

"Mercenary."

"Call it whatever you want."

Stone nodded. "What was the drug? You kept it in your pendant, didn't you?" She was still wearing the blue gem pendant, but its sparkle had dulled somewhat.

She gave him a sly grin. "I couldn't count on having anything else on at the time. I didn't figure you'd bother taking my necklace off."

"And the drug?"

"I don't know. They gave it to me. Said it would knock you out fast and keep you unconscious for at least a couple hours, which should give me plenty of time to search."

Stone made a mental note to try salvaging some of the wine so he could give it to Verity and Hezzie for analysis. "What were you looking for?"

"You already know."

"Tell me anyway." He watched her aura.

She paused, looking away, but finally sighed. "A small, black pyramid with writing on the sides."

"Ah. The one from Hiram Drummond's collection."

"I don't know. They didn't tell me anything about where it came from. They just showed me a photo."

Stone perched on the edge of the desk. Raider, who'd been watching the proceedings with faint interest, crawled into his lap and settled there. "I thought that was what you were looking for. And as I said before, you're lucky I caught you."

"Why is that?"

"Well, first of all, as I said before, it's not here because I haven't got it. So you wouldn't have found it."

"And second?"

"When I woke up from your concoction, it would have been inconvenient to have to locate your body and figure out what to do with it."

Another aura flare. "You're bluffing this time."

"I'm not. I take the security of my home very seriously, Ms. Newman." He lied without a second thought, confident she wouldn't catch him in it. He did have some nasty traps in the magically concealed areas of his home, but none of them were deadly. Not like the ones back home in Surrey. "If you did manage to find it, what were you supposed to do with it?"

"I don't know. They said they'd contact me. That's the truth," she added with more force.

"Oh, I believe you." He leaned in closer, meeting her gaze straight on. "And now comes the important question: who hired you?"

"I don't know. They didn't say."

He raised his hand again and moved it toward her forehead.

"I don't *know*!" she yelled again. "I'm telling the truth!"

"What did they look like? How did they contact you?" Stone did believe her, and had already come to terms with the fact that he probably wouldn't find out. If it was Portas Justitiae, they could have contacted her through one of their quisling mages under an illusion, used an intermediary, or even reached her remotely.

"It was a man. That's all I know. He wore a mask, and the room was mostly dark. I met him in San Francisco."

"What did he sound like?"

"What do you mean?"

"How did he speak? Did he use any phrases that seemed odd or unusual? Anything religious, perhaps?"

She shook her head. "Definitely nothing religious. He was…I don't know…well-spoken, I guess. Kind of condescending, like he didn't really want to be working with me. Like he thought he was better than I was. But I don't care—as long as the payments clear, I'll work for anybody."

Condescending. That didn't bode well. It was only a tenuous clue, but Stone hoped he was wrong about his suspicion. If he was right, it meant another player had possibly entered the game. "Did he pay you anything up front?"

"Yeah. Through a secure bank transaction." She glared. "You can't trace it, so don't bother trying."

"Probably not. And I don't care. How much did he pay you? And how much were you supposed to get when you delivered the item? Don't lie to me. I'll know."

Her gaze cut away, and for several moments she didn't answer. "Ten thousand up front," she finally mumbled. "I'm supposed to get another twenty-five on delivery."

Stone snorted. "That's not a lot for the risk you were taking."

"Not a bad take for a couple hours of work," she said, eyes flashing again. "We're not all as rich as you are."

"I suppose it isn't—assuming everything went as you expected. Which it didn't."

"Yeah," she said. "I got that." Her voice dripped with sarcasm, but she was clearly still wary. "That's all I know. It's the truth, whether you want to believe me or not. I didn't take any oath."

"Oh, I know that," Stone said cheerfully.

Her gaze sharpened. "What? But you said—"

"I know what I said. I was lying. The difference is, *I* can tell when *you're* lying."

"You're a bastard, Stone."

"So I've been told, on occasion." He tipped Raider off his lap and stood. "But that still leaves the matter of what to do with you. I can't just let you go and send you back to whoever hired you. The easiest thing would be to let you have the pyramid and track you back to your employers—but unfortunately I can't do that because I don't have it." He wished he'd asked Eddie's friend to make a second fake copy, but it was too late for that now.

"You could be lying about that, too."

"I could be—but I'm not. It's not here, so I can't let you take it."

"So what do we do, then?"

Her aura showed her continued wariness. She was tough and smart, that was clear, but Stone wondered if she'd ever gone against a mage of his level before. He studied her for a moment, remembering the last time he'd questioned a thief suspended in midair by magic. He'd been at Kolinsky's shop then, and Zack Beeler had been a lot more terrified than this woman was.

Hmm. But perhaps Kolinsky had the right idea.

He smiled.

Her eyes narrowed, and her aura blipped. "What are you smiling about?"

"I just came up with an idea for what to do with you."

"Oh?"

"You're a mercenary. In your own words, 'as long as the payments clear, you'll work for anybody.' Were you serious about that?"

"It's how I make my living."

"Well…you're not going to be collecting that twenty-five thousand for stealing the item from my home, obviously."

"Obviously," she said dryly.

"I don't know who you're working for, but your comments gave me a clue about who it might be. And I promise, if I'm correct, they will not respond well to failure—especially if they found out I caught you."

Her gaze sharpened. "You think you know who hired me?"

"As I said, just a guess. But if it's who I think it is, they don't hold mundanes in high regard. They'll use them as tools, but when they're no longer useful, they'll discard them without a second thought. And in case you don't know what I mean by 'discard,' remember when I said I could kill you and no one would find the body?"

She didn't answer, but she was definitely still listening.

"Well…they can do that too. And the difference between them and me is that they *will* actually do it."

"Okay," she snapped. "So, I'll run. I have plenty of places to hide, to lie low until they give up looking. Friends who will help me stay under the radar."

Raider, thinking he'd heard his name, poked his head up and yawned.

Stone ruffled his fur. "But they'll *never* give up looking, Ms. Newman. If you run, they *will* find you. I guarantee it. I could be wrong about who they are—if it's the other group it could likely be, they probably won't kill you. But is it worth it to you to take the chance?"

She was silent for a long time, obviously mulling over the possibilities. "So, what do you propose?"

"Simple. I'll hire you myself."

"*What?*" Her eyes got big, and she snorted. "You're crazy."

"I've been called that too, but in this case I'm not. You're smart, you're capable, and you've got skills I don't have. They paid you ten thousand to break into my home. I'll pay you fifteen to contact them and tell them you searched the place from top to bottom and didn't find what you were looking for."

"But you said they wouldn't respond well to failure."

"They won't respond well if you run. But you can't find what isn't there. Tell them you still want to earn that twenty-five thousand dollars. Professional pride and all that. Tell them that after you failed to find the pyramid, you decided to remain with me and see if you could learn anything else. Is there a reasonable chance I wouldn't have caught on that you'd drugged me if you'd been successful?"

"Yes, actually. They told me when it wore off, you'd just wake up from what you thought was a deep sleep."

"Brilliant. So, tell them that happened, and when we talked the following morning, I invited you to my home in England later this week. Tell them I'm smitten with you. They won't be able to pass that up—and they won't have trouble believing it. I wasn't lying when I told you I haven't had a date in months, and I do have a bit of a reputation."

She gave him a sly, sideways smile. "You're a sneaky one."

"Thank you. Coming from you, I'll take that as a compliment. So—what do you think? Are you willing to give it a go? You still get paid, we both get what we want, and I buy some time to get a few steps ahead of your employers."

"You'd trust me, after what I did to you? How do you know I won't just run back to them as soon as you let me leave?"

"Several reasons. First, I consider myself a good judge of character, and I believe you're what you say you are: a professional doing a job. Second, it won't do you any good to go back to them empty-handed. This way, you've got another shot, so with luck they'll leave you alone for a while. Third, even if you do go back to them and tell them, they'll be no farther along than they were before. Obviously I won't fall for the same trick again, which means you'll hurt yourself more than you hurt me. Fourth, you've already fulfilled your contract: you got into my house, did your best to drug me, and searched the place." He stopped in front of her again, clearly pausing before continuing.

"And fifth?"

"Fifth. Yes. That's the sticky one, isn't it?" He hardened his expression. "You're not entirely right that I won't kill you. I won't do it *now*. But you're going to leave a bit of yourself behind with me— one that guarantees if you *do* betray me, there won't be anywhere on Earth you can hide from me. I *will* find you, and I *will* kill you. Quickly, without a trace, and with no remorse."

He paced away, pleased at the new flare in her aura, and returned to his conversational tone. "But I don't want to do that, and that's the truth. So it would be better for both of us if you accepted my offer. What do you say, Ms. Newman? It's a good offer, and I give you my word that if you don't betray me, you'll never hear from me again after this is over."

She was silent for almost a full minute, her eyes fixed on his face. "You know," she said at last, slyly, "there's one other thing you're not thinking about."

"What's that?"

"Well…" Her smile widened. "If you're supposed to be 'smitten' with me, and if we're going to fool anyone who might be watching, it might be better if we played our parts."

"Played our parts?"

"How about if you let me down now? I'm not going to run, and even if I did, you could catch me. You've proven that."

Stone gave her aura one last once-over, then shrugged and released the spell, lowering her to the floor. "What do you mean about our parts?"

"We should be seen together. I wouldn't object to that…would you?"

He tilted his head and frowned.

She moved closer. A few of the red flashes were back. "I accept your offer, Dr. Stone. And do you know why I won't betray you?"

"Because I'm paying you fifteen thousand dollars not to?"

She chuckled, crossing the room to sit in his chair, where she stroked Raider. "Well, yes. There's that. But there's also another reason."

"What's that?"

"You're right—I'm a professional. I do what I need to do to get the job done. So I was fully expecting tonight that I'd have to sleep with you before I drugged you."

Stone drew breath to speak, but she held up her hand. "And that wouldn't have been such a bad thing. You're hot, you're smart, you have a sexy accent, and you play a mean guitar. I could do a lot worse, you know—and have, to be honest. But when I said I wanted to stop—even after we were as far along as we were—you did it. You stopped. Just like that. No whining, no protests."

"Of course I did. You thought I wouldn't?"

"A lot of guys wouldn't. Especially not that far in. But you did. And that's a big deal."

He said nothing, but thought of the man back at the bar. Sure, he was a plant, but Stone had met plenty of other guys of a similar type.

"So…" she continued, rising from the chair and approaching him, "what I'm getting at here is…maybe we should finish what we started."

He blinked, then shifted to magical sight. The red flashes were back. She wasn't messing with him. "Don't you want to complete our…financial transaction first?"

"That can wait until morning. You're not paying me for this." She tilted her head up and kissed him, then pulled back, her eyes glittering with challenge.

He smiled. "You've told me why you won't betray me. Shall I tell you why I trust you not to?"

"Yeah. Tell me." Her voice was low and husky again as she took his arm.

He nodded toward the desk. "Because Raider likes you. And he's an excellent judge of character."

CHAPTER TWENTY-EIGHT

S HE WAS GONE when he woke the following morning. Raider was still there, curled in the crook of his arm. On the nightstand was a note, held down with his phone. It included a phone number, a bank account number, and the message: *Call me soon. Let's do this again. E.*

He smiled, shaking his head in amusement. "I hope I haven't made a big mistake," he told Raider. But he knew he hadn't. Even if she *were* inclined to betray him, there was no way she could get to anything interesting in his house.

Also, he wasn't a complete trusting fool: he'd put a discreet, simple ward on the bedroom door when he'd gone to take a quick shower last night. If she'd left the room, he'd have known it—and she hadn't. Not until this morning, when the tiny, full-body buzz awakened him. As he swung out of bed, he felt another faint buzz as the front door opened.

He took care of the transfer right away—one thing he was well-versed in was moving money around without anyone catching on—and headed back to the bathroom to shower and shave.

His phone chirped, indicating a text.

It was from Gina. *Hi Dr. Stone. Got something for you, if you want to come by today. G.*

Finally. *Be there in an hour,* he sent back.

He hoped she'd found something he could use. The auction was coming up fast, and he hadn't made nearly as much progress as he'd liked.

As he stood under the hot water in his shower, he thought about Eleanor Newman—almost certainly not her real name. If she wasn't working for Portas Justitiae, there was only one other group he knew of who would both be interested in the device and have the kind of money to throw around thirty-five thousand dollars to hire someone to steal it.

He knew Ordo Purpuratus was active in the United States— he'd run into two of their members in Massachusetts while dealing with the eldritch horror in Lake Nepahauk. Had they made it all the way out to California? Or had they, like Portas, kept someone in their employ to watch for interesting auctions, estate sales, and other potential sources of magical treasures? It made sense.

Either way, though, he had no idea if they *were* behind Eleanor's plan. But given her comments about the man she'd spoken with being condescending and acting like he was better than she was, it made sense.

Which made it all the more urgent that he find the other half of the device. And the book Kolinsky referred to, if it even existed.

He arrived at the agency at eleven a.m.

Gina looked up from her screen with a bright smile. "Hey, Doc."

"Where's Jason?"

"Out again. He's got a big case he's been spending all his time on over the last few days."

"You said you've got something for me? I hope it's something good."

She grimaced. "Well…not sure how *good* it is. But you said you wanted anything I could find, so…"

He strode over and stood behind her. "What have you got?"

"I think I told you the company that did McGrath's auction got bought by another company in the Nineties, right?"

"Yes…"

"Okay. And *that* company said the stuff was probably stored in hardcopy in a warehouse somewhere?"

"Yes…"

She rolled her eyes at him. "This has been a *mess* to trace, I hope you know."

Stone made a *go on* gesture.

She picked up a legal pad and consulted some notes. "Well, they finally got back to me. They identified the warehouse where the records from that period were stored, and surprisingly it still exists. Knowing your luck, I was half-expecting it to have burned down, or been overrun by mutant space rats or something."

"Mutant space rats can be inconvenient," Stone agreed. His heart was beating faster. "So, what *did* you find?"

She gave him an airy wave. "Just hang on, boss. It took me a long time to find this, so I want to give it to you in the right order."

He pulled a chair over and dropped into it. "Fine. You've got a captive audience."

"Okay. That's better." She grinned, but then sobered. "Okay, so here's the part you might not like."

"That doesn't sound good."

"Don't know yet. By the way, you owe five hundred dollars for the search fee. Apparently, some flunky had to spend several hours digging through a bunch of seriously dusty old files to get this info. I charged it to the agency, but Jason's gonna want it back."

"I'll write him a check," he said impatiently. "What did they find?"

She turned back to her screen and pulled up a file. It looked like a photo of a handwritten list. "Fortunately, everything was arranged by lot number, and that catalog entry you gave me had the lot number." With a loud sigh, she added, "but this is the part you won't like."

"Why is that?" He leaned closer, trying to read the tiny text.

She hit a key several times, paging through the document. "The lot number for the thing you're looking for was 1723548. Believe me, I've got that memorized after all this time."

"Okay. And did you find it?"

"Just look." She reached the page she was looking for, scrolled down, and zoomed in on several rows. Then she backed away so he could move in closer.

Each row showed a lot number, a brief description of the item, the starting bid, the final selling price, the name of the purchaser, and a signature and date showing it was picked up. As soon as he got close enough to read the lines, Stone saw the source of Gina's evasion.

There it was: lot number 1723548. The description read, "black stone pedestal with markings." The starting bid was listed as twenty-five dollars.

The rest of the rows were blank. There was no selling price, purchaser name, or signature.

"Bugger," Stone murmured. "There's nothing about the purchaser. What does that mean? It was put up but nobody bought it?"

"I wondered about that too. It's the only one in the McGrath collection that doesn't have that info." She paged back slowly, then forward. "There are three pages of his stuff here, and every bit of it sold."

"So…I don't understand. Are you saying it *did* sell, but they didn't include the data?"

"That's what I thought, too. But I figured I'd better check for sure before I contacted you, so I called the auction people back and asked them." She zoomed in further on the page. "See this?"

The writing on the rows was so small and close together, Stone had missed another tiny field next to the opening bid. "It's a tick box. What's it mean?"

"See how all the other ones are checked, but this one isn't?"

"Yes…"

"That means it *wasn't* sold. As in, it wasn't even offered for sale."

He frowned. "You mean it wasn't included in the auction?"

"That's what they said. If that box is checked, it means it was put up for sale. No check, no sale."

Damn. "Did they have any ideas why?"

"No good ones, given that the auction happened fifty years ago and by a different company. But you're in luck—I got a person who actually gave half a damn about her job, so she did a little more digging for me. I think she was bored." She swung her chair around to face him. "Her best guess is that, since this was such a big collection, maybe the item was included in error. Like maybe they wrote up the descriptions from a photo, or worked off a list provided by the relatives, or something like that. Either that, or McGrath's relatives pulled that one at the last minute, after the paperwork was all completed and it was too late to delete it. I don't think you're ever going to find out for sure, unless you've got a TARDIS or something. Sorry, Doc. I think we've hit a dead end, unfortunately."

Stone sighed loudly. "Damn." It had been a long shot, for sure, but after he'd managed to find the catalog, he'd hoped they could trace the auction.

"Sorry…" Gina bowed her head, clearly dejected at her failure.

"No, no, Gina," he said hastily. She was usually so confident, almost cocky, that he sometimes forgot how young she was. "Don't worry about it. You did a brilliant job. You can't find what isn't there to find. You got us a lot farther than I expected to get, honestly. Thank you for your efforts."

She brightened. "Yeah. I just wish I could have found something better for you."

"Eh, we don't always get what we want. And I've still got a couple other leads to pursue." He stood. "Thanks again. And don't worry—I'm keeping a tab for what I owe you."

Stone's frustration overshadowed his thoughts as he drove back to Encantada.

That was it, then. The catalog had been his last solid lead to the second piece, but without the auction record showing who'd purchased it, the object could be anywhere. It could be hidden away in someone's private collection anywhere in the world, languishing in someone's attic, or even in a landfill somewhere. As much as he wanted to, there was no way, not even with all his magic, to go back fifty years and see what had happened to the thing.

He pictured the white-bearded Leander McGrath laughing at his efforts, reveling in pulling off one last disappearing act before he died, and wondered what the old man would have made of some twenty-first-century mage chasing all over the country trying to find what he probably thought of as a useless bit of kitsch.

The image reminded him of where he'd first seen the photos of McGrath—the grainy, black-and-white ones in the book Eddie had shown him back at the Library.

What if Leander McGrath actually *had* been a mage?

If he'd known the item was both magical and potentially dangerous, he might not have kept it out on display—especially if he'd realized its true nature later on.

What if he'd stored it away somewhere? Somewhere his mundane relatives didn't know about and couldn't find?

Stone tightened his grip on the steering wheel.

It wasn't possible. He was grasping at straws again. The whole thing was starting to take on all the aspects of an unhealthy obsession.

I should let this go, and concentrate on finding the people who tried to steal the pyramid.

But he was already pulling his phone out and hitting a number. He tapped the speaker button and put the phone on the dashboard.

Eddie answered on the second ring. "Evenin', Stone."

Stone heard the low hubbub of conversation, music, and clinking glasses in the background. "Are you at the Dragon?"

"Yeah, 'ere with Ward and a few other mates. What's up?"

"Listen—" He took a couple breaths and slowed his voice. "Remember that book you showed me before? The one with the writeup on Leander McGrath?"

"Yeah, why?"

"I need to look at it again."

"Right now?"

"It's important, Eddie."

Eddie sighed. "Yeah, yeah, it's always important wit' you. You seriously need to take up knittin' or origami or summat." He didn't sound annoyed, though—more amused. "Fine. You do whatever that poppin'-over thing o' yours is, and I'll meet you there in a 'alf-hour. That soon enough for ya?"

"That's fine. That's great. Rounds are on me next time."

"Too right they are. See you then."

Stone was already waiting at the Library door when Eddie's cab pulled up.

"Bloody 'ell, you *are* impatient, aren't you?" The librarian was dressed in jeans, West Ham jersey, and brown corduroy jacket. His unsteady gait as he approached told Stone he must have been at the Dancing Dragon for quite some time prior to his call. He leaned to the side in an exaggerated motion, staring at Stone from the side. "Well, your arse isn't on fire, so that's a good thing, I s'pose."

"Thanks for coming on such short notice. I had a brainwave, and I want to pursue it while it's fresh."

"Yeah, okay." He used magic to open the door and led Stone inside and back to the sitting area. "Sit ycrself down and I'll fetch it."

Stone was far too keyed up to sit, so he wandered the room, examining the collection of dusty, nonmagical books on the shelves.

"'Ere we go." Eddie swept back into the room, moving more steadily now, and dropped the heavy tome on the table. "'Ave at it."

Stone noticed with more amusement that he didn't seem in any hurry to leave. "You can go back to your mates now if you like. I'll lock up, and you know I haven't got a clue how to get to the stacks even if I wanted to."

"'S'allright. Now you've got me curious." Eddie plopped down on the brocade sofa.

"What *doesn't* get you curious?" Stone was already paging through the volume.

"Oi! This is *you* what's sayin' that? Shut up and get on with it."

He opened the book to the pages on McGrath, looking over the photos with a new eye. "Got a magnifying glass?" he asked without looking up.

Eddie levitated one over to him. "You see somethin'?"

"Not yet. Give me a moment."

At first, he didn't think he'd find anything. He studied the images from the magic shows, looking for any sign of the black pedestal in the background, but didn't see it. The photo with McGrath's son was taken outside, in a grove of trees. The others appeared to be inside McGrath's home, usually taken in front of impressive-looking bookshelves with strange artifacts on them.

Stone bent low over each of them, trying to make out anything unusual.

"What are you lookin' for?" Eddie asked. "Maybe I can 'elp."

Continuing to pore over the photos and the text, Stone told him about what Gina had discovered. "I was just thinking if the item was never sold, it might be because it was never included as part of the collection in the first place. If McGrath was a mage and had even an inkling about what it was, maybe he concealed it somewhere in his house."

Eddie leaped off the couch. "Wait!" he yelled.

"What?"

"'Old on. Be right back!" He ran out of the room, as usual without a word of explanation.

Stone was used to it by now. He returned his attention to the book, wishing the photos weren't so grainy. Half the time, it was hard to make out what was part of a bookshelf and what was merely streaks or flaws in the images.

It took Eddie longer to return this time, carrying what looked like an old periodical box.

Stone had given up squinting at the photos by that point and was reading through the text again. "What did you find?"

"Maybe nothin'. Just…do what you're doin' for a few more minutes." He slid the box out of its slipcase and spread a series of magazines across the table. The title on each of them read *The Sphinx* in old-fashioned script. He ran his gaze over them, then snatched up the first one and began riffling through it.

Stone had a hard time focusing on what he was doing, since he'd already examined the photos and the text in his book several times and nothing new was popping up. Instead, he watched Eddie gently toss aside the first magazine and pick up the second. He worked with quick efficiency, but Stone noticed the care in which he handled each one.

He got through four before he jerked his head up with a triumphant grin. "'Ere we go!" He thrust the open magazine across the table. "This is a publication for magicians, from the early part of last century. 'Ave a butcher's at this! And pay particular attention to the third paragraph in the second column on page thirty-three."

Handling the magazine with the same care Eddie had, Stone looked at the open pages. The date on the header was March, 1912. On the left side was an obviously staged publicity photo of McGrath the Magnificent in full magician's regalia: top hat, black tailed suit, and satin cape. His hands were raised in a "spellcasting" pose. On the right side, page thirty-three, another photo—somewhat more candid this time—showed McGrath in a normal suit, gripping the shoulders of a smiling boy. The caption read *Famed Midwest magician Leander McGrath hopes his son Willie, twelve years old, will follow in his magical footsteps.*

Stone soberly shifted his attention to the second column, trying not to think about how Willie McGrath had never had the chance to follow in his father's footsteps, magical or otherwise. It was a shame, but…

He tensed.

"You see it, don't you?" Eddie leaned forward eagerly.

"Bloody hell."

He read the words again, aloud this time: "*McGrath has been teaching some of his simpler tricks to his twelve-year-old son, Willie, who has lived among the trappings of magic since babyhood. The boy responded with enthusiasm when asked about his father's vocation. 'Dad's been teaching me some tricks already,' he said. 'And he lets me practice with his props as long as I'm careful. I even get to play in his hidden room at the house sometimes, but only when he's around.'*

"'*Now, now,' the elder McGrath admonishes with a chuckle. 'That's a secret, Willie, remember?'*"

He dropped the magazine and looked at Eddie. "There's a secret room in his house. Eddie—*how* did you remember this article was here? You've got copies of an obscure magazine from 1912...and you *remembered* them?"

Eddie grinned. "What can I say? We've all got our talents."

"One of these days I'm going to make you take me down to those stacks of yours. They've got to be bloody amazing." He leaped up. "Thanks. I'm running up quite a tab with you, aren't I?"

His friend waved him off. "Eh—you know you can always pay me in beer. And you've gotta tell me what you find out."

"Count on it. I've got quite a few stories to tell you, actually. But for now—I've got a house to track down. Hopefully that will be easier than what you've found here."

CHAPTER TWENTY-NINE

STONE MADE A QUICK CALL as soon as he got back to Encantada, on his way over to a second errand.

"Gina. It's Stone again. I've got an easy one for you this time."

"That'll be a change."

"I need to know where Leander McGrath's house was in Tilley, Nebraska. And please don't tell me they tore it down, or I might cry."

She laughed. "Well, we wouldn't want that. I'll find out and get back to you."

His next stop was Kolinsky's shop. To his relief, the door was unlocked this time. He found the dragon seated at his familiar rolltop desk, a large tome open in front of him.

"Good morning, Alastair," he said without turning or looking up.

"Morning. I won't take much of your time today."

Kolinsky swiveled his chair around. "I am pleased to hear that, as this new acquisition is fascinating, and I plan to spend the day perusing it."

"Not a problem. Do you remember what we discussed the other day, about helping me travel more conveniently?"

"Of course."

"Have you made any progress yet? I've got to go back to Nebraska soon, and given what happened last time I went there, I'd rather get a rental car than take a taxi."

"I have not. The individual I will be contacting is very busy, unfortunately."

"Damn." Stone sighed, even though he knew trying to get Kolinsky to do anything quickly was an exercise in futility and there wasn't anything he could do about it. "All right. Thanks, Stefan. Sorry to bother you." He turned to leave.

"Alastair."

He stopped. "Yes?"

"I might be able to help you, at least as a short-term solution."

"Oh?"

"Perhaps. For…the right inducement."

Stone frowned. "What do you have in mind?"

"I would like to examine the object you have obtained."

Ah. That wasn't a surprise. "I should have known. Sure, I'll let you do that. Not right now, though. And I won't leave it with you. It's not that I don't trust you, but I've worked too hard to keep that damned thing in my possession. I hope you understand."

"Of course."

It was almost a relief. In truth, Stone not only had no objection to the dragon taking a look at the pyramid, but he actually welcomed it. Maybe Kolinsky would come up with something he'd missed—if his luck was running particularly hot, he might even know how to make the thing work without any operating instructions that might exist. "Right, then. I'll bring it by after I get back. So, what can you do for me?"

Kolinsky turned back to his desk. "Where are you going?"

"Kearney, Nebraska. That's the nearest ley line to where I need to be. It's a ninety-minute drive to a small town called Tilley, and I'd rather not take another cab."

The dragon scanned the numerous small cubbyholes on his desk, and after a moment withdrew an envelope. He sorted through the contents and offered Stone two cards.

Stone looked them over. One was a standard company credit card in the name of "Mark Goranson" of "Azarion Holdings, Inc." The other was a driver's license with the same name, showing an address in Chicago. The photo was a generic-looking white man in his middle thirties with short brown hair. "What—? Who is this guy?"

"He does not exist." Kolinsky held up the envelope, which Stone could now see contained more cards. "Azarion Holdings is a shell corporation—one the mundane authorities would find impossible to trace back to any individual. Mr. Goranson is an employee of the corporation."

Stone grinned. "This is bloody brilliant, Stefan. So then, all I've got to do is use an illusion so I look like this bloke?"

"Just so."

"Brilliant," he said again, pocketing the cards. Then he narrowed his eyes at Kolinsky. "Is that what you're cooking up for me with your elusive friend? My own shell corporation? Is that why it's going to take so long?"

The dragon inclined his head. "Consider what you would like to name it. If you choose to proceed, my associate will require a flat fee, payable annually, to maintain the organization and create a number of available personas. Any additional personas or work outside the scope of the original agreement will incur additional expense."

Stone didn't know what to say. He wasn't sure what he'd been expecting, but having a dummy corporation set up to help him keep his increasingly-frequent travel secret wasn't it. He shook his head in wonder. "I'm not sure why I thought you'd be setting me up with some bloke in a back alley with a coat full of fake ID cards…you'll have to forgive me, Stefan. I'm clearly thinking too small."

Kolinsky gave a thin smile. "It is a habit I suggest you break as soon as possible." He nodded toward Stone's pocket, where he'd stashed the cards. "In any case, those should serve you sufficiently for a brief trip to Nebraska. I will contact you when my associate is ready."

"Thank you. I'll bring the pyramid by in the next few days—probably after the auction's over. Maybe I'll get lucky and somebody completely unrelated to any of this mess will buy the fake I swapped in."

As Stone drove through the gate to his house, his phone buzzed with a text from an unknown number.

Hey, lover, it said. *Last night was amazing. We should do it again.*

He pulled into the garage and sent an answer: *It was indeed, and we absolutely should. How are things with you?*

Everything's great. Been thinking about you all morning.

Stone smiled. He couldn't be certain, of course, but he was fairly sure she was telling him obliquely that the Ordo people who'd hired her were buying her story. If so, that gave them some breathing room, but he'd still have to remain on his guard and maintain the charade. *And I, you. I'm busy today, but dinner tonight?*

Not just dinner, I hope.

That's up to you, love. I'll call you later?

Can't wait.

Stone didn't doubt for a moment that Kolinsky's fake IDs would work as billed, and to his delight he wasn't disappointed. After tweaking his disguise amulet so he matched the Mark Goranson photo on the driver's license, he had no trouble renting a car in Kearney.

The drive from there to Tilley was much more pleasant when he was in control of both the vehicle and the musical selections, though he did get a small shiver when he passed the site of the roll-over accident on the way. He hoped the cabdriver hadn't suffered any severe or permanent injuries.

The Tilley Museum was open. Stone sat in his car in the parking lot and watched a small troop of hyperactive uniformed boys shepherded inside by a frazzled-looking woman. He waited fifteen minutes, altering his amulet illusion again to match the young man he'd been last time he'd come here, then headed inside.

To his relief, Mrs. Hodges was there, sitting behind her desk with a cup of tea and a celebrity-gossip magazine.

She smiled when she spotted him, her eyes twinkling. "Well, hello, Mike! I hadn't expected to see *you* again. I thought you said you were just passing through."

"Hello, Mrs. Hodges. I was. But then I had another thought while I was working on my paper, so I decided it was worth coming back."

"What's that, dear?"

He gave her aura a brief glance. She seemed genuinely glad to see him—probably because of the generous donation he'd made—and not at all stressed. Apparently, she was well accustomed to dealing with squirrely herds of small boys. "Well...I was looking through the auction catalog, and I thought it might be nice to include a few photos of Mr. McGrath's home in my paper. It's...still here, isn't it? It didn't burn down or anything?"

She laughed. "Oh, no, dear. It's still here. It's over on Elm Street, at the end."

That matched with what Gina had told him when she texted earlier that day.

"But I'm afraid you won't be able to get inside. The people who own it aren't here. They're visiting their grandchildren in Arizona for the month. Lovely people. The Welbergs, they're called."

"Oh, that's too bad. But I guess I could still get some photos of the outside, right?"

"I don't see why not, as long as you don't go into their yard."

"No, of course not. I wouldn't trespass." He considered. "Mrs. Hodges…you said you knew Mr. McGrath when you were young, right?"

"I did. As I said, he was a sweet, kind man."

"Did you ever…go inside his house? Did he show you any of his magic gear? I mean, I know it wouldn't have been proper for a young woman to visit an older man on her own, of course."

Again, she laughed. She had a friendly, grandmotherly laugh. "I did visit once, actually. But I wasn't alone. His wife was there too. Both of them were very kind, and sad. As I said, I don't think either of them ever got over the loss of Willie, their son."

Stone had asked Eddie to make him copies of the pages from the *Sphinx* magazine. He pulled them out now. "I found this old magazine—it had an article about Mr. McGrath in it, and I found something that really fascinated me." He pointed. "Right here, Willie says he got to play in the hidden room, and Mr. McGrath says it's supposed to be a secret." He met her gaze, trying to look as sincere and eager as possible. "Did you see it, Mrs. Hodges? *Did* he have a secret room in there?"

Her eyes widened. "Oh, my. We don't have that magazine as part of our collection. I've never seen that article before. You're quite the detective, young man."

"Thanks. I wish I could give it to you to add to the exhibit, but it's not mine. Anyway—have you ever heard about the secret room?"

"Oh, yes." She leaned in closer and whispered conspiratorially, "Now that you mention it, I've even seen it."

"No kidding?" Stone grinned. "Can you tell me about it?"

She considered. "Oh, my—I haven't thought about that room in…it must be forty years. I suppose I can tell you what I know, which isn't much. It's not like the secret can cause him trouble anymore, since the whole family line died out. Also, I doubt it's there anymore at all. The house has been sold two or three times since Mr. McGrath died, and remodeled at least once. I don't think too many people knew about the room."

Stone wondered if she was right. Even if Leander McGrath had been a genuine mage and magically concealed the room's entrance, magic faded. Especially with no ley line to sustain it. "Can you tell me about it? That story would make a great addition to my paper, too." He pulled out a notebook and a pen.

"Not much to tell, really. Like I said, I haven't thought about it since well before you were born. I barely remember it anymore. I think…" She rubbed her chin and stared off into space past him. "Yes…I think it was downstairs in the basement, hidden behind a big, built-in bookshelf. I didn't see how he opened it—he wouldn't show me that—but the room itself was about the size of a small bedroom. He kept some of his more valuable magical tricks in there, and the ones he was most afraid somebody would steal. We only spent a few moments inside, and then—"

"Hey, Lady!" A shrill voice sounded, followed an instant later by a small, wide-eyed boy pounding down the stairs.

Mrs. Hodges spun her chair around. "What is it, dear?"

"Jacob puked in the Zachary Muldoon room! All over the floor! Mrs. Torelli wants to know if you got a mop and a bucket."

"Oh, dear." Mrs. Hodges sighed. "I'm sorry, Mike, but I've got to handle this."

"That's fine," he said hastily. "Thanks for your stories. They'll be a big help. Take care."

He got out of there as the boy took the old woman by the hand and was already trying to drag her up the stairs.

This time, he didn't wait for full darkness. He saw no point. The faster he got in and out of the McGrath house, the better. At least he wouldn't have to worry about anyone being home.

As he drove over to Elm Street, he tried not to let his mind wander, but he couldn't help thinking if things went as he hoped they would, in less than an hour he'd have the other half of the magical blocker. Sure, he wouldn't have the book, if there was one—unless he got much luckier than he had a right to and McGrath had that too—but he had confidence that between himself, Eddie, and Ward, they could work out how to make the thing function.

And if not, he'd take it to Kolinsky.

Elm Street was a typical Midwest lane, lined with light snow, tall, leafless trees, and staid, middle-class houses set back from well-tended yards. As both Gina and Mrs. Hodges had indicated, Leander McGrath's former home was all the way at the end, at the edge of a grove of trees. There was more space between it and its nearest neighbor than most of the others, and a low, white-painted wrought-iron fence surrounded it. The house itself was a sprawling, two-story structure, yellow with white trim. The yard was full of whimsical birdbaths, stone statuary, and other folksy decorations.

Stone turned the car around and parked several doors down, then summoned his disregarding spell and walked back, maintaining a confident, easygoing gait that wouldn't draw any suspicion.

Getting inside was easy: brief invisibility combined with levitation got him around the back and up to one of the second-story windows. He unlocked it and slipped inside in less than ten seconds.

Using levitation once again to keep from leaving any footprints in the carpet, he drifted silently downstairs to the ground floor. It took him a little longer to find the stairs to the basement, but eventually he located the door near the pantry in the kitchen. He didn't pay much attention to the décor, except to note that it was more homespun, country kitsch and involved a lot of chickens. He wondered what Leander McGrath would have thought of the new owners' decorating style.

The basement was obviously Mr. Welberg's domain. Unlike the busy, old-fashioned style of the upper floors, this space was furnished as a "man cave," with a comfortable couch, big-screen TV, bar, pool table, and Cornhuskers and Denver Broncos memorabilia.

Still hovering, Stone turned slowly around, scanning the walls. Mrs. Hodges had said the secret room was behind a bookshelf. There was still one here, built into the left-side wall. Mr. Welberg had lined it with sports trophies, photos of himself and his buddies, stacks of hunting and fishing magazines, and a number of dusty old books he'd probably never read.

First, Stone checked with magical sight, but nothing showed up. No surprise there. If there *had* been any magic in the house, it would long ago have faded.

This would be the hard part.

To his surprise, though, it turned out not to be nearly as hard as he'd expected. He started on the far side of the shelves, using a light spell to methodically examine each one in turn and more magic to move items out of the way so he wouldn't leave any fingerprints.

The catch, when he finally located it, was on the bottom of the second shelf from the floor on the middle section. Stone had to give McGrath credit: there was no way anybody would have found it if they weren't specifically looking for it. Operating it required him to press a tiny, concealed button flush with the underside of the shelf, listen for a tiny *click,* and then pull the whole section out from the wall.

"There we go," he murmured, smiling. Finally, something was going his way. He raised his hand, shining his light spell into the space he'd revealed.

The hidden room was small—as Mrs. Hodges had said, barely the size of a tiny bedroom. It, too, was lined with shelves along three of its walls, with a wooden table in the center. Dust covered every surface, and decades-old cobwebs hung from the ceiling and the shelves.

It was quickly obvious that most of it was empty.

Only a few items, as dusty as everything else, remained on the shelves. Several boxes were piled at the room's rear, and a few more random objects—an old top hat, some battered magic props, and a small, faded empty box—lay on the table.

Stone floated closer, holding his breath to avoid a coughing fit from the dust he'd disturbed with his entry.

Was the stand not here after all?

None of the boxes were large enough to contain it, nor was it small enough to fit on the shelves. He crouched and peered under the table, but found nothing but more dust and an old pair of slippers.

No, damn it, I was so sure it was here...

He rose again, trying not to let his despair get the better of him. It *had* been a long shot, after all. Just because it made every bit of sense in the world that the object would be here didn't mean it actually was.

As he scanned the tabletop again, though, he spotted something he hadn't noticed before.

There was a square, dust-free space in the center of the table, measuring approximately one foot on each side, as if someone had recently removed something.

He tensed, remembering the dimensions he'd seen for the stand in the McGrath auction catalog.

At its base, it had measured twelve inches square.

But if it had been here, who had taken it?

He held up his hand, moving the light spell over the table's full surface, and only then did it reveal the answer.

Someone had used a finger to draw a symbol in the dust, directly below where the object had been removed.

"No…" Stone murmured, clenching his fists. "Damn it, no…"

He knew that symbol all too well—and also knew why whoever had beaten him here had left it there.

Ordo Purpuratus had gotten here first.

And now they were taunting him.

CHAPTER THIRTY

THE DRIVE BACK TO KEARNEY seemed to take considerably longer than the one to Tilley had, mostly because Stone had been full of hope before and now he was brimming with frustration and a growing sense of defeat.

Until he'd seen the contents of the secret room, he'd had only a speculation that Ordo Purpuratus had joined the search for the magic nullifier. Now he was sure of it.

He was also sure they knew *he* was after it.

That was probably why they'd sent Eleanor after him. They had the bottom part now, and they needed the top part to make the thing work. Stone had no doubt their people were as capable of figuring out its workings as he and his friends were, even if the book did exist and they didn't have it.

Or maybe they *did* have it.

If so, they had two out of the three pieces, and would be even more desperate to get their hands on the third.

As he drove, he pulled out his burner phone and tapped in a number. "Hello, Jason."

"Hey, Al. I'm guessing you're somewhere you shouldn't be if you're calling from one of your burners."

"I'm in Nebraska again. There was a secret room in McGrath's old house, so I checked it. I thought what I was looking for might be there."

"I'm also guessing from your tone that it didn't go well. You okay?"

"Define 'okay.' Nobody attacked me, if that's what you mean."

"But it wasn't there?"

"It *was* there. Operative word: 'was.'"

"I don't get it."

"Somebody beat me to it."

Jason let out a long sigh. "Shit. How do you know it was there, if you didn't find it?"

"Because there was a spot on the table exactly the same size as the bottom of it. And because whoever took it left a message in the dust right next to it."

"A message?"

"For whoever got there after they did. They were taunting me—or whoever they expected to show up after them."

"Do you know who it was?"

"I do. It was the Ordo."

Long pause. "You mean those rich asshole mages your family used to be connected with?"

"The very ones. They're operating in America now, apparently, and they're after this thing. And now they've got part of it."

"Yikes. So there are three groups after it now—you, them, and those Portas people."

"Possibly four. Don't forget that government organization that contacted Blum."

Another long pause. "Damn, Al, you really *can't* do anything the easy way. So what do you want to do now?"

"I've got to get back home, and I've got some plans for later to-night. I suppose our next step is to attend the auction. It's this Saturday at six p.m. in San Francisco. Can you and Amber make it? I'd like to have as many eyes on the place as possible."

"Yeah, sure, of course we can be there. Have you contacted V yet?"

"Not yet. Can you do that for me? I need to call Blum, too. I don't know if he'll want to go, but as I said, the more the merrier."

"Sure, I'll talk to V. I doubt she'll want to miss it."

"Thank you, Jason."

He was about to hang up when Jason spoke again. "Wait—where did you say you were?"

"Nebraska."

"There's no portal near there, right? I thought you said you had something to do tonight. How are you gonna get home from there that fast?"

"Sorry—line's cutting out. Rubbish reception. Talk to you soon." He flipped the little phone shut and tossed it on the passenger seat.

When he got home, he debated whether to call Eleanor. On the one hand, he did need to maintain the charade that he'd fallen for her, for her own safety. On the other—what if her employers had known all along that things weren't as they seemed, and they were playing him every bit as much as he thought he was playing *them?*

What if *she* was playing him?

Bugger it, he thought. If he let himself spin off wild speculations like that, he'd second-guess himself into inaction. He couldn't afford to do that.

He retrieved his real phone and sent a text: *Still up for dinner tonight?*

Her answer came quickly: *Sure. I've been looking forward to it.*

Brilliant. He realized she hadn't told him where she was staying; he doubted she actually lived in Sunnyvale. High-end mercenaries didn't live in Sunnyvale. *Where shall I pick you up?*

I'll meet you there. My place is a mess.

He smiled. That was an easy way to get around revealing her location to him.

"You seem preoccupied tonight." Eleanor tilted her head at him from across the table.

"Long day, I suppose."

"I didn't think teaching college would be so draining." She sipped her wine and shot him a challenging glance.

"You'd be surprised."

He'd been watching her surreptitiously throughout the meal, sneaking peeks at her aura when he thought she wasn't looking. So far, he hadn't spotted any sign of deception or duplicity. If anything, she seemed amused by their little game, as if she was enjoying putting something over on her former employers.

She'd done her research, in any case, spending part of the main course telling him a funny story about how the CEO and the lead engineer got sloshed at her tech start-up's holiday party and ended up standing on the conference table singing "Who Let the Dogs Out?".

"Maybe you should add that one to your setlist," she suggested. "I crack up every time I hear it now."

"I'll suggest it."

"No, you won't."

"No, I won't."

They continued their light banter through dinner, and didn't drop the act until they were back at Stone's house, safely behind his wards.

"Did they give you any trouble when you told them you were unsuccessful?" he asked as they sipped more wine in front of the fireplace downstairs, with Raider curled on the top of the sofa behind them.

"No. They were disappointed, but I'm pretty sure they weren't surprised."

"But they still think I've got the pyramid."

"I get that impression. They think you might have taken it overseas. The guy I talked to kind of lit up when I mentioned you'd invited me to your place in England." She snuggled against him. "So, you were serious about that—you actually *have* a place in England?"

"I do."

"*Is* that where you're keeping this thing?"

He checked her aura again, but it hadn't changed beyond showing mild curiosity. "I told you before—I haven't got it. As far as I know, it's being sold at auction this Saturday."

"Why don't I believe you?"

He shrugged. "You don't have to believe me. Regardless of whether I'm telling the truth, if I *did* have it, it's somewhere your employers will never get their greedy little hands on it. So there's no point discussing it, is there?"

"Hey, I don't care. Your bank transfer came through, so as far as I'm concerned, I'm working for you." She rolled her head around to face him. "One of my better jobs, actually. Especially the fringe benefits. Speaking of which…"

"You're reading my mind."

CHAPTER THIRTY-ONE

*I*s everyone in position?

Stone sent the text from his seat at the end of a row, half-way back along the bank of chairs in the San Francisco auditorium where the auction was being held. He shifted to magical sight again and scanned the crowd in front of him, but aside from the expected baseline anticipation, he didn't see anything that caught his attention.

Ready, Verity sent. She was in the back row, where she could watch the remainder of the crowd. *People are still taking their seats.*

I'm good, came Jason's reply. He loitered at the back of the hall, keeping an eye on the double entrance doors where people were coming in.

Good to go. Amber was the floater; she was stationed in the lobby now, but after the auction began her job was to patrol the perimeter and watch for anything unusual outside.

I'm set. Blum was near one of the hall's two side exit doors.

Good, Stone said. *Say something right away if you see anything out of the ordinary.*

If we even know what that is, he thought, glancing up to scan the old auditorium's high rafters for any sign of invisible or lurking people.

He had tried to focus on his work for the rest of the week, but the effort hadn't been much help.

When he'd called Blum a couple days ago, the detective had immediately agreed to come along and help keep watch, but he hadn't heard anything about anyone breaking in to the location where the Drummond collection was being stored.

"That's good, I suppose," Stone told him when they spoke again on the day of the auction. "I'm not sure whether it means they're all biding their time, or they've managed to sneak in there and nick the thing without anyone noticing. I suppose we'll find out soon." In truth, it didn't matter either way: if someone had stolen it, they'd soon find out it was a fake. So even if the thieves were from the Ordo, that still didn't put them any closer to reuniting the two pieces.

"I'm not sure exactly what you're planning to do, and that makes me a little nervous if you want the truth."

"Yes. Well." Stone had hoped he wouldn't catch on to that. "If you *do* want the truth, *I'm* not exactly sure what I'm planning either, other than to post our group in various strategic areas and try keeping an eye on as many people bidding on that pyramid as possible."

"Okay, but what then? Are you going to chase down whoever ends up buying it? What if it's not somebody from the groups you're after? As a cop, I can't exactly condone snatching somebody off the street. Especially since we both know the thing they're buying is a fake."

"I'm…planning to play that part by ear. It will be useful to identify the players, even if all we do is watch."

"I guess. Are you gonna bid on the thing?"

"I am, yes. I doubt it will fool anyone who thinks I've already got it, but it would look odd if I *didn't* bid."

Now, he sat in his seat next to a large, intense-looking woman, alternating between his magical-sight checks and flipping through the auction program they'd given him along with his bid paddle when he'd registered. There was another large collection before

Drummond's and still another after; the pyramid's lot number was halfway through the Drummond set. That was promising, he supposed. He hoped the fact that it hadn't been removed meant the fake was still where it belonged. He glanced at his watch. One way or another, he'd know in about an hour.

·The time passed slowly. The collection before Drummond's had nothing to do with either the occult or magic—it was a bunch of paintings, sculptures, and other art objects belonging to some wealthy deceased couple from Atherton. Stone paid more attention to the crowd than the items for sale, but it didn't help much. Clearly, quite a few people in the audience were very interested in these objects, and their auras flared their excitement every time a bid was increased. It was hard to spot auric anomalies among this much background disturbance.

His phone buzzed with a message from Blum. *Don't look, but the guy two rows back from you in the middle is checking you out.*

It took all Stone's willpower not to turn around, but he managed. *What does he look like?*

Hard to tell from here. White guy, blond hair, wearing a blue sweater.

Can you see him from where you are, Verity?

Several seconds passed. The auctioneer droned on with his fast-talking spiel, as all around Stone people raised their paddles to bid on a large, framed oil painting of a pastoral scene.

Yeah, she finally responded. *I see him. He's not watching just you, but he's definitely shot a couple glances in your direction. Can't see his face from here. His aura's orange, only one that color in the row.*

All right, he sent back. *Keep an eye on him, but don't lose sight of everything else. Jason? Amber?*

Nothing out here, Amber sent back. *Pretty quiet.*

Same here, Jason sent. *Not too many people coming in now.*

Stone looked at his program. There were still several more items to go in the previous collection. *Going to get coffee and see if I can spot Blue Sweater.*

He dropped his program on his chair to indicate it was taken, shot a confirming glance at the woman next to him, then got up and took a quick scan of the crowd while walking toward the rear of the auditorium. He switched to magical sight, and immediately identified the orange aura Verity had mentioned. He couldn't take more than an instant's look, but that was all it took to be sure he'd never seen the man before.

He shook his head at Verity and continued on to buy a cup of coffee from the small concession area set up in the lobby. By the time he returned to his seat, the auctioneer was on the final item from the collection before Drummond's.

Here we go, he sent to the group. *Eyes open.*

A few people got up and left, including the large woman sitting next to Stone, and a few more came in and took their seats. Stone didn't need magical sight to pick up the change in the room's ambient energy—the crowd interested in Drummond's occult collection didn't have much in common with the mostly older, wealthy types bidding on the Atherton couple's conventional art collection.

A thin woman in a stylish jacket slipped past Stone and took the seat next to him, nodding politely as she went by. He paid her no attention until his phone buzzed again.

That lady next to you has a two-tone aura, Verity sent. *Careful.*

Once again, Stone had to fight the temptation to take a look with magical sight. Instead, he merely turned a little as if scanning the crowd so he could catch a mundane glimpse. She had dark hair, a pinched, pale face, and sharp gray eyes. He didn't recognize her. She seemed to be pointedly ignoring both him and the man sitting on her other side.

On stage, the auctioneer began with the first item in the Drummond collection—a life-sized, carved wooden skull decorated with striking primitive artwork. Bidding was brisk, with several people around the room raising their paddles. The auctioneer was about to close the sale when a murmur rose from the other end of Stone's row. Someone else had increased the bid at the last second before the gavel came down.

Nobody contested, so the skull went to the late bidder.

Stone's phone buzzed again.

You know who that is? Blum asked.

No, why?

That's Chaz DaCosta.

He almost said "who?" but then the name clicked. *Are you sure?*

Pretty sure. Wonder why a famous magician's bidding on this junk? Think he knows?

Stone pondered. Chaz DaCosta was indeed a famous mundane magician—his shows had been featured on cable television, and he had a standing gig at one of the mid-sized Las Vegas casinos. In his act, he was known for being flamboyant and high-energy, with wild costumes and pounding music. He was also known for being a collector of all sorts of odd, magic-related paraphernalia.

Apparently, a few other people had recognized DaCosta too, judging from the hubbub at the other end of Stone's row. Even the severe woman next to him glanced in his direction.

Don't know. Keep an eye on him, Stone sent to the group.

It was a good call. As the next few items came up and were quickly handled, Chaz DaCosta bid on most of them—and won every one he bid on. He used the same method every time: waiting until the bids slowed down and then raising his own paddle to swoop in and take the prize. Sometimes, he'd bark a triumphant laugh when he won.

Stone scanned the crowd with magical sight again, and immediately noticed a few red flashes of frustration he hadn't seen before. DaCosta clearly had more money to throw around than most of these casual bidders who'd expected to pick something up for a pittance, and it wasn't sitting well.

The auction progressed in much the same way for the next several items, with DaCosta winning the bids for all but a few he didn't seem interested in.

And then the black pyramid was the next item. Stone tensed, his heartbeat picking up, and focused on keeping his aura under control. Next to him, the severe-looking woman seemed more watchful too. He shielded his phone screen and sent to the group: *Heads up. Here we go.*

"Next," the auctioneer said, "we've got Lot 265436, a black pyramid-shaped stone sculpture measuring six inches on a side, decorated with carved symbols." He indicated the table next to him, where an assistant had brought the pyramid out and placed it on a lighted stand. "We'll start the bid at twenty-five dollars."

As Stone had expected, bidding was brisk and fast. He tried to identify everyone involved, but from his seat he had to rely on his friends to do it. Once, when he glanced over at Blum, he saw the detective surreptitiously snapping photos with his phone.

The bid was up to five hundred dollars now, and the crowd rumbled with anticipation. So far, nothing in the collection had gone for anything close to that much, or had that much interest. Most of the casual bidders had dropped out by now.

Other people were craning their necks to spot the major bidders, so Stone felt more secure doing the same thing now. He quickly identified five people vying for the pyramid aside from himself: the severe woman seated next to him; Chaz DaCosta, who had given up his sniping strategy and was looking grumpy; the blond man in the blue sweater; a middle-aged man who looked like someone's suburban dad, near the front row; and a young, red-haired woman at the rear of the auditorium. Stone also noticed that all five of them seemed as interested in each other—and him—as they were in raising their bids.

"Five hundred."

"Five-fifty."

"Six hundred."

Stone raised his paddle when the auctioneer called for six-fifty. All around, the spectators were getting more excited, almost like a crowd at a closely-contested football game.

Finally, it seemed that Chaz DaCosta had grown impatient with the slow pace. He thrust his paddle up and yelled, "Two thousand dollars!"

The crowd gasped. Surely, that would put an end to this crazy bidding run-up for an obscure and mostly unimpressive-looking gewgaw from a collection that had otherwise generated lackluster interest.

But no, the woman next to Stone raised her paddle again. She wore an even grimmer expression than normal.

"Twenty-one hundred from the lady in the sixth row!" the auctioneer called. "Do I hear twenty-two?"

Blue Sweater's paddle went up.

"Twenty-two! Do I hear twenty-three?"

"Three thousand!" Chaz DaCosta cried. He was looking downright angry now, shooting glares at the other bidders. Next to him, a young man was trying to talk some sense into him. Clearly, he didn't respond well to having his whims thwarted.

Stone, who had no intention of winning the bid for the fake pyramid, decided to see if he could throw a spanner in the works and hasten the end of the auction. He raised his paddle. "Five thousand dollars," he called in a clear voice. He aimed an amused, satisfied smile at nobody in particular.

The crowd gasped even louder, and he heard a whispered "holy shit!" from a couple rows back. Even the auctioneer looked shocked.

If looks could kill, Chaz DaCosta would have turned Stone into a fine red mist about this point. Pretending not to notice, Stone glanced at the woman next to him and then back around to look at Blue Sweater and the red-haired woman.

They were both glaring at him, narrow-eyed and grim.

"Six thousand!" DaCosta yelled, poking his paddle up like he was trying to puncture a balloon hovering above his head.

Stone realized most of the crowd—including, most likely, DaCosta—had no idea why such an obscure little item had garnered so much interest. Even if some of them had heard about the break-in at the University, as far as he knew nobody except himself and his friends were aware the pyramid had been the subject of that break-in. Blum, who'd been keeping watch on the case since shortly after the theft occurred, had told Stone no one had ever discovered what the thief had been after. The auction people had no doubt catalogued the entire collection prior to the auction and found nothing missing.

"Do I hear sixty-one hundred?" The auctioneer, clearly aware now that he had no idea where this whole mess was going, seemed to be having a good time with it now.

The redhead raised her paddle.

Stone made a show of looking disappointed, as if he'd just realized he'd nearly won a bid he couldn't cover, and lowered his hand. He didn't smile, but he wanted to: now, as a failed bidder disappointed at being priced out of the fun, he had every justification to turn around and watch the other bidders. No doubt at least some of them knew who he was, but what were they going to do—tell him to stop looking at them? It wasn't as if he was the only one doing it. Not even close. The whole crowd was into the spirit of the thing now, living vicariously through this bunch of rich weirdos who'd drop serious cash on some stupid shelf trinket.

"Sixty-two! Do I hear sixty-two hundred?"

Stone scanned the crowd. For the first time, nobody else seemed to be bidding. Was the red-haired woman going to get it for that price?

"Okay, we have sixty-two hundred. Going once! Going—"

"Ten thousand dollars, damn it!"

Chaz DaCosta didn't just raise his paddle this time. He leaped out of his chair, whirling around to glare defiance at the other bidders.

For the first time, Stone got a good look at him. He was in his late twenties, his pale cheeks flushed with adrenaline, his eyes flashing, his mop of dark hair flopping over his forehead. Instead of one of the trademark flamboyant outfits he wore in his shows, he was dressed in slacks and a leather jacket. His bright-yellow aura was awash in red patches. Whether he knew the pyramid was more than it appeared or merely wished to own every part of Hiram Drummond's collection that interested him, he obviously had his sights set on winning it.

Stone—and most of the rest of the crowd—swiveled their heads to check out the remaining four bidders. All of them wore variations on the same expression: frustrated annoyance, tinged with confusion. Stone was sure all of them had come here to try obtaining the prize quietly and without fanfare, and now here was this glitzy, show-biz idiot doing his best to draw the entire crowd's attention to the whole thing.

"The bid is ten thousand dollars," the auctioneer was saying, his gavel hovering over his podium. "Ten thousand going once. Ten thousand going twice…"

The crowd held its collective breath.

The gavel slammed down with authority. "*Sold* for ten thousand dollars to bidder number eighty-seven!"

"Yes!" DaCosta pumped his fist and shot a fierce, gloating grin around the room. He didn't say, "Take *that,* losers!" but he might as well have.

Stone was more interested in what the other bidders would do. Would they remain, now that the pyramid was no longer available?

Would they try stealing it before DaCosta, who was already focused on the next object up for sale, could collect it?

Or, even worse, would they lie in wait for DaCosta *after* he picked it up?

The woman next to Stone got up and slipped past him with a sour look and no "excuse me." After she'd stalked away toward the rear of the auditorium, Stone pulled out his phone.

A message immediately popped up from Jason. *That was weird. Are we staying?*

Yes, he sent back. *Blum, keep an eye on the backstage area where they're holding the sold items. Jason and Verity, watch the other bidders. I'll watch DaCosta. Amber, a woman with dark hair is leaving. Make sure she doesn't hide somewhere.*

You think they're gonna jump him? Jason sent.

Thought has crossed my mind.

The auction progressed. By the end, Stone was convinced Chaz DaCosta was not only what he appeared to be—a mundane with an interest in odd artifacts and more money than sense—but also that he had no idea there was anything unusual about the pyramid. He continued bidding on a large number of remaining items in the Drummond collection, mostly winning them for fairly low prices because nobody wanted to bid against him. He did get into one more bidding war, over the non-Egyptian sarcophagus Stone had seen in the storeroom back at the University, but the woman opposing him wasn't part of the group interested in the pyramid. Stone bid on, and won, the magical herbalism tome, which DaCosta showed no interest in.

His phone buzzed again. *Blue Sweater is leaving,* Verity sent.

Other woman left, Amber sent. *I followed her to her car. She drove off.*

Watch Blue Sweater, Stone sent. *And keep an eye on the others. Going to pick up my purchase.*

He had an ulterior motive for bidding on the book, aside from thinking it would be a useful gift for Verity: it gave him an excuse to be in the small side chamber where they were handling payments and collections. From previous affairs like this he'd attended, he knew the winning bidders, once they'd paid for their purchases, had the option to either pick them up on site or have them shipped. DaCosta, most likely, would choose the latter since he'd bought so many things. Unless his frazzled assistant had brought a truck, anyway.

Stone took his place in line as the auction continued with the last, non-Drummond lot. DaCosta was already there, standing off to the side while his assistant held his place in the queue. The young magician was basking in the attention he was getting from several other buyers, but he grinned at Stone when he spotted him.

"Sorry for outbidding you, man. Shouldn't have gone so high. I get what I want, y'know?"

Stone shrugged. "It's not a problem. You probably saved me from spending more than I wanted to anyway."

"Yeah, no hard feelings."

"Of course not." Stone moved up a couple positions as others collected their items. When the assistant was next in line, he motioned DaCosta over.

The magician came reluctantly, unwilling to move away from his little group of admirers. "What?"

"I'd keep an eye on that pyramid, if I were you."

His eyes narrowed. "Why do you say that?"

Again, Stone shrugged. "A lot of people seem interested in it. I'm just saying you should keep it somewhere safe."

"You think someone's going to steal it?" He laughed contemptuously. "Do you know who I am? I've got full security on my collection. Anybody'd be an idiot to try breaking in."

"Suit yourself. I'm sure you're right."

DaCosta drifted off, but Stone didn't miss the sudden uncertainty in his aura. When the assistant reached the front of the line, he swapped places with his boss.

"I'll bring the car around to the front," he told DaCosta.

"Yeah, okay. I'll be there when I'm done."

Stone pulled out his phone and sent a text. *Anything?*

Blue Sweater left, Verity sent back. *Redhead and Dad Bod are in the lobby. Not together.*

Nothing happening back here, Blum sent. *They've got heavy security watching the stuff.*

Good, Stone sent. *DaCosta's assistant just left to get their car. Amber, can you watch? Skinny young man in a sport jacket and jeans. Make sure nobody's got eyes on the car.*

On it.

Satisfied that everything outside was being handled, Stone waited for DaCosta to finish. It took quite some time since he had so many items to pay for and sign off on. To Stone's surprise, though, when the magician finished, he stepped aside and a few moments later a security guard came out carrying a box.

DaCosta took it, peeked inside, and flashed Stone a grin. "Later, man." He headed out, the guard following him.

The other two other people ahead of Stone in line quickly completed their business. Only five minutes had passed when Stone had taken possession of the herbalism tome. He stepped out of line and texted again:

Report? Amber?

I'm on the roof of the auction building. The assistant brought the car around. Silver Mercedes sedan. Nice ride. DaCosta was carrying a box. He came out with a guard and got in, and they drove off. The guard went back inside. I don't see any sign of anyone following them.

Verity? Are the others still here?

Dad Bod is back in the auditorium. Redhead still in the lobby.

I'm keeping an eye on her, Jason sent. *She seems to be waiting for somebody.*

Still nothing backstage, Blum sent. *Pyramid's gone. Okay to come out now?*

Yes. Stone frowned. This wasn't going anything like he expected. He'd been certain that either one of the groups after the pyramid would have won the bid, or else somebody would have assaulted or followed DaCosta on his way out. He'd obviously taken the pyramid with him in the box, probably spooked by Stone's words.

Stone left the side room, walking slowly and deep in thought. Something was wrong here.

"Hmm…" he muttered under his breath. "What if…?"

Maybe the oddness he was looking for was DaCosta himself. What if the magician had been the X-factor, and nobody else had expected him to show up and be interested in the collection? From the look on the other bidders' faces, they were annoyed about it—but why did they suddenly drop the bid and let DaCosta have the pyramid? If he was right and the Ordo and Portas were among the bidders, those organizations certainly had enough money to put up a lot more than ten thousand dollars to secure something this valuable to them.

But what if they didn't need to?

Stone smiled mirthlessly. Of course—it made sense. Why draw attention to themselves by spending insane amounts of money for something most of the crowd thought was relatively worthless, when they could let the eccentric DaCosta draw all the eyeballs, spend his own money, and then conveniently arrange to relieve him of what they wanted later?

DaCosta had said he had heavy security on his collection, though—which meant if he had the pyramid on him now, their safest option would be to catch him before he got it home.

Stone's phone buzzed.

He pulled it out and was about to check the message and text the others when a voice called from in front of him: "Dr. Alastair Stone?"

All he saw before he jerked his head up was that there were two messages, from Jason and Verity. When he saw who was standing in front of him, he thought he probably knew what those messages had been about.

The two individuals Verity had dubbed "Dad Bod" and "Redhead" were watching him with calm interest, but their auras were on high alert.

"Er...do I know you two?"

"You don't." Redhead nodded toward the book under his arm. "I see you won at least one of the things you were bidding on."

"Oh. Yes. It's a tome on the practices of herbalism in various occult traditions. I think it will be fascinating reading." He scanned the auditorium. The auction was still going on, so most of the crowd was focused on the auctioneer. He didn't see Blum or Amber, but Jason and Verity were near the exit doors, watching him with concern.

"Not nearly as fascinating as that black pyramid, though," Dad Bod said conversationally. "Are you upset that you lost it to the magician kid?"

"Ten thousand dollars is a lot of money for something that's probably just gonna sit on a bookshelf somewhere looking cool," Redhead added.

"No, not at all. I'm actually relieved, to be honest. I...er...got a bit ahead of myself. Heat of the moment, you know?" Stone kept his voice light to hide his inner turmoil. The longer these two held him off, the longer it would be before he could share his ideas with his friends. Someone could already be hijacking DaCosta's car. "Is there something I can do for you two? I've really got to get going—"

"Oh, sure, no problem. We won't keep you long."

Stone noticed that both of them had subtly moved to block his forward progress—not enough that he couldn't get past them or flank them if he was sufficiently motivated, but he'd have to make more of a commitment than he knew he should. "What do you want?"

"We're just curious," Dad Bod said. "We know there was a break-in at Stanford a while back. Someone got into the storeroom where Hiram Drummond's collection was being stored."

"Yes. It was in all the papers." By now, Jason was approaching cautiously from the side.

"You were inside that storeroom, weren't you?"

Stone narrowed his eyes. "Is this an interrogation, Mr.—"

"No, no, of course not. We're just curious, is all. You've got nothing to hide, do you?"

"Of course I don't."

"So, you wouldn't mind answering a few questions?" Redhead asked.

"Not until you tell me who you are. As far as I know, you could be reporters for some dodgy publication."

Dad Bod chuckled. "No, nothing like that." He pulled out a wallet and flashed a badge.

"You're police?"

"Not exactly police," Redhead said. "We work for a government agency."

"Ah. And clearly you can't reveal which one, or you would have. Which is unfortunate, because you could have bought that badge at a second-hand store."

Dad Bod sighed. "Dr. Stone, we're not your enemies. If anything, from everything I've heard about you, we're on the same side. And to be honest with you, we think that black pyramid is more than it seems—and we're pretty sure you do too."

Stone tilted his head. "I've got no idea what you're talking about...er...what should I call you? Agent? Officer? Captain?"

The two exchanged glances.

Jason approached. "Al, we need to go. Everything okay?"

"Everything's fine. I'll be there in just a moment. I'll meet you in the lobby."

"Yeah, okay." He headed off with obvious reluctance.

Stone focused back on the two agents. "Listen—I don't know what you think, but I know nothing about it. I'm just a university professor with a bit too much money and an interest in occult artifacts. That's why I'm here. Now, if you'll excuse me—"

"Of course. Sorry to bother you, Dr. Stone. Have a good day."

Stone slipped past them and hurried out to the lobby. His heart was pounding, but not entirely from stress. So, one of the players in this little game had revealed themselves at last. Sort of, at least. He still didn't know exactly who or what they were, but at least now his suspicion that somebody in the mundane government had taken an interest in the pyramid had proven correct. If they knew what it was, that could make things even more interesting.

Verity, Jason, and Blum were already in the lobby when Stone arrived.

Verity hastened up to him. "Are you okay?"

"Of course."

"Who were those people?"

"They were from the government…though I'm not at all sure they were here to help me." He aimed a significant glance at Blum. "But that's irrelevant at the moment. We've got to find DaCosta."

Verity frowned. "Why?"

At that point, Amber strode inside. "They're gone," she said. "I watched them through my binoculars as long as I could, and nobody bothered them. Not surprising, given the traffic around here."

"You think DaCosta's in danger?" Blum asked, glancing toward the door.

"Quite possibly," Stone said. "He's a mundane, and unless I miss my guess, he took the pyramid with him. I doubt those other groups are going to give up so easily, and it would be nothing for either of them to overpower him. I could do it in a heartbeat, and I suspect they have fewer scruples than I do."

He glanced at Amber, who seemed distracted, sniffing the air. "Something wrong?"

She didn't answer right away. Instead, she raised her head and sniffed again, looking like a wolf who'd caught a scent. Her expression turned grim. "I think I smell blood."

Everyone stared at her. "Blood?" Blum looked around in confusion. "Where? I don't see anything."

She still looked preoccupied, barely paying attention to her friends as she turned slowly. "Not far. Definitely blood. This way." She pointed toward a closed door behind the concession table.

The older woman behind the table stood as they tried to move past her. "You can't come back here," she protested.

"We think our friend is there," Jason said, ignoring her. Amber had already reached the door.

"Nobody's back here, young man." Now she was looking angry. "That door is locked."

"Are you sure?" Stone asked. He shielded Verity with his body so she could pop the lock.

"It's not locked," Verity said brightly, shoving it open. "Look, see? Open."

"Now, just a moment!" the woman protested. "If you don't leave right now, I'm calling security!"

For all the difference her words made, she might as well have been talking to her coffee urn. Stone, Verity, Jason, Amber, and Blum all swept by.

"It's definitely here," Amber said. "It's stronger now."

They were standing in a hallway with two doors along it. Amber immediately pointed to the one directly in front of them. It was unlabeled—probably an office. "There."

Stone tried the door, expecting it to be locked. Instead, it swung open readily. He strode inside, magical sight active.

It wasn't necessary. It was easy to spot what Amber had smelled. Chaz DaCosta's assistant lay on the floor, his hands and feet bound, clearly unconscious. A small, spreading puddle of dark blood stained the floor under his head.

"Oh, no," Verity muttered, already rushing over to drop next to him.

"Is he dead?" Blum already had his phone out.

"No," Amber said. "But he needs help fast."

Stone crouched next to the young man. He looked pale, but his breathing seemed regular. "Can you help him, Verity? We won't have much time."

"I'll try."

The door flew open to admit the coffee woman, now accompanied by a uniformed security guard.

"What the hell—?" the guard began. "Hey! Get away from that guy!"

Blum flashed his badge. "SFPD. We've got this under control. Already called for help. Watch the door, and make sure nobody comes in here except the people who need to be here."

"But—" the coffee woman spluttered, her sharp gaze darting between all the people in the room. "How did you—?"

The security guard was already obeying orders. "I got this," he told Blum, and began gently herding the coffee woman back outside.

"What happened?" Jason demanded. He backed off to give Verity room to work as Stone broke the zip-ties binding the assistant. "Amber, I thought you said you saw the guy leave with DaCosta."

"I *did.* Clear as day."

"But she was on the roof," Stone said grimly. "Too far for a good scent. And she never got the real assistant's scent in the first place."

"Illusion?" Verity didn't look up from her work.

"Has to be. Not quite sure how they managed it, but they must have waylaid him somehow and stashed him in here, then used illusion to impersonate him."

"Damn," Jason said. "So they could be anywhere by now. If DaCosta doesn't catch on that it's not his real assistant in the car with him..."

Blum got on his phone again. "I'll put out a BOLO on the car and both of them. Amber, did you get a plate number?"

"Yeah." She gave it to him. "Silver Mercedes S-Class, a year or two old."

He looked surprised she'd noticed. "Good job."

"They won't stay in the car any longer than they have to," Stone said. "We do have one thing working in our favor, though."

"What's that?" Jason asked.

"I don't think whoever did this expected DaCosta to be here—and certainly didn't expect him to keep raising the bid for the pyramid. I'm guessing they had to deviate from their original plan. That might make them sloppy."

"That's a pretty slim hope."

"It's all we've got right now. We can do a ritual to try finding DaCosta if we can get something of his, but that will take time. How's the assistant doing, Verity?"

She rose from her crouch, looking tired but satisfied. "I think he'll be okay. I caught it fast and it actually wasn't as bad as it looked. Head wounds can bleed a lot, even when they're not |serious."

Stone didn't want to wait around for the ambulance and other emergency personnel to arrive, but he didn't have a lot of choice. It would look suspicious if he left now, and in any case there wasn't much they could do since they didn't have anything to use as a tether object to track DaCosta. Nonetheless, he itched to get out there and do something.

They were in the middle of San Francisco, so it didn't take long for the ambulance to arrive, accompanied by a pair of uniformed SF cops. The EMTs hurried in with a gurney and immediately set about examining the assistant, while the cops took Stone and the others to the other side of the room.

Blum showed them his badge. "Detective Leo Blum," he said, and gave them his station name.

The cops exchanged glances. "What are you doing here, Detective? This isn't your end of town."

"Off duty. Attending the auction with some friends." He introduced Stone and the others. "Dr. Stone's a professor down at Stanford. Occult stuff's his specialty, and a lot of it was up for auction earlier."

"You know who this guy is?" one of the EMTs spoke up. "I can't find any ID on him."

"I don't know his name," Stone told him. "But he's the assistant to Mr. Chaz DaCosta, who may have been abducted."

"Oh, right," one of the cops said. "Is that the silver Mercedes we just got the BOLO about?"

"Yeah." Blum paced as he talked.

"So who whacked this guy?"

"We don't know yet. How's he doing?" he called to the EMTs.

"Not too bad." They were already loading him on the gurney. He hadn't regained consciousness yet, but he looked better than before, following Verity's healing. "I thought it was gonna be a lot worse, but he seems stable. Just a little banged up. Excuse us, please."

Stone and the others stood back as they wheeled the assistant out.

"Okay," said the other cop. "Just need to ask you some questions, and then you can go."

Stone sighed and exchanged frustrated glances with Blum. There was no helping it, though. He leaned against the edge of the desk and waited.

"Well…that was a lot weirder than I expected," Verity said.

She, Jason, Amber, and Stone were walking to the parking garage across the street. The cops' "few questions" had ended up taking nearly half an hour, and by the time they were allowed out of the office, the third auction was over and most of the attendees had left. Only a few remained, resisting the security guards' efforts to move them out.

"No kidding," Jason said. "Al, do you know who all those people were? The ones we were watching?"

"Not specifically. Though I'd be quite surprised if they didn't include members of the Ordo, Portas…and as I said before, some sort of government agency, apparently."

"Are those the two who were talking to you before?" Amber asked. "The ones Verity called Dad Bod and Redhead?"

"Yes, so it would seem. They wouldn't tell me which agency, though. I suspect they've got some idea that the pyramid is something special." Stone realized he was still carrying the book under his arm, and offered it to Verity. "Oh—here. Got this for you."

She stared at the cover in wonder. "For me? Why?"

"Thought you and Hezzie might find it interesting." He gave her a sideways glance. "You didn't think *I* was interested in magical horticulture, did you?"

"Well, I'll admit I *did* wonder," she said dryly. "Thanks, Doc. I think it'll be a great reference for our alchemy stuff."

"You guys want to go get some dinner?" Jason asked, glancing at his watch. "I'm starving."

Stone didn't think he could sit still long enough for dinner. "I'm going to beg off, I think. Still got a few things to do tonight. Thank you—all of you—for helping out with the auction. I owe you. Later, after all this is over, I'll take you out for a truly memorable dinner."

"Right now," Jason said, "I'd just settle for a big plate of burgers."

Stone used the ley line to return home, but couldn't focus on much. His mind was stuck on wondering what had become of DaCosta, and what would happen when whoever had hijacked his car discovered the pyramid was a fake.

When his phone rang around nine o'clock and he saw it was Blum's number, he snatched it up from his desk, startling Raider.

"Yes? Have you got anything?"

"Yeah." He sounded tired.

"DaCosta?"

They found him and the car. He's okay. They think somebody used knockout gas on him or something, and stashed him and the car in a garage. He came stumbling out into the street and nearly got hit by a taxi."

Stone let his breath out. That was a relief, at least. "But he'll be all right?"

"Yeah. They're keepin' him in the hospital overnight, all hush-hush, to make sure. And the assistant's okay too. Whacked upside the head, but not hurt as bad as your guy down at Stanford."

"Thanks to Verity, anyway."

"Yeah, probably."

"I take it the pyramid was gone."

"Oh, yeah. No surprise there. I hear DaCosta's hopping mad. He tried to blame his assistant for selling him out until he found out the guy in the car fooled him."

Stone frowned. "What does he think about that?" It wouldn't be good to have a relatively famous person blabbing on the news about illusionary disguises.

"Don't worry—you got nothin' to worry about there, thankfully. DaCosta barely noticed the guy in his car. Saw the hair, the jacket, and figured it was his guy. Probably feels a little embarrassed about it. Anyway, apparently it's not a new thing. He's a pretty self-centered guy, so he doesn't pay a lot of attention to other people unless they're in his way."

"Well…thank the gods for that, I suppose." Stone sighed. "But that doesn't leave us anywhere, does it?"

"Not really, unfortunately. At least the pyramid's a fake. How long do you think it'll take 'em to figure that out?"

"Who knows? Obviously they'll know it's not what it's supposed to be…but then again, nobody ever said it *was*. They might think the one in the storeroom was just a mundane object after all."

"You think that'll happen, honestly?"

"Honestly? Not a chance. Which means they'll probably be coming after me next."

"Well…take care, Stone. I know you can look after yourself, but if you need anything, feel free to call."

"Thank you, Detective. This day didn't go anywhere near as I expected it to, so it's time for me to have a good think about my next steps."

CHAPTER THIRTY-TWO

S TONE GOT NO FARTHER in his investigations over the next few days. That was frustrating, but even more frustrating was the constant, low-level feeling of a sword hanging over his head. Whoever had snatched the pyramid must know by now that it was a fake.

Or did they? The longer it went without anyone trying to come after him or his friends, the more he began to convince himself the thieves had reached the conclusion that either the pyramid *hadn't* been the other half of the magic-blocking device or, more likely, that its magic had faded over the years. They'd never known for sure it ever even *had* magic, after all.

Chaz DaCosta had been making a lot of noise in the media about the theft, offering a twenty-thousand-dollar reward for information leading to the arrest of the people who'd attacked him. When asked why he wanted to pay twice the (probably hyperinflated) price he'd paid for the pyramid in the first place, he'd responded angrily that it was "the principle of the thing" and that he wasn't going to "let those lowlifes get away with this."

Stone, for his part, had also mostly convinced himself that Portas Justitiae was behind the theft. They'd obviously sent at least one mage after DaCosta, so they could easily have killed him and made him disappear, rather than simply drugging him and stashing him with his car in a garage. And Verity had pointed out that even the assistant hadn't been hurt badly before she got to him. In other words, they'd gone out of their way not to kill any mundanes. Stone didn't think the Ordo would have been so careful.

He continued to see Eleanor off and on, to maintain the fiction of their relationship if the Ordo was still watching. It wasn't difficult—he liked her, and was reasonably sure she wasn't faking that she liked him too. It wasn't as if the sham relationship had any chance of becoming a real one, but the company and the sex were both good, so neither of them was in a hurry to put a stop to it yet.

When he was alone, though, Stone had to admit to himself that his prospects of getting hold of the other half of the device were growing weak at this point. If the Ordo had it—and he was convinced they did—they had the capacity to keep it as well hidden and protected as he did the pyramid. His only consolation was that at least neither of them would have a chance of reuniting the two pieces.

He also had to do a bit of soul-searching as to *why* he wanted to reunite the parts. As long as he had the pyramid, the Ordo or whoever had the other piece couldn't re-create the device and use it for its intended purpose. Maybe it was better if things stayed that way. Better for nobody to have it than people who would use it for the wrong purpose. And what did he want with it, anyway?

He knew the answer, though: he wanted it because it existed. Even if he ended up stashing it where no one would ever see it again, his curiosity had been activated, and he planned to do his best to see the thing through.

He'd already filled Eddie and Ward in on the latest developments the day after the auction, and neither had had any suggestions at the time. On Wednesday morning, though, Stone's phone buzzed as he was preparing to go out for a run. He stopped at the front door when he saw Eddie's number.

"Morning, Eddie. Have you got anything for me, or just want to collect on those rounds I owe you?"

"Well, both, actually—but I might 'ave somethin'. Can you pop over to the Library?"

"I was about to have a run, but I can do that later. Give me a few minutes to change into something respectable, and I'll be there."

Eddie laughed. "You? Respectable? Not much chance o' that, mate."

"Sod off."

Both Eddie and Ward were waiting for him in the workroom when he arrived at the Library twenty minutes later. A closed folder was on the table between them.

Eddie shook his head in wonder. "Gonna be a while before I get used to that speedy new travel thing o' yours, not gonna lie."

Stone didn't sit. "What have you got? Did you find something? Have you got a line on the other half of the device?" He realized he sounded almost as breathless as if he *had* gone for that run, and took a moment to calm down.

"No luck on that," Ward said. "To be honest, we haven't really been trying, except to put a few discreet feelers out."

"We're not ready to tangle with the Ordo yet," Eddie agreed. "Though we *did* discover one thing you might find of interest."

"Is this what you called me about?"

"Nope, this is extra. About the Ordo."

"What about it?" Stone paced, pausing to study the books on the shelves without consciously registering their titles.

"Them, actually."

He stopped and turned back to them. "Them?"

"Yep. There are two. At least two. Maybe more."

"Two...*what?*"

"Ordos."

Stone flung himself into the nearest chair and glared at his friends. "Eddie, what the *hell* are you on about?"

Eddie and Ward exchanged smug glances. They always loved it when they knew something Stone didn't—which was far more often than he would have liked.

"Well," Eddie said, stretching back in his chair, "there's the European version we all know an' love, of course. It doesn't appear they've changed much from the old days. Bunch o' rich wankers who think magic and money let you get away with anythin' you want."

Stone thought about Elias Richter, who was most likely dead by now, and James Brathwaite. They both definitely fit the mold. "And the other one?"

"The American version," Ward said. "Almost certainly including the two men you encountered in Massachusetts a while back."

"Kroyer and Lang?" Stone narrowed his eyes. "So...there are *different* Ordos?"

"Near as we can figure—and trust me, this kind of info is thin on the ground if you're not in bed with 'em—the two broke off from each other sometime in the early nineteen-'undreds," Eddie said. "They have a different organizational structure, different leadership...and it doesn't seem they're too fond of each other."

That was news to Stone—but then again, he hadn't even known the Ordo existed at all up until a couple of years ago. Stefan Kolinsky had mentioned previously that the organization had a U.S. arm, but he'd thought they were simply another branch office answering to the European higher-ups. "So...what...they each do their own thing and don't communicate much?"

"That's what we think," Ward said. "They also have different...priorities."

"What do you mean?"

Eddie shrugged. "The American Ordo doesn't seem to be as concerned with breeding and family and all those other things we get our knickers in a knot about on this side of the pond. Their focus seems to be on advancing magical scholarship—by any means necessary. They don't give a rat's arse who your family were or where you went to school, as long as you bring the magic and you've got a good brain." He tilted his head, shooting Stone a quirky grin. "You'd fit right in with 'em, mate. We probably would, too."

"Except for the 'by any means necessary' bit," Stone said. Once again, he was thinking of the extradimensional horror the kids were trying to summon from Lake Nepahauk. Kroyer and Lang hadn't helped with that effort, but they'd certainly arranged to be johnny-on-the-spot to study it once it was here.

"Well, yes," Ward agreed soberly.

"So you're saying they're basically mad scientists."

"That's a good way to describe 'em," Eddie said. "The good news is, they may not be as bloodthirsty as the European version. The bad news is, they might be willing to go even farther in pursuit of things man wasn't meant to know."

Stone pondered that. "And they're the ones who nicked the bottom piece out from under my nose at McGrath's place."

"Sounds that way, yeah."

He sighed. "It doesn't matter, though, does it? Who cares which branch has it, when they've both got the resources to keep it hidden?" He rose and began pacing again. "I might have to give this one up as a bad job. I don't like it, but I'm out of ideas."

Eddie gave a sage nod. "Of course you are. That's why you keep *us* around."

"Wait." Stone spun back around, hardly daring to hope. "You're telling me you *have* an idea?"

"Maybe. Don't get yourself all wound up about it yet. It was just somethin' we were knockin' around, and honestly I don't think it's got much chance of workin'."

"Tell me. It's better than I've got."

"Well…" He leaned forward, clasping his hands on the table. "The thing is, somebody 'ad to build this thing originally, right?"

"Yes…"

"We've already got one 'alf of it, and we're reasonably sure, from examinin' the thing and extrapolatin', that the second 'alf serves as a kind of amplifier. It makes sense, then, that the pyramid is probably the…control module, I guess you'd call it. The base provides the punch, and the top part provides the targeting."

"Or the fine control," Ward said.

"Okay…" Stone still didn't see where they were going with this. "But the pyramid on its own doesn't have enough power to do much of anything except erase magical documents."

"Right," Eddie said. "But you missed the important part o' what I said. *Somebody 'ad to build the original.*"

One of the things Stone liked most about Eddie and Ward— and one of the things that frustrated him the most about them— was that they kept him humble. He was used to being the smartest person in the room, but with these two, that was never a certainty. "Come on, Eddie—spit it out."

He grinned. "Simple, mate: somebody built it. So, somebody can build it again. Why not us?"

Stone stared at him. "You're…saying you want to build our own version of the amplifier, to work with the pyramid?"

"Why not? No idea if it's possible, but it's worth a go, isn't it? If anybody can do it, the three of us can."

For a moment, Stone let himself get caught up in his friends' enthusiasm. Maybe Eddie was right. Maybe they *could* build it. They certainly had the magical knowledge and more than enough brainpower between them. They could—

His shoulders slumped. "No," he said, dejected. "We can't."

"Why not?" Eddie looked confused. "I mean, I know we might not succeed, but why not at least give it a go? You said you didn't 'ave any other ideas."

"Because it won't work."

"Why won't it work?" Ward asked.

He looked at his hands. "Remember I've mentioned Stefan Kolinsky before?"

"The bloke with the tatty shop back in California, yeah. What about him?"

"I didn't tell you this before—it sort of got lost in everything else. But he's the only person I know who probably surpasses you two in magical knowledge. At least the only one who isn't trying to kill me."

Now it was his friends' turn to be perplexed. "So?" Eddie asked.

"So…I talked to him about this a while ago. He'd actually heard of these devices."

"That right?" Both of them leaned in now, interested. "'Ow?"

"Kolinsky is a very secretive bloke. He doesn't tell me everything—not even close. But he's also reliable. If he says he knows about something, he does. And he told me what makes them work."

Eddie's gaze was laser-sharp now. "And what's that?"

"A substance. A very rare extradimensional one that, as far as he knows, doesn't exist on Earth anymore. He said the reference he'd heard to the devices was very old, and he was as surprised as you were to find out there might be one existing in modern times."

"Bloody 'ell, mate—not somethin' to be leavin' out of the story," Eddie grumbled.

"Sorry. Like I said, I was planning to tell you, but a lot's been going on lately. But it doesn't matter, because if we don't have it, there's no way we'll have a chance at recreating the original base."

"Damn." Eddie opened the folder and fanned out the photos he'd taken of the pyramid from all its sides. "And 'ere was me 'opin' if we could suss out these markings, maybe we could get somewhere."

"Sorry, Eddie. Believe me, I wish you were right."

"And you're certain there's no other place to find this substance?" Ward asked.

Stone shrugged. "I don't know where it would be. The only place that *might* be possible is in the room under my house that has the same symbols, but that's buried. Even if the room itself is still intact down there, there's no way to get to it, without—"

He jerked his head up.

Eddie and Ward both stared at him, startled.

"Y'okay, mate?" Eddie ventured.

Stone didn't answer. Something had taken hold of him—a crazy idea that for a moment he couldn't even articulate.

No…that's insane.

Even if you could *manage it, it's too dangerous.*

But what if it worked?

But what if it didn't?

"Stone?"

He snapped out of his thoughts. They were still looking at him. "Er…never mind. It was nothing."

"It was *not* nothin'." Eddie glared at him. "Come on, don't insult us—out wi' it. What are you cookin' up in that mad brain of yours?"

He couldn't lie to them—why bother trying? He sighed. "I was just thinking…I still can't give you all the details, but…it might be possible for me to get inside that room."

"What?" Ward's eyes widened. "How? That whole catacomb was buried during the cave-in. We saw it."

"It is…but it's possible the chamber didn't cave in. If it was that magically potent, it was probably heavily reinforced. And if there's anywhere on Earth we might have a chance of finding some of that substance, it's there."

"Wait." Eddie gripped the table, never taking his eyes off Stone. "Are you sayin' this…new travel thing you've got that you won't tell us about…might let you pop into that room?"

Stone inclined his head. "Possibly. I don't know for sure." True, the whole house was at the confluence of three ley lines, so if there was any chance, that might be the best place to do it. And Kolinsky *had* told him that it was impossible to pop into solid rock, so if the chamber was buried, the attempt simply wouldn't work.

But if he *did* manage to travel into the room and something went wrong, he'd be trapped. There was no chance anyone else could get in there to rescue him. Even if his growing suspicion that it was impossible to kill him was true, it would take days to dig down to him—assuming his friends could convince anyone to do it.

Eddie seemed to be thinking along the same lines. He shook his head emphatically. "No. It's too risky. You could get stuck down there, and then what would we do? Tell Aubrey we've got to dig up 'alf the house to get to you?"

Stone got up and paced. "You've got a point…but bloody hell, what if it *is* there? What if we *can* get hold of it? We might not *need* to find the other piece."

"I don't think it's a good idea," Ward said. He looked unusually sober, even for him. "I think we're caught up in our zeal to solve this problem. But we don't need this thing. What would we do with it if we had it? I'm not sure I'm comfortable with it existing in the world at all, if I'm being completely honest."

"Still…" Eddie rubbed his chin. "It would've been nice to find out if we could manage it. Ah, well. You're right, of course." He slid the photos of the pyramid back into the folder and closed it with an emphatic *thump*. "That's that, then. Unless you get a new lead on the platform, we'll have to chalk this one up to 'insufficient resources' or summat."

Stone nodded slowly. "I suppose so…" he murmured, but his thoughts were whirling again.

"Stone…" Eddie's voice held a warning tone.

He didn't answer.

"You're gonna do it, aren't you? You're not foolin' anybody. You're gonna leave here, pop down to Surrey, and do it."

Was he? His friends were right—it *was* too risky.

But would he let himself rest if he didn't know?

"I'm afraid so," he said.

"Stone—" Ward began.

He snapped back to reality with a decisive jerk of his head. "Yes. I'm going to do it. I know it's dangerous, but I've got to know. Are you coming with me? You don't have to come inside—in fact you can't, because I've got no way to bring you along. But I'd feel safer knowing someone was there besides Aubrey."

"Right now?" Eddie and Ward exchanged glances.

"Have you got a better time? It's not like we need any preparation."

They didn't like it—he could tell. He felt guilty asking them to be party to this. But he could also tell by their troubled expressions that part of them wanted to see if they could make this work too.

"Fine," Eddie said with a sigh. "No talkin' you out of it, so *somebody's* gotta be there to keep watch over your reckless arse." He shoved the folder aside. "Let's do it, then, before I get some sense and change my mind."

Aubrey didn't come out to greet them when Stone, Eddie, and Ward came through the portal to the mausoleum outside the Surrey house. A quick glance at the garage on the way past showed no lights on in his apartment, and his old pickup truck missing from its usual spot.

"Probably down the pub with Susan, his lady friend," Stone said, smiling fondly. "I'm so glad he's finally met someone."

"Yeah, 'bout time," Eddie said. "Selby here?"

"It's his day off, so probably not. We've got the place to ourselves."

"Brilliant." He didn't sound pleased about it. Stone wondered if he'd hoped the caretaker would talk him out of his plan.

"Okay," Stone said when they got inside the house. "Give me a moment—I need to work out exactly where the chamber is from up here."

"That's easy," Eddie said immediately, pointing. "The room where we initially went down is at the far end of the east wing." He set off at a fast stride down the hall until he found the room. The floor and collapsed wall had long since been repaired. He faced outward, toward the grounds to the side of the house. "The big chamber with the altar where we found Brathwaite should be about fifteen feet out from 'ere, so it's gotta be buried. Same with the catacombs further out." He turned and pointed the opposite direction, back toward the interior of the house. "But the rest of the catacombs, includin' the one with the chamber at the end, are gonna be this way, and this part didn't collapse. You've got a good shot, Stone. I still don't like it, though. The air down there isn't gonna be great."

"You should at least wear some kind of safety equipment," Ward said. "Eye protection and a dust mask at minimum."

"I'd be more comf'table with full oxygen, like a bleedin' scuba tank," Eddie muttered. "But Stone's not gonna sit still that long."

"I swear, you two are like a couple of old women," Stone grumbled. "Fine. Stay here."

He jogged out to Aubrey's garage workshop and retrieved a mask, safety glasses, and a Maglite. When he returned, he found Eddie and Ward talking softly in the corner. They both looked somber. "Something wrong?"

"Nah," Eddie said, waving him off. "Just talkin' about how barmy you are. Nothin' new. Come on—if we're gonna do this, let's get on wi' it. Then we can pop up to the Dragon and 'ave a laugh about the whole thing afterward. You're buyin', so make sure you don't get stuck in there to get out of it."

Stone shivered a little at the word "Dragon." This chamber had been built to contain one. The ley-line travel was a draconic technique. What if he got down there and something was still operational, preventing him from returning?

You can still back out, he told himself. *We don't need this. We probably can't re-create the thing even if we had it.*

He took a deep breath and shook his head. They were here now, and he had to know. And besides, Aldwyn had gotten out once he awakened, which meant the earthquake must have disrupted the room's magic enough for his abilities to work.

But he's an actual dragon, and you're not.

Eddie and Ward were watching him with nervous expectation.

"Okay," he said. "Just be quiet and let me concentrate."

"Quiet as church mice, mate," Eddie murmured. He didn't sound flippant now.

Stone turned away from them, closing his eyes and letting his breathing settle to a soft, even cadence. The ley-line technique was a bit more difficult when shooting for a specific spot instead of just a point roughly in the desired location. It got much easier the more familiar he was with the spot, so he could pop into the Encantada, Surrey, and London houses with ease, along with Caventhorne. But he'd only seen this chamber briefly, over a year ago. He pictured it in his mind's eye, gritted his teeth, and released the magical energy.

Nothing happened.

Damn. Missed the mark. Still, it was good that nothing *had* happened, if the alternative was materializing in the middle of solid rock.

He gathered himself, focused harder, and tried again.

Nothing.

"All right, Stone?" Ward called softly.

"Yes. Just…let me do this."

He tried twice more, and twice more nothing happened. He felt a faint resistance, but nothing else. Could it be that he *was* getting it right, but something inside the chamber was pushing back? The technique didn't work against wards, but as far as he knew, the wards around the chamber had been broken. The house wards shouldn't be an issue—not merely because they were inside them already, but because they were *his*.

He let his breath out, and his shoulders slumped. "It's not working."

"Eh." Eddie sounded relieved. "That's all right. Maybe it wasn't meant to be. Let's just—"

"Hush. One more try."

This *would* have to be the last try. He could already feel his body's fatigue from the previous attempts, and didn't think it would be safe to keep pushing. If this didn't work, he'd admit his friends were right and accompany them to the Dancing Dragon. He could use a pint or two—or three—about now.

Focus.

He visualized the inside of the chamber, tightened his grip on the Maglite, and released the energy.

Instantly, he knew he'd been successful this time. Even with his eyes still closed, he could feel and smell the difference in the air.

He snapped on the flashlight and opened his eyes.

The chamber appeared just as he'd remembered it, with the pedestal and the blasted box in the middle and the broken door on one side. Every one of the walls, the ceiling, and the floor were covered with intricate carved symbols. The dry, dusty air smelled dank and seemed to press in on Stone from every side. When he pointed the flashlight out through the door, he saw that rubble had come down to fill most of the hallway leading out. Nobody was getting out there without a lot of effort.

He pulled out his phone and tried to get a signal. He didn't expect to, and wasn't surprised to see no bars. Stuffing it back in his pocket, he moved to the pedestal.

Don't have long. I'll need to do this fast.

He shifted to magical sight, looking for any sign of leftover energy, but found none. With a sudden sense of panic, he wondered if that was because there wasn't any to find, or if somehow the chamber was still functioning to block his power. A quick glance at his hand dispelled that fear, though: his aura shone as bright as ever. He let out his breath in relief.

Already, the air felt wrong. He wasn't experiencing any light-headedness or any other indication he wasn't getting enough oxygen, but he knew better than to waste time down here.

Moving fast but methodically, he directed the flashlight beam to first the box, then each of the walls in turn. He wasn't even sure what he was looking for: was it something in the carved symbols? A hidden alcove in one of the walls? Something about the box or embedded in the pedestal it rested on?

After ten minutes, he was breathing hard. Sweat beads had broken out on his forehead and more were creeping down the back of his neck. He knew it wasn't because he was physically tired—he hadn't expended enough effort for that—but even more than before, he felt the oppressive air pushing against him.

He couldn't stay down here much longer. He wasn't sure if most of the problem was in his head or if the air really was getting bad, but he couldn't risk waiting around to find out. Already, the swimmy feeling in his brain was growing noticeable. He couldn't afford to pass out.

Damn it. He spun in place, pointing the flashlight in every direction, shifting once again to magical sight, but nothing new presented itself. Maybe, possibly, he could come back down here with better gear and spend more time looking, but right now, he had to get out.

Bugger it. Give it up. There's nothing here. Stop chasing ghosts before you get yourself killed—or worse.

He closed his eyes and reluctantly concentrated on the pattern, hoping it wouldn't take as many attempts as it had to get down here.

An instant later, he reappeared in the same room where he'd left, looking straight into Eddie's and Ward's worried faces. He staggered forward, letting his breath out in a rush of relief and frustration.

His friends surged forward and caught him, hustling him to a chair.

"Y'all right, mate?" There was still no sign of humor in Eddie's voice.

Stone nodded. "Yes, I'll…be fine in a moment."

"Did you find it?" Ward asked. "Did you make it to the room?"

He nodded again, wearily. The lightheadedness was already lifting with the influx of fresh air, but he felt as tired as he did after a long run. He suspected his disappointment was part of it.

"I'm guessin' you didn't find anything, though," Eddie said.

"No. Not a damned thing. If it's in there, it's well hidden."

"Or it got ruined when the enchantment broke," Ward said.

"Or it was never there in the first place, and they did it some other way." Eddie sighed. "I 'ate to say it—you know 'ow I feel about givin' up on a juicy problem like this—but it might just be worth puttin' this one on the shelf, this time. We can examine that pyramid some more if you want, but other than that, I don't see where else we can go."

Stone sighed and lowered his head. "I don't want to admit it either," he said, his tone thick with dejection. "But you might be right." He looked up. "Anyway, thanks for coming with me. I appreciate your putting up with my mad schemes, even when you don't approve."

Eddie shrugged. "It was a good idea. But sometimes even good ideas don't pan out." He brightened. "So, you up for a few pints, or are we gonna 'ave to take you upstairs and put you to bed wi' some warm milk and yer teddy bear before Aubrey gets 'ome?"

Stone flashed a faint, tired grin. "I'll never turn down a few pints. Even if I *am* buying."

CHAPTER THIRTY-THREE

AFTER A FEW MORE DAYS had passed with no further developments on any of the fronts Stone was keeping watch on, he became increasingly convinced that perhaps no developments were coming.

Blum had reported that even Chaz DaCosta's offered reward hadn't brought any takers out of the woodwork with information about the pyramid. As far as Stone could tell, neither the Ordo, Portas, nor the nameless government organization had made any efforts to break into his home or bother any of his friends, and he was sure none of them had tried contacting him. The original thief was still listed as a John Doe, and Brandon Greene had returned to work without any apparent long-term ill effects from getting his bell rung.

In fact, everything had grown so quiet it was almost unsettling.

Had whoever had stolen the pyramid from DaCosta decided they'd been wrong about it being magical in the first place, and directed their search elsewhere? It seemed unlikely, but Stone supposed it was possible. Not everybody was as curious as he was.

Even Eleanor didn't think things were going anywhere.

"They're not bugging me about when you're going to take me to England anymore," she told him one night while they were at his house on one of their less frequent sham dates. "They told me I could keep on watching you if I wanted, and they'll pay me if I report back with anything interesting, but I don't think their heart's in it anymore." She gave him a rueful smile and leaned in to kiss him. "This has been fun, but I think it might be time to move on."

He was surprised at his disappointment. "I suppose it was inevitable at some point. Where will you go?"

She shrugged. "Wherever the jobs take me. But hey, you've got my number. If you ever need my services again, give me a call."

"You'll stay tonight, though, right?"

Her smile grew less rueful and more sly. "Try to send me away."

Later that week, a couple days after Stone had awakened in the morning to find Eleanor gone, Jason called him as he was leaving his afternoon class.

"Hey, Al. Just wanted to check with you on something."

"What's on your mind?"

"I got a case that's taking me down to L.A. tonight. I figured I'd take Amber along to help out, and maybe we'd stay a couple extra days for a little R&R. You need us for anything? You haven't said much about this pyramid thing—is it over?"

He sighed. "I think it is, much as I don't like to admit it."

"So, you sure you don't need us?"

"No, no. You go. Have fun. You two need a holiday."

"Yeah, we kinda do. Okay. Take care, Al. You could use a holiday too. Try to relax. I know you suck at that, but try."

That same evening, Verity texted him. *Got a minute? Give me a call if you do.*

"Hey," she said when she answered. "Jason was telling me he and Amber were going to L.A. for a few days. He said you told him the pyramid thing was over."

"Far as I know, yes. It's been days since I've heard anything."

"I know you're disappointed about it, but I'm kinda relieved, to be honest. Anyway, that's not what I wanted to talk about."

Stone leaned back on the sofa and carefully nudged Raider away from his Guinness pint. "So what is it?"

"Well…I wasn't gonna do it because I didn't want to leave you alone in case you needed me, but if it's really over, Scuro's got a tattoo job he wants me along on."

He frowned. "Why are you calling about that? I'm sure you've got all sorts of tattoo jobs."

"Yeah, but this one's in Australia. There's a portal in Sydney, but Scuro says the client's really reclusive and is paying big bucks on top of the regular fee for a house call. She lives about an hour out."

"Ah. And he wants you to go along to heal."

"Yeah. He's offered me a nice bonus if I'll do it. Enough so I could put some serious money away." She paused. "Plus, I've never been to Australia. He said he'd show me around Sydney a little after the job."

Stone chuckled. "I absolutely think you should go, then. Can't turn down money like that, and I'm sure you'll quite like Australia. If you get a chance to investigate them, there are some fascinating magical traditions among the Indigenous people in that area."

"That sounds awesome." Another pause. "You sure you'll be okay, though? With Jason, Amber, and me all away at the same time—"

"Verity, come on. I'm quite capable of taking care of myself. I did it for years before I ever met you lot. And besides, all I've got planned is spending some time working on papers with Raider. Not very exciting, I promise."

"Famous last words," she said with a laugh. "Okay, then. I'll tell Scuro it's a go. You be good while I'm gone. I'll ask Raider when I get back, and you know he'll rat you out in a second for a few kitty treats and a tummy rub."

The following day, Stone had no classes. He slept late, drove up to campus for a meeting in the afternoon, and ran a few errands he'd been putting off. It had been a while since his life was this normal; he'd gotten a bit used to it during the last quarter, but he still wasn't sure he liked it. Was this the way most mundanes spent the majority of their lives? He couldn't imagine it.

Verity, Jason, and Amber were all gone by now, and he hoped they were doing something more productive than he was. He thought about giving Eleanor a call to see if she'd left the area yet, but decided against it. Their relationship, as fake as the pyramid that had disappeared following the theft, had run its course, served its purpose, and now the best thing to do was let it go.

Instead, he picked up some take-out from his favorite Thai place in Menlo Park, then drove back to the Encantada house. "Well, Raider," he said as the cat wound around his legs and demanded his own dinner, "I guess it's just you and me tonight."

Raider didn't seem to mind that at all. He tore into the plate of cat food Stone set on the kitchen floor for him, then followed him out to the living room and hopped onto the couch. Stone picked at his own dinner, realizing he wasn't nearly as hungry as he'd thought he was, and half-listened to the Zombies tune playing in the background.

He was trying to decide between going upstairs to work on research for his latest paper or giving Brandon Greene a call to see if he wanted to get a beer and catch up when his phone buzzed on the table.

He glanced at it, figuring it was probably one of his friends updating him on their adventures. But this was a call, not a text, and the number showed as *UNKNOWN*.

"Yes, hello?"

"Dr. Stone?"

It was a male voice, and he didn't recognize it. "Yes, who's this?"

"You don't know me, but you probably know the organization I represent." The man sounded calm, at ease—maybe even a little smug.

"Is that right? And which organization is that?" Stone sat up straighter.

"I think I've got something you're interested in. And I'm fairly sure *you've* got something *I'm* interested in. I'm calling to make you an offer."

CHAPTER THIRTY-FOUR

STONE TIGHTENED HIS HAND on the phone. At this point, he wasn't seeing anything else in the room. "What are you talking about? What kind of offer?"

The man chuckled. "Don't play stupid, Dr. Stone. It's not a good look for you. We both know you know exactly what I'm talking about."

"Suppose I did. You'd be mad to think I'd entertain any offer from anyone connected with your…organization."

"I don't see why not. We're not your enemies, Dr. Stone. In fact, I suspect we see eye to eye about more things than you'd care to admit. One of them being the particular subject of our current interest."

"It doesn't matter if we do. Even if I *did* have what you think I've got, you must know I'd have it hidden and protected well enough that you lot will never find it."

"Oh, no doubt. I'm certain of that. But you can be equally certain that we likewise have our part hidden where *you* won't ever find it."

Stone leaned back into the couch cushions. "Maybe that's for the best. If you know anything about the item and its function, I don't know why you'd even want it."

"Probably the same reason you do—curiosity. We want to know how it works. And…"

"And what?"

"And we want to keep it out of the hands of those who shouldn't be meddling with things they don't understand."

"Oh? And who would those be? Anyone who isn't you?"

"Of course you know I'm talking about mundanes." The man made a little clucking *tsk*. "Come now, Dr. Stone—you can't tell me that you're any more comfortable about having it in mundane hands than we are."

Stone didn't answer that. "What makes you think I've even got it? Last I heard, it was up for auction in San Francisco, and someone nicked it from the man who paid far too much money for it. Was that you?"

"You and I both know that item was a fake. A well-made fake, for certain, but a fake nonetheless."

Stone gave a wolfish grin. "Bet your people were surprised when they found out. I can picture them hopping about like a bunch of angry chickens."

"You think that was us?" The man snorted. "Hardly. We wouldn't dirty our hands with such a thing. And you know as well as I do that if it *had* been us, the unfortunate Mr. DaCosta and his assistant would not have fared as well as they did."

"What do you want?" Stone snapped. "I'm not going to waste my evening nattering on with you. I've got better things to do."

"I told you before: I'm offering you a deal."

"And I'll ask again: what kind of deal?"

"A chance for both of us to satisfy our curiosity."

"Sorry, I still don't follow."

The man *tsk*ed again. "I'll make it clearer for you, then: we want to see how this thing functions—or *if* it functions. We believe you do too. Thus, my proposal is that we meet somewhere neutral, in a public place, and discuss the situation. You bring your piece of the device, I bring ours, and we…put our heads together."

Stone barked a laugh. "You must think I'm a complete idiot, if you think I'd agree to something like that."

"I know you're not an idiot, Dr. Stone. I know you have reason to be apprehensive. But I assure you—in this case, we have no malicious intentions. You may choose the venue, with the only requirement that it be a public place not associated with you. And of course you must come alone, as will I."

"And…what? We both bring our pieces and we sit there out in front of everyone trying to put the thing together?"

"Surely you're capable of an illusion that would hide our efforts. I know I am."

Stone had to allow that he was right. Those kinds of small illusions were easy.

He let his breath out. This was an inopportune time for this to occur, when Jason, Verity, and Amber were away. He wondered if the Ordo had planned it that way on purpose. He had to admit, though, that despite his reservations, his curiosity had poked its head tentatively up for a look around.

"I might be interested," he said. "But not tonight. Call me again in a few days."

"I'm sorry, Dr. Stone, but that won't be possible. The offer exists only for this evening."

Of course it does. "How do I even know you've got the thing? Assuming I have my half, this whole thing could be a ploy to get me somewhere you can get your hands on it."

"I could say the same of you—though we're willing to trust our intelligence reports that you *do* have your part. And as a good faith gesture, I will send you this."

The phone beeped again, and an image popped up on the screen.

Stone studied it, narrowing his eyes. He'd never seen the platform part of the device before, but the item in the photo matched the description in the McGrath auction catalog. The symbols carved into the two shiny black, visible sides were clearly in the same ancient language as those on the pyramid. The background was indistinguishable: a corner with white walls and a white floor. He could barely see the twin protuberances extending from the top. Sure, it could be a fake too—but if it was, it was a damn good one.

"Assuming you're not lying to me—what then? We show up, do whatever it is we can do with it, and…what? I've got no intention of letting you take the completed device with you, and I doubt you'd fancy letting me take it with me."

"Simple—once we've assembled it and determined whether it's possible to make it function, we separate it once again. You take your piece, I take ours, and we return them to their respective secure storage locations."

Stone narrowed his eyes. "What's the point of that, then?"

"I'm surprised you don't see it. You're right about something: we don't have a compelling reason to possess the functional device. I'm sure you know who I represent, and we are…shall we say…rather famously pro-magic. The last thing we want to do is *interfere* with magic. In fact, it would be in our best interests if the device *were* stored in separate pieces, far away from any chance a mundane organization like those ridiculous religious zealots might get hold of it. Doesn't that make sense?"

Once again, Stone had to admit it did. He remembered what Eddie had told him about the American branch of the Ordo—that they were more mad scientists than raging magical chauvinists.

"You want us there alone? Just the two of us? How do I know you won't have the place under surveillance, and be ready to jump me as soon as I show up?"

"Technically, you don't," he admitted. "It's a risk you'll have to take. But think about it—we know how good you are…and more to the point, how adept you are at getting out of traps. Why would we risk it? We want to know about this thing as much as you do. Possibly more. Not only how it works, but how, perhaps, we might defend against it should we encounter it in the future. And in any case, that's why we're allowing you to choose the venue, so you'll know we won't have time to prepare anything ahead of time. What do you say, Dr. Stone? Will you take a chance on satisfying your curiosity?"

This was madness. He knew it. It was a huge risk. But on the other hand, the Ordo man was probably telling the truth: they wanted to study the thing too. And what was the worst thing that could happen if they *did* manage to get hold of it? The old Ordo, the European version, might have been a bigger threat, but unless this lot planned to start kidnapping mages, they'd probably just do exactly what Stone had done with it: store it away somewhere and spend the next several years trying to work out what made it tick so they could counter its effects. It wasn't as if they could build another one, since the substance necessary for its function appeared to be extinct on Earth.

He was rationalizing, he knew.

But still…

"All right," he said at last. "This is against my better judgment, but honestly I think it would be difficult for your lot to take me down before I could make life quite unpleasant for you."

The man chuckled. "You're probably right. We're scholars, not fighters. So, do we have a deal?"

"I suppose we do."

"Name the place. Oh—one more requirement. Please forgive me, but unfortunately I must disqualify A Passage to India for obvious reasons."

Stone didn't argue. If this whole thing went pear-shaped, he didn't plan to put Marta in danger, or bring unwanted attention down on the portal location. He thought for a moment, trying to come up with a place that was still open and would be difficult to surround, with good sight lines and lots of windows. *You're starting to think like Jason.*

"How about University Perk, on University Avenue?" It had been his favorite spot for morning coffee when he still lived in Palo

Alto, and popular with local workers. He knew from experience, though, that it wouldn't be crowded this late.

"Done. I'll meet you there in an hour."

"How will I recognize you?"

"I don't think it will be difficult. I'll be the one carrying the large box."

It wouldn't take anywhere near an hour for Stone to get to University Perk—that was part of why he'd chosen it—but another thing Jason had taught him was to do a little recon prior to potentially dangerous meetings.

First things first, though.

The meeting would be a risk, but he could minimize the risk to at least some extent. He thought about texting or emailing Jason and Verity, but decided against it. There was no point in interrupting their plans, especially since there was no way they could get home fast enough to be of any help even if they wanted to. Instead, he wrote them a note explaining what he was planning to do, enchanted everything but the names on the outside to require magical sight to read, and left it prominently displayed on the breakfast bar.

He also considered contacting Ian, but likewise chose not to. His son was probably still off on the other side of the world with Gabriel, and dragging him into this mess at this late date didn't seem to be a good idea even if he was close enough to a portal to make it here in time.

Kolinsky was pointless. He'd already told Stone he wouldn't involve himself in anything to do with the device, and Stone was sure he wouldn't change his mind now.

He was on his own, then, which meant he'd have to be especially careful.

He was about to pop over to Caventhorne to retrieve the pyramid when another idea occurred to him.

He paused to send a single text and wait for a reply before stroking Raider's head and disappearing from the kitchen.

As Stone had expected, University Perk wasn't crowded at nearly nine p.m. Most of the retail stores along University Avenue had either already closed or were in the process, leaving only the restaurants, bars, and a few coffee shops open. It was a drizzly, unpleasant evening, and most of the remaining window-shoppers had already fled to the various eateries and watering holes.

Stone, under a disregarding spell, watched the coffee shop from across the street. The place was well lit, revealing clearly through the full-length front window that two customers lingered near the counter while waiting for take-out orders. Two more, a man and a woman who looked like students, sat at one of the back tables, each with a laptop open. When he shifted to magical sight, their calm, untroubled auras all sprang into being: blues, yellows, greens, oranges, with no sign of red flashes, nervousness, or discomfort. As far as he could tell, none of them were waiting for anything other than their orders.

He lifted his head, scanning along the roof, and then checked out the few other people on the street. Aside from a pair of young men who appeared to be having an ambulatory lovers' spat, nothing stood out. He watched them until they disappeared around a corner, still arguing.

Stone faded into the background and waited, occasionally slipping his hand into his coat pocket to verify the pyramid was still there. He'd retrieved it from Desmond's vault at Caventhorne and paused to leave another note for Eddie and Ward, inside their workroom. They wouldn't see it until a few hours from now, but at least they'd know his plans if anything went wrong.

The meeting was set for nine forty-five. At nine-forty, he dropped the disregarding spell and jogged across the street. The two take-out customers had already left, and no one else had come in to take their place. The couple with the laptops might as well have been in another world for all the attention they paid to their surroundings.

Stone pushed open the door and entered the shop.

"Welcome," the barista, a smiling young woman, called. "What can I get started for you?"

Stone didn't recognize her, but that wasn't surprising. He rarely frequented the place anymore, and when he had, it had been in the morning. Aside from her, the only other employee was a man about the same age wearing a white T-shirt, jeans, and an apron. He came out of the back and began fiddling with the espresso machine.

"Er—nothing at the moment, thank you. I'm waiting for a...friend."

"Sure, no problem." She laughed. "Plenty of room. Just let me know if you need anything."

Stone took a seat at the table nearest the window, where he could keep an eye on the door and the people walking by outside. Aside from the small, chunky vase containing a fresh flower, the only thing on the table was a copy of the *Palo Alto Weekly* someone had left behind. He glanced at the headline, then tossed the paper onto the table behind him. He didn't want anything distracting him.

A few more people ambled by before he spotted what he was looking for. A dark-haired man of medium height approached slowly from the right. He wore a buttoned overcoat and slacks, and carried a large green shopping bag. The top of a brown cardboard shipping box poked out of the top.

Stone narrowed his eyes, continuing to watch the man. Oddly, he seemed nervous. His aura was watchful, and a couple times he glanced behind him as if expecting someone to be there.

Either he was a damned good actor, or he was twitchier about this meeting than Stone was.

Maybe they're scared of me. He could use that to his advantage, perhaps. But it still didn't mean he could afford to get sloppy.

The man pushed open the door, scanned the shop's interior with obvious magical sight, and entered. His shoulders dropped a bit with relief when he spotted Stone, and he hurried over to take the seat across from him.

"Did you bring it?" he muttered.

"Did you?"

He patted the bag. "Right here."

Stone patted his pocket.

"Do you want to get some coffee or something?"

Stone snorted softly under his breath. "Thank you, no. Forgive my lack of trust, but—well—I don't trust you, so I won't be eating or drinking anything."

The man gave a thin smile. "I don't blame you. I don't trust you either. Shall I do the illusion, or do you want to?"

"I'll do it." He glanced around first. The male barista had returned to the back. The woman was rinsing blender pitchers with her back to the room. The laptop couple were still oblivious. Quickly, he summoned an illusion around the table to make it appear that the two of them were sharing an innocuous conversation.

"We'll have to be careful," he muttered. "If we actually *do* get this thing working, it's likely to interfere with the illusion."

"If we get it working, I won't care."

He had a point. They weren't doing anything wrong or illegal, even if someone did spot them messing with a two-foot-tall black obelisk. "All right—let's get on with it. I don't plan to stay here long."

"Nor I." He reached down, pulled the box from the shopping bag, and set it on the table. "Show me yours."

Stone didn't laugh, but it was a close thing. Instead, still keeping an eye around him, he withdrew the pyramid and placed it in front of him.

The man gazed at it a moment, then lifted a larger black object free of the box.

Now it was Stone's turn to stare. The base looked identical to the pyramid in materials and construction. The lines of symbols and sigils along its sides were clearly in the same language. The two nubs at the top appeared to exactly match the holes on the bottom of the pyramid. Even without magical sight, he could tell it was the real deal; in fact, being near it made him feel vaguely uncomfortable.

The man seemed to notice Stone's discomfort. "I don't like being around it either. It's making my head hurt. Let's do this quickly."

"Do you have the instructions?"

He tilted his head. "Instructions?"

"From what I understand, there might be a set of instructions explaining how to make it work. I don't have them—and it appears you don't, either. So I hope my understanding is wrong."

"Let's put it together and find out." The man looked around again, nervously. Stone's illusion allowed them to see the room as it was while hiding their activities from the outside world. So far, nothing had changed.

Moving with caution and keeping magical sight up, he lifted the pyramid and settled it on top of the base, lining up its holes with the projections on the larger piece.

Both he and the Ordo man leaned closer in anticipation.

Nothing happened.

Stone narrowed his eyes. Both pieces were still putting out the unsettling anti-magic field, but it didn't seem to be any more powerful or reach out any farther than it had when the pieces were separate. The illusion remained strong, unaffected.

"It isn't working," the Ordo man said. "The symbols line up perfectly. It's obvious the two sections were meant to fit together."

"Yes." Stone sighed. "But if there's some sort of ritual required to get it started, I haven't got a clue what it is. I wouldn't know where to start looking for it."

The man looked up sharply, almost as if trying to determine whether he was lying. "We don't have it either, obviously, or I'd have brought it." He looked at the black obelisk in frustration. "This was pointless. If you thought there was another component, why did you call me if you didn't have it?"

It took only a second for that to sink in. Stone jerked his head up and fixed a hard stare on the man. "What? *I* didn't call *you*. *You* called *me*."

They got it at exactly the same instant—but by then it was too late. Next to the obelisk, the chunky flower vase emitted a powerful cloud of shifting green gas. So did the ones on the two tables next to them.

The Ordo man moved fast. Stone moved faster. Both of them lunged free of their chairs, trying to get out of the cloud's reach, but neither made it. Stone's legs seemed to belong to someone else, for all the control he had over them. He crashed to the floor, twitching.

The instant before he passed out, he spotted two things: the Ordo man lying unconscious next to him, and the sly, triumphant grin of the barista as she came around the counter toward them.

CHAPTER THIRTY-FIVE

S TONE NOTICED THREE THINGS when he regained consciousness, all of them without opening his eyes.

First, he was cold.

Second, wherever he was, it wasn't the coffee shop. Instead of
the pleasant aromas of coffee and baked goods, the air smelled
dank and sour.

Third, his head swam like he'd just awakened from general
anesthesia. His thoughts moved sluggishly, foggy and disorganized.

A moment later, he noticed something perhaps more important
than all three of the others: stout bracelets encircled his wrists.
When he lifted his hand, something rattled against the floor.

Chains.

It seemed this evening wasn't going well at all.

He opened his eyes, and confirmed it.

He lay on the concrete floor of a small room, perhaps eight feet
on a side. There were no windows. The room's only illumination
came from a bare lightbulb hanging from the ceiling. The concrete
explained part of why he was cold—the rest came from the fact that
he wore nothing but his black boxer briefs.

As he'd surmised, someone had locked thick metal manacles
around his wrists. Chains attached to them extended a short distance to the room's center, where a metal cage protected a familiar
object. The chains were fastened to a thick metal anchor bolted to
the floor.

"Bloody hell…" Stone murmured.

The black obelisk was inside the cage, which had also been bolted to the floor. Both parts were still there, but it somehow seemed more complete than before. It was hard to tell through the narrow spaces between the cage bars from Stone's angle, but it appeared the faint line between them was gone, as if the two pieces had been fused into a single whole.

From the other side of the cage came a soft groan.

Stone snapped his gaze up. He'd been so focused on his own misery and his shock at seeing the obelisk that he hadn't noticed he wasn't alone in the room. He sat up a little, setting off a cascade of swirling confusion inside his head, and lowered himself back down again. All he could see of his cellmate from that position were the light-blue plaid boxer shorts and pale, hairy legs of a white man.

"Who's over there?" he croaked. His voice echoed hollowly in the small space.

The other man moaned again, but didn't reply.

Stone took in the rest of the room with a quick glance. The walls, floor, and ceiling were all water-stained gray concrete, with a drain in the floor near the cage. On the wall closest to his feet, a heavy metal door was currently closed. Aside from the cage, the obelisk, the chains, the lightbulb, and the two occupants, the room had no other features. No furniture, nothing on the walls.

It was indeed a cell—and not a very hospitable one.

At least there weren't any cameras he could see. If they were present, they were well hidden.

His brain was clearing now, at least enough so he could recall his last memories before he'd passed out.

The coffee shop.

The green gas erupting out of the flower vases.

The barista's nasty, triumphant smile.

Had the Ordo planned an ambush? Had they somehow managed to hide their presence from him, lure him in, and drug him?

That didn't make sense, though. He clearly remembered the Ordo man falling next to him, looking as shocked as he'd been. Was that a ploy? Was the man even now off in another room, watching him through a hidden camera and laughing at how gullible he'd been?

But why would they even bother with all this if all they wanted was the device? Why bring him…where?

Snippets of their conversation flooded into his mind:

Why did you call me if you didn't have it?

And his own reply: *What? I didn't call* you. *You called* me.

He let his breath out, sinking back to the cold floor.

They'd been played.

Both of them had been played.

And now he was sure he knew who his fellow captive was.

The chains were barely long enough to allow him to sit upright, but nothing more. He wrenched himself up, shivering, noting it didn't seem his captors had injured him physically beyond the effects of the gas and the cold. It didn't matter how he felt, though— he needed to get out of here before whoever had done this to him returned.

He shifted himself until he was as far away from the cage and the obelisk as he could manage, then attempted to switch to magical sight.

Nothing happened.

No, no, no…

Bright panic stabbed at him, increasing his heart rate, but he drove it back down. If he panicked now, everything would be lost.

Just focus. You can do this. You're stronger than they are.

He closed his eyes and concentrated, trying to open the familiar connection to Calanar. Even if his captors had managed to get the obelisk functioning, it shouldn't work against Calanarian magic, right? Even in Windermere, when his mad grandmother's people had dosed him with an alchemical concoction to block his magic, it hadn't stopped him from pulling power from Calanar. All he'd need to do was keep his focus, pop off these manacles, and then whoever had done this would quickly learn the consequences of messing with him. If he could free his cellmate too, maybe he'd add his magic to their effort.

The enemy of my enemy is my friend, after all…

He took several slow, deep breaths, did his best to clear his mind, and visualized the pattern that would connect him with Calanar's burgeoning wellspring of energy.

Nothing.

It was as if someone had built a solid wall between him and what he was trying to reach. He couldn't even *feel* it anymore.

No…

With a growl of sudden rage, he yanked hard on the chains in an attempt to pull them loose from the anchor with nothing but physical force.

They didn't budge. All he accomplished was to scrape his wrists and wrench the muscles in his shoulders.

He lunged forward, trying to force his hands between the cage bars. Maybe if he could knock the obelisk over, it would break apart again. But the bars were thick, and the spaces between them were too narrow to fit more than his fingertips past.

Clearly, whoever had done this had planned it with care.

His gaze fell on his cellmate again. Now that he was seated, he could see it was the dark-haired Ordo mage from the coffee shop, as he'd suspected. The man's eyes were closed, his face pale and blotchy, his breathing slow.

Stone shifted his body as close to the cage as he could, then reached out with a foot and prodded the man's leg. "Oi. Wake up."

The Ordo mage groaned, louder this time. "What…?" he muttered.

"Wake up. We're in a bit of a pickle here."

"What…?"

Stone poked him with his toe again, harder. "Come on. Wakey wakey. We've got to figure something out before they come back to check on us."

A terrifying thought stabbed at his brain: *what if they* aren't *coming back to check on us? What if they've left us here to die?* He squelched it fast, though. If they were going to get out of here, he'd need his brain focused on the problem, not on wasting time worrying about hypotheticals.

The man pulled his legs away, rolled over, and stiffened. "I'm…chained."

"Yes, do keep up. Are you all right otherwise? Did they hurt you?" Stone tried to speak briskly, but his voice shook with the cold. Although it wasn't freezing in here, they hadn't bothered to turn on the heater, either. Concrete held cold well, especially when all you had on was your shorts.

"C-cold."

"Yes. That too." Stone supposed he should give the man a few moments to get caught up, but they didn't have time. "Look—do you remember anything about the coffee shop?"

The man glared at him. "You…tricked me."

"No. And you didn't trick me. Somebody else tricked us *both*. And if you haven't noticed yet, it seems they've got our little device functioning, though I can't imagine how. Does your magic work? Try it now, please."

"Ugh…" The man blinked a few times, trying to clear his head, and aimed a dirty look at Stone. But then he took a deep breath and assumed the thousand-yard stare that clearly indicated an attempt at magical sight.

Stone didn't have to wait for his look of panic to see it wasn't working. He sighed. "You too, then."

"What's…happening? How did we—"

"Look—I don't know much more than you do. I woke up five minutes before you did. We're in a concrete room, chained to the floor in our pants, and that thing inside the cage is preventing us from using magic."

"Who did this?" His voice was clearer now, but like Stone's, it shook with cold. He, too, scrambled around until he was seated upright, staring at Stone through the bars of the cage.

"Don't know."

"How are we going to get out of here?"

Despite Stone's opinions of the Ordo in general, he couldn't help feeling a bit of sympathy for this particular representative of the organization. This was objectively a terrifying situation, and if whoever had impersonated him had been telling the truth, the man was a scholar, not an adventurer. He looked like a middle-aged accountant who was a long way out of his comfort zone. "Just— don't get yourself all wound up just yet. We'll figure something out. What should I call you?"

"Richard."

"Richard, then. And you already know who I am, so there's introductions sorted."

Richard narrowed his eyes. "How are you so damned *calm?*"

"Calm? Me?" Stone snorted. "Obviously you can't see what's flying around inside my head if you think that. But if we're going to have a chance of getting out of here, we can't let panic take over."

"We're not getting out of here. Not as long as our magic doesn't work."

"Now, see, I used to be like you, thinking magic was the only answer to everything. Fortunately, though, I got rather forcibly disabused of that notion."

"So what are you going to do, then?" Richard twisted around so he could get a straight-shot glare at Stone. "Rip the chains out with your massive muscles?"

"Well...no. You've got me there." Despite his regular, post-Calanar gym routine, massive muscles and Stone weren't two concepts that were ever likely to coexist.

"What, then?"

"You're right about one thing: we've got to get our magic back. So, since we can't rip the chains out, I think our best bet is to see if we can dislodge this cage and knock the obelisk over." He shifted position, moving as far as the chains would allow toward the back of the cage. "Shall we give it a go?"

"You want to *push* on it? Can't you see it's bolted down?"

"Yes, but who knows how well? Between the two of us, we might have a chance. Not a good one, admittedly, but would you rather sit there on your arse and do nothing?"

Richard shot him a sour look, but sighed loudly and hitched himself backward on his butt. "This isn't going to work. We're going to die here."

"That's the spirit. Now belt up and push."

Unfortunately, they soon discovered that whoever had bolted the cage to the floor had apparently taken their plan into account. Despite pressing their combined weight into the side, the thing didn't even move. The bolts stayed solidly in place, and the black obelisk seemed to mock them from inside, like a Christmas tree fortified against mayhem-minded kittens.

Richard slumped back to the floor. "This is hopeless."

This man was getting tiresome in a hurry. "We're still alive. That means it's not hopeless. I just wish I knew who's done this."

Almost as if someone had been waiting for his words, a key rattled in the door lock. An instant later, the door swung outward to reveal a shadowy, broad-shouldered male figure framed in the opening.

"Well," the new man said. "Settling in, I see. Good." His voice was deep, serious but somehow also amused. The voice of a man who was certain he had the upper hand.

"Bugger off," Stone said. "Who the hell are you, and why did you bring us here?"

The man stepped into the light. He was tall, of middle age, dressed in a severe black shirt, jacket, and slacks. His graying hair was cut short and his face clean-shaven. He watched Stone and Richard with a calm, unruffled expression and a steady gaze. "Who I am doesn't matter," he said. "I am but one of many. And as for why you're here? To face retribution, of course."

Stone clenched his fists. "Of course. I should have known. You're one of those Portas prats, aren't you?"

The man offered a thin, beatific smile. "Call us what you like, Dr. Stone. Your words mean nothing to us."

"Couldn't manage to get what you wanted on your own, so you had to take it from us, is that the way it is?"

He chuckled in the manner of a father listening to a child babble nonsense. "Why should we do the work when we could allow you to do it for us?" Nodding toward the obelisk, he added, "And in any case, you might note that *we* were the ones who managed to make it function. And function it does, clearly. Or would you care to try using some of your Satanic powers on me?" He spread his hands invitingly. "Go ahead, if you can."

"You won't get away with this," Richard said. "We'll be found, and you'll regret your actions."

"Oh, I don't think so. We did a few tests on our new device before we put you in here. It's working even more impressively than we'd hoped."

"Tests?" Stone frowned. "What kind of tests?"

"We couldn't trust it to hold you until we were sure it would work, of course. And as it happened, we had more than one volunteer—fellow followers of our ways ashamed of their own disgusting powers—who were all too eager to test it first. Sadly, they were disappointed to discover it doesn't eliminate such powers, as we'd hoped, but merely suppresses them when in proximity to it. That would have been truly a miracle, if it had. We could have removed your powers and simply released you, free to live your lives in a godly way, free of Satanic influence."

He sighed, rubbing his chin. "But as I said, that was not to be. We did discover, however, that being near the obelisk prevents outside tracking. So if you're expecting your demonic companions to come to your rescue, I'm afraid you're quite out of luck."

"How did you make it work?" Stone asked. As long as the man was willing to talk, best to get as much information from him as possible.

He smiled. "We had something you didn't."

Stone went still. "The instructions."

"Ah, so you know about them? Indeed. The book containing the foul ritual necessary to activate the obelisk has been in our possession for decades, in a secret library in Rome. We haven't been actively looking for the obelisk, of course, but when word reached us that the pyramid had surfaced, we knew others would be seeking it as well."

"You nearly killed a good friend of mine," Stone growled. "A mundane. How do you reconcile that with your holier-than-thou moral code?"

"You're correct—and that was truly regrettable. Unfortunately, one of your demonic kind who'd pledged himself to our cause proved unable to resist his evil nature."

"So you had him hit by a truck. More murder."

"No, Dr. Stone. That wasn't murder. That was justice. As the sacred word of God says, 'thou shalt not—'"

"Yes, yes, thou shalt not suffer a witch to live. You lot bang on about that until we're all tired of hearing it. Your quisling even had it tattooed on his body."

"I'm aware. Many of us do, as you have your demonic ways tattooed upon yours."

Stone looked down, only now realizing that the tattoo on his chest, which he normally covered with an illusion, was now visible.

"Come on," he said impatiently. "We can keep on with this until we're all old, but I don't think that's what you want. Where are we, by the way?"

"I won't tell you that. It doesn't matter anyway—you won't be getting out."

"You can't cure us of our 'affliction,' so you're going to kill us. Is that the way it is?"

"Exactly. The world will be better off with two less demon-tainted beings in the world. But first, as long as we've got you here, we might as well make use of you."

Stone and Richard exchanged glances.

"What the hell does that mean?" Richard demanded. He seemed to have gained at least some of his fire back.

"Do not speak blasphemy," the man snapped. Brief anger flashed across his face and he took a step into the room, but then stopped and resumed his original position and expression. "Though I should expect nothing less of your kind."

"What *are* you planning to do with us?" Stone asked. "What do you mean, 'make use of us'?"

The man's smile was smug. "One thing I have found to be true about you demons: when somehow deprived of your evil powers, your sense of superiority evaporates like morning dew." He tilted his head at Stone. "You, I'm well acquainted with, Dr. Stone. You have been a thorn in our side in the past, and I relish the chance to punish you for your transgressions."

"I can hardly wait to see what you come up with." Inwardly, Stone wasn't nearly as enthusiastic about the prospect, but these Portas people were like predatory animals: you couldn't show weakness around them.

"You won't have long to wait. But I think we'll start with your friend here." He turned away from Stone and faced Richard. "I don't know you personally. But I *do* know the organization you represent. That is one thing I have to say in Dr. Stone's favor: he does most of his work alone, or with a few friends. You, on the other hand, belong to an entire *nest* of demons, dedicated not only to destroying God's true children, but also to advancing demonic knowledge."

"We're scientists," Richard protested. "That's all. We're harmless."

Stone didn't snort, but he wanted to. Portas might be the immediate threat, but he suspected everyone in the room knew the Ordo were about as harmless as a tank of piranhas.

"Of course you would tell lies. That's what Satan and his minions do, after all. You lie in the same way as godly people breathe. But at any rate, you are avoiding the subject at hand. As long as I have one viper as my captive, that presents a truly promising opportunity to gain some useful information about his fellow vipers."

Stone was watching Richard, who tensed.

The man smiled. "Remain here. I will return soon, and we will...talk. Until then, I suggest you spend your time in prayer and reflection, asking God's forgiveness for your many sins."

He backed out of the room and closed the door. An instant later, the lights in the cell went out, plunging the space into impenetrable darkness.

"Bloody hell..." Stone murmured. "He's full of himself, isn't he?"

Richard didn't reply, but Stone could hear his harsh, fast breathing.

"Richard?"

"They're going to kill us." His whisper shook with more than cold.

"They are if we don't come up with a plan." Stone blinked a few times, trying to accustom his eyes to the blackness, but it didn't work. With no light, it seemed even more frigid in here than before.

"Don't you *get* it, you fool? There *isn't* any plan! We're chained! We don't have any magic! We're freezing our asses off! You heard him—he's going to torture us, and then he's going to kill us!" The bright edge of incipient panic sluiced through the Ordo man's voice.

"Richard!" Stone snapped. "Pull yourself together!"

Richard let his breath out in a long, shuddering exhalation. "It doesn't matter…" he mumbled. "No one's going to find us here. We don't even know where *here* is. We don't know how long we were unconscious, or far they've taken us. We could be anywhere in the world by now."

"I doubt it."

"Why?"

Stone pressed his back against the cage. "Think about it. These Portas tossers are anti-magic. Even their mages hate themselves. In the first place, there was only one portal near where we were, and do you honestly think they'd try bringing two unconscious people through it? I doubt they've got the cream of the magical crop working for them. They probably don't even *use* the portals."

"That's a lot of speculation. And they were good enough to catch *us*, weren't they?" His voice held bitterness now.

"I didn't say they weren't smart. I said they're likely not powerful. Illusions are easy, and we both got sloppy. That's on us."

"Great." He snorted. "I'll keep that in mind while they're killing me."

Stone said nothing. The cage bars were cold, but no colder than the concrete floor. He tried not to shiver. In truth, despite his confident words, he wasn't convinced they *were* going to get out of here alive. The obelisk's magic-blocking ability worked just fine against Calanarian magic—did that mean it would also block whatever strange arcane forces that had thus far kept him from dying? If they did kill him and then moved his body away from the device, would it kick back in and bring him back from the brink? Or would he be irrevocably dead, beyond even its ability to revive him?

He bowed his head until his chin touched his chest, and tried to think. There had to be *something* they could do. There was always a way out.

Until there wasn't.

"I should never have gotten involved in this whole mess," Richard muttered.

"What?"

His chains rattled against the floor. "This. Everything to do with this vile device."

"I won't argue with you there. Was that you in the car, in Tilley? Were you the one who tried to kill me?"

"No." He sounded defeated. "Those were…agents the organization hired to retrieve McGrath's half of the device."

Agents. The words made Stone think of Eleanor Newman. Had *she* been the one who'd shot at him? He couldn't let himself believe that. "Your people weren't behind the attack on DaCosta, were you?"

"No." This time, the word was contemptuous. "That time, they beat us to it." A long silence, and then: "The woman was working for us, though. Did you know that?"

"The woman?" Stone raised his head and made sure his voice held the proper amount of confusion.

"The one who seduced you. The one you've been sleeping with."

"No." He made himself sound shocked. "Eleanor? No! That's not possible. You're lying."

"Why else would I know about her?" Richard snorted again. "Your…proclivities are well known in our organization, Stone. We took advantage of them."

He sighed. "Bloody hell. I should have caught on to that."

"We were surprised you didn't, honestly. We'd heard rumors that your libido has led you to unwise decisions in the past, though, so we took a chance."

"Didn't pay off, though, did it?" Stone was glad the room was dark—it was a lot easier to feign shocked betrayal when all he had to control was his voice. "She didn't find a bloody thing. Wait…she drugged me that first night, didn't she? I knew I felt odd in the morning."

"She did. But unfortunately, you're right: she *didn't* find anything. We were quite surprised and pleased when you didn't catch on."

Stone let out a loud sigh. "And I was going to take her home to England with me…" He paused. "But why are you telling me this now?"

"What difference does it make? We're both dead. They've got the device. It doesn't *matter* anymore." The chains rattled again. "I don't want to talk. It's pointless. Just…let me try to rest."

Stone lowered his head back down. He had no idea how long it would be before the Portas man came back—perhaps this time with friends. He tried pulling on the chains again, getting no better results than before. He pressed his back harder against the cage, but it still didn't move.

He closed his eyes and concentrated as hard as he could, trying to scrounge up the tiniest hint of magic. He had so much power— surely the obelisk couldn't block *all* of it.

But nothing happened. Not even a faint, minuscule shred of power responded to his call.

Perhaps Richard was right: they *were* going to die. And there was nothing either of them could do about it this time. Every story had to end at some point. Every streak of luck had to run out.

As he sat, shivering in the cold with his hands clasped around his drawn-up legs, he wondered if this was finally that time for him.

CHAPTER THIRTY-SIX

To Stone's surprise, he must have managed to sleep for at least a brief time despite the chill and the discomfort in the cell. He jerked his head up when a harsh light sprang to life above his head.

"Wake up, demons."

Stone winced away from the light, which spiked pain into his eyes after the total darkness. "What…?"

"Wake up. It is the hour of your retribution." It was the same man, but there was no lightness or bantering in his tone now.

"What are you on about?" Stone twisted around to watch as the man entered the cell and moved to Richard's side. The Ordo man lay stretched on the floor, shivering, his chained hands twisted awkwardly behind him.

"Your time will come soon. For now, watch and contemplate your fate."

The Portas man was now dressed in simple black pants, pullover shirt, and boots. He pulled something from his belt, then bent and deftly zip-tied Richard's legs together at the ankles. The he waved toward the door.

Another man, younger this time but no less serious-looking, pushed a rack of implements into the room and shoved it against the wall. He had a chubby, sullen face, with a light dusting of acne across his lower jaw. He left and returned with a wooden chair, which he placed next to the rack.

"Thank you, Caleb," the Portas man said. "You may remain, but do not enter the room. I hope this will be instructional for you. These demons must not be given any leeway. They are snakes, even when deprived of their Satanic powers."

"Yes, sir," the young man said. He glanced at Stone, then back at Richard. His expression was rapt, almost hungry. He was looking forward to what was to come.

"If we're so Satanic," Stone snapped, "why hasn't Satan come to rescue us from your tender mercies?"

"Shut up!" the older man ordered. "Your judgment will come. Do not be in such a hurry to hasten it."

"I'm just saying—if we were in his service, do you honestly think you deluded wankers could keep him out of here?"

"*Silence!*"

On the ground, Richard did his best to move away from the thundering voice, pressing himself against the cage.

The Portas man glared daggers at Stone. "In answer to your question, demon—Satan has forsaken you. He knows the power of God is stronger than his own, and God rules here."

"You wouldn't know God if he ran you down with a truck. Which apparently is something you lot like to do."

Caleb, apparently having reached his limit of listening to his superior being insulted by a heathen, strode in and backhanded Stone across the face with a blow that rocked his head back. "He said shut up!"

Stone licked his lips, tasting a little blood, but smiled thinly. "Fine," he murmured. "For now." He couldn't miss the red flush on both the young man's and the older one's faces. Perhaps they weren't as calm and placid as they were trying to project. He filed that away for future use.

"Outside, Caleb," the Portas man murmured. "I understand and appreciate your fervor, but you must understand these demons hold no power over us. Let them rail and babble. It won't do them any good."

"Yes, sir. Sorry, sir." The young man returned to his spot in the doorway.

"Now," the older man said, "let us begin." He sat in the chair, leaned his elbows on his knees, and looked down at Richard. "We can do this the easy way, or the hard way. It is entirely up to you."

Stone studied the implement rack. It included a coiled whip, several truncheons of varying lengths, rope, knives, and candles. A platform attached to it held some kind of electrical device with two cables ending in clamps. "Planning to indulge in a spot of BDSM, Reverend? I didn't know you had it in you."

The man clenched his fists, but otherwise ignored him. "What's it going to be, Richard? Easy or hard? Believe me, I hope you choose easy. I truly have no desire for you to suffer unnecessarily."

Stone didn't believe that. The kid in the doorway was looking positively orgasmic, and for a moment, Stone wondered if some of the leftover Evil hadn't found a welcome home among the Portas crowd.

Richard didn't answer.

The man didn't seem to find that surprising. "Let me explain them for you, so you'll understand, demon. Your choices are these: You repent and can betray your fellows, providing us with their names and locations. If you give us enough information we can use to hunt down more of your vile kind, your death will be swift and merciful."

Stone didn't miss Richard's body tensing, and he knew why. The Ordo was famous for requiring their members to accept magical oaths that prevented them from revealing any substantive knowledge to non-members. If this was true, Richard literally *couldn't* betray his fellows. No matter how much this man tortured him, it wouldn't matter.

Did the Portas man know this, and was choosing to toy with him?

"Not very godly of you, is it?" Stone asked, injecting a full measure of sarcasm into his words.

"What would you know of godliness, demon?" Caleb snapped.

"Caleb, please." The Portas man's voice was still calm, almost fatherly.

Stone shrugged. "The whole thing just seems a bit dodgy to me. I've been to an S&M dungeon before—purely as an observer, you understand—and they had a lot of similar implements there. When you combine that with chaining us here in our underwear...one has to wonder what the Reverend's true motives are."

"Shut *up!*" Caleb screamed. His whole face was red now. "Sir, are you going to allow this...this *filth* to—"

"Shh..." The man made a quelling motion with one hand, and selected a whip with the other. "I promise, he'll suffer for his sins. But first things first. All must be done in its appropriate order. We are better than they are. Do you understand?"

"Yes, sir." His whisper didn't sound like he did, entirely.

"*I* don't," Stone said. "I don't see a bloody thing about you that makes you better than anyone. You're nothing but a pair of jumped-up sadists. If I were God, I'd be ashamed of both of you."

The man ignored him, but Caleb continued to glare at him in righteous rage. The kid couldn't have been more than eighteen or nineteen.

Ian's age, when they'd first met.

Get them while they're young, indeed...

"Last chance, demon..." the man said smoothly, raising the whip.

Richard said nothing.

"All right, then. You've made your choice. I'd ask God to have mercy on your soul, but you demons don't *have* souls. That's why what we're doing here isn't murder."

The whip came down with a *crack* that ricocheted around the small cell.

Richard screamed.

Stone looked away.

There was nothing he could do—he knew that now. Nothing he said or did would make a difference in what happened to Richard. These people were the worst kind of zealots, convinced their twisted version of "faith" justified anything they chose to do in the name of their equally twisted "God." He'd never been much for religion himself, but he'd always respected Aubrey's devotion to his own faith, and his efforts to be a good and kind person. These people were nothing like that. They were beyond help.

Clearly, so was Richard. Stone lowered his head and closed his eyes as the Ordo mage's screams pitched higher, turning to desperate cries for mercy as the whip continued to crack, the truncheon to find its mark, and the electronic device to buzz with sinister purpose. Richard could have lied, perhaps—given the Portas man fake names. It might even have worked, at least for a while. But if he'd ever considered doing that, he was much too far gone to do it now.

Stone remained where he was, head bowed and eyes closed, until Richard's screams gradually quieted, first to soft moans and then to silence.

"Weak," Caleb said with contempt. "Both of them are weak."

"Demons *are* weak. That is the most important lesson I hope you will take from this example. This demon has paid the first installment of his debt for his sins," the Portas man said. "He will be consigned to the pits of Hell where he will suffer for all eternity."

Stone raised his head, but didn't look at Richard. "So, what now?" he asked softly. "Is it my turn? Are you going to clean those things first, at least? Your sanitary practices are appalling."

The man chuckled. "In such a hurry, Dr. Stone? Don't worry—it won't be long now. We'll leave you in here with your friend for a while, and perhaps that will quiet your tongue and help you see the wisdom of your choices."

"What wisdom? What choices? You want me to take the easy way? If I do that, you won't get your sadistic jollies torturing me."

Another laugh. "That's a choice you won't have. You don't know anything we care about, but you've committed far more transgressions—against us and against godly people in general—than our unfortunate friend here. Your death will neither be slow nor easy. Think about that for a while. We'll be back shortly."

He motioned to Caleb, who wheeled the rack of implements back outside and retrieved the chair. He fixed his gaze on Stone as he passed, and a slow smile spread across his face. "Foul demon," he said. "I look forward to hearing you scream."

The door slammed shut, and the lock clicked.

Stone waited for the light to go off, but it didn't.

Of course not. They want me to see.

He didn't want to see. He didn't want to look at Richard. There was nothing he could do for the man—even if by some miracle he still clung to life, Stone couldn't reach him. And even if he *could* reach him, without his magic or any medical supplies, he'd be helpless to do anything.

The room smelled like blood now. Blood and urine and fear.

Stone swallowed hard, steeled himself, and twisted his body so he could see beyond the cage.

Richard was dead. There was no doubt about it, so at least that was a kind of mercy.

He lay on his back in a puddle of blood, his left chained arm wrenched under him. His pale body was covered in bloody whip stripes, bruises, and burns. His face was twisted into a rictus of pain and terror, his unseeing eyes staring up toward the bright overhead bulb. Stone didn't doubt the Portas man had tried out every toy on his vile little cart.

He settled back into his previous position, with his back against the cage. He didn't need to look at the scene. It wouldn't bring Richard back.

Yes, it was true that Richard had been a member of the Ordo—a group whose members thought nothing of killing mundanes when they got in the way of their plans. Maybe the American branch was less bloodthirsty, but Stone had no doubt the man across from him was no saint, by anyone's standards.

Still, that didn't mean he deserved *this*. Nobody deserved this. The fact that the Portas people had inflicted this kind of treatment on another human being said far more about them than it did about their victim.

And soon, all too soon, they were going to come back here and inflict it on *him*.

Caleb would watch in righteous fervor while his boss tortured Stone the same way he'd tortured Richard. He would walk away untroubled, believing with all his heart that the punishment was justified, that a demon had been removed from the world, that the ways of godliness were restored. Maybe he'd go and have a meal, drink a beer, watch some television. Maybe he even had a girlfriend (of course he wouldn't have a boyfriend—Portas wouldn't stand for that. Maybe they wouldn't even stand for the beer).

Nonetheless, Stone couldn't feel sorry for him. Not even because he'd probably been raised among these horrible people and hadn't had much agency about where his life path took him. It didn't matter. Evil was evil.

None of that was relevant now, though. Any time now, they were going to return with their rack of torture implements and their pious sense of superiority. Without his magic, he had no way to fight back. His arms were chained, his body was so cold now it hurt to move at all, and they would bind his ankles so he couldn't even kick. Physically and magically, he had no chance.

He rested his forehead on knees and knew there was only one answer.

It would be a long shot—a *very* long shot.

He had no way to know if it would work. He was beginning to realize there were a lot of things he didn't know.

But it was his only chance.

And if nothing else, if only part of it worked, at least he'd die quickly, instead of in slow, screaming agony like poor Richard had.

Small victories, but right now they were all he had.

CHAPTER THIRTY-SEVEN

WHEN THE DOOR OPENED AGAIN, Stone was still seated as he had been, his back pressed against the cage with his legs drawn up, his arms wrapped around them, and his forehead on his knees.

"Saying a little prayer, demon?" the familiar deep, resonant voice called. "I regret to inform you it won't work. God doesn't answer prayers from Satan's foul servants."

Stone raised his head. "Just having a bit of a rest."

Caleb snickered. "You'll have your *eternal* rest soon, filth. You'll burn in Hell for all eternity."

"You know..." Stone said slowly, with a confused head-tilt, "one thing I don't quite get. Maybe you can help me work it out."

"What is that?" the Portas man asked.

"Well...you and your pimply little lickspittle here keep banging on about how we're going to end up in Hell, like that's a bad thing. But if we really *are* working for Satan, aren't you just sending us home? You know—kick off our boots after a job well done, have a pint, get our performance evaluation and a few days' holiday before our next assignment?"

Both men glared at him.

Stone shrugged. "Don't mind me—I've just had a while to think about these things. So if I *am* a demon, you're not consigning me to eternal punishment at all. But if you're wrong—if I'm *not* a demon—then what's that say about your methods?"

"Of course you're a demon!" Caleb snapped. "You have demonic powers. Thou shalt not suffer a witch to live!"

"Ah! There we go. I was wondering when we were going to trot out the slogan again." Stone looked the boy directly in the eye and made a little *tsk* noise. "But shame on you, Caleb. You should be old enough by now to recite the company motto in its proper Latin. Come on, say it with me now, slowly: *Maleficos... non... patieris... vivere.* Got that? Let's hear you try it on your own now." He regarded the boy expectantly. "If you get it right, maybe the Reverend will pat your head and give you a gold star. Or better yet, a gold cross."

"Enough!" the older man thundered. "The demon is toying with you, boy! We are not here to listen to him spout his foul swill."

"No. You're here to torture me, like you did with poor Richard there—except this time you don't even have the excuse of trying to get information out of me." As cold as he was, it was hard to keep his voice from shaking. He mostly managed, but not entirely. "You already said I don't know anything you'd find useful—which is doubtful, honestly. But if it's true, what does *that* say about you?" He flashed a fierce grin. "Let's spell it out, for the people in the back row: it says there's nothing at all righteous or godly about you. You're sadists, pure and simple. Come on, Reverend—at least have the bollocks to own it."

"*Shut up!*" Caleb screamed. "You will not mock your betters!"

"My betters? That's debatable. But what have I got to lose? You're going to kill me either way—you've already said so, and God's favorite twisted little children never *lie,* do they? Why shouldn't I have a bit of fun before you snuff me?"

The boy glared at Stone, then at the older man. "Sir—let me do it. Please. Let me have him! I saw what you did with the other one—and I've got some other ideas, too."

"Oh, brilliant idea," Stone said brightly. "Let Caleb do it, Reverend. Watching's great, but torture's a sort of hands-on discipline, isn't it? He'll never get it right if you don't let him get his hands dirty."

"Out of the question."

He'd been addressing Caleb, but Stone replied as if he'd been speaking to him directly. "Why? Are you afraid he won't do the job properly? That's fair." He aimed a conspiratorial chin-jerk at Caleb. "He does strike me as a bit…you know…*slow*. But you work with what you've got, don't you? And if he botches the job, you can always come along behind him and clean up." He rattled his chains. "It's not like I'm going anywhere."

"Let me do it, sir," Caleb growled. "He's mocking us! Let me shut his foul mouth!" He clenched and unclenched his fists as he said it, and the look on his face was a combination of rage and fervor.

The man considered, looking back and forth between Stone and Caleb. "Very well," he said at last. "Soon, you will be dealing with demons on your own. You may proceed, Caleb. I will observe from the hallway. Be careful, though—these demons are treacherous. Do not allow him to get away with anything."

"Oh, don't worry, sir." Caleb's face split in a smug, satisfied smile. "I'll teach him God's plan for demons like him."

"I can hardly wait," Stone said. "Do instruct me."

The boy returned to the hallway and pushed the familiar cart inside. This time, he rolled it to Stone's side of the room, careful to avoid getting close to him, and placed it against the wall.

Stone feigned interest, looking over the implements. "Where shall we start, where shall we start?"

"Immobilize his legs," the man called from the doorway. "He will kick you if he gets a chance."

Stone didn't fight as Caleb pulled out a thick zip-tie and dropped down next to him. "Oh, yes," he murmured. "You should absolutely immobilize my legs. Although, while aiming a sad little kick at you would be satisfying, I doubt it would be of much use. It won't get me out of here."

Caleb grabbed one of his ankles, wrenched it next to his other leg, and deftly trussed them together.

"Good job!" Stone said, in the tone of a preschool teacher praising a child for using the potty properly. "Oh, I can see this is going to be fun, Caleb. You've got the touch." He leaned forward a little and murmured under his breath, "But then, you *like* the touch, don't you?"

"Shut up!" Caleb reached around, pulled a knife from the cart, and waved it in Stone's face. "Shut up, or you'll regret it, demon!"

"No doubt I will." He smiled. "But I'm not wrong, am I? You like the touch. Tell me—was it your idea to strip us down to our underwear? Maybe it's not about the cold at all. Maybe it's because you like to look? Maybe you wish you hadn't had to stop there?"

"Shut *up!*" Caleb backhanded him again with the hand holding the knife.

"Caleb—" the man called from the doorway.

"It's all right, sir." The boy's voice shook with rage. "I've got this."

"Do you?" Stone whispered. "You know, it *is* all right. Truly, it is." He didn't like using this approach, but desperate times justified a little inappropriateness. Especially because he could tell it was working. "I won't blame you at all, if it's true. It's absolutely natural."

Caleb's hand tightened on the knife. "You will not speak to me this way, demon! The power of God will cast you out, and I will be the vessel that administers His punishment!"

"That's the way!" Stone leaned forward a little more and dropped his voice back to a whisper. "Make him believe you." He leaned in closer. "Maybe you can get him to go away—to leave us alone together. *Then* we can have fun. You'd like that, wouldn't you, before you kill me? Once you go demon, you'll never want to go back. Trust me. I can show you things that would curl your hair."

The boy was gripping the knife so hard his hand was shaking now, his chest heaving with his short, sharp breaths. "You—I—"

"You know you want it, Caleb!" Stone yelled in his face with sudden, shocking ferocity. "You know it! Admit it! Surrender to your true desires!" He fixed a crazy-eyed stare on the boy, lunged at him to the limits of his chains, and began screaming in a guttural magical language. The words were nonsense: something about *your ox is green* and *the circle is full of cheese,* but their deep, harsh cadence could easily have been the speech of some foul demon from the depths of hell.

And all the while he was silently thinking, *Please let this work...*

Caleb jerked back as if Stone had hit him with a hot poker. "No! You will not tempt me! Begone, foul demon!"

"Caleb!" the Reverend shouted from the hallway. He rushed into the room toward the boy.

But it was too late. With a wild scream of fear mixed with righteous rage, Caleb flung himself forward, raised the knife, and plunged it into Stone's chest.

"*Die, demon!*" he shrieked.

The knife struck true. Stone felt only a quick flare of pain as the blade pierced him, before a tide of grayness rose to overwhelm his vision. His body slumped sideways, held half-upright by the chains, and the instant before everything drifted away into blackness, he heard the Reverend scream, "*NO!*"

If he was truly going to die, he hoped he'd done it with a smile on his face.

That would piss them off.

CHAPTER THIRTY-EIGHT

HE DRIFTED IN AND OUT of consciousness, never quite reaching the level where he was sure whether the world around him was real, in his mind, or somewhere in between.

Angry screaming.

Blackness.

He was moving, bouncing as if someone was dragging him over an uneven surface.

Blackness.

A bolt of agonizing pain flaring in his chest.

Blackness.

He landed hard and rolled.

But…*not* blackness this time. Grayness. Confusion. Pain.

He had no idea how long it lasted.

He was cold.

He was hungry.

How could he be dead if he was hungry?

And then, miraculously, a voice.

A woman's voice, speaking in a harsh whisper.

"Oh, god, what have they done to you?"

Cold, strong hands seized his shoulders and rolled him onto his back.

The voice gasped.

Opening his eyes was the hardest thing he'd ever done. It felt as if he were trying to lift a two-ton roll-up door with the strength of a toddler. But something deep in the back of his mind told him he had to do it anyway.

His eyelids flickered, then opened to slits.

Above him, it was dark. But not fully dark, as it had been in the cell. There were lights. There were stars.

The hanging bulb was gone.

The concrete under his back was gone, too. Instead, he felt something uneven, parts of it soft, parts poking into him.

A figure crouched over him, blurry and indistinct.

He tried to blink.

He thought he managed a faint moan.

"You're alive…"

He thought the voice might sound familiar, but he couldn't be sure. Things weren't making sense right now, no matter how hard he tried to wrangle his chaotic thoughts.

"Okay…okay…" The woman seemed to be talking to herself now. "Need to call an ambulance…get you to a hospital…"

The word *hospital* grabbed hold of some of the errant thoughts and wrenched them into focus. "No…" he whispered, or tried to. It came out as a dry croak. He tried again: "No…"

Her head snapped up. "Did you say something?"

"No…hospital."

"But you're dying! I thought you were already dead." She definitely sounded concerned, but there was no panic in her tone.

"No…not…dying." It was so hard to summon the breath to force the words out. Something in his chest felt tight, and he couldn't get a deep breath.

"Alastair, listen to me. I know dying when I see it."

At the sound of his name, it came to him—who she was, and possibly why she was here. "Eleanor…you…you came." He managed a faint, arch smile. "But your…timing is…rubbish."

"Yeah, well, you didn't tell me they were taking you somewhere I couldn't trace. It took me longer to find them than I thought." She had her phone in her hand now. "I'm calling somebody. I'll be damned if I let you die on me out here in your underwear in the middle of a vacant lot full of trash."

He raised a shaky hand and reached for her arm. The manacles were gone now. More memories tumbled back.

He'd done it.

His desperate gamble had paid off.

"What the hell are you *smiling* about? Damn it, you look like absolute crap."

"Feel...like it, too." He stared at her. His memories were like a box full of puppies, popping up with no discernable order or chronology. "We've got to...find them."

"Find who?"

"Portas. Where...are we?"

"North San Jose. Like I said, in a vacant lot full of trash. Some-body dumped you here. Come on—do you think you can stand if I help you? Let me get you to my car so we can get out of here. There's a blanket in the back."

He remembered the knife, and patted his chest. It wasn't there now. Had the Portas people removed it before they dumped his body?

"What's wrong?"

Magic.

His breath came faster, and his heart pounded harder. The obelisk wasn't here anymore. Did he dare hope he could—

"Alastair?"

"Shh. A moment, please," he whispered.

He'd thought opening his eyes was hard, but it was nothing compared to this. He had to concentrate, to focus, and everything seemed to be conspiring against that.

But he had to know.

He held up a shaking hand and stared hard at it, reaching out with everything he had.

Come on…come on…

A faint, flickering purple-and-gold nimbus sprang up around his hand. As he watched it, it grew stronger, and even the tiny band of silver around the edge showed up for a second before he lost his concentration and the whole thing collapsed again.

"What are you doing? We have to go."

He let his breath out in a rush of relief. "Magic."

"Magic? What are you talking about?"

He snapped his gaze to fix on her. "Where are they? The people who took me? We can't let them get away—"

"They're not going to get away."

She was avoiding something—he could see it in her face. "What—? Did you—?"

"I didn't do anything. They got raided."

That was almost enough to make him ignore the pain in his chest. "Raided?"

"Come *on.*" She slipped her arm around his shoulders. "Help me here. Let's get you back to the car and then I'll tell you everything."

He resisted. "No hospital."

"No hospital, you stubborn son of a bitch. I'll take you back to your house. Okay?"

"Yes. All right."

Her car, a rented sedan, wasn't parked far away, but she had to do most of the work to get him there. He tried to help—she'd either already cut the zip-tie around his ankles or the Portas people had removed it before they dumped him—but his legs refused to obey his commands. It was a good thing she was strong.

Finally, he lay slumped across the back seat with a blanket over him.

"Are you sure you're not going to die on me?" She peered in at him accusingly.

"I'm sure." *If I haven't died by now, I'm not going to.* He lifted his head a little to see that his chest was covered in dried blood, but the knife wound had already begun to knit together. "What do you mean…they got raided?"

She climbed into the driver's seat and drove off. "Just what I said. I tracked those people to an abandoned church not too far from here. When I got inside and roughed up one of their guys, they told me you were dead—that they'd dumped your body in a lot a mile or so away. He was pretty smug about it, but he folded like a cheap card table when I threatened him. By the way, I've got your phone, but I think they burned the rest of your clothes."

"What about the obelisk?" Stone tried to sit up, but didn't have the energy to do it.

"The what?"

"The black pyramid, and the base. They put them together."

"You mean the weird-looking thing inside the cage?"

"Yes."

"I don't know what happened to it. That's when the other people showed up, and I had to get my ass out of there. I managed to sneak out the back before they got inside, but it was a close thing."

Damn. "Who were they? Your employers?" Had someone else been tracking the meeting at the coffee shop, and gone in with the intent to rescue Richard?

"No. These were law enforcement. Several local cops, but there were a couple others, too, who seemed to be in charge. Plainclothes, but you can't miss the type. Feds, maybe. They were good."

"Oh, bloody hell…"

"You know them?"

"Not…exactly. Was one of them a woman with red hair?"

"Yeah. The other one looked like a middle-aged dad."

Stone let his breath out. "They were after the obelisk too. If they were behind the raid on Portas's lair…"

"They might have it now."

"Yes."

She twisted around and flashed him a quick smile. "Maybe we can do something about that. But we have to do something about *you* first."

"What are you talking about?"

"Tell you soon. You're in no shape to be doing anything yet. Let's get you home."

He could tell from her tone that she wasn't going to say anything else now, and in any case, he was so tired he could barely keep his eyes open. At least the blanket was warm. "Eleanor…?" he mumbled.

"Yeah?"

"Thank you…"

She snorted. "Hey, you're paying me. And I'm getting a bonus for this one."

"You're worth every penny."

By the time they reached the Encantada house, Stone was feeling marginally better. Only marginally, though. His chest still hurt, and he still had next to no energy.

The car stopped. "How do I get the gate open?"

Damn. The fob was in his car, which was probably still parked back in Palo Alto. At least he hoped it was. He dragged himself up, focused, and used a little magic to open it, then sank back down. "How long has it been? What time is it?"

"Uh…it's around three a.m."

"What day?"

"Friday."

He let his breath out. The meeting had been Thursday night—so Portas hadn't held onto him and Richard for long before they began their little torture party. But that also meant Verity was still in Australia, and Jason and Amber were in Los Angeles. No help from either of them.

It was a good thing whoever had dumped his body had pulled the knife out before they did it. If they hadn't, his strange accelerated healing ability wouldn't have been able to start working on him, and he'd be in a lot worse shape than he was now.

The car crawled up the graveled drive and stopped in front of the house.

"Getting you inside isn't going to be easy. You don't happen to have a gurney in there, do you?"

"I'm afraid not."

Already, he was feeling somewhat better. Still not great, but well enough he could provide a bit of help as she hustled him into the house and settled him on the sofa. Raider immediately appeared, leaping to a nearby chair to watch with worried eyes.

"It's all right, mate," Stone rasped. "I know I smell like blood and rubbish."

Eleanor considered. "Okay. Now what? I can't just leave you here like this. You need attention. I can do a bit of field-medic stuff, but I'm no nurse."

She was right—he *did* need attention. The wound in his chest was healing, but the knife had pierced deep. It would be slow if he left it alone, even if he didn't move around. He could try to heal it himself, but he didn't trust his abilities on something like this. And Verity was well out of reach…

An idea struck him. He looked up at Eleanor. "Listen…I need to ask you a big favor."

"You mean bigger than retrieving your mostly-dead carcass from a vacant lot in the middle of the night?" she asked dryly.

"Potentially, yes."

"What?"

"You said something about dealing with the people who raided Portas later. What did you mean by that?"

Her sly smile returned. "I put a tracker on their car before I took off. If they didn't find it, we might be able to find *them*. But you're in no shape to go anywhere, and no offense, I'm not going up against the Feds on my own, without any of your special kind of assistance. I'm a mercenary and I'm damn good, but I'm not an idiot. Unfortunately, they'll probably be long gone before we get to them."

"Maybe not." Now it was Stone's turn for a sly smile. "That's where the favor comes in."

"Mate, I do *not* know what to do with you."

Eddie grabbed hold of one of Stone's arms, and Ward the other, as he appeared in front of them and immediately pitched forward.

"Long…story," he got out between harsh breaths. "Thanks, both of you. Did you…find somebody?"

They helped him to a sofa and laid him down. "Yeah," Eddie said. "It's that strange kind of luck o' yours, I think—one of the best 'ealers in the UK 'as been 'ere at Caventhorne doin' some research, and we convinced 'im to do the job. You're gonna owe 'im, though—not just for 'ealin'. For silence. He's a right grumpy bugger, and 'e's blowin' off a nice lunch invitation for this."

Stone nodded wearily. "Good. Good. Send him in, please. I'll pay whatever he wants."

"And then you're gonna tell us what's got you into this state, right?"

"Yes…but later. Time is short."

Both of them looked dubious. "Okay," Eddie finally said. "I'll get 'im. You rest. You look like you're 'alf dead. Keep an eye on 'im, Ward. Make sure 'e doesn't do a runner on us."

There was no danger of that. He *felt* half-dead. The trip to Caventhorne had taken what little energy he had left, but at least he'd kept it together long enough for Eleanor to help him clean up and put on some fresh clothes after he called Eddie. "Help" might have been a bit optimistic—she did most of the work.

Eddie hurried out, and Ward sat on the chair across from the sofa. "This has something to do with the pyramid, doesn't it?" he asked.

Stone nodded wearily. "Haven't got the energy to tell the whole story now…and it needs a few pints anyway. I promise, I'll tell you everything after it's over."

"It isn't over yet?"

"That…remains to be seen. Depends on how fast I can get back into action."

Ward looked dubious about that being anytime soon, but didn't comment.

Eddie returned five minutes later with an older, cranky-looking man in a suit even more old-fashioned than Stefan Kolinsky favored. He had a florid face, small eyes beneath impressively-bushy eyebrows, and a bald, shiny pate.

The man took one look at Stone, narrowed his eyes to slits, and asked, "What happened to *you*?" His accent was thickly Scottish.

"Got myself stabbed."

He shook his head. "Damned fool kids. Okay. Take your shirt off and let's have a look."

Stone needed Eddie's help to comply. He lay back, propped against the sofa arm, and waited.

By now, the wound didn't look like much to the naked eye. The man dragged a chair over, sat, and fuzzed out as he shifted to magical sight. After a few moments, he opened his eyes and stared at Stone in shock. "How the hell are you alive?"

"Er—"

"No, I'm serious. Ye said ye got stabbed, but this looks like it hit ye square in the heart. Ye shouldn't be alive."

Stone managed a small shrug. "What can I say? Lucky, I guess. Can you fix it?"

"Depends on what ye mean by 'fix.' How long ago did this happen? Why'd ye let it go so long before gettin' help? This looks like it's been healin' up for days."

Here was the tricky part. "Eddie said I'm paying for your silence...and your discretion. Is that right?"

"Yeah, and payin' dear. This is gonna take some careful work."

"That's fine." He glanced at Eddie, who nodded once. He trusted this guy, and Stone didn't have much choice but to follow suit. "The thing is...I've got some...er...rather special tricks up my sleeve. This happened about..." He paused, then forged ahead. "Two hours ago."

The man's bushy eyebrows met in the middle as he frowned deeply. "Don't lie to me, boy."

"I'm not. Can you do it or not? I'm in a bit of a hurry."

The healer barked something between a laugh and a snort. "Ach, I can do it all right. But ye won't be hurryin' anywhere for quite some time if ye've got any sense."

"'E 'asn't got much sense, and that's the God's-honest truth," Eddie said.

Stone shot him a tepid glare. "Just do it. I'll worry about the rest later."

Clearly, the man had his doubts. But finally he shrugged. "Whatever. It's your money."

Fifteen minutes later, he sat back in his chair with a loud sigh. "There. That's the best I can do. Ye're damned lucky it's a single wound—those are easier to heal, even bad ones like this."

Stone, who'd been lying back and luxuriating as the pain lessened and it got easier to get a full breath, opened his eyes and sat up. He still didn't feel a hundred percent—not even close. But this man was good, without a doubt. Better than Verity. Possibly better than Edna Soren, and that was saying a lot. "Thank you, sir."

The healer *harrumph*ed. "Don't do nothin' so daft next time."

"I'll...keep that in mind." He sat up and pulled his shirt back on. It didn't hurt, which was nice. "Let me know where to send your payment."

Eddie and Ward eyed him severely after the man left. "Don't tell me you're plannin' on 'eadin' out again already."

"No choice. As I said, haven't got much time." His stomach rumbled, and he realized he'd had neither food nor drink since early the previous evening. "But first—have you got something to eat? And something non-alcoholic to drink?"

Barely thirty minutes had passed when Stone popped back into his bedroom in Encantada. Between the healing and the sandwich and tea Ward had found for him, he felt better than he had since the beginning of his Portas ordeal. That was still only about seventy percent of normal, but he'd take it.

Eleanor was waiting for him downstairs, seated on the sofa with Raider, drinking a Guinness and watching a monster movie on the TV.

"You're still here," he called.

"You expected I wouldn't be?" She studied him with a critical eye. "You look a lot better. Whatever you did up there, it worked."

"Mostly worked. Best I can hope for." He sat across from her. "Please tell me they didn't find your tracker yet."

She raised her phone and smiled. "Not yet. I'm disappointed, actually. If they're Feds, they're getting sloppy."

"Their sloppiness is our gain. Where are they?"

"Still in San Jose—near downtown. Looks like they're in a hotel. One of those long-term residence inns."

Stone frowned. "That's odd. I wonder what they're doing there. Are they *based* in this area?"

"No idea. If I had to guess, I'd say they're waiting for morning so they can catch a plane somewhere. The hotel isn't far from the airport."

"So it's possible they still have the obelisk with them?"

"Unless they handed it off to somebody else, yeah. But we'd better hurry." She narrowed her eyes. "You sure you're up for this? If you keel over in the middle of the operation, I can't promise I'll be able to save you again."

Stone wasn't sure he was, but at this point he didn't have a lot of options. All the people he would normally call for help weren't available, so it was up to him. "I'll make it. We've got to do this."

"Okay. Let's go, then. We'll take my car. It's less conspicuous, and I don't trust you to drive."

"We'll have to, anyway—mine's still parked down by University Perk. If they haven't towed it yet."

"So," Eleanor said as they drove down 280 toward San Jose. "Tell me about this obelisk. Why is everybody after it?"

"They didn't tell you?" Stone sat with his cheek pressed against the passenger-side window, conserving his energy and watching the traffic. By now it was just after five a.m., the leading edge of the brutal Bay Area morning commute. So far, they were still moving at a decent speed in the HOV lane.

"I didn't care before. It was just a job. But now...I feel like I want to know. I assume it's some kind of big-deal magical doodad."

"It's a magic blocker. And a powerful one."

"Blocker?" She glanced his way. "You mean it can mess up magic? Stop it from working?"

"Yes. That's how they caught me. They tricked me and your employer by impersonating both of us and setting up a meeting between us." He tilted his head. "His body wasn't in that vacant lot too, was it?"

"No. I didn't see any other bodies. Maybe they dumped him somewhere else. I'm sure they'll spill when they're questioned."

He nodded. He still felt bad about Richard's fate, especially when he remembered assuring the other mage they'd both survive. "Anyway...yes, it's very powerful when the two pieces are combined—the pyramid and the base part—to form the obelisk. Powerful enough to completely interfere with my magic."

"Ah, I see now. That's how they managed to hold you."

"Yes. It was quite unsettling."

"So, what are you going to do with it if you get it back?"

He thought about it. He didn't know yet, not ultimately. "I'll work that out once we have it."

"It's dangerous to keep it around, isn't it? If it messes with your magic…"

"It is, if I can't break it apart. It could be that the ritual that fused it made the fusion permanent."

"And whoever ends up with it has a lot of potential power."

"Yes." He shot a glance her way, and shifted to magical sight to check her aura. It hadn't changed, which he hoped was a good sign. She *was* a mercenary, after all, and if she realized the kind of money she could make if she took the obelisk for herself and sold it to the highest bidder…

"Don't worry," she said, almost as if she'd read his mind. "I'm not going to steal it, if that's what you're thinking. I'm a simple girl. I do jobs, I get paid, I move on. You're lucky I still had a couple things to do in the area, or I'd have been long gone when you texted me. I don't have either the desire or the inclination to get involved in all that behind-the-scenes cloak-and-dagger stuff—especially not against your types. I'm not an idiot. You can keep the thing, and you're welcome to it…*if* we can get hold of it."

It was a big *if*. As they approached the location her tracker pointed at, Stone's tension grew. What if Redhead and Dad Bod *had* discovered Eleanor's tracker, but had chosen to leave it in place to see who it might lure in?

Stop it, he told himself. *You're overthinking again.*

But was he?

"Okay, we're getting close." Eleanor's voice cut into his uneasy thoughts. "The hotel's just up the street here. What's the plan?"

"How precise is your tracker? It will just find their car, right? Not their room?"

"Yeah. And I'm guessing you don't have any way to track the item itself?"

"Not a good one."

"I guess we could wait for them to come out and jump them."

Stone shook his head as she pulled into the hotel's parking lot. "Too dangerous. As long as they've got that obelisk, my magic is useless."

She cruised past the line of cars, switching her gaze between them and her phone screen. Halfway down the row, she pointed. "There it is. The light-blue Ford."

"Keep going. Park in the back. They might be watching it."

She did as directed, pulling the car to a stop next to a dumpster. "Well, we need *something* we can do. I doubt they'd leave the thing in their car."

"Unlikely." Stone unbuckled his seatbelt, but didn't get out yet. He still didn't feel well enough to waste unnecessary energy. He thought of Gina. "Are you any good with computers? If I could distract the desk clerk, could you get into their system and figure out which room goes with that car?"

"Sorry. Not really my thing. I'm more a woman of action." She waggled her eyebrows at him suggestively.

It was a testament to how tired and focused Stone was that he didn't respond to her obvious flirtation. "Bugger. I know someone who could, but it would take too long to get her here."

"That sucks." She twisted around to look back toward the hotel. "The place isn't very big—just three stories. Maybe you could—I don't know—wander around and see if you pick up any vibes from the thingamabob?"

Stone almost waved that off as absurd, partly because the last thing he wanted to do when he was feeling this trashed was plod up and down hotel hallways.

Although...

If the obelisk was still whole, it had to be putting out some fairly significant power. Otherwise, there was no way it could have blocked all of Stone's considerable magical strength.

It *might* reach to the edge of a small hotel room... "You might be on to something."

"Yeah? I was actually kidding."

"No, it might work." Energized, he opened the door. "I think it's got a chance. Come on. Let's give it a go."

She got out as well. "Give me a few minutes. I'll catch up with you. And keep your head down, so you don't show up on any cameras."

"What are you going to do?"

"Make sure if they sneak out, that car isn't going anywhere. Be careful. No keeling over—you promised." Without giving him a chance to reply, she took off toward the building, then moved along the edge of it and around the corner.

Stone watched her go, then headed for the hotel's back door. He didn't feel as bad as he feared—maybe adrenaline was doing its job. He couldn't count on that forever, though. He'd have to hurry.

The back door was locked, but only a small bit of magic was necessary to open it. He slipped inside.

The hotel wasn't large. It was three stories tall, composed of two wings on either side of a central lobby containing the front desk, the elevators, and a small sitting area. This early in the morning, nobody was there except a bored-looking clerk playing with her phone. Stone put up a disregarding spell and walked past her with purpose; she didn't even look up.

He didn't bother keeping the spell going. Nobody here knew him, and if his plan worked, the obelisk's field would interfere with it anyway. Instead, he summoned a tiny light spell around his hand and walked down the left-side hallway, trailing his fingers along the wall as he went. As Eleanor had directed, he kept his head down and did his best to avoid the security cameras.

If his luck ran the same way as usual, he expected he wouldn't find anything until he reached the final wing of the third floor—if then. To his surprise, though, the little spell flickered and died halfway down the right-side, first-floor hall, in front of room 114.

His phone vibrated in his pocket, with a text from Eleanor: *Find it?*

114, he sent.

That was fast. Be right there.

Less than thirty seconds later, she appeared at the door at the outside end of the hall. He hurried down and opened it for her.

"You seriously found it already?" she whispered.

"This isn't a thriller movie, where we've got to drag out the suspense to the last possible moment," he muttered back.

"*Touché.* So what do we do now?"

"This is your show, I think. I can't open the door with magic, and I can't use any to sneak around inside the room. You said you're good at this kind of thing—now's the time to demonstrate that. I'll keep watch out here. Leave your phone on in your pocket so I'll hear if there's any trouble."

She frowned. "You want me to sneak in there and jack the thing out from under their sleeping noses?"

"You don't think you can do it?"

The frown changed to a grin. "Just watch me." She pulled a compact, leather-wrapped kit from one of her jacket pockets, and plugged a tiny device into the keycard lock. "Keep an eye out for anybody coming."

It took her less than ten seconds to open the lock. She took a deep breath and flashed another grin. "Here goes nothing. Think happy thoughts."

Stone remained in the hallway, his ear glued to the phone and his tension increasing, but there was no sound from inside the room. He didn't feel as helpless as he had when he was chained in Portas's cell, but knowing his magic would do him no good here wasn't helping his stress level.

A movement at the lobby-side end of the hall caught his attention. A maid was rolling her cart in his direction. So far she seemed not to notice him, but if she kept coming, she couldn't miss him. *Bloody hell, not now…*

He sidled toward the next room, closer to the exterior door. When he felt his magic return, he cast a disregarding spell and remained quiet, hoping Eleanor wouldn't choose that moment to exit the room.

Come on…hurry… He dared not say anything and risk someone else inside hearing him. All he could do was wait.

The maid left her cart in the hallway and turned off into an alcove, probably to gather more supplies.

Stone switched his gaze between the cart and room 114's door, tapping his foot with growing impatience.

Come on…

114's door opened silently, and Eleanor slipped out. She carried a black duffel bag.

Stone hurried back to her as she closed the door just as silently. "You got it!" He didn't need to say it, though—already, he could feel the thing interfering with his magic.

"Yeah, I checked. It's in there. Let's get out of here before they catch on."

They turned toward the outside door, but at that moment it opened and two young men in suits entered, carrying overnight bags and briefcases.

"Bugger!" Stone snapped. "They might be more feds."

Eleanor shoved the bag into his hands. "You go the other way. I'll go out the side and bring the car around to the front."

Stone wasn't crazy about that solution, since having the bag in his possession meant he couldn't use any magic, but she was already moving down the hall.

"Morning!" she said cheerfully to the young men as she passed them.

Stone started down the hall the other direction, but risked a quick glance over his shoulder to see if the men were headed his way.

They weren't paying any attention to him. Instead, one of them opened the door to a room near the side exit, and both of them went inside.

Stone didn't let himself relax yet, though. He backed down the hall toward the lobby, keeping a close eye on the door to 114.

He'd only need to make it a short distance more, and then he could head out the front, get in the car, and he and Eleanor would be home free with the obelisk.

The door opened.

Damn! Stone almost panicked. He didn't know where Redhead and Dad Bod had stored the duffel bag in their room, so he had no way to know if they'd already missed it. If they *did* miss it, all they'd have to do was look his way and they'd see him standing there holding it. Without magic, there was nowhere for him to hide.

He darted his desperate gaze back and forth, heart pounding, trying to remain calm.

The maid's cart was still there, two steps behind him. A quick glance into the alcove revealed she wasn't there anymore, but there was a door—perhaps a restroom for the employees? Maybe she'd ducked in there.

Either way, Stone didn't have a lot of choice. He jammed the duffel bag into the pile of dirty sheets on the cart, pulled a couple over top of it, and ducked into the alcove. As he reached the back wall, his magic flickered to life. He quickly pulled up an illusion to make himself look like a maid, and waited. He couldn't see the cart from where he was, so he had to hope Redhead and Dad Bod wouldn't have any reason to check it.

The wait seemed to take forever, but in reality it was only a few seconds. Redhead and Dad Bod swept past the opening to the alcove, paying no attention to the "maid" fiddling with a stack of folded sheets. Stone didn't miss their expressions, though—they looked focused and stressed. They *had* noticed. That was fast.

Quickly, he pulled out his phone and tapped out a text: *They're coming to front. Go side door.* Then he peered out of the alcove.

Dad Bod and Redhead were gone. That was good.

So was the cart. That was bad.

Damn, damn, damn! Had they taken it? How could they have *known?* Was one of them a mage?

But then he spotted the propped-open door to room 101 and let out the breath he was holding.

With a last look toward the lobby, Stone darted out and headed for 101. Immediately, his illusionary disguise dropped.

The cart was inside the room, along with the maid. Apparently she *hadn't* gone through the door in the alcove, but somewhere else, and now she was back and ready to begin her rounds.

The room was a suite, with a small kitchenette/sitting area combo in the front and a bedroom in the back. The maid, earbuds in and head bopping to whatever unseen music she was listening to, had her back to Stone, busily stripping the sheets off the bed. The cart was in the kitchenette.

Stone's phone vibrated in his pocket, but he didn't spare the time to look at it now. He'd need to get out of here fast. Heart pounding harder than ever, he hurried forward and plunged his hand into the pile of dirty sheets, all the while keeping his gaze fixed on the maid.

She never even looked up. He grabbed the duffel bag, took a quick peek outside the door to make sure Dad Bod and Redhead weren't coming back, then lowered his head like a football running back and dashed toward the side door. As he did, he remembered the joking comment he'd made earlier that they weren't in a thriller movie. If Eleanor hadn't gotten his text and was waiting for him at the front instead of the side—

But no, there was her rental car, idling impatiently just outside the door. Stone shouldered it open and ran out, flinging the passenger door open and throwing the duffel bag into the back seat in one smooth motion. He barely had his own door shut before Eleanor took off, driving quickly but not erratically.

Stone let out a long breath. "Bloody *hell!* That was much closer than I hoped!"

"They're awake already? They were sleeping like babies when I went in there."

"I've got no idea, but they're out now, and they know it's gone."

"I hope you stayed off the cameras."

"I did my best."

"And you can't do anything to conceal us?" She exited the parking lot and turned onto the frontage road next to the freeway.

"Not magically. Not with *that* in the back seat."

"Well, we'll just have to hope they didn't notice us, then."

Stone didn't have a lot of faith in that. He spent the rest of the trip back to Encantada swiveling his head around, checking the mirrors, and stressing out every time a car seemed to get too close to them.

"Calm down," Eleanor said, patting his knee in amusement. "I do this all the time. Even if they're on to us, it doesn't happen instantly. By the time they catch on, I'll have ditched the rental car, which was rented under a fake ID, and be long gone, and you'll have that thing stashed where they'll never have a chance of finding it."

Stone nodded, but he didn't believe it. Maybe it was his leftover fatigue from the injury talking, but he wouldn't be truly relaxed until the obelisk was safely under lock and key. And that, he realized, was going to be a lot harder than he thought, depending on whether he could successfully separate the two pieces. If he couldn't, that meant all his normal avenues of concealment wouldn't be available to him.

He couldn't take it through the portal—that would be too risky. What if it did something to interfere with the conduit, stranding him halfway between two points—or worse? Likewise, he couldn't use ley-line travel, which he understood even less well. He couldn't store the thing behind an illusion, or in his warded safe. Hell, what if it messed with the wards on his house?

He twisted around, grabbing the duffel bag and dragging it to his lap.

"What are you doing?" Eleanor demanded.

"I've got to see something."

"Can't it wait until we're inside?"

"No." He unzipped the bag. They were almost to the house now.

"What do you want me to do? I can't get past your gates."

He was barely paying her any attention now. "Just—pull over for a moment, and keep an eye out for anyone watching us."

She sighed loudly and kept driving past the house. "I'm not stopping here. We're too exposed, especially if they know you're involved. What are you trying to do?"

He pulled the obelisk out of the bag. He felt strange and uncomfortable even touching it—it made his fingers tingle, and his whole body squirmed uneasily—but he tried his best to ignore it. Instead, he took hold of the top part with one hand and the bottom with the other, and tried to pull the two pieces apart.

They didn't budge. In fact, when he looked closer, he saw that there was no line, not even the thinnest of cracks, indicating where the pyramid ended and the base began. The whole thing was a single, unified whole now.

Stone sighed. He'd been afraid of that.

"What is it?"

"I can't break it."

"What do you mean, you can't break it? I thought it was two pieces."

"It *was*. But now it's not. Those Portas tossers did something to fuse it."

"Maybe there's something in the book?"

Stone jerked his head up. "What book?"

"Look in the bottom of the bag. I noticed it was in there when I checked, but I didn't pay any attention to it. All I wanted to do was make sure the thingamabob was there."

Stone's heart pounded harder. *Could it be possible?* He stuffed the obelisk back in the bag and fished around in the bottom, coming up with a small, leatherbound book tied with a leather cord.

With shaking hands, he untied the cord and opened the book, then carefully paged through it.

It wasn't written in English. In fact, it wasn't in any language Stone had ever seen, and definitely not the same as the symbols on the sides of the obelisk. But his grip tightened as he turned another page and saw the series of carefully rendered drawings of the device. They included several each of both the pyramid and the base, a cross-section showing the inside of both and revealing small, hollow chambers inside, and more of all sides of the finished obelisk. Below it were more paragraphs of the strange language, interspersed with blocks of familiar symbols.

Stone grinned. "Eleanor, I could *kiss* you! You're brilliant!"

"Hey, I'm not going to argue, though this probably isn't a good time. What is that thing? Is it important?"

"Bloody *right* it is! Maybe even more important than the obelisk itself. And I doubt those two Feds even knew what they had."

"That's great. Really. But what the hell are we doing? We can't just drive around here forever. I need to ditch this car and get out of here."

Stone fought to focus. He didn't have a lot of options. The obelisk was here, and it wasn't coming apart anytime soon. Even if the little book *did* contain instructions for how to separate the pieces, he couldn't read it. Maybe Eddie and Ward could, but he couldn't take the obelisk to them. It was dangerous to hold on to it this long when he couldn't protect it.

Who could he trust, who'd be strong enough to keep it safe and wouldn't be tempted to use it against him?

When the answer came to him, he didn't like it.

He didn't like it at all.

But he couldn't see a better one, and time was ticking.

He jammed the book into his inner coat pocket. "Keep driving," he told Eleanor, and gave her an address.

It was barely seven a.m. now—far earlier than Stone had ever visited Kolinsky's shop in the past.

"Where the hell are we?" Eleanor asked, looking around the shabby business district with distaste. "What are you planning to do, pawn the thing?"

"No. Listen—I've got to leave you for a few moments, and I have to leave the obelisk in the car."

"Why? I don't like that idea very much." She glanced in the mirror as if expecting someone to pull up behind them.

"There's no helping it. I need magic to get where I'm going."

"You're not afraid I'll drive off with it?" Her words were joking—but not entirely.

"No. At this point, I trust you. And besides," he added with a feeble attempt at a grin, "I'm paying you, remember?"

"Well, hurry up. If I see anything that looks wrong, I'm out of here."

"Five minutes. Ten at the most."

Stone, still with the book in his pocket, got out and darted across to Kolinsky's shop. He slipped past the wards, unlocked the door, and dashed down the stairs.

As he expected, the place was empty, the illusion of the threadbare shop in place. He barely paid it any attention.

"Stefan!" he called. "I know it's early, but trust me, you're going to want to show up for this one."

For a few agonizing seconds, he thought Kolinsky would ignore his plea. But then the door to the back part of the shop opened and the dragon strode through, looking as well put together as if he'd just finished lunch at a fine restaurant.

He narrowed his eyes and frowned at Stone. "Alastair. It is early."

"Yes, I know. I hope I didn't get you out of the shower or anything. But I need your help—and I don't think you're going to mind this time."

"My help?" Kolinsky's brow furrowed. He glanced up, staring off into the space like a dog catching a distant scent. "Something is…odd."

"You sense it from here?" Stone was impressed. "You're good. *Bloody* good." He glanced over his shoulder, mindful of the time passing. "Remember the thing we talked about before? The device?"

"The one that can interfere with magic? Yes, of course. I will remind you that you have not yet fulfilled your part of our agreement by providing the pyramid for me to study."

"I've done better than that—I've got the whole thing."

Kolinsky's eyebrows rose. "Indeed."

"Yes—and that's what I need your help with. It works, Stefan. It works better than I ever expected. I'm not even going to *tell* you what I've been up to for the past several hours. Maybe later, over a nice dinner which I'll buy. But right now, I need you to take this thing off my hands and make it disappear before anyone catches on I've got it."

"Take it…off your hands?"

"I don't want it. I don't want to be *near* it. But there are a lot of nasty people who *do* want it, and I don't want *them* to have it either. I figure you're the safest bet for making sure it doesn't end up somewhere it shouldn't be."

Kolinsky couldn't keep his interest entirely hidden. "So, you propose to simply…give it to me?"

"Yes. I hope you'll let me study it, and that it will tilt our balance sheet back in my direction for a while. But aside from all that, I just want it safe. Will you take it? *Can* you keep it safe? Will anyone give you trouble for having it?" With a sinking feeling, he remembered what Kolinsky had told him before—why he couldn't help Stone look for the device. If he refused to take it now—

"Of course. And…yes, I can keep it safe."

"What about the other dragons?"

Kolinsky smiled thinly. "Do not concern yourself with them. I have not provided you any aid in seeking the device, and I did not ask you to bring it to me. Where is it?"

Stone smiled too. Dragons would make lawyers look like amateurs, the way they wormed their way around the loopholes in their agreements. "Outside, with my...associate. You'll have to take down the wards long enough to let us bring it inside."

Kolinsky shook his head. "No. Do not bring it here. One moment." He pulled a notebook from his pocket and wrote something on a page. "Take it to that address. I will meet you there."

Stone didn't like that—he didn't like having the thing in his possession any longer than necessary—but he sighed and nodded. "All right. Hopefully nobody will bother us on the way, because my magic's useless around it."

Eleanor was waiting impatiently when he slipped back into the car. "What was all that about?"

"Drive. I'll navigate. Did anyone suspicious turn up?"

"Not yet. I've been listening to the police channels. We might have gotten lucky—they didn't spot the car at the hotel, or at least not the license plate. I always rent generic-looking cars for just that reason." She pulled away from the curb. "So where is this we're going?"

"I just talked to a friend. He's going to take the obelisk and hide it where nobody can get hold of it."

"You're just going to...give it away to somebody? After everything we went through?"

"Not give it away, exactly. I'll still have access to it. But I can't keep it, and I don't want Portas or the Feds or your former employers to have it."

She sighed. "About that. They think I'm still working for them. What do I tell them if they ask me what happened?"

"Tell them…our relationship didn't work out, and the pyramid is in safe hands. Tell them I don't have it anymore. They'll probably trace Richard—that's the man Portas killed—and then the trail will die out. At least the one pointing to me, and as far as I'm concerned that's all I care about."

"Yeah. Okay." She stretched her arms, pressing back against the steering wheel. "This has been a wild ride, I'll have to say that."

"It has. And it's not quite over yet."

Nobody approached them as they drove out of East Palo Alto and into an old, wealthy neighborhood near downtown Palo Alto. The address was a two-story house on a corner, only a few blocks from Stone's old townhouse.

"Here we are," Stone said.

She pulled off at the curb. "Okay. And here's where we say goodbye, I think."

He bowed his head. She was right, of course, but that didn't mean he had to like it. "Already?"

"My job here's done. I need to ditch this car and be on the other side of the country by tomorrow. I've got another job starting the day after, which is going to take me to western Africa."

He chuckled. "You do get around."

"I do. Hey, this isn't the end. If I'm in the area again, I'll look you up. Or give me a call sometime. If we're on the same continent, maybe we can get together for a little fun."

"I'll make sure your payment—and a nice bonus—makes it to your account."

"That's appreciated. But I want the other part of my payment, too."

He tilted his head. "What's that?"

"You promised me a kiss. I'd like more, but—" She indicated the car. "Not really practical right now."

He smiled, leaning toward her. "I always pay my debts…" he murmured. "And as for the rest…will you take an I.O.U.?"

CHAPTER THIRTY-NINE

"HOLY SHIT," VERITY SAID, and looked troubled. "If only I hadn't gone off to Australia…"

They were seated around a big table at the Dancing Dragon in London—Verity, Jason, Amber, Eddie, Ward, and Stone. It was three days after Eleanor had left.

"Now, come on," Stone assured her. "You've got your own life, and I can't expect you to hang about on the off chance I might need patching up."

"But you could have—" She sighed. "Okay, I guess it's looking like you *couldn't* have died. But still—that's horrible. They could have tortured you, which maybe would have been worse."

"Yeah," Jason agreed. "Damn, those Portas guys are hardcore. I thought they were just a little fringe thing, but it sounds like they aren't."

Stone nodded, only half listening as the group continued talking among themselves. He still hadn't quite gotten past looking over his shoulder for Portas, or the Ordo, or even Redhead and Dad Bod, but he was finally starting to think things might finally be returning to normal.

Kolinsky had the obelisk, and had promised Stone he would keep it somewhere none of those people—or anyone else—would ever get hold of it. Stone hadn't asked him where that place *was*, or how he planned to get around the obelisk's powerful anti-magic field, but he trusted the dragon to keep his word.

What he *hadn't* done, though, was give Kolinsky the book—or even tell him it existed. As soon as he'd dropped off the obelisk, he'd called a rideshare to take him back to his own car near University Perk (which, wonder of wonders, hadn't been towed). Then he'd returned home to Encantada and immediately popped over to the Surrey house for a nice, long nap that ended up lasting the better part of the day. When he awakened, feeling much better and almost back to his normal self, he'd headed to Caventhorne to drop the book off with Eddie and Ward.

"See what you can do with it," he'd told them. "I can't make heads nor tails of it, but from the look of those diagrams, it might contain instructions not only for the ritual to get the device working, but also for how to build another one. Not that we could—or would necessarily want to—since the substance that powers them seems to be unavailable, but…"

"…but more knowledge is always nice," Eddie said, his eyes shining with curiosity as he took the book. "We'll sort it out, mate. It might take some time, but we're on it."

When Stone got back from that trip, he'd made one more call, to Leo Blum. He hadn't given the detective all the details about what had happened to him, but he asked him to keep a lookout for both anything about the raid on the Portas facility and anything indicating the cops were looking for Stone.

"I don't know what you did," Blum had told him when he called back an hour later. "But whatever it is, none of it's on my radar."

"Nothing?" That was a surprise. Eleanor had told him other law enforcement had been involved in the raid. "Are you sure?"

"Trust me, I'm sure. I checked all the calls in the San Jose area for hours around the time you gave me. Nothing at all."

Stone wondered if Dad Bod and Redhead's shadowy organization was powerful enough to expunge anything from the local record. "Okay, thanks for letting me know."

"You think somebody's after you?"

"No way to know. I'll have to keep an eye out for a while, I suppose."

"You do that. I'm just glad this whole mess is over and I can get back to some *normal* police work, like tracking con men up trees and dogs killing their mistresses."

"Hey, Al?"

Stone snapped out of his drifting thoughts and focused back on the present. Jason was regarding him expectantly. "Yes?"

"I was just sayin', you said something about all of us going out for a nice dinner after this was all over. We should plan that—but how about you let *us* take *you* out for a change?"

He smiled. "Sounds brilliant."

He took a healthy swallow from his pint and sat back, feeling content—mostly, anyway. He caught himself thinking about Eleanor, and wondering what part of west Africa she was in and what kind of dangerous, high-adrenaline job she was doing. He wondered if he truly would ever see her again.

He hoped so.

EPILOGUE

WHEN THE SHADOWY FIGURE appeared in the dusty underground room, he had to stand still for a moment and take a few deep breaths to get his anger under control.

Fortunately, the bad air here didn't affect him in the slightest.

The last time he had been here, aware of his surroundings, it had been after he had clawed his way out of a sealed sarcophagus. He'd been skeletally thin, desperately weak, disoriented, thoroughly lost as to where—and *when*—he was.

Aldwyn Stone did not like being out of control. The only thing liked even less were the people who had put him in that state in the first place.

The people who had conspired against him—his own son included—and designed this room in secret to immobilize him, to block his defenses, to contain his power.

They couldn't kill him. They might not have known that for certain, but they'd strongly suspected it. Thus, they'd done the next best thing, interring him in this bespoke prison and leaving him to languish in a state of suspended animation for nearly two hundred years.

The worst part might have been that he couldn't have his revenge against them. Not when they were long dead, their bones turned to dust in the ground by now.

All but one, as he'd recently discovered.

Not many people in this modern age knew Aldwyn even existed. He'd kept quiet on purpose, concealing not only his presence but his existence from all but a few people. He'd revealed himself to his descendant, the powerful mage who owned the family property now, and whom he had not yet given up on the hope of turning to his side despite an inconvenient association with his sworn enemy. By necessity, the others of his kind knew of his return, but their complicated and carefully wrought agreements meant they couldn't interfere with him any more than he could interfere with them. None of them were pleased about this, but thus went the agreements. Breaking them would cost more than any of them were prepared to pay.

And so, Aldwyn had waited. He was good at waiting. He'd always been patient, willing to spend years, decades, even centuries setting up his plans within plans to ensure everything would go as he expected. He'd settled in to a new location deep in the mountains of Scotland, surrounded by forests and illusions, and set about learning the ways of this new world. He'd already retrieved some of his hidden fortune, and by various untraceable proxies he'd hired a series of individuals to instruct him in history and technology, to gather information for him, and to multiply his already vast holdings into something that had grown many times larger even in this relatively short period of time.

He'd also kept track of his descendant. The manor house in Surrey had been his, after all—he knew its secrets better than anyone, including its current master. He didn't keep constant watch, nor did he need to. But when it had come back to him that the younger Stone had discovered a smaller version of the device that had imprisoned him, his interest had naturally been piqued.

He'd also discovered something else through his secret ways: that one of his betrayers had, beyond all possible reason, remained alive. His spirit had persisted after his own compatriots had betrayed *him,* remaining a fellow prisoner with Aldwyn in the catacombs beneath the house until the same small earthquake had released him as well. And now, somehow, he'd managed to find a descendant of his own and take over her body so he could continue practicing his foul, necromantic magic.

Aldwyn had smiled when he found that out—the sort of smile nobody on this Earth would ever want to see—but he had been even more pleased when he heard of the device's existence.

What more fitting way to exact revenge upon his betrayer than to use the man's own tricks against him? Except he would not limit himself to merely imprisoning James Brathwaite without his magic. Suffering could be extended for a very long time when the one committing it had the power to heal a frail human body to full health at the end of each session.

Brathwaite would indeed regret the day he'd ever made his unwise decisions.

The whole thing would have been perfect—except his fool descendant, in a fit of weakness, had chosen to give the device to his enemy! Aldwyn's rage had burned bright when he'd discovered that, and it had probably been good that no one else had been in his presence.

But his anger hadn't lasted long. He didn't blame his descendant for what he'd done, inconvenient though it had been. It made things more difficult for him, but he still had another way around it. It might take him longer, but that was fine.

Time, he had.

It had been easy for him to breach the wards at the London library, and easier still to borrow the book his descendent had left in the care of his two friends. After making his own copies of all the pages—there was nothing inherently magical about the book or its contents—he'd returned it to its place so no one would suspect it had been gone. Aldwyn preferred operating in full secrecy. The fewer people who were aware of his plans, the smaller the chance one of them would interfere with them.

And now here he was, back in the place of his initial incarceration.

But now his rage had faded and he was smiling, because it would also be the place where he would begin his revenge.

He raised a hand, summoning a light spell around it, and looked around at the symbols on the wall. They were all familiar to him, but he paid them little notice. This place was broken, and would never function as it was designed again...but that didn't mean it couldn't still be useful.

What he was looking for was a single, small symbol near the center of each of the four walls, indistinguishable from the others in size, type, and method of carving. He moved to each of these in turn, using a bit of magic to activate it.

The first three proved to be disappointments. The tiny alcoves opened to his touch and his magic, but the small vials of quicksilver liquid in each one were broken, their contents long since dried and useless. He began to wonder if his plan would work at all.

But then the fourth alcove revealed another vial, this one whole and sealed, glittering in the light of his spell. Sparks of multicolored energy danced around it like flecks of metal in a kaleidoscope.

His wolfish, unwholesome smile spread once again across his face as he plucked the little vial from the nook and put it carefully in his pocket.

It had taken four of them to contain him—four tiny vials of an immensely potent substance that did not originate on Earth.

It would only take one—if that—to contain Brathwaite's pathetic human shell.

As he faded from view, leaving all four alcoves open, his last thought was of his descendant. Alastair Stone hated Brathwaite as much as he did.

Perhaps this would finally be the hook that would allow him to persuade the young one to his way of thinking.

But that was for later.

He had plenty of time.

**Alastair Stone Will Return in
Alastair Stone Chronicles
Book Twenty-Six**

Look for it in Summer 2021

WE LOVE REVIEWS!

If you enjoyed this book, please consider leaving a review at Amazon, Goodreads, or your favorite book retailer. Reviews mean a lot to independent authors, and help us stay visible so we can keep bringing you more stories. Thanks!

If you'd like to get more information about upcoming Stone Chronicles books, contests, and other goodies, you can join the Alastair Stone mailing list at **alastairstonechronicles.com**. You'll get two free e-novellas, *Turn to Stone* and *Shadows and Stone!*

WHO IS THIS R. L. KING, ANYWAY?

R. L. King lives the kind of exotic, jet-set life most authors only dream of. Splitting her time between rescuing orphaned ocelots, tracking down the world's most baffling cheese-related paranormal mysteries, and playing high-stakes pinochle with albino squirrels, it's a wonder she finds any time to write at all.

Or, you know, she lives in San Jose with her inordinately patient spouse, three demanding cats, and a crested gecko. Which, as far as she's concerned, is way better.

Except for the ocelots. That part would have been cool.

You can find her at *rlkingwriting.com*, and on Facebook at www.facebook.com/AlastairStoneChronicles.

Printed in Great Britain
by Amazon